R. Barry O´Brien

The Autobiography of Theobald Wolfe Tone

1763-1798

The Autobiography of Theobald Wolfe Tone

1763-1798

R. Barry O´Brien

The Autobiography of Theobald Wolfe Tone
1763-1798

ISBN/EAN: 9783742833846

Manufactured in Europe, USA, Canada, Australia, Japa

Cover: Foto ©Raphael Reischuk / pixelio.de

Manufactured and distributed by brebook publishing software
(www.brebook.com)

R. Barry O´Brien

The Autobiography of Theobald Wolfe Tone

The Autobiography of Theobald Wolfe Tone

THE AUTOBIOGRAPHY

OF

THEOBALD WOLFE TONE

1763—1798

EDITED WITH AN INTRODUCTION BY

R. BARRY O'BRIEN

AUTHOR OF "FIFTY YEARS OF CONCESSIONS TO IRELAND," "THOMAS DRUMMOND, LIFE AND
LETTERS," "IRISH WRONGS AND ENGLISH REMEDIES," &c.

VOLUME I

London

T. FISHER UNWIN

PATERNOSTER SQUARE

MDCCCXCIII

CONTENTS OF VOLUME I.

CHAPTER IX.

CHAPTER X.

CHAPTER XI.

CHAPTER XII.

CHAPTER XIII.

CHAPTER XIV.

CHAPTER XV.

CHAPTER XVI.

CHAPTER XVII.

CHAPTER XVIII.

ILLUSTRATIONS.

EDITOR'S NOTE.

In 1826 the "Life of Theobald Wolfe Tone, edited by his son William Theobald Wolfe Tone," was published in Washington. The work consisted (chiefly) of two short autobiographical sketches ; of an account of the Catholic Convention of 1793 ; of Tone's diaries, letters, and political writings ; concluding with an account, by his son, of the last French expedition to Ireland, and of the fate of Tone's family after his death. In the present edition Tone's political writings are omitted. They are of little interest or importance now. The letters, and the account of his family after his death, are omitted to meet the exigencies of space. The rest is preserved. The words "Autobiography of Theobald Wolfe Tone" have been substituted for the words "Life of Theobald Wolfe Tone" on the title-page. The narrative has been divided into chapters, and arranged in chronological order, with dates and head-ings on each page ; explanatory notes [in brackets] have been added with an Introduction by the Editor.

The aim of the Editor has been to preserve all of the original work essential to show the character of the man, and give a history of the events in which he played so important a part.

INTRODUCTION.

THEOBALD WOLFE TONE has a distinct place in Irish
history. He is the Irish Separatist *par excellence*. Irishmen there have been who began as Constitutional agitators
and ended as rebels. Such men were among Tone's own
colleagues in the United Irish movement; and such men
gathered around Thomas Davis and Gavan Duffy half a
century later. Irishmen there have also been who began
as rebels and ended as Constitutional agitators. They are
in our midst to-day. But Tone began and ended as a
rebel. His disciples are the founders of the Fenian
organisation.

Tone was a formidable rebel. A competent authority
bears testimony to the fact. "Wolfe Tone," says the Duke
of Wellington, "was a most extraordinary man, and his
history is the most curious history of those times. With
a hundred guineas in his pocket, unknown and unrecom-
mended, he went to Paris in order to overturn the British
Government in Ireland. He asked for a large force, Lord
Edward Fitzgerald for a small one. They listened to
Tone;" and the Bantry Bay expedition was the result.
For the failure of that expedition Tone was not respon-

sible. He had organised victory; an incompetent French
general contrived defeat. "The army was composed of
fifteen thousand of the very best troops which France
possessed, with heavy trains of field artillery, and sufficient
spare muskets and powder to arm half the peasants in
Ireland. The reputation of General Hoche [the Com-
mander] was second only to that of Napoleon. The
next officer in command was Grouchy."[1] The ship bearing
Hoche never reached the Irish coast. But on December
21, 1796, Grouchy with thirty-five sail opened Bantry
Bay. "At any time during that day or the next had [he]
ventured to act on his own responsibility, he might have
chosen his own point of landing, and Cork must inevitably
have fallen. It had no land defences, and on the side
of the sea no batteries which a couple of line-of-battle
ships could not have silenced." But "then, as twenty
years later, on another occasion no less critical, Grouchy
was the good genius of the British Empire. He continued
to cruise as he was directed, standing off and on upon that
uncertain coast"[2] until a storm arose and swept his fleet to
sea. His incapacity to grasp a great opportunity lost
Ireland as it lost Waterloo. Recalling these events, one
may well repeat what Mr. Goldwin Smith has said of
Tone. "Though his name is little known among English-
men, he, . . . brave, adventurous, sanguine, fertile in
resource, buoyant under misfortune, . . . was near being
as fatal an enemy to England as Hannibal was to Rome."

Wolfe Tone was born in Dublin in 1763. A graduate

[1] Froude, "English in Ireland."   [2] Ibid.

of Trinity College and a member of the Bar, he entered politics in 1790-1. Catholic Emancipation and Parliamentary Reform were the questions of the hour. The Catholic organisation had just fallen under the influence of a great Catholic democratic leader—John Keogh ; and a secret political society, pledged to reform, had been established in Belfast. Tone flung himself into the Catholic cause and joined the Ulster Reformers. Visiting Belfast in 1791, he met the members of the secret political society and co-operated with them in founding the United Irish movement. This movement was, in the beginning, Constitutional. The majority of its founders were Parliamentary Reformers. But, as I have said, Tone was always a rebel ; he has himself placed the fact beyond controversy. "To subvert the tyranny of our execrable Government," he says, "to break the connection with England, the never-failing source of our political evils, and to assert the independence of my country—these were my objects. To unite the whole people of Ireland, to abolish the memory of our past dissensions, and to substitute the common name of Irishmen in place of the denomination of Protestant, Catholic, and Dissenter—these were my means."

Tone strove earnestly to bring the United Irishmen and the Catholic Committee into touch. He succeeded. In 1792 the Catholic leaders visited Belfast, and then and there was sealed the bond of union between them and their Ulster brethren.

In the same year Tone became assistant secretary to the Catholic Committee. Catholics and United Irishmen now worked together for a common cause. Catholic Emancipation and Parliamentary Reform was the cry of both. The Catholics were organised as they had never been organised before. Agents of the Committee were sent throughout the country. Communications were opened between Dublin and the provinces. There was a consolidation of forces, and a concentration of aims which made the agitators formidable. "I have made men of the Catholics," said Keogh. It was no idle boast. He had infused a spirit of independence into the Catholic body, which gave life and energy to the Catholic movement. The country was roused. The Ministers were alarmed. The union between Northern Presbyterians and Southern Catholics sent a thrill through the Cabinet. Troubles on the Continent increased. England's allies were routed by the soldiers of France.

The principles of the Revolution spread to Ulster.

Protestant Volunteers marched through the Protestant capital, cheering for the French Republic, and bidding defiance to England. The victory of Valmy gave joy to many a northern and many a southern heart. Belfast illuminated. Dublin illuminated. " Huzza ! huzza ! " writes Tone in his diary. " Brunswick and his army are running out of France with Dumouriez pursuing him. If the French had been beaten it was all over with us." The Government felt that the United Irishmen and the Catholics were driving in the direction of Separation. How were they to be stopped ? By policy of conciliation which would break up the union of their forces, satisfying

the one and isolating the other. So thought Pitt, and
acting on the conviction, he resolved to grant the most
urgent demands of the Catholics. In 1793 they were
accordingly admitted to the Parliamentary Franchise. At
the last moment Tone urged the Committee to insist on
complete emancipation. But Keogh refused to move
from the line of battle originally drawn up. The Franchise was within his reach. He would take it, and bide
his time for the rest. "Will the Catholics be satisfied
with the Franchise?" says Tone; and he adds, "I believe
they will, and be damned." He was disgusted with
Keogh's moderation. "Sad, sad!" he notes. "Merchants I see make bad revolutionists."

But Tone was not conciliated. No concession would
satisfy him. His goal was separation; and he was not
checked for an instant in his onward course. In 1794
he plunged more deeply into treason, and others followed
or anticipated his example. Measures were then taken
for reorganising the United Irish Society on a rebellious
basis. But the work of revolution was checked by the
arrival of Lord Fitzwilliam in December, 1794. He
came with a message of peace. He was sent to emancipate the Catholics. In February, 1795, a bill for this
purpose was read a first time in the House of Commons
practically without opposition. The hopes of the people
were raised to the highest pitch, and then they were
dashed suddenly to the ground. The King revolted at
the notion of further concessions to the Catholics. Pitt
flinched. Fitzwilliam was recalled. The policy of con-

cession was abandoned. An era of terror and revolution commenced. Fitzwilliam left Ireland on the 25th of March, 1795, amid the sorrow and the blessings of a grateful people. On March 31st the new Viceroy, Lord Camden, made his State entry through the streets of Dublin amid the angry growls of a sullen and despairing multitude. The policy of concession was replaced by a policy of coercion. But the work of revolution was not stopped. On the contrary, it grew apace under the new *régime*. Camden began his reign by a State prosecution. On the 23rd of April the Rev. William Jackson, a Protestant clergyman, who had been sent in 1794 by the French Government on a mission to the United Irishmen, was put on his trial for high treason. There was a clear case against him, and he anticipated the sentence of the law, dying in the dock by his own hand. On May 10th the United Irish Society became a distinctly rebellious organisation. Soon afterwards Tone, who had been in direct communication with Jackson, and was under the *surveillance* of the authorities, resolved to leave for America. Before departing he explained his plans to the United Irish leaders, Thomas Addis Emmet, Thomas Russell, Neilson, Simms, McCracken, and to the Catholic leader, John Keogh. In Dublin he saw Emmet and Russell. " I told them that my intention was immediately on my arrival in Philadelphia to wait on the French Minister, to detail to him fully the situation of affairs in Ireland, to endeavour to obtain a recommendation to the French Government ; and if I succeeded so far to leave my family in America, and to set off instantly for Paris, and apply, in the name of my country, for the assistance of France, to enable us to assert our independence."

A few days later, on the summit of McArt's Fort, near Belfast, he, Neilson, Simms, McCracken, and Russell " took a solemn obligation never to desist in our efforts until we had subverted the authority of England over our country and asserted our independence."

On June 13th Tone sailed from Belfast for America. He was true to the duty he had undertaken, and, after a short stay in the United States, set out for France. Arriving at Havre in January, 1796, he immediately placed himself in communication with the French Government, established close relations with De la Croix, Carnot, General Clarke, and Hoche, and finally persuaded the Directory to send an expedition to Ireland.

On December 16, 1796, the expedition, consisting of forty-three sail, with an army of fifteen thousand men under the command of Hoche and Grouchy, left Brest. Tone, who now held the rank of Adjutant-General in the French service, was on board the *Indomptable*. In the night the ships were scattered. The *Fraternité*, with Hoche on board, never reached Ireland. But Grouchy with thirty-five sail, including the *Indomptable*, made Bantry Bay on the evening of December 21st. Tone urged him to land. But he hesitated, standing off and on the coast until, at length, the elements warred for England and swept the French fleet from the Irish shore. " It is sad," says Tone, "after having forced my way thus far, to be obliged to turn back, but it is my fate, and I must submit. Notwithstanding all our blunders, it is the dreadful stormy weather and easterly winds, which have been blowing furiously since we made Bantry Bay, that have ruined us. Well, England has not had such an escape since the Spanish Armada, and that expedition, like ours, was defeated by the weather; the elements fight against us, and courage here is of no avail."

Buoyant under misfortune, Tone did not relax his efforts. He urged the French Government to despatch another expedition. He was supported in his appeal by delegates from Ireland, and backed by the great influence of Hoche. Another expedition was prepared by the Dutch Republic in union with France.

But the Dutch fleet, under De Winter, was destroyed by the English fleet, under Duncan, at Camperdown, on October 11, 1797. A month before the battle, Hoche, in whom Tone had kindled a real interest for Ireland, died.

Tone's cup of disappointment was filled to the brim ; but he did not despair. He applied himself with fresh vigour to persuade the French Government to make one last attempt in the cause of Irish freedom. Meanwhile events had been moving rapidly in Ireland.

The policy of coercion had borne fruit. Martial law, " half hangings," indiscriminate torture, and wholesale oppression and cruelty had done their work. The United Irish leaders found their ranks filled by a harassed and a desperate peasantry. North joined hands with South ; Catholic combined with Protestant. The timid and the fearful for very safety sought refuge in revolution. The people were dragooned into treason. "Every crime, every cruelty, that could be committed by Cossacks or Calmucks has been transacted here." So wrote Sir Ralph Abercrombie when he took over the command of the troops early in 1798. Shortly afterwards he was forced to resign. His humanity was too great a strain upon the endurance of the Ascendancy faction.

Grattan and the Constitutional party begged the Government at least to temper coercion with concession. But a stern *non possumus* was the only reply. "We have offered you our measure," Grattan said to the Ministers in the House of Commons in 1797 ; "you will reject it. Having no hope left to persuade, or dissuade, and having discharged our duty, we shall trouble you no more, and from this day we shall not attend the House of Commons."

As the doors of the constitution closed, the path of revolution opened. In 1796 the United Irish Society had become a military organisation. Before the spring of 1797 a supreme executive had been established in Dublin, and Provincial Directories were formed in Ulster and in Leinster. A competent military chief had taken command. Lord Edward Fitzgerald had joined the rebels. Arrangements were pushed forward for an insurrection. The Ulster Directory proposed the end of 1797 for the rising ; the Leinster Directory the beginning of 1798 : the last date was fixed upon. But the Government struck suddenly and struck hard. Before the end of March, 1798, all the leaders in Ireland except Lord Edward Fitzgerald and McCracken were seized and imprisoned. But Fitzgerald and McCracken resolved to take the field. May 23rd was the day appointed for the commencement of hostilities. But on May 19th Fitzgerald's place of hiding was discovered, and, after a desperate resistance, he was dragged to jail, surrounded by a troop of dragoons. The insurrection, nevertheless, broke out on May 24th.

Left without leaders, the insurgents fought wildly and desperately, sometimes rushing into excesses, which were, however, exceeded by the forces of the King. The rebels overran the county of Kildare and the bordering parts of Meath and Carlow. They seized Dunboyne, Dunshaughlin, and Prosperous, and took possession of Rathangan, Kildare, Ballybore, and Narraghmore. But the troops made a stand at Naas and Carlow, drove back their assailants, and reoccupied the captured towns. The rebels rallied on the hill of Tara, but were once more routed and dispersed. On June 7th, McCracken, with a strong force, attacked the town of Antrim. Successful in the first onset, he was ultimately repulsed after a fierce battle, and some days later arrested, tried by court-martial, and hanged.

But the rebels of county Wexford made the stoutest fight of all. Taking the field on May 27th, they seized Oulart, marched on Ferns, captured Enniscorthy, and occupied Wexford itself. In a few days the whole county was in their hands, with the exception of the fort of Duncannon and the town of New Ross. On June 4th New Ross was attacked. The battle raged for ten hours. The town was taken and re-taken ; but in the end the rebels were defeated and forced back on Gorey. A few days later they took the offensive again, and advanced on Arklow. Reinforcements were despatched from Dublin to succour the garrison. On June 9th Arklow was attacked. Another fierce battle, closing only with sunset, was fought. Victory remained still doubtful, when, at 8 p.m., the rebel captain was struck down, killed by a cannon-ball. Then his men, who had throughout the day maintained the struggle with desperate courage, retreated sullenly, falling back once more on Gorey.

Fresh troops now arrived from England, and General Lake, who had succeeded Abercrombie as commander-in-chief, took the field in person. On June 21st the rebel army was attacked in its last stronghold on Vinegar Hill, and annihilated. The insurgents, retreating through the counties of Dublin and Wicklow, were hunted down with merciless vengeance. " The carnage was dreadful," wrote Lake to Castlereagh ; " the determination of the troops to destroy every one they think a rebel is beyond description." Before the end of July the fire was put out in Wexford. But before the end of August an attempt was made to rekindle it in the West.

When news of the insurrection reached France, the Government, yielding to the importunities of Tone, resolved to despatch another expedition to Ireland. The plan was to send detachments from various French ports. For this purpose General Humbert was quartered at Rochelle, with 1,000 men ; General Hardy at Brest, with 3,000 men ; General Kilmaine was held in reserve, with

9,000 men. At the last moment the Government grew
dilatory, and Humbert determined to strike at once on his
own responsibility. Accompanied by Tone's brother Matthew and another United Irish exile, Bartholomew Teeling, he left Rochelle towards the middle of August, and
landed in Killala on the 22nd of the same month. General
Lake hastened to meet him. A pitched battle was fought
at Castlebar on August 22nd. Lake was beaten and driven
from the field. He retreated so rapidly, that the battle is
to this day known as the " Races of Castlebar." Cornwallis, who had become Viceroy in June, came quickly to
Lake's help, and forced Humbert to surrender at Ballinamuck on September 8th. Matthew Tone and Teeling
were arrested, and, despite the protestations of Humbert,
hurried to Dublin and hanged.

Yet another effort was to be made. On September 20th
the last French expedition sailed from Brest. It consisted
of a fleet of one sail of the line the *Hoche* (74 guns), eight
frigates *Loire*, *Resolue*, *Bellone*, *Coquille*, *Embuscade*, *Immortalité*, *Romaine*, *Semillanté*, and one schooner the
Biche, under the command of Admiral Bompard; and of an
army of 3,000 men under General Hardy. Tone was on
board the Admiral's ship, the *Hoche*. As on the previous
occasion, the ships were scattered on the voyage; but on
October 10th Bompard arrived at the entrance of Lough
Swilly with the *Hoche*, the *Loire*, the *Resolue*, and the
Biche. He was instantly signalled from the shore. At
daybreak next morning a British squadron, consisting of
six sail of the line, one razee (60 guns), and two frigates,

under the command of Sir John Borlase Warren, hove in sight. Bompard signalled the French frigates and the schooner to retreat, and cleared the *Hoche* for action. A boat from the *Biche* came alongside the *Hoche* for last orders. The French officers gathered around Tone, and urged him to escape. "The contest is hopeless," they said. "We shall be prisoners of war; but what will become of you?" He answered, "Shall it be said that I fled when the French were fighting the battles of my country? No; I shall stand by the ship." The British admiral having despatched two sail—the razee and a frigate—to give chase to the *Loire* and the *Resolue*, bore down on the *Hoche* with the rest of the squadron. The French ship was surrounded; but Bompard nailed his colours to the mast. For six hours the *Hoche* stood the combined fire of the British ships. Her masts were dismantled; her rigging was swept away; the scuppers flowed with blood; the wounded filled the cock-pit. At length, with yawning ribs, with five feet of water in the hold, her rudder carried away, her sails and cordage hanging in shreds, her batteries dismounted, and every gun silenced, she struck. Tone commanded a battery, and fought like a lion, exposing himself to every peril of the conflict. The *Hoche* was towed into Lough Swilly, and the prisoners landed and marched to Letterkenny. The Earl of Cavan invited the French officers to breakfast. Tone was among the guests An old college companion, Sir George Hill, recognised him. "How do you do, Mr. Tone?" said Hill. "I am very happy to see you." Tone greeted Hill cordially, and said, "How are you, Sir

George? How are Lady Hill and your family?" The police, who suspected that Tone was among the prisoners, lay in waiting in an adjoining room. Hill went to them, pointed to Tone, and said, "There is your man." Tone was called from the table. He knew that his hour had come, but he went cheerfully to his doom. Entering the next apartment, he was surrounded by police and soldiers, arrested, loaded with irons, and hurried to Dublin. On November 10th he was put on his trial before a court-martial.

He said to his judges : " I mean not to give you the trouble of bringing judicial proof, to convict me, legally, of having acted in hostility to the Government of his Britannic Majesty in Ireland. I admit the fact. From my earliest youth, I have regarded the connection between Ireland and Great Britain as the curse of the Irish nation, and felt convinced that, whilst it lasted, this country could never be free nor happy. My mind has been confirmed in this opinion by the experience of every succeeding year, and the conclusions which I have drawn from every fact before my eyes. In consequence, I determined to apply all the powers which my individual efforts could move, in order to separate the two countries."

He made but one request. He asked to be shot like a soldier. The request was refused, and he was ordered to be hanged within forty-eight hours. On the morning of the 12th of November Curran moved the Court of King's Bench for a writ of *habeas corpus.*

" I do not pretend," he said, " that Mr. Tone is not guilty of the charges of which he is accused. I presume

the officers were honourable men. But it is stated in this
affidavit, as a solemn fact, that Mr. Tone had no commission under his Majesty, and therefore no court-martial
could have cognisance of any crime imputed to him whilst
the Court of King's Bench sat in the capacity of the
Great Criminal Court of the land. In times when war
was raging, when man was opposed to man in the field,
courts-martial might be endured ; but every law authority
is with me, whilst I stand upon this sacred and immutable
principle of the Constitution, that martial law and civil law
are incompatible, and that the former must cease with the
existence of the latter. This is not, however, the time for
arguing this momentous question. My client must appear
in this court. He is cast for death this very day. He
may be ordered for execution whilst I address you. I call
on the Court to support the law, and move for a *habeas
corpus,* to be directed to the Provost-Marshal of the barracks
of Dublin, and Major Sandys, to bring up the body of
Tone."

Chief Justice. "Have a writ instantly prepared."

Curran. "My client may die whilst the writ is preparing."

Chief Justice. "Mr. Sheriff, proceed to the barracks,
and acquaint the Provost-Marshal that a writ is preparing
to suspend Mr. Tone's execution, and see that he be not
executed."

The Sheriff hastened to the prison. The Court awaited
his return with feverish suspense. He speedily reappeared.

"My lord," he said, "I have been to the barracks, in

pursuance of your order. The Provost-Marshal says he must obey Major Sandys. Major Sandys says he must obey Lord Cornwallis."

Curran. "My lord, Mr. Tone's father has just returned after serving the writ of *habeas corpus*, and General Craig says he will not obey it."

Lord Chief Justice Kilwarden. "Mr. Sheriff, take the body of Tone into custody, take the Provost-Marshal and Major Sandys into custody, and show the order of the Court to General Craig."

The Sheriff hastened once more to the prison. He returned quickly. He had been refused admittance, and was told that Tone had attempted suicide and that he lay in a precarious state. A surgeon was called to corroborate the Sheriff's statement.

Lord Chief Justice. "Mr. Sheriff, take an order to suspend the execution."

At the prison Tone lay on his pallet dying. On the evening of the 11th of November, while the soldiers were erecting the gallows before his window, he cut his throat with a penknife, inflicting a deep wound. At four o'clock next morning a surgeon came and closed the wound. As the carotid artery was not cut, he said that Tone might recover. "I am sorry," said Tone, "that I have been so bad an anatomist." He lingered till the morning of November 19th. Standing by his bedside, the surgeon whispered to an attendant that if he attempted to move or speak he would die instantly. Tone overheard him, and making a slight movement, said, "I can yet find words to thank you, sir; it is the most welcome news you can give me. What should I wish to live for?" Falling back with these expressions upon his lips he instantly expired. So perished Wolfe Tone. So ended the rebellion of 1798.

It has well been said that Tone needs to be defended against himself. He is, in truth, ridiculously outspoken. He carries frankness to an extravagant pitch. He not only confesses his faults; he exaggerates them. But the judicious reader and the generous critic need scarcely be told that the evidence of a man against himself is not always to be taken *au pied de la lettre;* and there is no other evidence against Wolfe Tone. Harsh use has been made of his confessions by his enemies. But had he possessed only a tithe of the hypocrisy and solemn self-love characteristic of his censors, he might now appear before us as a hero *sans reproche*, as he certainly is a hero *sans peur*. He wrote for his friends. He knew that they would not misjudge him. He was profoundly indifferent to the approbation of those "superior" persons who represent what for the want of a better (or a worse) name is called "the world."

Tone loved adventure and romance. In early life he sought an outlet for his restless energy in odd enterprises. He sometimes went to bed drunk and got up ill; and he swore frightfully. These are his faults. It is a grave thing to mix wine with politics. But is the thing unknown in British history? In the days of the great General Monk drinking, we are told, was "a sport, and the first of sports.

A good drinker was held in as high esteem as a good
player at any fashionable game is held now. 'Pray excuse my style,' says Courtin [French Ambassador to
England in 1665]; 'I have been writing all the night,
and drank more than I ought.' Monk himself was a
hard drinker. He attracted the attention of Cominges
[another French Ambassador] by the unparalleled splendour of his drinking capacities. In one of his dis-
patches the Ambassador describes a little fashionable
fête, the style of which looks now very old-fashioned
indeed. 'An amusing affair happened last week in this
Court. The Earl of Oxford, one of the first noblemen of
England, Knight of the Garter and an officer of the Horse
Guards, asked to dinner General Monk, the High Cham-
berlain of the kingdom, and some few other Councillors of
State. They were joined by a number of young men of
quality. The entertainment rose to such a pitch that every
person happened to become a party to quarrels, both as
offended and offender ; they came to blows and tore each
other's hair ; two of them drew their swords, which luckily
had a cooling effect on the company. Each then went
away according as he pleased. Those who followed the
General wanted some more drink, and it was given them.
They continued there till evening, and therefore wanted
food. Having been warmed by their morning and after-
dinner doings, each resolved to see his companion aground.
The General, who is obviously endowed with a strong
head, struck a master stroke ; he presented to each a
goblet of the deepest. Some swallowed the contents, and

some not; but all peaceably remained where they were till the following morning, without speaking to each other, though in the same room. Only the General went to Parliament as usual, with his mind and thoughts nothing impaired. There was much laughter at this.'"[1]

In Tone's own day the British statesman was not above his bottle or more of port.

But it is sorry business exhuming the foibles of the dead. Let a man be broadly judged by the mark which he has left on the history of his time.

The Duke of Wellington's measure of Tone is the true measure. With a hundred guineas in his pocket, un-recommended and without friends, he went to France and persuaded the French Government to send an army of 15,000 men to overthrow the British authority in Ireland. This was an achievement of genius. The hero of the enterprise was indeed " near being as fatal an enemy to England as Hannibal was to Rome." Tone was light-hearted, full of fun and frolic, witty, genial, gay, but beneath all lay the serious purpose of an earnest man. Monk sat up drinking with brawlers. But he brought back the Stuarts. Pitt, according to tradition, reeled even under the Speaker's eye, but he ruled England for twenty years. Tone enjoyed a carouse with his friend Russell, but he almost wrested Ireland from England's grasp. The Duke of Wellington is assuredly right. This was the work of an " extraordinary man."

Tone was not born into Irish politics like Grattan,

---

[1] Jusserand, " A French Ambassador at the Court of Charles II."

O'Connell, Davis. He was nearly thirty years of age before Irish affairs occupied his thoughts. But when, at length, he threw in his lot with his country, he bore himself courageously and unselfishly, acting throughout with a singleness of purpose and a steadiness of aim which made amends for the heedlessness of youth.

He saw more clearly than any one of his time the great blot on the Irish Constitution. There was an independent Parliament, but a foreign Executive ; and the Parliament and the Executive were almost constantly in conflict. " I called a Parliament in Ireland," pleaded Strafford, when accused of arbitrary government. " Parliaments," said Pym, "without parliamentary liberties, are but a fair and plausible way to servitude." The liberties of the Irish Parliament were fettered by the action of the English Executive. No doubt the Parliament did some good work both before and after the revolution of 1782. But that work was accomplished by the help of outside forces which, for the time being, awed the Executive into submission. Free Trade (1779) and Legislative Independence (1782) were won by the Volunteers, and the Franchise Act (1793) was obtained by the rebellious combination of the United Irishmen and the Catholic Committee. When the strength of that combination was impaired by the concession of 1793, and by the hopes raised by the promise of further redress, the Executive once more gained the ascendancy. The recall of Lord Fitzwilliam, and the abandonment of the policy of conciliation and justice was the result. The remedy for this condition of things, Tone saw, was in the destruction of the Executive. But the Executive could not, he felt, be destroyed while the connection between the two countries lasted. He therefore went straight for separation, struggling to unite all classes and creeds of Irishmen in the common cause of Irish independence.

The overthrow of established government is a serious affair. The man who attempts it must be judged not only by the intrinsic justice of his cause, but by the practical character of his plans. To attempt an insurrection without the faintest hope of success is worse than a blunder. Bentham has, I think, fairly stated the ethical aspect of the case. He says, "[Governments rest on no other foundation than their utility ; their so-called right to make laws depends on the utility of the laws they make ;] and it is allowable, if not incumbent on every man, as well on the score of duty as of interest, to enter into measures of resistance when, according to the best calculation he is able to make, the probable mischiefs of resistance (speaking with respect to the community in general) appear less to him than the probable mischiefs of submission." Writing on an earlier period of Irish history, Mr. Froude says, "The Irish were not to be blamed if they looked to the Pope, to Spain, to France, to any friend in earth or heaven, to deliver them from a power which discharged no single duty that rulers owe to subjects." These words are applicable to the condition of Ireland in the eighteenth century. "America has been lost," said Lord Camden, "because she has had bad governors, and Ireland may one day be lost for the very same reason—bad government." "What does Ireland want?" said Pitt to Grattan, in 1794. "What would she have more?" At that time the Catholics, constituting the vast mass of the population, were shut out from all part in the government of the country. A Catholic could not be governor, nor deputy-governor, nor commander-in-chief of the forces. Catholics were excluded from Parliament, from the Judicial Bench, from the Privy Council, and from the rank of King's Counsel. A Catholic could not be sheriff, nor sub-sheriff, nor lord-lieutenant of a county. The peasantry were sunk in the lowest state of degradation, and the Protestant Ascendancy faction was maintained in defiance of popular opinion by British bayonets. Enlightened Irish Protestants felt that this condition of things should cease, and in 1795 an earnest attempt was made by the Irish House of Commons to end it. But the British Minister interposed, and upheld the infamous system of monopoly and exclusion by which he hoped to divide, and to enslave. "Rebellion against tyrants is obedience to God," and rebellion against English rule in Ireland was obedience to the first instinct of man's nature—the instinct of self-preservation; for English rule was killing the body and the soul of the nation.

Was there hope of success? That is the final question. Mr. Froude and Mr. Goldwin Smith answer it in the affirmative. There can be no doubt of the fact. Had Grouchy been equal to the situation; had he yielded to the importunities of Tone and landed at Bantry Bay in

December, 1796, Ireland would have then been lost to Britain.

Tried, then, by the intrinsic merits of the cause and the practical character of his plans, Tone must stand justified to posterity.

We live in better times, and brighter prospects still are dawning on us, but we should never forget the men who

> "Rose in dark and evil days
> To right their native land."

And a pitiful creature, indeed, must be the Irish Constitutional agitator who refuses to sing with the Young Ireland poet—

> "Who fears to speak of Ninety-Eight?
> Who blushes at the name?
> When cowards mock the patriot's fate,
> Who hangs his head for shame?
> He's all a knave, or half a slave,
> Who slights his country thus;
> But a *true* man, like you, man,
> Will fill your glass with us."

R. BARRY O'BRIEN.

April, 1893.

THE AUTOBIOGRAPHY OF
THEOBALD WOLFE TONE.

CHAPTER I.

BIRTH, FAMILY, AND EARLY LIFE.

Paris, *August 7, 1796.*

As I shall embark in a business,[1] within a few days, the event of which is uncertain, I take the opportunity of a vacant hour to throw on paper a few memorandums relative to myself and my family, which may amuse my boys, for whom I write them, in case they should hereafter fall into their hands.

I was born in the city of Dublin, on the 20th of June, 1763, My grandfather was a respectable farmer near Naas, in the county of Kildare. Being killed by a fall off a stack of his own corn, in the year 1766, his property, being freehold leases, descended to my father, his eldest son, who was, at that time, in successful business as a coachmaker. He set, in consequence, the lands which came thus into his possession to his youngest brother, which, eventually, was the cause of much litigation between them, and ended in a decree of the Court of Chancery, that utterly ruined my father ; but of that hereafter. My mother, whose name was Lamport, was the daughter of a captain of a vessel in the West India trade, who, by many anecdotes which she has told me of him, was a great original ;

[1] [French Expedition (under Hoche) to Bantry Bay, *post.*—ED.]

she had a brother who was an excellent seaman, and served as first
lieutenant on board of the *Buckingham*, commanded by Admiral
Tyrrel, a distinguished officer in the British service.

I was their eldest son; but, before I come to my history, I must
say a few words of my brothers. William, who was born in August,
1764, was intended for business, and was, in consequence, bound
apprentice, at the age of fourteen, to an eminent bookseller. With
him he read over all the voyages he could find, with which, and
some military history, he heated an imagination naturally warm
and enthusiastic, so much that, at the age of sixteen, he ran off to
London, and entered, as a volunteer, in the East India Company's
service; but his first essay was very unlucky; for, instead of
finding his way out to India, he was stopped at the Island of
St. Helena, on which barren rock he remained in garrison for six
years, when, his time being expired, he returned to Europe. It is
highly to his honour, that, though he entered into such execrable
society as the troops in the Company's service must be supposed
to be, and at such an early age, he passed through them without
being affected by the contagion of their manners or their principles.
He even found means, in that degraded situation and remote spot,
to cultivate his mind to a certain degree, so that I was much surprised, at our meeting in London, after a separation of, I believe,
eight years, to find him with the manners of a gentleman, and a
considerable acquaintance with the best parts of English literature:
he had a natural turn for poetry, which he had much improved, and
I have among my papers a volume of his poems, all of them
pretty, and some of them elegant. He was a handsome, well-made
lad, with a very good address, and extremely well received among
the women, whom he loved to excess. He was as brave as Cæsar,
and loved the army. It was impossible for two men to entertain
a more sincere, and, I may say, enthusiastic, affection for each
other than he and I; and, at this hour, there is scarcely anything
on earth I regret so much as our separation. Having remained in
Europe for three or four years, my father being, as I have above
alluded to, utterly ruined by a lawsuit with his brother Will took
the resolution to try his fortune once more in India, from which,

my own affairs being nearly desperate, I did not attempt to dissuade him. In consequence, he re-entered the Company's service in the beginning of the year 1792, and arrived at Madras towards the end of the same year. With an advantageous figure, a good address, and the talents I have described, he recommended himself so far to the colonel of the battalion in which he served, that he gave him his discharge, with letters to his friends at Calcutta, and a small military command, which defrayed the expense of his voyage, and procured him a gratification from the Company of £50 sterling for his good behaviour on his arrival. The service he performed was quelling, at some hazard, a dangerous mutiny which arose among the black troops who were under his command, and had formed a scheme to run away with the ship. He had the good fortune to recommend himself so far to the persons at Calcutta to whom he had brought letters, that they introduced him, with strong recommendations, to a Mr. Marigny, a French officer, second in command in the army of the Nizam, who was then at Calcutta, purchasing military stores for that prince. Marigny, in consequence, gave him a commission in the Nizam's service, and promised him the command of a battalion of artillery (the service to which he was attached), as soon as they should arrive at the army. The stores, &c., being purchased, Will marched with the first division, of which he had the command, and arrived safely at the Nizam's camp. After some time, Marigny followed him, but, by an unforeseen accident, all my brother's expectations were blown up. A quarrel took place between Marigny and the Frenchman first in command, in which my brother, with an honourable indiscretion, engaged on the side of his friend. The consequence was that Marigny was put in irons, as would have been Will also, if he had not applied for protection as a British subject to the English Resident at the Nizam's court. This circumstance, together with the breaking out of the war between England and France, utterly put an end to all prospects of his advancement, as all the European officers in the Nizam's service were French, and he determined, in consequence, to return to Calcutta. On his journey, having travelled four hundred miles, and having yet two hundred

to travel, he alighted off his horse, and went to shoot in a jungle,
or thick wood, by the roadside ; on his return, he found his servant
and horses in the hands of five ruffians who were plundering his
baggage ; he immediately ran up and fired on them, by which he
shot one of them in the belly ; another returned the fire with one
of his own pistols, which they had seized, and shot him through
the foot ; they then made off with their booty, and, in this condition, my brother had to travel two hundred miles in that burning
climate, at the commencement, too, of the rainy season, badly
wounded, and without resources ; his courage, however, and a good
constitution, supported him, and he arrived at length at Calcutta,
where he got speedily cured.   His friends there had not forgotten
him, and, after some time, an opportunity offering of Major Palmer
going up to Poonah as Resident at the court of the Peshwa of the
Mahrattas, they procured him strong recommendations to that
court, and he set off with Major Palmer in high health and spirits,
with expectations of the command at least of a battalion of
artillery.   Such is the substance of the last letter which I received
from him.   Since that time I am utterly ignorant of his fate.[1]   I
hope and trust the best of him ; he has a good constitution, un-
shaken courage, a fluent address, and his variety of adventures
must, by this time, have sufficiently matured his mind, and given
him experience.   I look, therefore, with confidence to our meeting
again, and the hour of that meeting will be one of the happiest of
my life.

[1] [William Tone became a distinguished officer in the Mahratta service, and
was killed in battle while fighting under Holkar, *circa* 1802.   He wrote a book
entitled, "Some Institutions of the Mahratta People," of which Mr. James
Grant Duff, in his "History of the Mahrattas," says : "I have examined minutely
all which that intelligent gentleman [William Tone] wrote respecting the
Mahrattas.   What he saw may be relied upon ; as to what he heard I am less
surprised that he should have fallen into error than that he should have
obtained information so nearly correct."   Lewis Ferdinand Smith, in his book
on "Europeans in the Service of the Native Princes of India," describes Tone
as a man "of undaunted valour and persevering enterprise ; an unfortunate
gentleman whose abilities and integrity were as great as his misfortunes had
been undeservingly severe."   An account of William Tone will be found in
an interesting book, recently published, by Mr. Herbert Compton, "Military
Adventurers of Hindustan."—ED.]

My second brother, Matthew, was of a temper very different from that of William ; with less of fire, he was much more solid ; he spoke little, but thought a great deal ; in the family we called him the Spectator, from his short face and his silence ; but, though he had not Will's volubility, and could not, like him, make a great display, with frequently little substance, and though his manner was reserved and phlegmatic, so as to be frequently absent in company, he had a rambling, enthusiastic spirit, stronger than any of us. He loved travelling and adventures for their own sakes. In consequence, before he was twenty-five, he had visited England twice or three times, and had spent twelve months in America, and as much in the West Indies. On his return from this last place, he mentioned to me his determination to pass over to France, and enter a volunteer in the service of the Republic, in which I encouraged and assisted him. This was in the month of August, 1794. In consequence, he crossed over to Hamburg, whence he passed to Dunkirk, and presenting himself as an Irishman desirous of the honour of serving in the French armies, was immediately thrown into prison on suspicion. There he remained until May, 1795, when he was discharged by order of the committee of public safety, and, going on to Havre de Grace, he took his passage to America, where he arrived in safety, for the second time, about Christmas, at which time I was actually at New York, waiting for my passage to France ; so that we were together in America, without knowing of each other, a circumstance which I regret most exceedingly, as, in the present situation of my affairs, it is at least possible that we may never meet again ; but I am not of a very desponding temper. The variety of adventures we have both gone through, and the escapes we have had in circumstances of great peril, have made me a kind of fatalist, and therefore I look with confidence to the day, and, I hope, not a very remote one, when the whole of my family shall be reunited and happy, by which time I think the spirit of adventure will, or at least ought to be, pretty well laid in all of us. My brother Matthew, like Will, is something of a poet, and has written some trifles, in the burlesque style, that are not ill done. He is a brave lad, and I love him most sincerely.

His age, at the time I write this, is about twenty-six or twenty-seven years. Matthew is a sincere and ardent republican, and capable, as I think, of sacrificing everything to his principles. I know not what effect his lying so long in a French prison may have had upon him, but, if I do not deceive myself, it has made no change in his sentiments. He is more temperate in all respects than William or myself, for we have both a strong attachment to pleasures and amusements, and a dash of coxcombry, from which he is totally free ; and, perhaps, a little, at least, of the latter foible would be of no prejudice to him, nor render him less agreeable.[1]

My third brother, Arthur, is much younger than any of us, being born about the year 1782 ; of course he is now fourteen years of age. If I can judge, when he grows up, he will resemble William exactly in mind and person. He is a fine, smart boy, as idle as possible (which we have all been, without exception), with very quick parts, and as stout as a lion. My father was bent on making him an attorney, for which no boy on earth was ever so unfitted. He wished, himself, having the true vagrant turn of the family, to go to sea; his father was obstinate, so was he, and the boy was in a fair way to be lost, when I prevailed, with some difficulty, on his father to consent to his going at least one voyage. In consequence, he sailed with a Captain Meyler to Portugal, being then about twelve years of age. On his return, he liked the sea so well that he was bound regularly apprentice to Captain Meyler, under whom he made a voyage to London and a second voyage to Portugal. On his return from this last trip, in June, 1795, he found me at Belfast on my departure for America, and he determined to accompany me. I was extremely happy to have him with us, and, in consequence, he crossed the Atlantic with me, and remained until I decided on coming to France, when I resolved to dispatch him to Ireland, to give notice to my friends there of what I was about. I put him, in consequence, on board the *Susannah*, Captain Baird, at Phila-

[1] [Matthew Tone accompanied the French Expedition (under Humbert) to Killala in 1798. Humbert landed, defeated the English General Lake at Castlebar, but surrendered to Cornwallis at Ballinamuck, September 8th. After the battle Matthew was taken prisoner, brought to Dublin, tried by court martial, and hanged, September 29th.—ED.]

delphia, on the 10th December, 1795, since which time, from circumstances, it has been impossible for me to have heard of him, but I rely, with confidence, that he has arrived safe, and discharged his commission with ability and discretion.[1]

My sister, whose name is Mary, is a fine young woman ; she has all the peculiarity of our disposition, with all the delicacy of her own sex. If she were a man, she would be exactly like one of us, and, as it is, being brought up amongst boys, for we never had but one more sister, who died a child, she has contracted a masculine habit of thinking, without, however, in any degree, derogating from that feminine softness of manner which is suited to her sex and age. When I was driven into exile in America, as I shall relate hereafter, she determined to share my fortunes, and, in consequence, she also, like the rest of us, has made her voyage across the Atlantic.[2]

My father and mother were pretty much like other people ; but, from this short sketch, with what I have to add concerning myself, I think it will appear that their children were not at all like other people, but have had, every one of them, a wild spirit of adventure, which, though sometimes found in an individual, rarely pervades a whole family, including even the females. For my brother William has visited Europe, Asia, and Africa before he was thirty years of age ; Matthew has been in America twice, in the West Indies once, not to mention several trips to England, and his voyage and imprisonment in France, and all this before he was twenty-seven. Arthur, at the age of fourteen, has been once in

[1] [Arthur Tone returned to America about 1797. In 1798 he came back to Europe, and entered the Dutch navy as a midshipman. He fell into the hands of the English about the same time as Wolfe Tone was taken, but escaped by the help of an Irish officer who found him weeping over an account of his brother's death. Promoted at the age of eighteen to the rank of lieutenant, Arthur sailed for the East Indies about 1799. He was not heard of afterwards.—ED.]

[2] [Mary Tone came from America to France with Tone's wife in 1796. In 1797 she married a Swiss merchant who settled in St. Domingo. There she died. According to one account she caught yellow fever while attending a sick friend who had been deserted by her family and servants; according to another, both she and her husband were killed by negroes during disturbances in the island.—ED.]

England, twice in Portugal, and has twice crossed the Atlantic, going to and returning from America. My sister Mary crossed the same ocean, and I hope will soon do the same on her return. I do not here speak of my wife and our little boys and girl, the eldest of whom was about eight, and the youngest two years old when we sailed for America. And, by all I can see, it is by no means certain that our voyages are yet entirely finished.

I come now to myself. I was, as I have said, the eldest child of my parents, and a very great favourite. I was sent, at the age of eight or nine, to an excellent English school, kept by Sisson Darling, a man to whose kindness and affection I was much indebted, and who took more than common pains with me. I respect him yet. I was very idle, and it was only the fear of shame which could induce me to exertion. Nevertheless, at the approach of our public examinations, which were held quarterly, and at which all our parents and friends attended, I used to labour for some time, and generally with success, as I have obtained six or seven premiums in different branches at one examination, for mathematics, arithmetic, reading, spelling, recitation, use of the globes, &c. In two branches I always failed, writing and the catechism, to which last I could never bring myself to apply. Having continued with Mr. Darling for about three years, and pretty nearly exhausted the circle of English education, he recommended strongly to my father to put me to a Latin school, and to prepare me for the University, assuring him that I was a fine boy, of uncommon talents, particularly for the mathematics ; that it was a thousand pities to throw me away on business, when, by giving me a liberal education, there was a moral certainty I should become a Fellow of Trinity College, which was a noble independence, besides the glory of the situation. In these arguments he was supported by the parson of the parish, Dr. Jameson, a worthy man, who used to examine me from time to time in the elements of Euclid. My father, who, to do him justice, loved me passionately, and spared no expense on me that his circumstances would afford, was easily persuaded by these authorities. It was determined that I should be a Fellow of

Dublin College. I was taken from Mr. Darling, from whom I parted with regret, and placed, about the age of twelve, under the care of the Rev. Wm. Craig, a man very different, in all respects, from my late preceptor. As the school was in the same street where we lived (Stafford Street), and as I was under my father's eye, I began Latin with ardour, and continued for a year or two with great diligence, when I began Greek, which I found still more to my taste ; but, about this time, whether unluckily for me or not the future colour of my life must determine, my father, meeting with an accident of a fall downstairs, by which he was dreadfully wounded in the head, so that he narrowly escaped with life, found, on his recovery, his affairs so deranged in all respects, that he determined on quitting business and retiring to the country, a resolution which he executed accordingly, settling with all his creditors, and placing me with a friend near the school, whom he paid for my diet and lodging, besides allowing me a trifling sum for my pocket. In this manner I became, I may say, my own master, before I was sixteen ; and as, at this time, I am not remarkable for my discretion, it may well be judged I was less so then. The superintendence of my father being removed, I began to calculate, that, according to the slow rate chalked out for me by Craig, I could very well do the business of the week in three days, or even two, if necessary, and that, consequently, the other three were lawful prize ; I therefore resolved to appropriate three days in the week, at least, to my amusements, and the others to school, always keeping in the latter three the day of repetition, which included the business of the whole week, by which arrangement I kept my rank with the other boys of my class. I found no difficulty in convincing half a dozen of my schoolfellows of the justice of this distribution of our time, and by this means we established a regular system of what is called *mitching;* and we contrived, being some of the smartest boys at school, to get an ascendency over the spirit of the master, so that when we entered the school in a body, after one of our days of relaxation, he did not choose to burn his fingers with any one of us, nor did he once write to my father to inform him of my proceedings, for which he most certainly was highly culpable. I must do myself and my school-fellows the justice to say, that, though we were abominably idle, we were not vicious; our amusements consisted in walking to the country, in swimming parties in the sea, and, particularly, in attending all parades, field days, and reviews of the garrison of Dublin in the Phœnix Park. I mention this particularly, because, independent of confirming me in a rooted habit of idleness, which I lament most exceedingly, I trace to the splendid appearance of the troops, and the pomp and parade of military show, the untamable desire which I ever since have had to become a soldier, a desire which has never once quit me, and which after sixteen years of various adventures, I am at last at liberty to indulge. Being, at this time, approaching to seventeen years of age, it will not be thought incredible that *woman* began to appear lovely in my eyes, and I very wisely thought that a red coat and cockade, with a pair of gold epaulets, would aid me considerably in my approaches to the objects of my adoration.

This, combined with the reasons above mentioned, decided me. I began to look on classical learning as nonsense; on a Fellowship in Dublin College as a pitiful establishment; and, in short, I thought an ensign in a marching regiment was the happiest creature living. The hour when I was to enter the University, which now approached, I looked forward to with horror and disgust. I absented myself more and more from school, to which I preferred attending the recruits on drill at the barracks. So that at length my schoolmaster, who apprehended I should be found insufficient at the examination for entering the college, and that he, of consequence, would come in for his share of the disgrace, thought proper to do what he should have done at least three years before, and wrote my father a full account of my proceedings. This immediately produced a violent dispute between us. I declared my passion for the army, and my utter dislike to a learned profession; but my father was as obstinate as I, and as he utterly refused to give me any assistance to forward my scheme, I had no resource but to submit or to follow my brother William's example, which I was too proud to do. In consequence, I sat

down again, with a very bad grace, to pull up my lost time ; and,
at length, after labouring for some time, sorely against the grain, I
entered a pensioner of Trinity College, in February, 1781 ; being
then not quite eighteen years of age ; my tutor was the Rev.
Matthew Young, the most popular in the University, and one of
the first mathematicians in Europe.[1] At first I began to study
Logic courageously, but unluckily, at my very first examination,
I happened to fall into the hands of an egregious dunce, one
Ledwich, who, instead of giving me the premium, which, as best
answerer, I undoubtedly merited, awarded it to another, and to me
very indifferent judgments. I did not stand in need of this piece
of injustice to alienate me once more from my studies. I returned
with eagerness to my military plan : I besought my father to equip
me as a volunteer, and to suffer me to join the British army in
America, where the war still raged. He refused me as before, and
in revenge I would not go near the college, nor open a book that
was not a military one. In this manner we continued for above a
twelvemonth, on very bad terms, as may well be supposed, without
either party relaxing an inch from their determination. At length,
seeing the war in America drawing to a close, and being beset by
some of my friends who surrounded me, particularly Dr. Jameson,
whom I have already mentioned, and a Mr. G. J. Brown, who had
been sub-master at Mr. Darling's academy, and was now become
a lawyer, I submitted a second time, and returned to my studies,
after an interval of above a year. To punish me for my obstinacy,
I was obliged to submit to drop a class, as it is called in the
University, that is, to recommence with the students who had
entered a year after me. I continued my studies at college as I
had done at school ; that is, I idled until the last moment of delay.
I then laboured hard for about a fortnight before the public examinations, and I always secured good judgments, besides obtaining
three premiums in the three last years of my course. During my

[1] [Matthew Young was born in the county Roscommon in 1750. Entering
Trinity College, Dublin, in 1766, he was elected Fellow, and took orders in
1775. He was an eminent mathematician, and wrote several scientific works.
In 1798 he was made Bishop of Clonfert by Lord Cornwallis. He died at
Whitworth in Lancashire in 1800.—ED.]

progress through the University, I was not without adventures. Towards the latter end of the year 1782, I went out as second to a young fellow of my acquaintance, of the name of Foster, who fought with another lad, also of my acquaintance, named Anderson, and had the misfortune to shoot him through the head. The second to Anderson was William Armstrong, my most particular friend, who is now a very respectable clergyman, and settled at Dungannon. As Anderson's friends were outrageous against Foster and me, we were obliged at first to withdraw ourselves, but after some time their passion abated, and I returned to college, whence this adventure was near driving me a second time and for ever. Foster stood his trial and was acquitted; against me there was no prosecution. In this unfortunate business the eldest of us was not more than twenty years of age.

At length, about the beginning of the year 1785, I became acquainted with my wife. She was the daughter of William Witherington, and lived, at that time, in Grafton Street, in the house of her grandfather, a rich old clergyman of the name of Fanning. I was then a scholar of the house in the University, and every day, after commons, I used to walk under her windows with one or the other of my fellow students; I soon grew passionately fond of her, and she also was struck with me, though certainly my appearance, neither then nor now, was much in my favour; so it was, however, that, before we had ever spoken to each other, a mutual affection had commenced between us. She was, at this time, not sixteen years of age, and as beautiful as an angel. She had a brother some years older than herself; and as it was necessary for my admission to the family that I should be first acquainted with him, I soon contrived to be introduced to him, and as he played well on the violin, and I was myself a musical man, we grew intimate, the more so as it may well be supposed I neglected no fair means to recommend myself to him and the rest of the family, with whom I soon grew a favourite. My affairs now advanced prosperously; my wife and I grew more passionately fond of each other; and, in a short time, I proposed to her to marry me, without asking consent of any one, knowing well it would be in vain to expect it; she accepted the proposal as frankly as I made it, and one beautiful morning in the month of July we ran off together and were married. I carried her out of town to Maynooth for a few days, and when the first *éclat* of passion had subsided, we were forgiven on all sides, and settled in lodgings near my wife's grandfather.

I was now, for a very short time, as happy as possible, in the possession of a beautiful creature that I adored, and who every hour grew more and more upon my heart. The scheme of a Fellowship, which I never relished, was now abandoned, and it was determined that, when I had taken my degree of Bachelor of Arts, I should go to the Temple, study the law, and be called to the bar. I continued, in consequence, my studies in the University, and obtained my last premium two or three months after I was married. In February, 1786, I commenced Bachelor of Arts, and shortly after resigned my scholarship and quit the University. I may observe here, that I made some figure as a scholar, and should have been much more successful if I had not been so inveterately idle, partly owing to my passion for a military life, and partly to the distractions to which my natural dispositions and temperament but too much exposed me. As it was, however, I obtained a scholarship, three premiums, and three medals from the Historical Society, a most admirable institution, of which I had the honour to be Auditor, and also to close the session with a speech from the chair, the highest compliment which that society is used to bestow. I look back on my college days with regret, and I preserve, and ever shall, a most sincere affection for the University of Dublin.

But to return. The tranquil and happy life I spent, for a short period after my marriage, was too good to last. We were obliged to break off all connection with my wife's family, who began to treat us with all possible slight and disrespect. We removed, in consequence, to my father's, who then resided near Clane, in the county of Kildare, and whose circumstances could, at that time, but ill bear such an addition to his family. It is doing him, however, but justice to mention, that he received and treated us with the greatest affection and kindness, and, as far as he

was able, endeavoured to make us forget the grievous mortifications
we had undergone.   After an interval of a few months, my wife was
brought to bed of a girl, a circumstance which, if possible, increased
my love for her a thousandfold ; but our tranquillity was again
broken in upon by a most terrible event. On the 16th October,
1786, the house was broken open by a gang of robbers, to the
number of six, armed with pistols, and having their faces blacked.
Having tied the whole family, they proceeded to plunder and
demolish every article they could find, even to the unprofitable
villainy of breaking the china, looking-glasses, &c. At length, after
two hours, a maidservant, whom they had tied negligently, having
made her escape, they took the alarm, and fled with precipitation,
leaving the house such a scene of horror and confusion as can
hardly be imagined. With regard to myself, it is impossible to
conceive what I suffered. As it was early in the night I happened to be in the courtyard, where I was seized and tied by
the gang, who then proceeded to break into the house, leaving
a ruffian sentinel over me, with a case of pistols cocked in his
hand. In this situation I lay for two hours, and could hear distinctly the devastation which was going on within. I expected
death every instant, and I can safely and with great truth declare,
that my apprehensions for my wife had so totally absorbed the
whole of my mind, that my own existence was then the least of
my concern. When the villains, including my sentry, ran off, I
scrambled on my feet with some difficulty, and made my way
to a window, where I called, but received no answer. My heart
died within me. I proceeded to another and another, but still no
answer. It was horrible. I set myself to gnaw the cords with
which I was tied, in a transport of agony and rage, for I verily
believed that my whole family lay murdered within, when I was
relieved from my unspeakable terror and anguish by my wife's
voice, which I heard calling on my name at the end of the house.
It seems that, as soon as the robbers fled, those within had untied
each other with some difficulty, and made their escape through a
back window : they had got a considerable distance from the house,
before, in their fright, they recollected me, of whose fate they were

utterly ignorant, as I was of theirs. Under these circumstances, my wife had the courage to return alone, and, in the dark, to find me out, not knowing but she might again fall into the hands of the villains, from whom she had scarcely escaped, or that I might be lying a lifeless carcase at the threshold. I can imagine no greater effort of courage; but of what is not a woman capable for him she truly loves? She cut the cords which bound me, and at length we joined the rest of the family at a little hamlet within half a mile of the house, where they had fled for shelter. Of all the adventures wherein I have been hitherto engaged, this, undoubtedly, was the most horrible. It makes me shudder even now to think of it. It was some consolation that none of us sustained any personal injury, except my father, whom one of the villains scarred on the side of the head with a knife: they respected the women, whose danger made my only fear, and one of them had even the humanity to carry our little daughter from her cradle where she lay screaming, and to place her beside my wife on the bed, whereon she was tied with my mother and sister. This terrible scene, besides infinitely distressing us by the heavy loss we sustained, and which my father's circumstances could very ill bear, destroyed, in a great degree, our domestic enjoyments. I slept continually with a case of pistols at my pillow, and a mouse could not stir that I was not on my feet and through the house from top to bottom. If any one knocked at the door after nightfall, we flew to our arms, and, in this manner, we kept a most painful garrison through the winter. I should observe here, that two of the ruffians being taken in an unsuccessful attempt, within a few days after our robbery, were hanged, and that my father's watch was found on one of them.

At length, when our affairs were again reduced into some little order, my father supplied me with a small sum of money, which was, however, as much as he could spare, and I set off for London, leaving my wife and daughter with my father, who treated them, during my absence, with great affection. After a dangerous passage to Liverpool, wherein we ran some risk of being lost, I arrived in London in January, 1787, and immediately entered my name as a student at law on the books of the Middle Temple; but this I may say was all the progress I ever made in that profession. I had no great affection for study in general, but that of the law I particularly disliked, and to this hour I think it an illiberal profession, both in its principles and practice. I was, likewise, amenable to nobody for my conduct; and, in consequence, after the first month I never opened a law book, nor was I ever three times in Westminster Hall in my life. In addition to the reasons I have mentioned, the extreme uncertainty of my circumstances, which kept me in much uneasiness of mind, disabled me totally from that cool and systematic habit of study which is indispensable for attaining a knowledge of a science so abstruse and difficult as that of the English code. However, one way or another, I contrived to make it out. I had chambers in the Temple (No. 4, Hare Court, on the first floor), and whatever difficulties I had otherwise to struggle with, I contrived always to preserve the appearance of a gentleman, and to maintain my rank with my fellow students, if I can call myself a student. One resource I derived from the exercise of my talents, such as they were. I wrote several articles for the *European Magazine*, mostly critical reviews of new publications. My reviews were but poor performances enough; however, they were in general as good as those of my brother critics; and, in two years, I received, I suppose, about £50 sterling for my writings, which was my main object; for, as to literary fame, I had then no great ambition to attain it. I likewise, in conjunction with two of my friends, named Jebb and Radcliff, wrote a burlesque novel, which we called "Belmont Castle," and was intended to ridicule the execrable trash of the Circulating Libraries. It was tolerably well done, particularly Radcliff's part, which was by far the best; yet so it was that we could not find a bookseller who would risk the printing it, though we offered the copyright gratis to several. It was afterwards printed in Dublin, and had some success, though I believe, after all, it was most relished by the authors, and their immediate connections.

At the Temple I became intimate with several young men of situation and respectability, particularly with the Hon. George

Knox,[1] son of Lord Northland, with whom I formed a friendship of which I am as proud as of any circumstance in my life. He is a man of inappreciable merit, and loved to a degree of enthusiasm by all who have the happiness to know him. I scarcely know any person whose esteem and approbation I covet so much; and I had, long after the commencement of our acquaintance, when I was in circumstances of peculiar and trying difficulty, and deserted by many of my former friends, the unspeakable consolation and support of finding George Knox still the same, and of preserving his esteem unabated. His steady friendship on that occasion I shall mention in its place; it has made an indelible impression of gratitude and affection on my heart. I likewise renewed an old college acquaintance with John Hall, who, by different accessions to his fortune, was now at the head of about £14,000 sterling a year. He had changed his name twice, for two estates; first to that of Stevenson, and then to Wharton, which is his present name. He was then a member of the British Parliament, and to his friendship I was indebted for the sum of £150 sterling, at a time when I was under great pecuniary difficulties. Another old college friend I recall with sentiments of sincere affection, Benjamin Phipps, of Cork. He kept a kind of bachelor's house, with good wine, and an excellent collection of books (*not law books*), all which were as much at my command as at his. With some oddities, which to me only rendered him more amusing, he had a great fund of information, particularly of political detail, and in his company I spent some of the pleasantest hours which I passed in London.

At length, after I had been at the Temple something better than a year, my brother William, who was returned a few months

---

[1] [Afterwards a prominent member of the Irish House of Commons. Knox was a staunch supporter of the Catholic claims. In 1793 he proposed that Catholics should be admitted to Parliament, but the House of Commons rejected the proposal by 163 to 69. In 1795 he supported Grattan's Bill for complete emancipation in a vigorous speech. "Take, then, your choice," he said; "re-enact your penal laws; risk a rebellion, a separation, or a Union, or pass this Bill." The Bill was rejected by 155 to 84. A rebellion and a Union both followed. Knox opposed the Union, sacrificing his post as a Commissioner of Revenue (worth £1,000 a year).—ED.]

before from his first expedition to St. Helena, joined me, and we lived together in the greatest amity and affection for about nine months, being the remainder of my stay in London. At this distance of time, now eight years, I feel my heart swell at the recollection of the happy hours we spent together. We were often without a guinea, but that never affected our spirits for a moment, and if ever I felt myself oppressed by some untoward circumstance, I had a never-failing resource and consolation in his friendship, his courage, and the invincible gaiety of his disposition, which nothing could ruffle. With the companionable qualities he possessed, it is no wonder that he recommended himself to Ben. Phipps, so that he was soon, I believe, a greater favourite with him than even I was. They were inseparable. It fills my mind now with a kind of tender melancholy, which is not unpleasing, to recall the many delightful days we three have spent together, and the walks we have taken, sometimes to a review ; sometimes to see a ship of war launched ; sometimes to visit the India-men at Deptford, a favourite expedition with Phipps. Will, besides his natural gaiety, had an inexhaustible fund of pure Irish humour ; I was pretty well myself, and Phipps, like the landlord of the " Hercules' Pillars," was *an excellent third man.* In short, we made it out together admirably. As I foresaw by this time that I should never be Lord Chancellor, and as my mind was naturally active, a scheme occurred to me, to the maturing of which I devoted some time and study : this was a proposal to the minister to establish a colony in one of Cook's newly-discovered islands in the South Sea on a military plan, for all my ideas ran in that track, in order to put a bridle on Spain in time of peace, and to annoy her grievously in that quarter in time of war. In arranging this system, which I think even now was a good one for England, I read every book I could find relating to South America, as Ulloa, Anson, Dampier, Woodes Rogers, Narborough, and especially the Bucaniers, who were my heroes, and whom I proposed to myself as the archetypes of the future colonists. Many and many a delightful evening did my brother, Phipps, and I spend in reading, writing, and talking of my project, in which, if it had been adopted, it was our firm resolution to have embarked. At length, when we had reduced it into a regular shape, I drew up a memorial on the subject, which I addressed to Mr. Pitt, and delivered with my own hands to the porter in Downing Street. We waited, I will not say patiently, for about ten days, when I addressed a letter to the minister, mentioning my memorial, and praying an answer, but this application was as unsuccessful as the former. Mr. Pitt took not the smallest notice of either memorial or letter, and all the benefit we reaped from our scheme was the amusement it afforded us during three months, wherein it was the subject of our constant speculation. I regret these delightful reveries which then occupied my mind. It was my first essay in what I may call politics, and my disappointment made such an impression on me as is not yet quite obliterated. In my anger I made something like a vow, that, if ever I had an opportunity, I would make Mr. Pitt sorry, and perhaps fortune may yet enable me to fulfil that resolution. It was about this time I had a very fortunate escape : my affairs were exceedingly embarrassed, and just at a moment when my mind was harassed and sore with my own vexations I received a letter from my father, filled with complaints, and a description of the ruin of his circumstances, which I afterwards found was much exaggerated. In a transport of rage, I determined to enlist as a soldier in the India Company's service ; to quit Europe for ever, and to leave my wife and child to the mercy of her family, who might, I hoped, be kinder to her when I was removed. My brother combated this desperate resolution by every argument in his power ; but, at length, when he saw me determined, he declared I should not go alone, and that he would share my fate to the last extremity. In this gloomy state of mind, deserted, as we thought, by gods and men, we set out together for the India House, in Leadenhall Street, to offer ourselves as volunteers ; but on our arrival there, we were informed that the season was passed, that no more ships would be sent out that year ; but that, if we returned about the month of March following, we might be received. The clerk, to whom we addressed ourselves, seemed not a little surprised at two young fellows of our appearance presenting ourselves on such a business, for we were extremely well dressed, and Will, who was the spokesman for us both, had an excellent address. Thus were we stopped, and I believe we were the single instance, since the beginning of the world, of two men, absolutely bent on ruining themselves, who could not find the means. We returned to my chambers, and, desperate as were our fortunes, we could not help laughing at the circumstance that India, the great gulf of all undone beings, should be shut against us alone. Had it been the month of March instead of September, we should most infallibly have gone off; and, in that case, I should most probably at this hour, be carrying a brown musket on the coast of Coromandel. Providence, however, decreed it otherwise, and reserved me, as I hope, for better things.

I had been now two years at the Temple, and had kept eight terms, that is to say, I had dined three days in each term in the common hall. As to law, I knew exactly as much about it as I did of necromancy. It became, however, necessary to think of my return, and, in consequence, I made application, through a friend, to my wife's grandfather, to learn his intentions as to her fortune. He exerted himself so effectually in our behalf that the old gentleman consented to give £500 immediately, and expressed a wish for my immediate return. In consequence, I packed up directly and set off, with my brother, for Ireland. We landed at Dublin the 23rd December, and on Christmas Day, 1788, arrived at my father's house at Blackhall, where I had the satisfaction to find all my family in health, except my wife, who was grown delicate, principally from the anxiety of her mind on the uncertainty of her situation. Our little girl was now between two and three years old, and was charming. After remaining a few days at Blackhall, we came up to Dublin, and were received as at first, in Grafton Street, by my wife's family. Mr. Fanning paid me punctually the sum he had promised, and my wife and I both flattered ourselves that all past animosities were forgotten, and that the reconciliation was as sincere on their part as it most assuredly was on ours. I now took lodgings in Clarendon Street, purchased about £100 worth of law books, and determined, in earnest, to begin and study the profession to which I was doomed ; in pursuance of this resolution, I commenced Bachelor of Laws in February, 1789, and was called to the bar in due form, in Trinity term following ; shortly after which I went my first (the Leinster) circuit, having been previously elected a member of the Bar club. On this circuit, notwithstanding my ignorance, I pretty nearly cleared my expenses ; and I cannot doubt, if I had continued to apply sedulously to the law, but I might have risen to some eminence ; but, whether it was my incorrigible habits of idleness, the sincere dislike I had to the profession, which the little insight I was beginning to get into it did not tend to remove, or whether it was a controlling destiny, I know not, but so it was, that I soon got sick and weary of the law. I continued, however, for form's sake, to go to the courts, and wear a foolish wig and gown, for a considerable time, and I went the circuit, I believe, in all, three times ; but, as I was, modestly speaking, one of the most ignorant barristers in the Four Courts, and as I took little, or, rather, no pains to conceal my contempt and dislike for the profession, and especially as I had neither the means nor the inclination to treat messieurs the attorneys, and to make them drink (a sacrifice of their respectability, which even the most liberal-minded of the profession are obliged to make), I made, as may well be supposed, no great exhibition at the Irish bar.

I had not been long a Counsellor, when the *coup de grâce* was given to my father's affairs by a decree in Chancery, which totally ruined him ; this was in a lawsuit between him and his brother, who was lieutenant of Grenadiers in the 22nd regiment. During the whole of this business I obstinately refused to take any part, not thinking it decent to interfere where the parties were both so nearly allied to me. When, however, my father was totally ruined, I thought it my duty, as it was most certainly my inclination, to assist him, even to distressing myself, a sacrifice which the great pains and expense he had bestowed on my education well merited. I, in consequence, strained every nerve to preserve a remnant of his property, but his affairs were too desperate, and I was myself too poor to relieve him effectually, so that, after one or two ineffectual efforts, by which I lost considerably with reference to my means, without essentially serving him, we were obliged to submit, and the last of his property, consisting of two houses, one in Stafford Street, and one on Summerhill, were sold, much under their value, to men who took advantage of our necessities, as is always the case. Soon after he had the good fortune to obtain a place under the Paving Board, which he yet retains, and which secures him a decent, though moderate, independence.[1]

[1] [Tone's father died about 1805 ; his mother about 1818.—ED.]

CHAPTER II.

ENTERS POLITICS.

As the law grew every day more and more disgustful, to which my want of success contributed, though in that respect I never had the injustice to accuse the world of insensibility to my merit, as I well knew the fault was my own, but being, as I said, more and more weary of a profession for which my temper and habits so utterly disqualified me, I turned my attention to politics, and, as one or two of my friends had written pamphlets with success, I determined to try my hand on a pamphlet. Just at this period the *Whig Club* [1] was instituted in Ireland, and the press groaned with publications against them on the part of Government. Two or three defences had likewise appeared, but none of them extra-ordinary. Under these circumstances, though I was very far from entirely approving the system of the Whig Club, and much less their principles and motives, yet, seeing them at the time the best constituted political body which the country afforded, and agreeing with most of their positions, though my own private opinions went infinitely farther, I thought I could venture on their defence without violating my own consistency. I therefore sat down, and in a few days finished my first pamphlet, which I entitled "A Review of

[1] ["Lord Charlemont, Mr. Grattan, Mr. Ponsonby, and Mr. Forbes were the originators of the Whig Club. It embraced various shades of politics, much diversity of talent, persons of great worth, great genius, and great abilities; men ardently attached to the monarchy—steady supporters of settled government—attached to the principles of the revolution of 1688 in England—and proud of that of 1782 in Ireland. The establishment of this body met with the warm approbation of Mr. Burke." Grattan said the object of the club was "to obtain an internal reform of Parliament, and to prevent the Union." (Grattan, " Memoirs.")—ED.]

the Last Session of Parliament!" To speak candidly of this performance, it was barely above mediocrity, if it rose so high;
nevertheless, as it was written evidently on honest principles, and
did not censure or flatter one party or the other, without assigning
sufficient reason, it had a certain degree of success. The Northern
Whig Club reprinted and distributed a large impression at their
own expense, with an introduction, highly complimentary to the
author, whom, at that time, they did not even know; and a very
short time after, when it was known that the production was mine,
they did me the honour to elect me a member of their body,
which they notified to me by a very handsome letter signed by
their Secretary, Henry Joy, jun., of Belfast, and to which I returned
a suitable answer. But this was not all. The leaders of the Whig
Club, conceiving my talents, such as they were, might be of service
to their cause, and, not expecting much intractability from a young
lawyer, who had his fortune to make, sent a brother barrister to
compliment me on my performance, and to thank me for the zeal
and ability I had shown. I was, in consequence, introduced to
George Ponsonby,[1] a distinguished member of the body, and who
might be considered as the leader of the Irish opposition; with
him, however, I never had any communication further than ordinary
civilities. Shortly after, the barrister above mentioned spoke to me
again; he told me the Ponsonbys were a most powerful family in
Ireland; that they were much pleased with my exertion, and
wished, in consequence, to attach me to them; that I should be
employed as counsel on a petition then pending before the House
of Commons, which would put an hundred guineas in my pocket,
and that I should have professional business put in my way, from
time to time, that should produce me at least as much per annum;
he added, that they were then, it was true, out of place, but that
they would not be always so, and that, on their return to office,

---

[1] [George Ponsonby was born in 1755. Called to the Irish Bar in 1780, he
soon entered Parliament, joining Grattan and the popular party. He was
favourable to the Catholic claims and an uncompromising opponent of the
Union. He became Lord Chancellor of Ireland under the second Grenville
Administration, 1806-7; entered the Imperial Parliament (on leaving office),
and died in 1817.—ED.]

their friends when out of power would naturally be first considered; he likewise observed, that they had influence, direct or indirect, over no less than two-and-twenty seats in Parliament; and he insinuated, pretty plainly, that when we were better acquainted it was highly probable I might come in on one of the first vacancies. All this was highly flattering to me, the more so as my wife's fortune was now nearly exhausted, partly by our inevitable expenses, and partly by my unsuccessful efforts to extricate my father. I did, it was true, not much relish the attaching myself to any great man, or set of men, but I considered, as I have said before, that the principles they advanced were such as I could conscientiously support, *so far as they went*, though mine went much beyond them. I therefore thought there was no dishonour in the proposed connection, and I was certainly a little dazzled with the prospect of a seat in Parliament, at which my ambition began to expand. I signified, in consequence, my readiness to attach myself to the Whigs, and I was instantly retained in the petition for the borough of Dungarvan, on the part of James Carrigee Ponsonby, Esq.

I now looked upon myself as a sort of political character, and began to suppose that the House of Commons, and not the bar, was to be the scene of my future exertions; but in this I reckoned like a sanguine young man. Month after month elapsed, without any communication on the part of George Ponsonby, whom I looked upon as most immediately my object. He always spoke to me, when we met by chance, with great civility, but I observed that he never mentioned one word of politics. I, therefore, at last concluded that he had changed his mind, or that, on a nearer view, he had found my want of capacity; in short I gave up all thoughts of the connection, and determined to trouble myself no more about Ponsonby or the Whigs, and I calculated, that as I had written a pamphlet which they thought had served them, and as they had in consequence employed me professionally in a business which produced me eighty guineas, accounts were balanced on both sides, and all further connection was at an end. But my mind had now got a turn for politics. I thought I had at last found my element,

and I plunged into it with eagerness. A closer examination into
the situation of my native country had very considerably extended
my views, and, as I was sincerely and honestly attached to her
interests, I soon found reason not to regret that the Whigs had not
thought me an object worthy of their cultivation. I made speedily
what was to me a great discovery, though I might have found it in
Swift and Molyneux, that the influence of England was the radical
vice of our Government, and consequently that Ireland would never
be either free, prosperous, or happy, until she was independent, and
that independence was unattainable whilst the connection with
England existed. In forming this theory, which has ever since
unvaryingly directed my political conduct, to which I have sacrificed
everything, and am ready to sacrifice my life if necessary, I was
exceedingly assisted by an old friend of mine, Sir Lawrence
Parsons,[1] whom I look upon as one of the very *very few* honest men
in the Irish House of Commons. It was he who first turned my
attention on this great question, but I very soon ran far ahead of
my master. It is in fact to him I am indebted for the first comprehensive view of the actual situation of Ireland; what his
conduct might be in a crisis, I know not, but I can answer for the
truth and justice of his theory. I now began to look on the little
politics of the Whig Club with great contempt; their peddling
about petty grievances, instead of going to the root of the evil, and
I rejoiced that, if I was poor, as I actually was, I had preserved
my independence, and could speak my sentiments without being
responsible to anybody but the law.

An occasion soon offered to give vent to my newly received
opinions. On the appearance of a rupture with Spain, I wrote a
pamphlet to prove that Ireland was not bound by the declaration
of war, but might, and ought, as an independent nation, to stipulate

[1] [Sir Lawrence Parsons (born in 1758) represented the King's County in the
Irish Parliament. He was an eloquent speaker, and a thoroughly independent
member. No one denounced more vigorously the recall of FitzWilliam, and
the consequent breach of faith with the Catholics in 1795 ; and no one was more
persistent in resisting the Union in 1799-1800. After the Union, Parsons sat in
the Imperial Parliament for the King's County until 1807, when, on the death
of his uncle, he became second Earl of Rosse, and died in 1841.—Ed.]

for a neutrality. In examining this question, I advanced the question of separation, with scarcely any reserve, much less disguise ; but the public mind was by no means so far advanced as I was, and my pamphlet made not the smallest impression. The day after it appeared, as I stood *perdu* in the bookseller's shop, listening after my own reputation, Sir Henry Cavendish, a notorious slave of the House of Commons, entered, and throwing my unfortunate pamphlet on the counter in a rage, exclaimed : " *Mr. Byrne, if the author of that work is serious, he ought to be hanged.*" Sir Henry was succeeded by a bishop, an *English* Doctor of Divinity, with five or six thousand a year, *laboriously* earned in the church. His lordship's anger was not much less than that of the other personage. " *Sir,*" said he, " *if the principles contained in that abominable work were to spread, do you know that you would have to pay for your coals at the rate of five pounds a ton ?*" Notwithstanding these criticisms, which I have faithfully quoted against myself, I continue to think my pamphlet a good one, but, apparently, the publisher, Mr. Byrne, was of a different opinion, for I have every reason to believe that he suppressed the whole impression, *for which his own gods damn him.*

Shortly after the premature end of my second pamphlet, which I have recorded, and which did not, however, change my opinion on its merit, for *Victrix causa Diis placuit, sed victa Catoni,* we came to an open rupture with my wife's family. It is not my intention to enter in this subject. One circumstance is sufficient to prove that the breach was not of our seeking, viz., that we had everything to lose and nothing to gain by a quarrel. . . .

About this time it was that I formed an acquaintance with my invaluable friend Russell,[1] a circumstance which I look upon as one

---

[1] [Thomas Russell was born in the county Cork in 1767. At the age of fifteen he went to India as a volunteer with his brother, a captain in the 52nd regiment. Returning to Ireland five years later, he himself became a captain in the 64th. He left the army in 1791, and was appointed Seneschal to the Manor Court of Dungannon, and a Justice of the Peace for the county Tyrone. Both offices were uncongenial, and he gave them up. He " could not," he said, " reconcile it to his conscience to sit as a magistrate on a bench where the practice prevailed of inquiring what a man's religion was before

of the most fortunate of my life. He is a man whom I love as a brother. I will not here attempt a panegyric on his merits; it is sufficient to say, that, to an excellent understanding, he joins the purest principles and the best of hearts. I wish I had ability to delineate his character, with justice to his talents and his virtues. He well knows how much I esteem and love him, and I think there is no sacrifice that friendship could exact that we would not with cheerfulness make for each other, to the utmost hazard of life or fortune. There cannot be imagined a more perfect harmony, I may say identity of sentiment, than exists between us; our regard for each other has never suffered a moment's relaxation from the hour of our first acquaintance, and I am sure it will continue to the end of our lives. I think the better of myself for being the object of the esteem of such a man as Russell. I love him and I honour him. I frame no system of happiness for my future life in which the enjoyment of his society does not constitute a most distinguishing feature, and, if I am ever inclined to murmur at the difficulties wherewith I have so long struggled, I think on the inestimable treasure I possess in the affection of my wife and the friendship of Russell, and I acknowledge that all my labours and sufferings are overpaid. I may truly say, that, even at this hour, when I am separated from both of them, and uncertain whether I may ever be so happy as to see them again, there is no action of my life which has not a remote reference to their opinion, which I equally prize. When I think I have acted well, and that I am likely to succeed in the important business wherein I am engaged, I say often to myself, " My dearest love and my friend Russell will be glad of this."

But to return to my history. My acquaintance with Russell commenced by an argument in the gallery of the House of Commons. He was, at that time, enamoured of the Whigs, but I knew these gentlemen a little better than he, and indeed he did not

going into the crime with which a prisoner was accused." One of the founders of the Society of United Irishmen, he was arrested by the Government in 1796 and kept in prison until 1802. Two months after his liberation he met Robert Emmet in Paris, entered into his plans for an insurrection, and returned to Ireland to prepare for action. But he was again arrested, tried for high treason, and hanged in October, 1803.—ED.]

long remain under the delusion. We were struck with each other, notwithstanding the difference of our opinions, and we agreed to dine together the next day, in order to discuss the question. We liked each other better the second day than the first, and every day since has increased and confirmed our mutual esteem.

My wife's health continuing still delicate, she was ordered by her physician to bathe in the salt water. I hired, in consequence, a little box of a house on the sea side, at Irishtown, where we spent the summer of 1790. Russell and I were inseparable, and, as our discussions were mostly political, and our sentiments agreed exactly, we extended our views, and fortified each other in the opinions to the propagation and establishment of which we have ever since been devoted. I recall with transport the happy days we spent together during that period ; the delicious dinners, in the preparation of which my wife, Russell, and myself were all engaged ; the afternoon walks, the discussions we had, as we lay stretched on the grass. It was delightful ! Sometimes Russell's venerable father, a veteran of near seventy, with the courage of a hero, the serenity of a philosopher, and the piety of a saint, used to visit our little mansion, and that day was a *fête*. My wife doted on the old man, and he loved her like one of his children. I will not attempt, because I am unable, to express the veneration and regard I had for him, and I am sure that, next to his own sons, and scarcely below them, he loved and esteemed me. Russell's brother John, too, used to visit us, a man of a most warm and affectionate heart, and, incontestably, of the most companionable talents I ever met. His humour, which was pure and natural, flowed in an inexhaustible stream. He had not the strength of character of my friend Tom, but for the charms of conversation he excelled him and all the world. Sometimes, too, my brother William used to join us for a week, from the county Kildare, where he resided with my brother Matthew, who had lately commenced a cotton manufactory at Prosperous in that county. I have already mentioned the convivial talents he possessed. In short, when the two Russells, my brother, and I were assembled, it is impossible to conceive of a happier society. I know not whether our wit was perfectly

classical or not, nor does it signify. If it was not sterling, at least
it passed current amongst ourselves. If I may judge, we were none
of us destitute of the humour indigenous in the soil of Ireland ; for
three of us I can answer, they possessed it in an eminent degree ; add
to this, I was the only one of the four who was not a poet, or at
least a maker of verses : so that every day produced a ballad, or
some poetical squib, which amused us after dinner, and, as our
conversation turned upon no ribaldry, or indecency, my wife and
sister never left the table. These were delicious days. The rich
and great, who sit down every day to the monotony of a splendid
entertainment, can form no idea of the happiness of our frugal
meal, nor of the infinite pleasure we found in taking each his part
in the preparation and attendance. My wife was the centre and
the soul of all. I scarcely know which of us loved her best ; her
courteous manners, her goodness of heart, her incomparable
humour, her never-failing cheerfulness, her affection for me and for
our children, rendered her the object of our common admiration
and delight. She loved Russell as well as I did. In short, a
more interesting society of individuals, connected by purer
motives, and animated by a more ardent attachment and friendship
for each other, cannot be imagined.

During the course of this summer there were strong appearances
of a rupture between England and Spain, relative to Nootka
Sound. I had mentioned to Russell my project for a military
colony in the South Seas, and, as we had both nothing better to
do, we sat down to look over my papers and memorandums
regarding that business. After some time, rather to amuse ourselves than with an expectation of its coming to anything, we
enlarged and corrected my original plan, and, having dressed up a
handsome memorial on the subject, I sent it enclosed in a letter to
the Duke of Richmond, then Master of the Ordnance. I thought
I should hear no more about it, but we were not a little surprised
when, a few days after, I received an answer from his Grace, in
which, after speaking with great civility of the merits of my plan,
he informed me such business was out of his department, but that,
if I desired it, he would deliver my memorial, and recommend it to

the notice of Lord Grenville, Secretary of State for Foreign Affairs whose business it properly was. I immediately wrote him an answer of acknowledgment, entreating him to support my plan, and, by the same post, I wrote also to Lord Grenville. In a few days I received answers from them both, informing me that the memorial had been received by Lord Grenville, and should be taken into speedy consideration, when, if any measures were to be adopted in consequence, I might depend on receiving further information. These letters we looked upon as leaving it barely possible that something might be done in the business, though very unlikely; and so indeed it proved, for, shortly after, a kind of peace, called a convention, was agreed upon between Spain and England, on which I wrote once more to Lord Grenville, enclosing a second memorial, in order to learn his determination, when I received a very civil answer, praising my plan, &c., and informing me that existing circumstances had rendered it unnecessary, at that time, to put it in execution, but that ministers would keep it in recollection. Thus ended, for the second time, my attempt to colonise in the South Seas, a measure which I still think might be attended with the most beneficial consequences to England. I keep all the papers relating to this business, including the originals of the minister's letters, and I have likewise copied the whole of them in a quarto book, to which I refer for further information. It was singular enough, this correspondence, continued by two of the King of England's cabinet ministers at St. James's, on the one part, and Russell and myself, from my little box at Irishtown, on the other. If the measure I proposed had been adopted, we were both determined on going out with the expedition, in which case, instead of planning revolutions in our own country, we might be now, perhaps, carrying on a privateering war (for which, I think, we have both talents) on the coasts of Spanish America. This adventure is an additional proof of the romantic spirit I have mentioned in the beginning of my memoirs, as a trait in our family; and, indeed, my friend Russell was, in that respect, completely one of ourselves. The minister's refusal did not sweeten us much towards him. I renewed the vow I had once before made, to make him, if I could, repent of it, in which Russell most heartily concurred. Perhaps the minister may yet have reason to wish he had let us go off quietly to the South Seas. I should be glad to have an opportunity to remind him of his old correspondent, and if I ever find one, I will not overlook it. I dare say he has utterly forgot the circumstance, but I have not. "*Everything, however, is for the best*," as Pangloss says, "*in this best of all possible worlds.*" If I had gone to the Sandwich Islands, in 1790, I should not be to-day *chef de brigade* in the service of the French Republic, not to mention what I may be in my own country, if our expedition thither succeeds.

But to return. Shortly after this disappointment, Russell, who had for two or three years revelled in the ease and dignity of an Ensign's half pay, amounting to £28 sterling a year, which he had earned before he was twenty-one, by broiling in the East Indies for five years, was unexpectedly promoted by favour of the commander-in-chief to an Ensigncy, on full pay, in the 64th regiment of foot, then quartered in the town of Belfast. He put himself, in consequence, in battle array, and prepared to join. I remember the last day he dined with us in Irishtown, where he came, to use his own quotation, "*all clinquant, all in gold!*" We set him to cook part of the dinner in a very fine suit of laced regimentals. I love to recall those scenes. We parted with the sincerest regret on both sides ; he set off for Belfast, and shortly after we returned to town for the winter, my wife's health being perfectly re-established, as she manifested by being, in due time, brought to bed of our eldest boy, whom we called William, after my brother.

This winter I endeavoured to institute a kind of political club, from which I expected great things. It consisted of seven or eight members, eminent for their talents and patriotism, and who had already more or less distinguished themselves by their literary productions. They were John Stack, Fellow of Trinity College, Dr. Wm. Drennan, author of the celebrated letters signed Orellana, Joseph Pollock, author of the still more justly celebrated letters of Owen Roe O'Neil, Peter Burrowes, a barrister, a man of a most powerful and comprehensive mind, William Johnson, a lawyer, also of respectable talents, Whitley Stokes, a Fellow of

Trinity College,[1] a man the extent and variety of whose knowledge is only to be exceeded by the number and intensity of his virtues, Russell, a corresponding member, and myself. As our political opinions, at that time, agreed in most essential points, however they may have since differed, and as this little club most certainly comprised a great proportion of information, talents, and integrity, it might naturally be expected that some distinguished publications should be the result ; yet, I know not how it was, we did not draw well together ; our meetings degenerated into downright ordinary suppers ; we became a mere oyster club, and, at length, a misunderstanding, or, rather, a rooted dislike to each other, which manifested

---

[1] [Of these men, the most remarkable were Drennan, Burrowes, and Stokes. Drennan (born 1754, died 1820), the son of a Presbyterian minister, and a medical doctor, was one of the founders of the United Irish Society, and the "penman" of the organisation. In 1794 he was tried for seditious libel, defended by Curran, and acquitted. Among his stirring lyrics the best known are "Erin to her own Tune," beginning with the words, "When Erin first rose ;" "Wake of William Orr" (a United Irishman hanged in 1797) ; "Wail of the Women after the Battle." Moore, in the Irish melody beginning with the lines :

> "Dear harp of my country, in darkness I found thee,
> The cold chain of silence had hung o'er me long,"

appends this note referring to Drennan : "In that rebellious but beautiful song, 'When Erin first rose,' there is, if I recollect right, the following line, 'The dark chain of silence was thrown o'er the deep.' In this song Drennan originated the phrase, 'Emerald Isle.' In 1800 Drennan returned from Dublin (where he resided since 1789) to his native town, Belfast. In 1808 he founded the *Belfast Magazine*, one of the ablest periodicals of its day." Peter Burrowes (born 1753, died 1841) was an eminent barrister and a distinguished member of the Irish House of Commons, a staunch supporter of the Catholic claims, and an unflinching enemy of the Union. "When I take into account," he said, in opposing that measure, "the hostile feelings generated by this foul attempt, by bribery, by treason, and by force, to plunder a nation of its liberties in the hour of its distress, I do not hesitate to pronounce that every sentiment of affection for Great Britain will perish if this measure pass, and that instead of uniting the nations, it will be the commencement of an era of inextinguishable animosity." He was one of Robert Emmet's council in 1803. Whitley Stokes (born 1763, died 1845), a physician and a distinguished Fellow of Trinity College, was a United Irishman up to 1792, but not afterwards. He was, however, suspected of revolutionary designs in 1797-8, and was deprived of his position at Trinity College for three years. Restored afterwards, he became Lecturer on Natural History and a Regius Professor of Physics.—ED.]

itself between Drennan and Pollock (who were completely Cæsar and Pompey with regard to literary empire), joined to the retreat of John Stack to his living in the North, and the little good we saw resulting from our association, induced us to drop off one by one, and thus, after three or four months of sickly existence, our club departed this life, leaving behind it a puny offspring of about a dozen essays on different subjects, all, as may be supposed, tolerable, but not one of any distinguished excellence. I am satisfied any one of the members, by devoting a week of his time to a well-chosen subject, would have produced a work of ten times more value than the whole club were able to show from their joint labours during its existence. This experiment satisfied me that men of genius, to be of use, must not be collected in numbers. They do not work well in the aggregate, and, indeed, even in ordinary conversations, I have observed that too many wits spoil the discourse. The dullest entertainment at which I ever remember to have assisted was one formed expressly to bring together near twenty persons, every one more or less distinguished for splendid talents, or great convivial qualities. We sat, and prosed together in great solemnity, endeavouring, by a rapid circulation of the bottle, to animate the discourse ; but it would not do, every man was clad in a suit of intellectual armour, in which he found himself secure it is true, but ill at his ease, and we all rejoiced at the moment when we were permitted to run home and get into our *robes de chambre* and slippers. Any two of the men present would have been the delight and entertainment of a well-chosen society, but all together was, as Wolsey says, "*too much honour.*" [1]

---

[1] NOTE BY TONE'S SON.—About this time, whilst his ideas on the evils resulting from the connection with Britain were fermenting in his mind (see the four essays addressed to the Club, in the Appendix, and his pamphlet on the Spanish war), my father wrote a letter to his friend Russell, where he expanded upon them, and concluded, " Such and such men (mentioning his friends and associates in the Club) think with me." This very innocent paper produced, about two years afterwards, in 1793, a most ridiculous alarm and disturbance. It would not have been noticed, at the time it was written, more than those pamphlets which were published ; but then, when the political fever raged at the highest, and when it was already forgotten by himself and his friends, it fell, by some chance or indiscretion, into the hands of the Government. The

In recording the names of the members of the Club, I find I have strangely omitted the name of a man whom, as well for his talents as his principles, I esteem as much as any, far more than most of them, I mean Thomas Addis Emmet, a barrister.[1] He is a man completely after my own heart; of a great and comprehensive mind ; of the warmest and sincerest affection for his friends ; and of a firm and steady adherence to his principles, to which he has sacrificed much, as I know, and would, I am sure, if necessary,

gentlemen mentioned, many of whom had since espoused the part of the administration, were all summoned before the Secret Committee. For that most illegal tribunal, the Star Chamber of Ireland, assumed the power of examining any suspected individuals on the opinions, as well as the actions, of themselves and of others; putting them on their oath, to answer all their questions, and imprisoning them arbitrarily. On this occasion these gentlemen were charged with being privy not only to a theoretical disquisition, but to a deep conspiracy against the Government, as far back as the year 1791. It is, however, remarkable that my father was not called before them. Perhaps he was deemed incorrigible.

This letter is alluded to in several parts of his subsequent memoirs, in Curran's Life by his son, and in several of Lord Clare's speeches to Parliament. His Lordship never lost an opportunity of alluding to that dangerous production, which disclosed the long meditation of those traitorous and rebellious designs, and it was laid before the British Parliament and Privy Council.

[1] [Thomas Addis Emmet (born in the city of Cork in 1764) was one of the most gifted men in the *United Irish* organisation. Having joined the medical profession, after a distinguished career at Trinity College, he ultimately (on the advice of Sir James Mackintosh, with whom he formed a fast friendship while studying medicine in Edinburgh) became a member of the Irish bar (1790). In 1795 he defended some prisoners charged with administering the *United Irish* oath, and, to strengthen his argument in support of his clients' innocence, took the oath himself in open court. In 1797 he was placed on the directory of the organisation, and in 1798 (before the rising) was arrested with his colleagues. When the insurrection was crushed, Emmet and the other prisoners, in order to save further bloodshed, agreed to give evidence (without implicating their comrades) before a Secret Committee of the House of Commons touching the history of the *United Irish* movement on condition that they were permitted to leave the country and that the public executions on account of the rebellion should be stopped. The evidence was given, but, as Emmet alleged, the Government broke faith with the prisoners. Emmet was kept in prison until 1802. In 1803 he urged Buonaparte to invade Ireland. In 1804 (when all his hopes for Ireland were blasted) he left France for America, where fame and fortune attended him. Rising rapidly to distinction as a member of the New York bar, he won golden opinions of all around him, and died in 1827 honoured by his profession and esteemed by a wide circle of admirers and of friends.—ED.]

sacrifice his life. His opinions and mine square exactly. In classing the men I most esteem, I would place him beside Russell, at the head of the list; because, with regard to them both, the most ardent feelings of my heart coincide exactly with the most severe decision of my judgment. There are men whom I regard as much as it is possible. I am sure, for example, if there be on earth such a thing as sincere friendship, I feel it for Whitley Stokes, for George Knox, and for Peter Burrowes. They are men whose talents I admire, whose virtues I reverence, and whose persons I love; but the regard which I feel for them, sincere and affectionate as it is, is certainly not of the same species with that which I entertain for Russell and Emmet. Between us there has been, from the very commencement of our acquaintance, a coincidence of sentiment, a harmony of feelings on points which we all conscientiously consider as of the last importance, which binds us in the closest ties to each other. We have unvaryingly been devoted to the pursuit of the same object, by the same means; we have had a fellowship in our labours; a society in our dangers; our hopes, our fears, our wishes, our friends, and our enemies, have been the same. When all this is considered, and the talents and principles of the men taken into the account, it will not be wondered at if I esteem Russell and Emmet as the first of my friends. If ever an opportunity offers, as circumstances at present seem likely to bring forward, I think their country will ratify my choice. With regard to Burrowes and Knox, whom I do most sincerely and affectionately love, their political opinions differ fundamentally from mine; and, perhaps, it is for the credit of us all three, that, with such an irreconcilable difference of sentiment, we have all along preserved a mutual regard and esteem for each other; at least, I am sure, I feel it particularly honourable to myself, for there are, perhaps, no two men in the world about whose good opinion I am more solicitous. Nor shall I soon forget the steady and unvarying friendship I experienced from them both, when my situation was, to all human appearance, utterly desperate, and when others, with at least as little reason to desert me, shunned me, as if I had the red spots of the plague out on me; but of that hereafter. With

regard to Whitley Stokes, his political opinions approach nearer to
mine than those of either Knox or Burrowes. I mention this, for,
in these days of unbounded discussion, politics unfortunately enter
into everything, even into our private friendships. We, however,
differ on many material points, and we differ on principles which do
honour to Stokes's heart. With an acute feeling of the degradation
of his country, and a just and generous indignation against her
oppressors, the tenderness and humanity of his disposition is such,
that he recoils from any measures to be attempted for her emancipation which may terminate in blood : in this respect I have not the
virtue to imitate him. I must observe, that, with this perhaps
extravagant anxiety for the lives of others, I am sure in any cause
which satisfied his conscience, no man would be more prodigal of
his own life than Whitley Stokes, for he is an enthusiast in his
nature, but "*what he would highly that would he holily*," and I am
afraid that in the present state of affairs that is a thing impossible.
I love Stokes most sincerely. With a most excellent and highly
cultivated mind, he possesses the distinguishing characteristic of
the best and most feeling heart, and I am sure it will not hurt the
self-love of any of the friends whose names I have recorded, when I
say that, in the full force of the phrase, I look upon Whitley Stokes
as the *very best man* I have ever known. Now that I am upon this
subject, I must observe that, in the choice of my friends, I have
been, all my life, extremely fortunate ; I hope I am duly sensible
of the infinite value of their esteem, and I take the greatest pride in
being able to say that I have preserved that esteem even of those
from whom I most materially differed on points of the last
importance, and on occasions of peculiar difficulty ; and this too
without any sacrifice of consistency or principle on either side—a
circumstance which, however, redounds still more to their credit
than to mine. But, to return to my history, from this long
digression, on which, however, I dwell with affection, exiled as I am
from the inestimable friends I have mentioned, it is a consolation to
my soul to dwell upon their merits, and the sincere and animated
affection I feel for them. God knows whether we shall ever meet,
or if we do, how many of us may survive the contest in which we

are, by all appearance, about to embark. If it be my lot, for one, to fall, I leave behind me this small testimony of my regard for them, written under circumstances which, I think, may warrant its sincerity.

The French Revolution had now been above a twelvemonth in its progress; at its commencement, as the first emotions are generally honest, every one was in its favour; but, after some time, the probable consequences to monarchy and aristocracy began to be foreseen, and the partisans of both to retrench considerably in their admiration: at length, Mr. Burke's famous invective appeared; and this in due season produced Paine's reply, which he called " Rights of Man." This controversy, and the gigantic event which gave rise to it, changed in an instant the politics of Ireland. Two years before, the nation was in lethargy. The puny efforts of the Whig Club, miserable and defective as their system was, were the only appearance of anything like exertion, and he was looked on as extravagant who thought of a parliamentary reform, against which, by the by, all parties equally set their face. I have already mentioned that, in those days of apathy and depression, I made an unsuccessful blow at the supremacy of England, by my pamphlet on the expected rupture with Spain; and I have also fairly mentioned that I found nobody who ventured to second my attempt, or paid the least attention to the doctrine I endeavoured to disseminate. But the rapid succession of events, and, above all, the explosion which had taken place in France, and blown into the elements a despotism rooted for fourteen centuries, had thoroughly aroused all Europe, and the eyes of every man, in every quarter, were turned anxiously on the French National Assembly. In England, Burke had the triumph completely to decide the public; fascinated by an eloquent publication, which flattered so many of their prejudices, and animated by their unconquerable hatred of France, which no change of circumstances could alter, the whole English nation, it may be said, retracted from their first decision in favour of the glorious and successful efforts of the French people; they sickened at the prospect of the approaching liberty and happiness of that mighty nation: they calculated, as merchants, the probable effects which the energy of regenerated France might have on their commerce ; they rejoiced when they saw the combination of despots formed to restore the ancient system, and perhaps to dismember the monarchy ; and they waited with impatience for an occasion, which, happily for mankind, they soon found, when they might, with some appearance of decency, engage in person in the infamous contest.

But matters were very different in Ireland, an oppressed, insulted, and plundered nation. As we well knew, experimentally, what it was to be enslaved, we sympathised most sincerely with the French people, and watched their progress to freedom with the utmost anxiety ; we had not, like England, a prejudice rooted in our very nature against France. As the Revolution advanced, and as events expanded themselves, the public spirit of Ireland rose with a rapid acceleration. The fears and animosities of the aristocracy rose in the same, or a still higher proportion. In a little time the French Revolution became the test of every man's political creed, and the nation was fairly divided into two great parties, the Aristocrats and the Democrats (epithets borrowed from France), who have ever since been measuring each other's strength, and carrying on a kind of smothered war, which the course of events, it is highly probable, may soon call into energy and action.

It is needless, I believe, to say that I was a Democrat from the very commencement, and, as all the retainers of Government, including the sages and judges of the law, were, of course, on the other side, this gave the *coup de grâce* to any expectations, if any such I had, of my succeeding at the bar, for I soon became pretty notorious ; but, in fact, I had for some time renounced all hope, and, I may say, all desire, of succeeding in a profession which I always disliked, and which the political prostitution of its members (though otherwise men of high honour and of great personal worth) had taught me sincerely to despise. I therefore seldom went near the Four Courts, nor did I adopt any one of the means, and, least of all, the study of the law, which are successfully employed by those young men whose object it is to rise in their profession.

As I came, about this period, rather more forward than I had hitherto done, it is necessary for understanding my history to take a rapid survey of the state of parties in Ireland; that is to say, of the members of the established religion, the Dissenters and the Catholics.

The first party, whom, for distinction's sake, I call the Protestants, though not above the tenth of the population, were in possession of the whole of the government, and of five-sixths of the landed property of the nation; they were, and had been, for above a century, in the quiet enjoyment of the church, the law, the revenue, the army, the navy, the magistracy, the corporations; in a word, of the whole patronage of Ireland. With properties whose title was founded in massacre and plunder, and being, as it were, but a colony of foreign usurpers in the land, they saw no security for their persons and estates but in a close connection with England, who profited of their fears, and, as the price of her protection, exacted the implicit surrender of the commerce and liberties of Ireland. Different events, particularly the revolution in America, had enabled and emboldened the other two parties, of whom I am about to speak, to hurry the Protestants into measures highly disagreeable to England and beneficial to their country, but in which, from accidental circumstances, they durst not refuse to concur. The spirit of the corps, however, remained unchanged, as they have manifested on every occasion since, which chance has offered. This party, therefore, so powerful by their property and influence, were implicitly devoted to England, which they esteemed necessary for the security of their existence; they adopted, in consequence, the sentiments and the language of the British cabinet; they dreaded and abhorred the principles of the French Revolution, and were, in one word, an aristocracy, in the fullest and most odious extent of the term.

The Dissenters, who formed the second party, were at least twice as numerous as the first. Like them, they were a colony of foreigners in their origin, but, being mostly engaged in trade and manufactures, with few overgrown landed proprietors among them, they did not, like them, feel that a slavish dependence on England was essential to their very existence. Strong in their numbers and their courage, they felt that they were able to defend themselves, and they soon ceased to consider themselves as any other than Irishmen. It was the Dissenters who composed the flower of the famous volunteer army of 1782,[1] which extorted from the English minister the restoration of what is affected to be called the constitution of Ireland ; it was they who first promoted and continued the demand of a parliamentary reform, in which, however, they were baffled by the superior address and chicanery of the aristocracy ; and it was they, finally, who were the first to stand forward, in the most decided and unqualified manner, in support of the principles of the French Revolution.

The Catholics, who composed the third party, were above two-thirds of the nation, and formed, perhaps, a still greater proportion. They embraced the entire peasantry of three provinces, they constituted a considerable portion of the mercantile interest, but, from the tyranny of the penal laws enacted at different periods against them, they possessed but a very small proportion of the landed property, perhaps not a fiftieth part of the whole. It is not my intention here to give a detail of that execrable and infamous code, framed with the art and the malice of demons, to plunder and degrade and brutalise the Catholics. Suffice it to say, that there was no injustice, no disgrace, no disqualification, moral, political, or religious, civil or military, that was not heaped upon them. It is with

---

[1] [Formed in 1778 (during the American War, when Ireland was denuded of troops) to protect the island from foreign invasion. There was no invasion, and the Volunteers turned their arms against England, demanding free trade and legislative independence. Both concessions were granted, 1779-1782. Thomas Davis has described the work of these "citizen soldiers" in stirring lines :—

> "When Grattan rose, none dared oppose
> The claim he made for freedom :
> They knew our swords, to back his words,
> Were ready, did he need them.
>
> *   *   *
>
> Remember still, through good and ill,
> How vain were prayers and tears—
> How vain were words, till flashed the swords
> Of the Irish Volunteers."—Ed.]

difficulty that I restrain myself from entering into the abominable
detail; but it is the less necessary, as it is to be found in so many
publications of the day.[1] This horrible system, pursued for above a
century with unrelenting acrimony and perseverance, had wrought
its full effect, and had, in fact, reduced the great body of the
Catholic peasantry of Ireland to a situation, morally and physically
speaking, below that of the beasts of the field. The spirit of their
few remaining gentry was broken, and their minds degraded; and
it was only in the class of their merchants and traders, and a few
members of the medical profession, who had smuggled an educa-

[1] [No one has summarised the provisions of the penal code so well as Mr.
Lecky:—

"To sum up briefly their provisions, they excluded the Catholics from the
Parliament, from the magistracy, from the corporations, from the university,
from the bench and from the bar, from the right of voting at parliamentary
elections or at vestries, of acting as constables, as sheriffs, or as jurymen, of
serving in the army or navy, of becoming solicitors, or even holding the position
of gamekeeper or watchman. They prohibited them from becoming school-
masters, ushers, or private tutors, or from sending their children abroad to
receive the Catholic education they were refused at home. They offered an
annuity to every priest who would forsake his creed, pronounced a sentence of
exile against the whole hierarchy, and restricted the right of celebrating the
mass to registered priests, whose number, according to the first intention of the
Legislature, was not to be renewed. The Catholics could not buy land, or
inherit or receive it as a gift from Protestants, or hold life annuities, or leases
for more than thirty-one years, or any lease on such terms that the profits of
the land exceeded one-third of the rent. A Catholic, except in the linen
trade, could have no more than two apprentices. He could not have a
horse of the value of more than £5, and any Protestant on giving him £5
might take his horse. He was compelled to pay double to the militia. In
case of war with a Catholic Power, he was obliged to reimburse the damage
done by the enemy's privateers. To convert a Protestant to Catholicism was
a capital offence. No Catholic might marry a Protestant. Into his own
family circle the elements of dissension were ingeniously introduced. A
Catholic landowner might not bequeath his land as he pleased. It was
divided equally among his children, unless the eldest son became a Protestant,
in which case the parent became simply a life tenant, and lost all power either
of selling or mortgaging it. If a Catholic's wife abandoned her husband's
religion, she was immediately free from his control, and the Chancellor could
assign her a certain proportion of her husband's property. If his child,
however young, professed itself a Protestant, he was taken from his father's
care, and the Chancellor could assign it a portion of its father's property. No
Catholic could be guardian either to his own children or to those of another."—
Macmillan's Magazine, January, 1873.—ED.]

tion in spite of the penal code, that anything like political sensation existed. Such was pretty nearly the situation of the three great parties at the commencement of the French Revolution, and certainly a much more gloomy prospect could not well present itself to the eyes of any friend to liberty and his country. But, as the luminary of truth and freedom in France advanced rapidly to its meridian splendour, the public mind in Ireland was proportionably illuminated; and to the honour of the Dissenters of Belfast be it said, they were the first to reduce to practice their newly-received principles, and to show, by being just, that they were deserving to be free.

The dominion of England in Ireland had been begun and continued in the disunion of the great sects which divided the latter country. In effectuating this disunion, the Protestant party were the willing instruments, as they saw clearly that if ever the Dissenters and Catholics were to discover their true interests, and, forgetting their former ruinous dissensions, were to unite cordially, and make common cause, the downfall of English supremacy, and, of course, of their own unjust monopoly, would be the necessary and immediate consequence. They therefore laboured continually, and, for a long time, successfully, to keep the other two sects asunder, and the English Government had even the address to persuade the Catholics that the non-execution of the penal laws, which were, in fact, too atrocious to be enforced in their full rigour, was owing to their clemency; that the Protestants and Dissenters, but especially the latter, were the enemies, and themselves, in effect, the protectors of the Catholic people. Under this arrangement the machine of government moved forward on carpet ground, but the time was, at length, come when this system of iniquity was to tumble in the dust, and the day of truth and reason to commence.

So far back as the year 1783, the Volunteers of Belfast had instructed their deputies to the convention, held in Dublin, for the purpose of framing a plan of parliamentary reform, to support the equal admission of the Catholics to the rights of freemen. In this instance of liberality, they were then almost alone; for it is their fate in political wisdom ever to be in advance of their countrymen. It was sufficient, however, to alarm the Government, who immediately procured from Lord Kenmare, at that time esteemed the leader of the Catholics, a solemn disavowal, in the name of the body, of any wish to be restored to their long lost rights. Prostrate as the Catholics were at that period, this last insult was too much ; they instantly assembled their General Committee,[1] and disavowed Lord Kenmare and his disavowal, observing at the same time that they were not framed so differently from all other men as to be in love with their own degradation. The majority of the volunteer convention, however, resolved to consider the infamous declaration of Lord Kenmare as the voice of the Catholics of Ireland, and, in consequence, the emancipation of that body made no part of their plan of reform. The consequence natural to such folly and injustice immediately ensued : the Government, seeing the convention, by their own act, separate themselves from the great mass of the people, who could alone give them effective force, held them at defiance, and that formidable assembly, which, under better principles, might have held the fate of Ireland in their hands, was broken up with disgrace and ignominy, a memorable warning that those who know not to render their just rights to others will be found incapable of firmly adhering to their own.

[1] [The Catholic Committee was formed between 1756–60 by Dr. Curry (author of the " Civil Wars in Ireland "), Charles O'Conor, of Ballenagar (author of " Dissertations on Irish History "), and Mr. Wyse, a country gentleman of culture and good sense. The Catholic aristocracy, as a body, timidly held aloof from the organisation, " scorning all connection with its members, laughing contemptuously at its labours, and interposing every obstacle to prevent, to discourage, to neutralise its success " (Wyse, " Catholic Association "). From the aristocracy, Curry, O'Conor, and Wyse turned to the Catholic merchants of Dublin who supported the movement heartily. But the Committee effected nothing, and melted gradually away in 1763. About 1773 it was reformed under the leadership of Lord Kenmare. But the co-operation of the aristocracy was worse than their neutrality or opposition. Kenmare proved an incompetent leader, and by his slavish submission to the Government brought about disunion and anarchy. But, in 1790, a great democratic leader came to the front, the aristocracy were pushed to the background, and, under the direction of John Keogh, the Catholic Committee soon became a real power in the country.—ED.]

The General Committee of the Catholics, of which I have spoken above, and which, since the year 1792, has made a distinguished feature in the politics of Ireland, was a body composed of their bishops, their country gentlemen, and of a certain number of merchants and traders, all resident in Dublin, but named by the Catholics in the different towns corporate to represent them. The original object of this institution was to obtain the repeal of a partial and oppressive tax called quarterage, which was levied on the Catholics only, and the Government, which found the committee at first a convenient instrument on some occasions, connived at their existence. So degraded was the Catholic mind at the period of the formation of their committee, about 1760, and long after, that they were happy to be allowed to go up to the Castle with an abominable slavish address to each successive Viceroy, of which, moreover, until the accession of the Duke of Portland, in 1782, so little notice was taken that his Grace was the first who condescended to give them an answer ; and, indeed, for above twenty years, the sole business of the General Committee was to prepare and deliver in those records of their depression. The effort which an honest indignation had called forth at the time of the volunteer convention in 1783 seemed to have exhausted their strength, and they sunk back into their primitive nullity. Under this appearance of apathy, however, a new spirit was gradually arising in the body, owing, principally, to the exertions and the example of one man, John Keogh,[1] to whose services his

---

[1] [John Keogh was born in Dublin in 1740. The younger Grattan describes him thus :—" He was the ablest man of the Catholic body ; he had a powerful understanding, and few men of that class were superior in intellect, or even equal to him. His mind was strong and his head was clear ; he possessed judgment and discretion, and had the art to unite and bring men forward on a hazardous enterprise, and at a critical moment. He did more for the Roman Catholics than any other individual of that body. He had the merit of raising a party, and bringing out the Catholic people. Before his time they were nothing ; their bishops were servile, and Dr. Troy, Archbishop of Dublin, though an excellent man, was under the influence of the Castle. . . . At the onset of his life Keogh had been in business, and began as an humble tradesman. He contrived to get into the Catholic Committee, and instantly formed a plan to destroy the aristocratic part and introduce the democratic. He wrote, he published, he harangued, and strove to kindle some spirit among the people"

country, and more especially the Catholics, are singularly indebted. In fact, the downfall of feudal tyranny was acted in little on the theatre of the General Committee. The influence of their clergy and of their barons was gradually undermined, and the third estate, the commercial interest, rising in wealth and power, was preparing, by degrees, to throw off the yoke, in the imposing, or, at least, the continuing of which the leaders of the body—I mean the prelates and aristocracy, to their disgrace be it spoken—were ready to concur. Already had those leaders, acting in obedience to the orders of the Government, which held them in fetters, suffered one or two signal defeats in the committee, owing principally to the talents and address of John Keogh; the parties began to be defined, and a sturdy democracy of new men, with bolder views and stronger talents, soon superseded the timid counsels and slavish measures of the ancient aristocracy. Everything seemed tending to a better order of things among the Catholics, and an occasion soon offered to call the energy of their new leaders into action.

The Dissenters of the north, and more especially of the town of Belfast, are, from the genius of their religion, and from the superior diffusion of political information among them, sincere and enlightened Republicans. They had ever been foremost in the pursuit of parliamentary reform, and I have already mentioned the early

(Grattan, "Memoirs"). Keogh has been called a revolutionist pure and simple, but, as I think, with insufficient proof. He co-operated with revolutionists, but was not a decided revolutionist himself. Indeed, nothing shows how great were his qualities as a leader more than his capacity of working with men of various political views and tendencies. He was the friend of Burke as well as the companion of Wolfe Tone ; the adviser of the Catholic bishops as well as the *confidant* of the United Irishmen. In fact, he combined almost all the forces favourable to the Catholic cause, and by this combination secured the admission of the Catholics to the parliamentary franchise in 1793. On the failure, in 1795, of all constitutional efforts to obtain further relaxation of the penal code, Keogh was more than tempted to throw in his lot with Tone, but he drew back in time, and took no active part in the revolutionary movement which followed. After the Union he still continued to labour in the Catholic interest, but gave way gradually to one who was destined to carry out his policy with complete triumph. He died in 1817, and was succeeded, as popular tribune, by the greatest of all Irish Constitutional leaders, O'Connell.--ED.]

wisdom and virtue of the town of Belfast in proposing the emancipation of the Catholics, so far back as the year 1783. The
French Revolution had awakened all parties in the nation from the
stupor in which they lay plunged, from the time of the dispersion
of the ever memorable Volunteer Convention, and the citizens of
Belfast were the first to raise their heads from the abyss, and to
look the situation of their country steadily in the face. They saw
at a glance their true object, and the only means to obtain it ;
conscious that the force of the existing Government was such as
to require the united efforts of the whole Irish people to subvert
it, and, long convinced in their own minds that to be free it was
necessary to be just, they cast their eyes once more on the long
neglected Catholics, and profiting of past errors, for which, however, they had not to accuse themselves, they determined to begin
on a new system, and to raise the structure of the liberty and
independence of their country, on the broad basis of equal rights to
the whole people.

The Catholics, on their part, were rapidly advancing in political
spirit and information. Every month, every day, as the revolution
in France went prosperously forward, added to their courage and
their force, and the hour seemed at last arrived, when, after a dreary
oppression of above one hundred years, they were once more to
appear on the political theatre of their country. They saw the
brilliant prospect of success which events in France opened to their
view, and they determined to avail themselves with promptitude of
that opportunity, which never returns to those who omit it. For
this the active members of the General Committee resolved to set
on foot an immediate application to Parliament, praying for a repeal of the penal laws. The first difficulty they had to surmount
arose in their own body ; their peers, their gentry (as they affected
to call themselves), and their prelates, either seduced or intimidated
by Government, gave the measure all possible opposition ; and, at
length, after a long contest, in which both parties strained every
nerve and produced the whole of their strength, the question was
decided on a division in the committee by a majority of at least
six to one in favour of the intended application. The triumph of

the young democracy was complete; but, though the aristocracy were defeated, they were not yet entirely broken down. By the instigation of Government they had the meanness to secede from the General Committee, to disavow their acts, and even to publish in the papers that they did not wish to embarrass the Government by advancing their claims of emancipation. It is difficult to conceive such a degree of political degradation; but what will not the tyranny of an execrable system produce in time? Sixty-eight gentlemen, individually of high spirit, were found, who, publicly, and in a body, deserted their party and their own just claims, and even sanctioned this pitiful desertion by the authority of their signatures. Such an effect had the operation of the penal laws on the minds of the Catholics of Ireland, as proud a race as any in all Europe!

But I am in some degree anticipating matters, and, indeed, instead of a few memorandums relating to myself, I find myself embarking in a kind of *history of my own times;* let me return and condense as much as I can. The first attempts of the Catholic Committee failed totally; endeavouring to accommodate all parties, they framed a petition so humble that it ventured to ask for nothing, and even this petition they could not find a single member of the Legislature to present; of so little consequence, in the year 1790, was the great mass of the Irish people! Not disheartened, however, by this defeat, they went on, and in the interval between that and the approaching session, they were preparing measures for a second application. In order to add a greater weight and consequence to their intended petition, they brought over to Ireland Richard Burke,[1] only son of the celebrated Edmund, and appointed him their agent to conduct their application to Parliament. This young man came over with considerable advantages, and especially with the *éclat* of his father's name, who, the Catholics concluded, and very reasonably, would, for his sake, if not for theirs, assist his son with his advice

[1] ["Mr. Richard Burke had acted as agent to the Catholic Committee during the year 1791 and to July, 1792. . . . His father's name and advice, and the influence he had in England, were the son's best recommendations. He had been spoiled by Mr. Burke, who greatly overrated his abilities; for he was vain and conceited, and wanted temper and modesty." (Grattan, " Memoirs.")—Ed.]

and directions. But their expectations in the event proved abortive. Richard Burke, with a considerable portion of talents from nature, and cultivated, as may be well supposed, with the utmost care by his father, who idolised him, was utterly deficient in judgment, in temper, and especially in the art of managing parties. In three or four months' time, during which he remained in Ireland, he contrived to embroil himself, and, in a certain degree, the committee, with all parties in Parliament, the Opposition as well as the Government, and, finally, desiring to drive his employers into measures of which they disapproved, and thinking himself strong enough to go on without the assistance of the men who introduced, and, as long as their duty would permit, supported him, in which he miserably deceived himself, he ended his short and turbulent career by breaking with the General Committee. That body, however, treated him respectfully to the last, and, on his departure, they sent a deputation to thank him for his exertions, and presented him with the sum of two thousand guineas.

CHAPTER III.

THE UNITED IRISHMEN AND THE CATHOLIC COMMITTEE.

IT was pretty much about this time that my connection with the Catholic body commenced in the manner which I am about to relate. I cannot pretend to strict accuracy as to dates, for I write entirely from memory ; all my papers being in America.

Russell had, on his arrival to join his regiment at Belfast, found the people so much to his taste, and in return had rendered himself so agreeable to them, that he was speedily admitted into their confidence, and became a member of several of their clubs. This was an unusual circumstance, as British officers, it may well be supposed, were no great favourites with the Republicans of Belfast. The Catholic question was, at this period, beginning to attract the public notice ; and the Belfast Volunteers, on some public occasion, I know not precisely what, wished to come forward with a declaration in its favour. For this purpose Russell, who by this time was entirely in their confidence, wrote to me to draw up and transmit to him such a declaration as I thought proper, which I accordingly did. A meeting of the corps was held in consequence, but an opposition unexpectedly arising to that part of the declarations which alluded directly to the Catholic claims, that passage was, for the sake of unanimity, withdrawn for the present, and the declarations then passed unanimously. Russell wrote me an account of all this, and it immediately set me on thinking more seriously than I had yet done upon the state of Ireland. I soon formed my theory, and on that theory I have unvaryingly acted ever since.

To subvert the tyranny of our execrable Government, to break the connection with England, the never-failing source of all our political evils, and to assert the independence of my country—these were my objects. To unite the whole people of Ireland, to abolish the memory of all past dissensions, and to substitute the common name of Irishman in place of the denominations of Protestant, Catholic and Dissenter—these were my means. To effectuate these great objects, I reviewed the three great sects. The Protestants I despaired of from the outset for obvious reasons. Already in possession by an unjust monopoly of the whole power and patronage of the country, it was not to be supposed they would ever concur in measures the certain tendency of which must be to lessen their influence as a party, how much soever the nation might gain. To the Catholics I thought it unnecessary to address myself, because, that as no change could make their political situation worse, I reckoned upon their support to a certainty; besides, they had already begun to manifest a strong sense of their wrongs and oppressions; and, finally, I well knew that, however it might be disguised or suppressed, there existed in the breast of every Irish Catholic an inextirpable abhorrence of the English name and power. There remained only the Dissenters, whom I knew to be patriotic and enlightened; however, the recent events at Belfast had showed me that all prejudice was not yet entirely removed from their minds. I sat down accordingly, and wrote a pamphlet addressed to the Dissenters, and which I entitled, "An Argument on behalf of the Catholics of Ireland," the object of which was to convince them that they and the Catholics had but one common interest and one common enemy; that the depression and slavery of Ireland was produced and perpetuated by the divisions existing between them, and that, consequently, to assert the independence of their country, and their own individual liberties, it was necessary to forget all former feuds, to consolidate the entire strength of the whole nation, and to form for the future but one people. These principles I supported by the best arguments which suggested themselves to me, and particularly by demonstrating that the cause of the failure of all former efforts, and more especially of the Volunteer Convention in 1783, was the unjust neglect of the claims of their Catholic brethren. This pamphlet, which appeared in September, 1791, under the signature of a Northern Whig, had a considerable degree of success. The Catholics (*with not one of whom I was at the time acquainted*) were pleased with the efforts of a Volunteer in their cause, and distributed it in all quarters. The people of Belfast, of whom I had spoken with the respect and admiration I sincerely felt for them, and to whom I was also perfectly unknown, printed a very large edition which they dispersed through the whole North of Ireland, and I have the great satisfaction to believe that many of the Dissenters were converted by my arguments. It is like vanity to speak of my own performances so much ; and the fact is, I believe that I am somewhat vain on that topic ; but, as it was the immediate cause of my being made known to the Catholic body, I may be, perhaps, excused for dwelling upon a circumstance which I must ever look on for that reason as one of the most fortunate of my life. As my pamphlet spread more and more, my acquaintance amongst the Catholics extended accordingly. My first friend in the body was John Keogh, and through him I became acquainted with all the leaders, as Richard McCormick, John Sweetman, Edward Byrne, Thomas Braughall,[1]—in short, the whole sub-committee, and most of the active members of the General Committee. It was a kind of fashion this winter (1791) among the Catholics to give splendid dinners to their political friends, in and out of Parliament, and I was always a guest of course. I was invited to a grand dinner given to Richard Burke on his leaving Dublin, together with William Todd Jones, who had distinguished himself by a most excellent pamphlet in favour of the Catholic cause, as well as to several entertainments given by clubs and associations ; in short, I began to grow into something like reputation, and my company was, in a manner, a requisite at all the entertainments of that winter.

[1] [Byrne was chairman, and McCormick secretary of the Catholic Committee. Sweetman was a United Irishman. Braughall and McCormick probably (some would say positively) belonged also to the society ; they were certainly trusted by its leading men. Sweetman and Braughall were arrested in 1798. Braughall was liberated on giving bail, "himself in £1,000 and two sureties in £500." Sweetman was kept in custody until 1802, and then liberated on condition of living abroad. He was ultimately allowed to return to Ireland. A reward of £300 was offered in 1798 for the arrest of McCormick (with others), but he escaped.—Ed.]

But this was not all. The Volunteers of Belfast, of the first or green company, were pleased, in consequence of my pamphlet, to elect me an honorary member of their corps, a favour which they were very delicate in bestowing, as I believe I was the only person, except the great Henry Flood, who was ever honoured with that mark of their approbation. I was also invited to spend a few days in Belfast, in order to assist in framing the first club of United Irishmen, and to cultivate a personal acquaintance with those men whom, though I highly esteemed, I knew as yet but by reputation. In consequence, about the beginning of October, I went down with my friend Russell, who had, by this time, quit the army, and was in Dublin, on his private affairs. The incidents of that journey, which was by far the most agreeable and interesting one I had ever made, I recorded in a kind of diary, a practice which I then commenced, and have ever since, from time to time, continued, as circumstances of sufficient importance occurred. To that diary I refer. It is sufficient here to say, that my reception was of the most flattering kind, and that I found the men of the most distinguished public virtue in the nation the most estimable in all the domestic relations of life : I had the good fortune to render myself agreeable to them, and a friendship was then formed between us which I think it will not be easy to shake. It is a kind of injustice to name individuals, yet I cannot refuse myself the pleasure of observing how peculiarly fortunate I esteem myself in having formed connections with Samuel Neilson, Robert Simms, William Simms, William Sinclair, Thomas Macabe : [1] I may as well stop

[1] [Samuel Neilson (the son of a Dissenting clergyman) was born in county Down in 1761. Having made a competence in trade, he retired from business and entered politics, a supporter of the Catholic claims, an advocate of Parliamentary reform. With him probably originated the idea of the United Irish Society. He also founded the *Northern Star*, the first organ of the society in the press. Though subjected to frequent Government prosecutions, Neilson conducted the paper successfully until September, 1796, when the office was "attacked and ransacked," and he himself arrested. The paper was finally suppressed in May, 1797. Neilson was kept in prison (without trial) until February, 1798. Then liberated, he worked with Lord Edward Fitzgerald in preparing for insurrection. But he was again arrested in May. Brought to trial in irons, he defied the authorities. Addressing the court, he said, " I scorn your power, and despise that authority which it shall

here ; for, in enumerating my most particular friends, I find I am, in fact, making out a list of the men of Belfast most distinguished for their virtue, talent, and patriotism. To proceed. We formed our club, of which I wrote the declaration, and certainly the formation of that club commenced a new epoch in the politics of Ireland. At length, after a stay of about three weeks, which I look back upon as perhaps the pleasantest in my life, Russell and I returned to Dublin, with instructions to cultivate the leaders in the popular interest, being Protestants, and, if possible, to form, in the capital, a club of United Irishmen. Neither Russell nor myself were known to one of those leaders ; however, we soon contrived to get acquainted with James Napper Tandy,[1] who was the principal of them, and, through him, with several others, so that, in a little time, we succeeded, and a club was accordingly formed, of which the Honourable Simon Butler[2] was the first

ever be my pride to have opposed. Why am I kept with these weighty irons on me, so heavy that three ordinary men could scarcely carry them ?" He was not tried, being one of the prisoners who entered into the honourable compact with the Government already mentioned (*ante*, p. 35). But he was kept in prison until 1802. Writing, after his liberation, to Hamilton Rowan, he says : " Neither the eight years' hardship I have endured, the total destruction of my property, the forlorn state of my wife and children, the momentary failure of our national exertions, have abated my ardour in the cause of my country, and of general liberty." Neilson finally went to America, where he died in 1803. The Simmses, Sinclair, and Macabe all took an active part in forming the United Irish Society. The Simmses were part proprietors of the *Northern Star.*—ED.]

[1] James Napper Tandy was born in Dublin in 1740. At first a Volunteer, afterwards a United Irishman, he took an active part in public affairs from 1779 to 1798. Suspected of treasonable practices, he fled to America in 1793. In September, 1798, he left for France, there raised a small force of Irish refugees, proceeded to Ireland, and landed on the island of Arran, near Donegal. But hearing of Humbert's defeat (*ante*, p. 6), he immediately sailed for Norway ; thence attempting to return to France was arrested at Hamburg and handed over to the English authorities in 1799. Tried for participating in the insurrectionary movement, he was acquitted on a point of law. Tried again in 1801 for his attempted invasion, he pleaded guilty and was sentenced to death. But he was pardoned, partly under pressure from Buonaparte, who claimed him as a French general, and partly on the intercession of Lord Cornwallis, who urged " the incapacity of this old man to do further mischief, the mode by which he came into our hands, his long subsequent confinement, and lastly, the streams of blood which have flowed in this island for these last three years." But Tandy had to leave Ireland. He died in France in 1803.

[2] In 1793 Butler was sentenced to six months' imprisonment and to a fine of

chairman, and Tandy the first secretary. The club adopted the declaration of their brethren of Belfast, with whom they immediately opened a correspondence. It is but justice to an honest man who has been persecuted for his firm adherence to his principles, to observe here, that Tandy, in coming forward on this occasion, well knew that he was putting to the most extreme hazard his popularity among the corporations of the city of Dublin, with whom he had enjoyed the most unbounded influence for near twenty years ; and, in fact, in the event, his popularity was sacrificed. That did not prevent, however, his taking his part decidedly : he had the firmness to forego the gratification of his private feelings for the good of his country. The truth is, Tandy was a very sincere Republican, and it did not require much argument to show him the impossibility of attaining a Republic by any means short of the united powers of the whole people ; he therefore renounced the lesser object for the greater, and gave up the certain influence which he possessed (and had well earned) in the city, for the contingency of that influence which he might have (and well deserves to have) in the nation. For my own part, I think it right to mention, that, at this time, the establishment of a Republic was not the immediate object of my speculations. My object was to secure the independence of my country under any form of government, to which I was led by a hatred of England, so deeply rooted in my nature, that it was rather an instinct than a principle. I left to others, better qualified for the inquiry, the investigation and merits of the different forms of government, and I contented myself with labouring on my own system, which was luckily in perfect coincidence as to its operation with that of those men who viewed the question on a broader and juster scale than I did at the time I mention. But to return. The club was scarcely formed before I lost all pretensions to anything like influence in their

£500 for presiding at a United Irish meeting where certain proceedings of the House of Lords (the inquiry into Defenderism) were declared to be illegal. On his release, he sent a challenge to Lord Clare, who had used offensive language in passing sentence on him. But both Clare's "friend," Colonel Murray, and Butler's "friend," Hamilton Rowan, agreed that Clare, "as Chancellor," could not fight. In the same year the Catholic Committee voted Butler £500 for his services in the Catholic cause.

measures, a circumstance which at first mortified me not a little, and
perhaps, had I retained more weight in their councils, I might have
prevented, as on some occasions I laboured unsuccessfully to
prevent, their running into indiscretions, which gave their enemies
but too great advantages over them. It is easy to be wise after
the event. So it was, however, that I soon sunk into obscurity in
the club, which, however, I had the satisfaction to see daily
increasing in numbers and consequence. The Catholics, particularly, flocked in in crowds, as well as some of the Protestant
members of corporations most distinguished for their liberality
and public spirit on former occasions ; and, indeed, I must do the
society the justice to say, that I believe there never existed a
political body which included amongst its members a greater
portion of sincere uncorrupted patriotism, as well as a very
repectable proportion of talents. Their publications, mostly
written by Dr. Drennan, and many of them admirably well
done, began to draw the public attention, especially as they were
evidently the production of a society utterly disclaiming all party
views or motives, and acting on a broad original scale, not sparing
those who called themselves patriots more than those who were
the habitual slaves of the Government ; a system in which I
heartily concurred, having long entertained a more serious contempt for what is called *opposition* than for the common prostitutes
of the Treasury bench, who want at least the vice of hypocrisy.
At length the Solicitor-General,[1] in speaking of the society, having

---

[1] [Toler, afterwards the notorious Lord Norbury (b. 1740, d. 1831). Toler's
words were : " I have seen papers signed by Tobias McKenna, with Simon
Butler in the chair, and Napper Tandy lending his *countenance;* I should have
thought they could have put a better *face* upon it. But, sir, such fellows are
too despicable for notice ; therefore I shall not drag them from their obscurity."
(Tandy had a very odd cast of countenance—hence the words in italics had a
personal sting.) In 1800 Toler was made Chief Justice of the Common Pleas,
and Baron Norbury. He is probably best known as the judge who tried Robert
Emmet (hanged for high treason in 1803). Many stories are told suggestive of
Norbury's severity on the bench. " Is that hung beef, Mr. Curran?" he once
said to the great advocate at dinner. " No, but if your lordship tries it, it will
be hung," was the ready reply. Norbury retired from the bench in 1827. He
had fallen asleep while trying a murder case. O'Connell seized the opportunity
to force his resignation by having Parliament petitioned for his removal.—ED.]

made use of expressions in the House of Commons extremely offensive, an explanation was demanded of him by Simon Butler, chairman, and Tandy, secretary. Butler was satisfied—Tandy was not ; and, after several messages, which it is not my affair to detail, the Solicitor-General at length complained to the House of a breach of privilege, and Tandy was ordered, in the first instance, into custody. He was in consequence arrested by a messenger, from whom he found means to make his escape, and immediately a proclamation was issued, offering a reward for taking him. The society now was in a difficult situation, and I thought myself called upon to make an effort, at all hazards to myself, to prevent its falling by any improper timidity in the public opinion. We were in fact committed with the House of Commons on the question of privilege, and having fairly engaged in the contest, it was impossible to recede without a total forfeiture of character. Under these circumstances I cast my eyes on Archibald Hamilton Rowan,[1] a distinguished member of the society, whose many virtues, public and private, had set his name above the reach of even the malevolence of party, whose situation in life was of the most respectable rank, if ranks be indeed respectable, and,

[1] [Archibald Hamilton Rowan (son of an Ulster landed proprietor) was born in London in 1751. He was educated at Westminster, and later on entered Cambridge University. After some years of travel he settled down in Ireland in 1784. Joined the Volunteers, the Whig Club, and finally the United Irishmen. At first an advanced constitutional reformer, he glided into treason. Tried in 1794 for seditious libel, he was defended by Curran, in a memorable speech, found guilty, and sentenced to two years' imprisonment and to a fine of £500. Knowing that, apart from the accusation of seditious libel, there was further incriminating evidence of a treasonable nature against him, he escaped from prison, by the connivance of his jailer, and got out of the country by the help of Sweetman. Two brothers, named Sheridan, agreed to man a "little fishing wherry" belonging to Sweetman, and to land Rowan in France. At the moment of departure one of the Sheridans pulled out of his pocket a Government proclamation offering £1,000 reward for the arrest of the fugitive. "It is Mr. Hamilton Rowan we are to take to France," he said. "Yes," answered Sweetman, "here he is." "Never mind," was the reply, "by —— we will land him safe !" And they did. In 1795 Rowan went to America, where he remained for five years. In 1803 he was allowed to return to England, and in 1806 to Ireland, where he died in 1834. ("Autobiography of Hamilton Rowan," ed. Drummond.)—ED.]

above all, whose personal courage was not to be shaken, a circumstance, in the actual situation of affairs, of the last importance. To Rowan, therefore, I applied ; I showed him that the current of public opinion was rather setting against us in this business, and that it was necessary that some of us should step forward and expose ourselves, at all risks, to show the House of Commons, and the nation at large, that we were not to be intimidated or put down so easily. I offered, if he would take the chair, that I would, with the society's permission, act as secretary, and that we would give our signatures to such publications as circumstances might render necessary. Rowan instantly agreed, and, accordingly, on the next night of meeting, he was chosen chairman, and I pro-secretary, in the absence of Tandy ; and the society having agreed to the resolutions proposed, which were worded in a manner very offensive to the dignity of the House of Commons, and, in fact, amounted to a challenge of their authority, we inserted them in all the newspapers, and printed 5,000 copies, with our names affixed.

The least that Rowan and I expected in consequence of this step, which, under the circumstances, was, I must say, rather a bold one, was to be committed to Newgate for a breach of privilege, and perhaps exposed to personal discussions with some of the members of the House of Commons ; for he proposed, and I agreed, that, if any disrespectful language was applied to either of us in any debate which might arise on the business, we would attack the person, whoever he might be, immediately, and oblige him either to recant his words or give battle. All our determination, however, came to nothing. The House of Commons, either content with their victory over Tandy, who was obliged to conceal himself for some time, or not thinking Rowan and myself objects sufficiently important to attract their notice, or perhaps, which I rather believed, not wishing just then to embroil themselves with a man of Rowan's firmness and courage, not to speak of his great and justly merited popularity, took no notice whatsoever of our resolutions, and, in this manner, he and I had the good fortune, and, I may say, the merit, to rescue the society from a situation of considerable difficulty without any actual suffering, though certainly with some personal hazard on our part. We had likewise the satisfaction to see the society, instead of losing ground, rise rapidly in the public opinion by their firmness on the occasion. Shortly after, on the last day of the sessions, Tandy appeared in public, and was taken into custody, the whole society attending him in a body to the House of Commons. He was ordered by the Speaker to be committed to Newgate, whither he was conveyed, the society attending him as before, and the Parliament being prorogued in half an hour after, he was liberated immediately, and escorted in triumph to his own house. On this occasion Rowan and I attended of course, and were in the gallery of the House of Commons. As we were not sure but we might be attacked ourselves, we took pains to place ourselves in a conspicuous situation, and to wear our Whig Club uniforms, which were rather gaudy, in order to signify to all whom it might concern, that there we were. A good many of the members, we observed remarked us, but no further notice was taken : our names were never mentioned ; the whole business passed over quietly, and I resigned my pro-secretaryship, being the only office I ever held in the society, into the hands of Tandy, who resumed his functions. This was in spring, 1792 : I should observe, that the day after the publication above mentioned, when I attended near the House of Commons in expectation of being called before them to answer for what I had done, and had requested my friend, Sir Lawrence Parsons, to give me notice, in order that I might present myself, the House took fire by accident, and was burned to the ground.

The Society of United Irishmen [1] beginning to attract the public

---

[1] [It has been said that the United Irish Society was, in its inception, a constitutional organisation. Some of its founders, however, were rebels from the outset, though others were not. But the "test" adopted at a meeting in Dublin in November, 1791, was certainly constitutional. " I, A. B., in the presence of God, do pledge myself to my country that I will use all my abilities and influence in the attainment of an adequate and impartial representation of the Irish nation in Parliament, and as a means of absolute and immediate necessity in the attainment of this chief good of Ireland, I will endeavour, as much as lies in my ability, to forward a brotherhood of affection, an identity of interests, a communion of rights, and a union of power among Irishmen of all

notice considerably, in consequence of the events which I have mentioned, and it being pretty generally known that I was principally instrumental in its formation, I was one day surprised by a visit from the barrister, who had about two years before spoken to me on the part of the Whig leaders, a business of which I had long since discharged my memory. He told me he was sorry to see the new line I was adopting in politics, the more so as I might rely upon it that the principles I now held would never be generally adopted, and consequently I was devoting myself without advancing any beneficial purpose; he also testified to me surprise at my conduct, and insinuated pretty directly, though with great civility, that I had not kept faith with the Whigs, with whom he professed to understand I had connected myself, and whom, in consequence, I ought to have consulted before I took so decided a line of conduct as I had lately done. I did not like the latter part of his discourse at all; however I answered him with great civility on my part, that, as to the principles he mentioned, I had not adopted them without examination; that, as to the pamphlet I had written in the Catholic cause, I had not advanced a syllable which I did not conscientiously believe, and, consequently, I was neither inclined to repent nor retract. As to my supposed connection with the Whigs, I reminded him that I had not sought them; on the contrary, they had sought me; if they had, on reflection, not thought me worth cultivating, that was no fault of mine. I observed, also, that Mr. George Ponsonby,

religious persuasions, without which every reform in Parliament must be partial, not national, inadequate to the wants, delusive to the wishes, and insufficient for the freedom and happiness of this country." The resolutions passed at Belfast in October, 1791, were also constitutional, with, however, an anti-English tone. 1. "That the weight of English influence in the government of this country is so great as to require a cordial union among all the people of Ireland, to maintain that balance which is essential to the preservation of our liberties, and the extension of our commerce." 2. "That the sole constitutional mode by which this influence can be opposed is by a complete and radical reform of the representation of the people in Parliament." 3. "That no reform is [just] which does not include Irishmen of every religious persuasion." It may, at least, be said that from 1791 to 1794-5 the society was avowedly constitutional; afterwards it became avowedly rebellious, *post.* —ED.]

whom I looked upon as principal in the business, had never spoken to me above a dozen times in my life, and then merely on ordinary topics ; that I was too proud to be treated in that manner, and, if I was supposed capable to render service to the party, it would only be by confiding in, and communicating with me, that I could be really serviceable, and on that footing only would I consent to be treated ; that probably Mr. Ponsonby would think that rather a lofty declaration, but it was my determination, the more as I knew he was rather a proud man.   Finally, I observed, he had my permission to report all this, and that I looked on myself as under no tie of obligation whatsoever ; that I had written a pamphlet, unsolicited, in favour of the party ; that I had consequently been employed in a business, professionally, which produced me eighty guineas ; that I looked on myself as sufficiently rewarded, but I also considered the money as fully earned ; that I had at present taken my party ; that my principles were known, and I was not at all disposed to retract them ; what I had done I had done, and I was determined to abide by it.   My friend then said he was sorry to see me so obstinate in what he must consider an indiscreet line of conduct, and protesting that his principal object was to serve me, in which I believed him, he took his leave, and this put an end completely to the idea of a connection with the Whigs.   I spoke rather haughtily in this affair, because I was somewhat provoked at the insinuation of duplicity, and, besides, I wished to have a blow at Mr. George Ponsonby, who seemed desirous to retain me as a kind of pamphleteer in his service, at the same time that he industriously avoided anything like communication with me, a situation to which I was neither so weak nor so mean as to suffer myself to be reduced : and as I well knew he was one of the proudest men in Ireland, I took care to speak on a footing of the most independent equality.   After this discussion, I for the second time dismissed all idea of Ponsonby and the Whigs, but I had good reason, a long time after, to believe that he had not so readily forgotten the business as I did, and indeed he was very near having his full revenge of me, as I shall mention in its place.

I have already observed that the first attempts of the Catholic

Committee, after the secession of their aristocracy, were totally unsuccessful. In 1790 they could not even find a member of Parliament who would condescend to present their petition. In 1791 Richard Burke, their then agent, had prepared, on their behalf, a very well-written philippic, but which certainly was no petition, which, after considerable difficulties, resulting in a great degree from his want of temper and discretion, after being offered to and accepted by different members, was at length finally refused, a circumstance which, by disgusting him extremely with all parties, I believe, determined him to quit Ireland. After his departure another petition was prepared and presented by . . . .[1] but no unfortunate paper was ever so maltreated. The committee in general, and its more active and ostensible members in particular, were vilified and abused in the grossest manner; they were called a rabble of obscure porter-drinking mechanics, without property, pretensions, or influence, who met in holes and corners, and fancied themselves the representatives of the Catholic body, who disavowed and despised them; the independence and respectability of the sixty-eight renegadoes who had set their hands so infamously to their act of apostacy were extolled to the skies, while the lowest and most clumsy personalities were heaped upon the leaders of the committee, particularly Edward Byrne and John Keogh, who had the honour to be selected from their brethren, and exposed as butts for the small wit of the prostitutes of the Government.[2] Finally, the petition of the Catholics, three millions of people, was, by special motion of David Latouche, taken off the table of the House of Commons, where it had been suffered to lie for three days, and rejected. Never was an address to a legislative body more unpitifully used. The people of Belfast, rapidly advancing in the

---

[1] [Mr. Egan, in 1792.—ED.]

[2] [Speaking of those times, Grattan said : "I could hardly obtain a hearing. As for Denis Browne (who always supported the Catholics), he could not be heard at all ; they would not listen to him. I spoke against the sense, Browne against the noise of the House, and he was abused, insulted, and covered with reproaches" (Grattan, " Memoirs "). Byrne was a wealthy merchant. In the course of this debate Colonel (afterwards General Lord) Hutchinson reminded the House that he paid £100,000 a year to the revenue.—ED.]

career of wisdom and liberality, had presented a petition in behalf of the Catholics much more pointed than that which they presented for themselves, for their petition was extremely guarded, asking only the right of elective franchise, and equal admission to grand juries, whereas that of Belfast prayed for their entire admission to all the rights of citizens. This petition was also, on motion of the same member, taken off the table and rejected, and the two papers sent forth together to wander as they might.

There seems from this time out a special providence to have watched over the affairs of Ireland, and to have turned to her profit and advantage the deepest laid and most artful schemes of her enemies. Every measure adopted, and skilfully adopted, to thwart the expectations of the Catholics, and to crush the rising spirit of union between them and the Dissenters, has, without exception, only tended to confirm and fortify both, and the fact I am about to mention, for one, is a striking proof of the truth of this assertion. The principal charge in the general outcry raised in the House of Commons against the General Committee was, that they were a self-appointed body, not nominated by the Catholics of the nation, and consequently not authorised to speak on their behalf. This argument, which in fact was the truth, was triumphantly dwelt upon by the enemies of the Catholics ; but in the end it would have, perhaps, been more fortunate for their wishes if they had not laid such stress upon this circumstance, and drawn the line of separation so strongly between the General Committee and the body at large. For the Catholics throughout Ireland, who had hitherto been indolent spectators of the business, seeing their brethren of Dublin, and especially the General Committee, insulted and abused for their exertions in pursuit of that liberty, which if attained must be a common blessing to all, came forward as one man from every quarter of the nation with addresses and resolutions, adopting the measures of the General Committee as their own, declaring that body the only organ competent to speak for the Catholics of Ireland, and condemning, in terms of the most marked disapprobation and contempt, the conduct of the sixty-eight apostates, who were so triumphantly held up by the hirelings of Government as the respectable part of the Catholic community. The question was now fairly decided. The aristocracy shrunk back in disgrace and obscurity, leaving the field open to the democracy, and that body neither wanted talents nor spirit to profit by the advantages of their present situation.

The Catholics of Dublin were at this period, to the Catholics of Ireland, what Paris, at the commencement of the French Revolution, was to the Departments. Their sentiment was that of the nation, and whatever political measure they adopted was sure to be obeyed. Still, however, there was wanting a personal communication between the General Committee and their constituents in the country, and, as the Catholic question had now grown to considerable magnitude, so much indeed as to absorb all other political discussion, it became the first care of the leaders of the committee to frame a plan of organisation for that purpose. It is to the sagacity of Myles Keon of Keonbrook, County Leitrim, that his country is indebted for the system on which the General Committee was to be framed anew, in a manner that should render it impossible to bring it again in doubt whether that body were or not the organ of the Catholic will. His plan was to associate to the committee, as then constituted, two members from each county and great city, actual residents of the place which they represented, who were, however, only to be summoned upon extraordinary occasions, leaving the common routine of business to the original members, who, as I have already related, were all residents of Dublin. The committee, as thus constituted, would consist of half town and half country members ; and the elections for the latter he proposed should be held by means of primary and electoral assemblies, held, the first in each parish, the second in each county and great town. He likewise proposed that the town members should be held to correspond regularly with their country associates, these with their immediate electors, and these again with the primary assemblies. A more simple and, at the same time, more comprehensive organisation could not be devised. By this means the General Committee became the centre of a circle embracing the whole nation, and pushing its rays instantaneously to the remotest parts of the circumference. The plan was laid in writing before the General Committee by Myles Keon, and, after mature discussion, the first part relating to the association and election of the country members was adopted with some slight variation; the latter part, relating to the constant communication with the mass of the people, was thought under the circumstances to be too hardy, and was accordingly dropped *sub silentio.*

About this time it was that the leaders of the committee cast their eyes upon me to fill the station left vacant by Richard Burke. It was accordingly proposed by my friend John Keogh to appoint me their agent, with the title of assistant-secretary, and a salary of £200 sterling a year during my continuance in the service of the committee. This proposal was adopted unanimously. John Keogh and John Sweetman were ordered to wait on me with the proposal in writing, to which I acceded immediately by a respectful answer, and I was that very day introduced in form to the sub-committee, and entered upon the functions of my new office.

I was now placed in a very honourable, but a very arduous situation. The committee having taken so decided a step as to propose a general election of members to represent the Catholic body throughout Ireland, was well aware that they would be exposed to attacks of all possible kinds, and they were not disappointed; they were prepared, however, to repel them, and the literary part of the warfare fell of course to my share. In reviewing the conduct of my predecessor, Richard Burke, I saw that the rock on which he split was an overweening opinion of his own talents and judgment, and a desire, which he had not art enough to conceal, of guiding at his pleasure the measures of the committee. I therefore determined to model my conduct with the greatest caution in that respect. I seldom or never offered my opinion unless it was called for in the sub-committee, but contented myself with giving my sentiments, without reserve, in private, to the two men I most esteemed, and who had, in their respective capacities, the greatest influence on that body—I mean John Keogh and Richard McCormick, secretary to the General Committee. My discretion in this respect was not unobserved, and

I very soon acquired, and I may say without vanity, I deserved the entire confidence and good opinion of the Catholics. The fact is, I was devoted most sincerely to their cause, and being now retained in their service, I would have sacrificed everything to ensure their success, and they knew it. I am satisfied they looked upon me as a faithful and zealous advocate, neither to be intimidated nor corrupted, and in that respect they rendered me but justice. My circumstances were, at the time of my appointment, extremely embarrassed, and of course the salary annexed to my office was a considerable object with me. But though I had now an increasing family totally unprovided for, I can safely say that I would not have deserted my duty to the Catholics for the whole patronage of the Government if it were consolidated into one office, and offered me as the reward. In these sentiments I was encouraged and confirmed by the incomparable spirit of my wife, to whose patient suffering under adversity, for we had often been reduced, and were now well accustomed to difficulties, I know not how to render justice. Women in general, I am sorry to say it, are mercenary, and especially if they have children, they are ready to make all sacrifices to their establishment. But my dearest love had bolder and juster views. On every occasion of my life I consulted her ; we had no secrets, one from the other, and I unvaryingly found her think and act with energy and courage, combined with the greatest prudence and discretion. If ever I succeed in life, or arrive at anything like station or eminence, I shall consider it as due to her counsels and her example. But to return. Another rule which I adopted for my conduct was, in all the papers I had occasion to write, to remember I was not speaking for myself, but for the Catholic body, and consequently to be never wedded to my own compositions, but to receive the objections of every one with respect, and to change without reluctance whatever the committee thought fit to alter, even in cases where perhaps my own judgment was otherwise. And trifling as this circumstance may seem, I am sure it recommended me considerably to the committee, who had been on former occasions more than once embarrassed by the self-love of Richard Burke, and, indeed, even of some of their own body, men of considerable talents, who had written some excellent papers on their behalf, but who did not stand criticism as I did without wincing. The fact is, I was so entirely devoted to their cause, that the idea of literary reputation as to myself never occurred to me, not that I am at all insensible on that score, but the feeling was totally absorbed in superior considerations; and I think I may safely appeal to the sub-committee, whether ever on any occasion they found me for a moment set up my vanity or self-love against their interests or even their pleasure. I am sure that by my discretion on the points I have mentioned, which, indeed, was no more than my duty, I secured the esteem of the committee, and consequently an influence in their counsels, which I should justly have forfeited had I seemed too eager to assume it; and it is to the credit of both parties that from the first moment of our connection to the last, neither my zeal and anxiety to serve them, nor the kindness and favour with which they received my efforts, were ever for a single moment suspended.

Almost the first business I had to transact was to conduct a correspondence with Richard Burke, who was very desirous to return to Ireland once more, and to resume his former station, which the committee were determined he should not do. It was a matter of some difficulty to refuse without offending him, and I must say he pressed us rather forcibly; however, we parried him with as much address as we could, and, after two or three long letters, to which the answers were very concise and civil, he found the business was desperate, and gave it up accordingly.

This (1792) was a memorable year in Ireland. The publication of the plan for the new organising of the General Committee gave an instant alarm to all the supporters of the British Government and every effort was made to prevent the election of the country members; for it was sufficiently evident that, if the representatives of three millions of oppressed people were once suffered to meet, it would not afterwards be safe, or indeed possible, to refuse their just demands. Accordingly, at the ensuing assizes, the grand juries, universally, throughout Ireland, published the most furious,

I may say frantic, resolutions against the plan and its authors,
whom they charged with little short of high treason. Government,
likewise, was too successful in gaining over the Catholic clergy,
particularly the bishops, who gave the measure at first very serious
opposition.   The committee, however, was not daunted : and,
satisfied of the justice of their cause, and of their own courage,
they laboured, and with success, to inspire the same spirit in the
breasts of their brethren throughout the nation.   For   this
purpose their first step was an admirable one.   By their order
I drew up a state of the case, with the plan for the organisation of the committee annexed, which was laid before Simon
Butler and Beresford Burton, two lawyers of great eminence, and,
what was of consequence here, King's counsel, to know whether the
committee had in any respect contravened the law of the land, or
whether, by carrying the proposed plan into execution, the parties
concerned would subject themselves to pain or penalty.   The
answers of both the lawyers were completely in our favour, and
we instantly printed them in the papers, and dispersed them in
handbills, letters, and all possible shapes.   This blow was decisive
as to the legality of the measure.   For the bishops, whose opposition gave us great trouble, four or five different missions were
undertaken by different members of the sub-committee into the
provinces, at their own expense, in order to hold conferences with
them, in which, with much difficulty, they succeeded so far as to
secure the co-operation of some, and the neutrality of the rest of
the prelates.   On these missions the most active members were
John Keogh and Thomas Braughall, neither of whom spared
purse nor person where the interests of the Catholic body were
concerned. I accompanied Mr. Braughall in his visit to Connaught,
where he went to meet the gentry of that province at the great fair
of Ballinasloe.   As it was late in the evening when we left town, the
postillion who drove us, having given warning, I am satisfied, to
some footpads, the carriage was stopped by four or five fellows at
the gate of the Phœnix Park. We had two cases of pistols in the
carriage, and we agreed not to be robbed. Braughall, who was at
this time about sixty-five years of age, and lame from a fall off his

horse some years before, was as cool and intrepid as man could be. He took the command, and by his orders I let down all the glasses, and called out to the fellows to come on, if they were so inclined, for that we were ready ; Braughall desiring me at the same time *not to fire till I could touch the scoundrels.* This rather embarrassed them, and they did not venture to approach the carriage, but held a council of war at the horses' heads. I then presented one of my pistols at the postillion, swearing horribly that I would put him instantly to death if he did not drive over them, and I made him feel the muzzle of the pistol against the back of his head ; the fellows on this took to their heels and ran off, and we proceeded on our journey without further interruption. When we arrived at the inn, Braughall, whose goodness of heart is equal to his courage, and no man is braver, began by abusing the postillion for his treachery, and ended by giving him half a crown. I wanted to break the rascal's bones, but he would not suffer me, and this was the end of our adventure.

All parties were now fully employed preparing for the ensuing session of Parliament. The Government, through the organ of the corporations and grand juries, opened a heavy fire upon us of manifestoes and resolutions. At first we were like young soldiers, a little stunned with the noise, but after a few rounds we began to look about us, and seeing nobody drop with all this furious cannonade, we took courage and determined to return the fire. In consequence, wherever there was a meeting of the Protestant ascendency, which was the title assumed by that party (and a very impudent one it was), we took care it should be followed by a meeting of the Catholics, who spoke as loud, and louder than their adversaries, and, as we had the right clearly on our side, we found no great difficulty in silencing the enemy on this quarter. The Catholics likewise took care, at the same time that they branded their enemies, to mark their gratitude to their friends, who were daily increasing, and especially to the people of Belfast, between whom and the Catholics the union was now completely established. Among the various attacks made on us this summer, the most remarkable for their virulence were those of the Grand Jury of

Louth, headed by the Speaker of the House of Commons;[1] of Limerick, at which the Lord Chancellor assisted; and of the corporation of the city of Dublin; which last published a most furious manifesto, threatening us, in so many words, with a resistance by force. In consequence, a meeting was held of the Catholics of Dublin at large, which was attended by several thousands, where the manifesto of the corporation was read and most ably commented upon by John Keogh, Dr. Ryan, Dr. MacNeven, and several others,[2] and a counter-manifesto being proposed, which was written by my friend Emmet, and incomparably well done, it was carried unanimously, and published in all the papers, together with the speeches above mentioned; and both the speeches and the manifesto had such an infinite superiority over those of the corporation, which were also published and diligently circulated by the Government, that it put an end, effectually, to this warfare of resolutions.

The people of Belfast were not idle on their part; they spared neither pains nor expense to propagate the new doctrine of the union of Irishmen through the whole North of Ireland, and they had the satisfaction to see their proselytes rapidly extending in all directions. In order more effectually to spread their principles, twelve of the most active and intelligent among them subscribed £250 each, in order to set on foot a paper, whose object should be

[1] [John Foster (b. 1740, d. 1828). Though an opponent of the Catholic claims, Foster is still fondly remembered as a steady enemy of the Union. "I declare from my soul," he said, "that if England were to give us all her revenues, I could not barter for them the free constitution of my country." After the Union he entered the Imperial Parliament, and accepted the post of Chancellor of the Exchequer for Ireland. In 1821 he was made Baron Oriel.]

[2] [John Fitzgibbon, Lord Clare (b. 1749, d. 1802). Called to the Bar in 1772, Fitzgibbon soon rose to eminence in his profession. In 1780 he entered Parliament. He then wrote: "I have always been of opinion that the claims of the British Parliament to make laws for this country is a daring usurpation on the rights of a free people, and have uniformly asserted the opinion in public and private." His subsequent career is well known. The enemy of the Catholics, the enemy of the Irish Parliament, he was honoured, though not trusted, by the British Government. In 1789 he became Lord Chancellor and Baron Fitzgibbon. In 1795 he was made Earl of Clare. No man was more able or more unscrupulous in supporting the Union.—Ed.]

to give a fair statement of all that passed in France, whither every one turned their eyes ; to inculcate the necessity of union amongst Irishmen of all religious persuasions ; to support the emancipation of the Catholics ; and, finally, as the necessary, though not avowed, consequence of all this, to erect Ireland into a republic, independent of England. This paper, which they called, very appositely, the *Northern Star*, was conducted by my friend Samuel Neilson, who was unanimously chosen editor, and it could not be delivered into abler hands. It is, in truth, a most incomparable paper, and it rose, instantly, on its appearance, with a most rapid and extensive sale. The Catholics everywhere through Ireland (I mean the leading Catholics) were, of course, subscribers, and the *Northern Star* was one great means of effectually accomplishing the union of the two great sects, by the simple process of making their mutual sentiments better known to each other.

It was determined by the people of Belfast to commemorate this year the anniversary of the taking of the Bastile with great ceremony. For this purpose they planned a review of the Volunteers of the town and neighbourhood, to be followed by a grand procession, with emblematical devices, &c. They also determined to avail themselves of this opportunity to bring forward the Catholic question in force, and, in consequence, they resolved to publish two addresses, one to the people of France, and one to the people of Ireland. They gave instructions to Dr. Drennan to prepare the former, and the latter fell to my lot. Drennan executed his task admirably, and I made my address, for my part, as good as I knew how. We were invited to assist at the ceremony, and a great number of the leading members of the Catholic committee determined to avail themselves of this opportunity to show their zeal for the success of the cause of liberty in France, as well as their respect and gratitude to their friends in Belfast. In consequence, a grand assembly took place on the 14th of July. After the review, the Volunteers and inhabitants, to the number of about 6,000, assembled in the Linen Hall, and voted the address to the French people unanimously. The address to the people of Ireland followed, and, as it was directly and unequivocally in favour of the

Catholic claims, we expected some opposition, but we were soon relieved from our anxiety, for the address passed, I may say, unanimously: a few ventured to oppose it indirectly, but their arguments were exposed and overset by the friends to Catholic emancipation, amongst the foremost of whom we had the satisfaction to see several dissenting clergymen of great popularity in that country, as Sinclair Kilburne, Wm. Dixon, and T. Birch. It was William Sinclair who moved the two addresses. It is the less necessary for me to detail what passed at this period, as every material is recorded in my diary. Suffice it to say, that the hospitality shown by the people of Belfast to the Catholics on this occasion, and the personal acquaintance which the parties formed, riveted the bonds of their recent union, and produced in the sequel the most beneficial and powerful effects.

APPENDIX TO CHAPTER III.

EXTRACTS FROM TONE'S DIARIES FOR THE YEARS 1789, 1790, 1791.

[Tone, in his diaries, calls his friends by "mock names." The key to these names may be given here.—ED.]

Mr. Hutton, or John Hutton—Tone.
P. P. Clerk of the Parish—Russell.
Blefescu—The City of Belfast.
The Draper—Wm. Sinclair.
The Jacobin—Samuel Neilson.
The Tanner—Robert Simms.
The Hypocrite—Dr. McDonnell.[1]

The Irish Slave—Mr. Macabe.
The Keeper—Whitley Stokes.
The Tribune—J. Napper Tandy.
The Vintner—Mr. Edward Byrne.
Gog—John Keogh.
Magog—R. McCormick.

1789.

June 21st. Fitzgibbon's want of temper and undoubted partiality will let in his resentments and his affections to bias his decisions. But Lord Earlsfort [2] is an ignorant man, and a stupid man, and a corrupt man.

[1] A distinguished Belfast Dissenter.

[2] [John Scott (b. 1739, d. 1798). Called to the Bar in 1765, made Chief Justice of the King's Bench and Baron Earlsfort in 1784 ; created Earl of Clonmel in 1793. Scott rose from the ranks of the people, and in early life took his stand in politics on the national side. But he was won over to the Government by Lord Townshend (Lord Lieutenant 1767-72). " My Lord," he said, " you have spoiled a good patriot."—ED.]

Mem. The committee for drawing up the address to the Chancellor, being headed by Egan [1] and Tom Fitzgerald, were said by Curran to be more like a committee for drawing a waggon, than for drawing up an address.

Mem. When the Chief Baron,[2] at the time of the King's illness, went over to London, his companions were Curran, Egan, and R. Barrett; on which Fitzgibbon remarked, that he travelled like a mountebank, with a monkey, a bear, and a sleight-of-hand man.

1790.

June 20*th.* My idea of political sentiment in Ireland is, that, in the middling ranks, and, indeed, in the spirit of the people, there is a great fund of it, but stifled and suppressed, as much as possible, by the expensive depravity and corruption of those who, from rank and circumstances, constitute the legislature. Whatever has been done, has been by the people, strictly speaking, who have not often been wanting to themselves, when informed of their interests by such men as Swift, Flood, Grattan, &c.

Mem. Michael Smith went six years round before he made half a guinea. Downes, in the year 1783, received his first brief in a record, by the joint influence and procurement of Dudley Hussey, Dennis George, and Michael Smith; but they engaged him in every cause on that circuit, and he had merit to sustain the recommendation.

---

[1] [John Egan (b. about 1750, d. 1810), a barrister, a member of Parliament, and a noted duellist. He is the subject of many stories, which are *ben trovate* if not *vere.* He and Curran had a hostile meeting. Egan said Curran had an unfair advantage: he was little of stature; Egan was big. "I'll tell you what, Mr. Egan," said Curran, "I wish to take no advantage of you whatever. Let my size be chalked out on your side, and I am quite content that every shot which hits outside the mark should go for nothing." Egan was made chairman of Kilmainham in 1799. He was threatened with the loss of his office if he voted against the Union. He did vote against the Union. "Ireland for ever," he said, "and damn Kilmainham!"—ED.]

[2] Barry Yelverton, Lord Avonmore (b. 1736, d. 1805). He took a foremost place in the struggle for Legislative Independence in 1782, but went over to the Government on the question of the Union.

Mem. Wolfe [1] is the Chancellor's private tutor in legal matters. Fitzgibbon has read Coke and Littleton under his papa; he has a very intelligent clerk to note his briefs; he has Boyd to hunt his cases; and he has some talents, great readiness, and assurance; and there is Fitzgibbon.

Mem. Erskine, who, in England, is not looked upon as a very sound lawyer, knows more law than the twelve Judges of Ireland, *plus* the Chancellor.

August 4th. Wogan Browne, Esq., foreman of the grand jury of county Kildare, sent down this evening to the bar-room a newspaper of the 3rd, containing the resolutions of the Whig Club, in answer to a printed speech, purporting to be that of the Chancellor, on the election of Alderman James.[2] It was enclosed

---

[1] [John Wolfe (b. 1739, d. 1803), afterwards Lord Kilwarden and Chief Justice of the King's Bench; a good judge, and a humane man. He was killed while driving through the streets of Dublin during Robert Emmet's insurrection (1803), by a ruffian whose brother (it is said) he had sentenced to death some time previously. While dying from his wound he overheard Major Swan say, "I will hang all the prisoners (arrested on suspicion of the murder) to-morrow." "What are you going to do, Swan?" he asked. "Hang these rebels, my lord." "Murder must be punished," said Kilwarden, "but let no man suffer for my death but on a fair trial and by the laws of his country."—ED.]

[2] ["Alderman James had been appointed Commissioner of the Police. He set up as candidate for the office of Lord Mayor under the patronage of the Government, and was chosen by the Aldermen, but rejected by the Commons, who selected Alderman Howison, a popular individual. In such a case the custom was that the aldermen should send down the name of another candidate. This they declined to do, and insisted that Alderman James was elected. The approbation of the Privy Council being necessary to confirm the election of the Lord Mayor, both parties appealed to that body on behalf of their respective candidates. The case was argued before them [George Ponsonby and Curran appearing for Howison]. . . . The Chancellor decided in favour of Alderman James, declaring 'that the case must come before the King's Bench, and by the time that the Commons had amused themselves there for three or four years it was probable they would be tired of it, and wish themselves out of the dispute. . . . The conduct of the Chancellor and Privy Council met with general disapprobation.' The resolution of the Whig Club ran: 'That the Whig Club cannot possibly have witnessed what has lately passed respecting the election of a Lord Mayor without expressing the deepest concern, and declaring that they will, both individually and as a body, co-operate with their fellow-citizens in every legal and constitutional measure which may tend to vindicate the laws, and to support the rights of this metropolis'" (Grattan, "Memoirs"). Ultimately a new election took place, and Howison was chosen Lord Mayor 1790-91.—ED.]

in the following letter : " Mr. Wogan Browne presents his compliments to the gentlemen of the Bar ; he encloses them this day's paper, which he has just now received ; he requests they will return it to him, and hopes they will find in the vindication of the Whig Club, principles similar to their own ; as honest and blunt men must look up to talents for the support of their most undenied rights, in times when they are so shamefully invaded."

This bold and manly epistle struck the Bar of a heap. The father, a supporter of opposition in Parliament, was here only solicitous how he should escape giving an answer, which, indeed, every man, save one or two, seemed desirous to shift on his neighbour. Burn and Burrowes were decided to meet the letter boldly ; Brownrigg and Lespinasse for taking no further notice than acknowledging the receipt ; the first, on the principle of preserving the harmony of the Bar ; the latter, for some time, could assign no reason for his opinion, other than that he did not know who Mr. Browne was ; but, at length, when pressed, he said, with equal candour and liberality, " that he did not like to receive anything from a reformed Papist." The general sense seeming to be for something in reply which should be perfectly insipid, I grew out of patience, and proposed, I confess without hope of its being adopted, a resolution to the following purport : That the Leinster Bar, in common with the Whig Club, and many other respectable societies, felt the warmest indignation and abhorrence of the late unconstitutional proceedings of the Privy Council, in the election of Alderman James—proceedings no less formidable to the liberties of the capital, than alarming to every city in the kingdom, as forming part of a system, evidently subversive of their franchises, whether established by custom, charter, or the statute law of the land.

This resolution the majority seemed determined to conceive that I was not serious in ; yet I was. However, being utterly hopeless of support, I did not press it. Two or three civil notes were proposed, of which the following, by Rochford, may serve as a sample. " The Leinster Bar present their compliments to Mr. Wogan Browne, and are thankful to him for his obliging communication of this day's paper, which they have the honour of returning."

However, the sense of shame in the majority was too high to admit so milky a composition, and, at length, after much irregular scuffling, the following was adopted as an answer, on my proposal, which I premised by stating that it had not my own approbation, as being too feeble : " The Leinster Bar return their thanks to Mr. Wogan Browne for his early communication of the resolutions of the Whig Club. However, individually, a majority of the gentlemen present may approve of the spirit of these resolutions, yet, as many respectable members are absent, the Bar, as a body, do not feel themselves authorised to give any further opinion on the subject of Mr. Browne's letter."

The words "majority of gentlemen present" being objected to by Mr. Moore, produced a division to ascertain the point, when nine were for continuing and five were for expunging them.

N.B.—Such is the public spirit and virtue of the Leinster Bar.

1791.

July 14*th*. I sent down to Belfast, resolutions suited to this day, and reduced to three heads. 1st, That English influence in Ireland was the great grievance of the country. 2nd, That the most effectual way to oppose it was by a reform in Parliament. 3rd, That no reform could be just or efficacious which did not include the Catholics, which last opinion, however, in concession to prejudices, was rather insinuated than asserted.

I am, this day, July 17, 1791, informed that the last question was lost. If so, my present impression is to become a red-hot Catholic ; seeing that in the party, apparently, and perhaps really, most anxious for reform, it is rather a monopoly than an extension of liberty, which is their object, contrary to all justice and expediency.

October 11*th*. Arrived at Belfast late, and was introduced to Digges, but no material conversation. Bonfires, illuminations, firing twenty-one guns, Volunteers, &c.

October 12*th*. Introduced to McTier and Sinclair. A meeting between Russell, McTier, Macabe, and me. Mode of doing business by a Secret Committee,[1] who are not known or suspected of co-operating, but who, in fact, direct the movements of Belfast. Much conversation about the Catholics, and their committee, &c., of which they know wonderfully little at *Blefescu*. Settled to dine with the Secret Committee at Drew's, on Saturday, when the resolutions, &c., of the United Irish will be submitted. Sent them off, and sat down to new model the former copy. Very curious to see how the thermometer of Blefescu has risen, as to politics. Passages in the first copy, which were three months ago esteemed too hazardous to propose, are now found too tame. Those taken out, and replaced by other and better ones. Sinclair came in ; read and approved the resolutions, as new modelled. Russell gave him a mighty pretty history of the Roman Catholic Committee, and his own negotiations. Christened Russell *P. P. Clerk of this Parish.* Sinclair asked us to dine and meet Digges, which we acceded to with great affability. Went to Sinclair, and dined. A great deal of general politics and *wine*. Paine's book, the Koran of Blefescu. History of the Down and Antrim elections. The Reeve of the shire a semi-Whig. P. P. very drunk. Home ; bed.

October 13*th.* Much good jesting in bed, at the expense of P. P. Laughed myself into good humour. Rose. Breakfast. Dr. McDonnell. Much conversation regarding Digges. Went to meet Neilson ; read over the resolutions with him, which he approved. Went to H. Joy's, to thank him for his proposing me at the Northern Whig Club. He invited Digges, P. P., and me for Friday next, which we accepted. Made further alterations in the resolutions, by advice of Digges. Went to Gordon's. Very respectable people, and a large company. Drank nothing. Went, at nine, to the card club, with Gordon and P. P. Came home early, much fatigued, and went to bed.

October 14*th.* Breakfasted with Digges at his lodgings. Met Capt. Seward, who carried out Mr. Pearce to America. Pearce

---

[1] [Before Tone's arrival in Belfast a political club, composed of Volunteers, and directed by a Secret Committee, was in existence. Among the members of the club were Neilson, Russell, the Simmses, Sinclair, McTier, Macabe, Digges, and Bryson.—ED.]

now living in President Washington's house. Met Macabe, who is going to England. He showed P. P. and me certain curious drawings. Met McTier, and showed him the resolutions, as amended. Curious discourse with a hair-dresser, one Taylor, who has two children christened by the priest, though he is himself a Dissenter, merely with a wish to blend the sects. Visited Jordan, who is an extraordinary young man, and lives in a baby-house. Walked all about the town, seeing sights. Four o'clock; went to dinner to meet the Secret Committee, who consist of Wm. Sinclair, McTier, Neilson, McLeary, Macabe, Simms 1st, and Simms 2nd, Haslitt, Tennant, Campbell, McIlvaine, P. P., and myself. P. P. and I made our declarations of secrecy, and proceeded to business. P. P. made a long speech, stating the present state and politics of the Catholic Committee, of which the people of Blefescu know almost nothing. They appeared much surprised and pleased at the information. Read the card of the Catholics and Stokes' letter. The Committee agree that the North is not yet ripe to follow them, but that no party could be raised directly to oppose them. Time and discussion the only things wanting to forward what is advancing rapidly. Agreed to the resolutions unanimously. Resolved to transmit a copy to Tandy, and request his and his fellow citizens' co-operation, from which great benefit is expected to result to the cause, by reflecting back credit on the United Irishmen of Blefescu. Settled the mode of carrying the business through the club at large, on Tuesday next. McTier to be in the chair; Sinclair to move the resolutions; Simms to second him; Neilson to move their printing; and P. P. and I to state the sentiments of the people of Dublin. Copies to be transmitted, with the usual injunction against newspaper publication, to Waterford, Leitrim, Roscommon, and McCormick, in Dublin. A civil letter to be written by P. P. or myself, to Tandy, enclosing the resolutions. The Secret Committee all steady, sensible, clear men, and, as I judge, extremely well adapted for serious business. Macabe asked us for Monday, Neilson for Tuesday, both which we did most graciously accept. Home at ten. P. P. in the blue devils—thinks he is losing his faculties; glad he had any to lose.

October 15th. Digges came in to supper. I had been lecturing P. P. on the state of his nerves, and the necessity of early hours ; to which he agreed, and, as the first fruits of my advice and his reformation, sat up with Digges until three o'clock in the morning, being four hours after I had gone to bed.

October 16th, Sunday. Breakfast, Digges, Jordan, and Macabe. Church—a vile sermon from Bristowe (called Caiaphas) against smuggling, &c., and about loyalty, and all that. P. P. in great sorrow and distress of mind ; resolved to leave off smuggling, which is injurious to the fair trader. Walked in the Mall with Digges and P. P. The ladies, one and all, *sneer* P. P. who is exceedingly fallen thereon, in his own good opinion. Put the plump question to Digges, relative to the possibility of Ireland's existence, independent of England. His opinion decidedly for independence. England would not risk a contest, the immediate consequence of which would be the destruction of her funds. Ireland supplies her with what, in case of a war, she could not possibly do without, as seamen and provisions. France would most probably assist, from the pride of giving freedom to one kingdom more. So would all the enemies of England. Nothing to be done until the religious sects here are united, and England engaged in a foreign war. If Ireland were free, and well governed, being that she is unencumbered with debt, she would in arts, commerce, and manufactures spring up like an air balloon, and leave England behind her at an immense distance. There is no computing the rapidity with which she would rise. Digges promised to detail all this, and much more, on paper. Home. Dinner at William Sinclair's, to meet Dr. Haliday, who could not come, being suddenly called out to attend a sick bishop. Much conversation about Foster's treatment of Macabe and Pearce. Sinclair in high wrath with Foster, of whom he told scurrilous anecdotes. The loom now in America, and a capital of 500,000 dollars subscribed to carry on the manufacture of linen ; workmen the great want in America, which this loom goes precisely to obviate. America improving, silently and unnoticed, in manufactures ; instance, in coarse linens, from 14d. to 8d., of which, seven years since, there was a large export from Ireland, but which they now are able to supply themselves. Danger, therefore, by the aid of Pearce's various and inexhaustible invention, that they may proceed in like manner in other fabrics. Washington has adopted Pearce as his *protégé*, and declares him to be the first man in America. Great superiority of Ireland and John Foster, who can afford to fling away what America and Gen. Washington are glad to pick up. One and all of us damn the Government. Home. P. P. sober. Find a large packet by the mail, which we rip open in haste, and find 2,000 prospectuses of the United Irishmen, instead of the pamphlet. Sat down in a pet, and wrote a tart letter to Chambers ; got up in a rage, cursed, stormed. P. P. very wise, quotes "Seneca," "Boethius de Consolatione," and many other good books ; enforces the folly of anger in many shapes ; I more and more enraged. Left the inn and went to sleep at Dr. McDonnell's. P. P. not quite honest ; owes me now several shillings, and makes no movement towards payment ; gave him a hint, on his observing how cheap Belfast was, and that he had not changed a guinea for some days, by assuring him that I had, and found it very expensive ; hope this may do. Bed.

October 17*th*. Breakfast, McDonnell, McAughtrey, Bryson, Digges, P. P., and I. Went to the inn ; P. P. paid the bill, by which my anxiety as to my shillings is completely removed ; believe I owe *him* now two or three, but shall not inquire. P. P. received a letter from C. O'Connor, an Irish *Papist ;* very good sense in it for all that ; read it to all persons when and where it did behove him. Walked out with Digges and P. P. to Macabe's, to dinner ; the old set ; nothing new under the sun. Came into town early ; went to the theatre ; saw a man in a white sheet on the stage, who called himself a Carmelite. P. P. whispered to me, with a very significant face, not to be too sure he was a Carmelite. Puzzled at this ; turned round in a little time with my doubts to P. P. P. P. asleep. N.B.—A gentleman, indeed a nobleman, on the stage, in a white wig, vastly like a gentleman whom I had seen in the morning, walking the streets in a brown wig ; one Mr. Atkins, a player. Query. Was he a lord or not ? P. P. incapable of resolving my doubts. Came home before the play was half over; the parties appearing all so miserable, that I could foresee no end to their woes. Saw a fine waistcoat on the man that said he was a Carmelite, through a tear in the sheet which he had wrapped about him; afraid after all that he was no Carmelite, and that P. P. was right in his caution. Home; whisky punch with P. P. Bed early.

October 18*th*. Breakfast; McDonnell, McAughtrey, Digges, called on us. Went to see the factory for sail-duck. Improvements on the warping machine. Dined with Neilson. Went, at eight, to the United Irishmen, McTier in the chair; twenty-eight members present; the club consists of thirty-six original members; six new ones proposed. William Sinclair moved the resolutions, which were adopted unanimously. Bryson very civil; resolved to print and issue an adequate number, but not to publish in newspapers. A copy enclosed in a letter from the secretary to be sent to J. N. Tandy, Richard McCormick, and Dr. McKenna. A committee of correspondence struck; the members are Sinclair, McTier, Haslitt, Neilson, and R. Simms, secretary. Read C. O'Connor's letter with great pleasure and satisfaction. Campbell made a flighty objection to one paragraph, relating to a renunciation of certain tenets falsely attributed to the Roman Catholics; answered with great ability by Bryson. Campbell angry because he was wrong, as is always the case; his objection overruled. P. P. and I made several orations on the state of the Roman Catholics, and the readiness of the citizens of Dublin to co-operate with the United Irishmen. The intelligence received with great applause. Broke up at eleven; came home; resolved to go to the coterie; dressed; went with P. P. P. P. changed his mind, after a quarter of an hour's fluctuation in the lobby, and calling a council of waiters, at which the chamber-maid assisted; *pleasant, but wrong;* came back again in something very like an ill-humour. At the door P. P. changed his mind again, and proposed to return to the coterie; refused him plump. P. P. severe thereupon; taxed me with many faults, one of which was giving advice; told P. P. I would do so no more. P. P. frightened; submitted. Went to bed with a resolution to attack him in my turn next morning. Could not sleep; a cat in the room; got up and turned her out; fell asleep at last.

October 19*th.* Breakfast; McAughtrey, Digges, and Bryson. Digges took me out to ask my opinion of the United Irishmen. I told him I thought them men of spirit and decision, who seemed thoroughly in earnest. He said he thought so too. I asked him whether they any way resembled the Committees of America in 1775, and afterwards. He said, " Precisely." In Digges' opinion, one Southern, when moved, equals twenty Northerns, but very hard to move them.—Digges, Secretary to the Baltimore Committee, in Maryland, for some years. He appears to take very kindly to P. P. and me.—Went, at one, to the Select men. Agreed on the mode of corresponding with the Volunteers of Dublin. Five hundred of the resolutions of the United Irishmen to be printed on little paper for distribution. Sinclair's idea that the citizens should everywhere precede the Volunteers in adopting similar resolutions. Dined at Getty's [1]; the old set. Went at eight to the Select men. Conversation as to the communication between the Belfast and Dublin Volunteers. Agreed that the North was not yet prepared for any strong and direct attack on the Armagh Grand Jury. The Dublin people should not go further in their answer than the Belfast men go in their declaration, as otherwise they of Belfast would be in a dilemma between doing too much and too little. Agreed that all communications, now, and for some time to come, should be through the medium rather of clubs than Volunteers, inasmuch as there are now many existing corps who might be influenced to oppose our present measures regarding the Catholics, but it would be impossible to raise a club differing in principles from the United Irish; besides, when the clubs are formed, the Volunteers will follow of course. Armagh not ripe for a deputation of Roman Catholics from Dublin, but every exertion to be made to prepare them, by letters, newspapers, &c. Wm. Sinclair to write, as President of the Volunteer Committee of Correspondence, an official letter to Tandy, with an account of their proceedings, &c., which is to be accompanied by a letter from P. P. or me, containing such

[1] An officer in the Belfast Volunteers.

facts as may not be proper to mention in official correspondence. Home at 10; a rainy night. P. P. in the rain, very like King Lear in the storm; came home in the character of the banished Kent. *Mem.* P. P. got up very early in the morning, this day, and wrote three letters before I was up; on which proof of the amendment of his life I remitted the attack which I had intended to make upon him.

October 20*th.* Breakfast, nobody; sad rainy day! McAughtrey called and sat awhile. Digges came in and stayed dinner. Wrote out queries for him, which he answered, relative to emigration. Conversation till 10 at night; extremely amusing, but no material business. Went to bed ill with a sore throat—very bad all night.

October 21*st.* Breakfast in bed, Digges, McAughtrey, and P.P. Did not get up till one o'clock. Met Tom Cleghorn, to my great surprise, fossilising in McDonnell's dining-room. Dressed; went in a chaise to Joy's, with Digges and P. P. An amazing battle after dinner on the Catholic question. For the Peep-of-day-boys,'

---

¹ [" About the year 1785 the North was again disquieted by tumults arising from religious and political animosity, and not from any local grievance. The Protestant party began by visiting the houses of Catholics, in order to search for arms, and from the time when these visits were made they derived their name of *Peep* or *Break-of-day-boys.* They did not, however, confine themselves simply to searching for arms, but attacked the houses and chapels of the Catholics, sometimes burning the building, and sometimes destroying all the furniture and property contained in it. The Catholics, on the other hand, organised themselves under the name of *Defenders,* and during a series of years many violent conflicts took place between the two parties, who were sometimes engaged to the extent even of thousands of armed men. The combats of these factions began in the county of Armagh, whence they spread to the neighbouring districts. The *Peep-of-day-boys* in 1795, or soon afterwards, changed their appellation, and were called Orange Boys or Orangemen. The *Defenders* having originally been (as their name purported) a defensive soon became an aggressive body; they extended their ramifications to counties where there were no strong bodies of Protestants to alarm them, and in many cases they became mere gangs of robbers, breaking into and plundering houses, and committing other outrages. The Secret Committee of the Lords in 1793 reported that the *Defenders* at that time ' were all, as far as the Committee could discover, of the Roman Catholic persuasion; in general poor, ignorant labouring men, sworn to secrecy, and impressed with an opinion that they were assisting the Catholic cause; in other respects they did not appear

MM. Joy, Williamson, and A. Stewart ; for the Defenders, P. P. and myself. The Defenders victorious after a hard battle. All the arguments on the other side commonplace, vague, and indefinite (vide *my pamphlet, in which I call my adversary Goose*). P. P. very clever ; led Williamson into a palpable absurdity by a string of artful questions. Williamson afraid of a bug-a-boo. Joy an artful and troublesome antagonist. Stewart half-way between both parties. The Peep-of-day-boys ashamed of their own positions. Agree to the justice of liberating the Catholics, but boggle at the expediency. Damned nonsense. P. P. eloquent ! ready to fight Williamson. The chaise—Digges of opinion that P. P. and I were victorious. *Mem.* All arguments over a bottle foolish. Home ; went to bed early. P. P. at the card club ; came home at two, and awoke me. P. P. perfectly polite ; went to sleep at last.

October 22*nd.* Breakfast, nobody ; my sore throat gone. Walked with P. P. and Jordan ; Jordan a very clever young man. Got one of my pamphlets [1] from Simms ; gave it to William Sinclair, another to Jordan, another to McAughtrey. Dressed—dinner at Mr. Ferguson's ; Bruce, Dr. Haliday, Waddel Cunningham, &c. ; Haliday pleasant. Home early ; no letters. P. P. in bed before me for the first time. *Mem.* Met the man who said on the stage he was a Carmelite, walking the streets with a woman holding him by the arm ; the woman painted up to the eyes ; convinced, at last, that he was no Carmelite ; made my apologies to P. P., who triumphed thereon. Read O'Connor's letter to Sinclair.

October 23*rd, Sunday.* Breakfast with Digges—Neilson came in. Long account of the proceedings of the delegates at Belfast on the question between Flood and Grattan. Spirit of Belfast in 1783, when convention was sitting. Artillery prepared with round and

to have any distinct particular object in view, but they talked of being relieved from hearth-money, tithes, county-cesses, and of lowering their rents.' At length the Defenders were partially dissolved, and partly absorbed into the body of United Irishmen, till they were finally lost in the more important movements, which gave rise to the rebellion of 1798, since which time their society has been revived under the name of Ribbonmen" (Sir G. Cornewall Lewis, " Irish Disturbances ").—ED.]

[1] Argument in behalf of the Catholics. (Tone's son.)

grape shot, vast quantities of ball cartridges, and at least five hundred men ready to march from Belfast, which they expected hourly. The same spirit almost universal in the North, all balked by the cowardice or wisdom of the representatives of Ireland in convention. Dinner at A. Stewart's, with a parcel of squires of county Down. Fox hunting, hare hunting, buck hunting, and farming. No bugs in the northern potatoes ; not even known by name, &c. A farm at a smart rent always better cultivated than one at a low rent ; *probable enough.* Went at nine to the Washington Club. Argument between Bunting and Boyd, of Ballicastle. Boyd pleasant. Persuaded myself and P. P. that we were hungry. Went to the Donegal Arms and supped on lobsters. Drunk. Very ill-natured to P. P. P. P. patient. *Mem. To do so no more.* Went to bed. Gulled P. P. with nonsense. Fell asleep.

October 24th. Wakened very sick. Rose at nine. Breakfast at Wm. Sinclair's, per engagement ; could not eat. Mrs. Sinclair nursed me with French drams, &c. Rode out with P. P. and Sinclair to see his bleach-green. A noble concern ; extensive machinery. Sinclair's improvements laughed at by his neighbours, who said he was mad. The first man who introduced American potash ; followed only by three or four, but creeping on. The rest use barilla. Almost all the work now done by machinery ; done thirty years ago by hand, and all improvement regularly resisted by the people. Mr. Sinclair, sen., often obliged to hire one and sometimes two companies of the garrison, to execute what is now done by one mill. Great command of water, which is omnipotent in the linen. Three falls of twenty-one feet each in ten acres, and ten more in the glen if necessary. A most romantic and beautiful country. Saw from the top of one mountain Loch Neagh, Strangford Loch, and the Loch of Belfast, with the Cave Hill, Mourne, &c., &c. Sinclair a man of very superior understanding. Anecdotes of the linen trade. Nearly independent of England. Seven years ago application made to Parliament for a bounty of 14d. per yard ; resisted by England ; carried at last. Before the bounty, not more than thirty or forty pieces shipped direct for the West Indies from Belfast ; now, always fifty, sixty, and seventy boxes in

every ship. England threatened then to take off the duty on
foreign linens, but did not venture it. Ireland able to beat any
foreign linens for quality and cheapness, as appears by the American market, which gives no preference by duties, and is supplied
entirely by Ireland. If England were disposed she might, for a
time, check the trade of Ireland in linens ; but she would soon give
up that system for her own sake, because she could not be supplied
elsewhere so good and cheap. German linens preferred, out of
spite, by some families in England, particularly by the royal family.
All the King's and Queen's linen, German, and, of course, all their
retainers. Sinclair, for experiment, made up linens after the German mode, and sent it to the house in London which served the
King, &c. ; worn for two years, and much admired ; ten per cent.
cheaper, and twenty per cent. better than the German linen. Great
orders for Irish German linen, which he refused to execute. All
but the royal family content to take it as mere Irish. *God save
great George, our King !* Home, after a delightful ride, quite well.
Admirable essay from Digges. Went to dinner at Simms' ; old
set ; tactics after dinner. Select men in the evening. Read a
letter, &c., from Tandy. Gave a list of names to send copies of the
resolutions. Home at ten.

October 25*th.* Went for Digges to breakfast. Walked out about
the town. Joy's ! paid my fees to the Northern Whig Club, and
signed the declaration. P. P. at home in the horrors ; thinks himself sick generally ; smoke the true cause, but no matter. Dinner
at McTier's ; Waddel Cunningham, Holmes, Dr. Bruce, &c. A
furious battle, which lasted two hours, on the Catholic question ;
as usual, neither party convinced. Seized with the liberality of
people agreeing in the principle, but doubting as to the expediency.
Bruce an intolerant high priest ; argued sometimes strongly, sometimes unfairly ; embarrassed the question by distinctions, and
mixing things in their nature separate. We brought him, at last,
to state his definite objection to the immediate emancipation of
the Roman Catholics. His ideas are, 1st. Danger to true religion,
inasmuch as the Roman Catholics would, if emancipated, establish
an *inquisition.* 2nd. Danger to property by reviving the Court of

Claims, and admitting any evidence to substantiate Catholic titles. 3rd. Danger, generally, of throwing the power into their hands, which would make this a Catholic government, incapable of enjoying or extending liberty. Many other wild notions, which he afterwards gave up, but these three he repeated again and again as his creed. Almost all the company of his opinion, excepting P. P., who made desperate battle, McTier, Getty, and me ; against us, Bruce, Cunningham, Grey, Holmes, Bunting, H. Joy. Ferguson *dubitante* and *cæteri*, all protesting their liberality and good wishes to the Roman Catholics. *Damned stuff.* Bruce declared that thirty-nine out of forty Protestants would be found, whenever the question came forward, to be adverse to the liberation of the Roman Catholics, as was the case when Lord Charlemont put in his veto, and seemed pleased with the idea. It may be he was right, but God is above all. Sad nonsense about scavengers becoming members of Parliament, and great asperity against the new-fangled doctrine of the Rights of Man. Broke up rather ill disposed towards each other. More and more convinced of the absurdity of arguing over wine. Went to the United Irish Club. Balloted in five men, amongst whom were Maclaine and Getty ; rejected one. Went to the coterie. Jordan pleasant, as usual. Home at two. Bed.

October 26th. Breakfast, Digges and Jordan. *Chat.* Jordan enraged at Bruce's theory. Walked out ; saw the glass-house, foundry, &c. Dinner at Sinclair's ; McTier, McAughtrey, P. P. and I. Bruce's theory again discussed. Sinclair much surprised at it. Catholic question. Assertion of Bruce relative to their behaviour at convention ; denied by P. P., who threatens to write a book. Promised to send Sinclair the debates of the convention, with notes. McTier asked what could we do against England. Sinclair hot. He and P. P. agree that the army in Ireland would be annihilated, and could not be replaced. Sinclair defies the power of England as to our trade ; admits that she could check it for a time, but that, after the revolution, it would spring up with inconceivable rapidity, Ireland being unencumbered with debt. (Singular that his opinion agrees with Digges, even in the very words.) My own mind quite made up. Sinclair bleaches annually 10,000 pieces of linen. P. P. of opinion that the weakness of England should be looked to, as well as that of Ireland ; also Mr. Digges, who says, " The first shot fired by England against this country, down go her stocks." Home early. P. P. pretty well on, but not quite gone. Bed.

October 27th. Rise for the purpose of packing. Assisted by Digges, and very much impeded by P. P., who has not yet slept off his wine, and is, besides, for certain reasons, much puzzled. Jordan and McDonnell stay with us. At one o'clock, leave Belfast with heavy hearts, having first taken leave of everybody on the road. McDonnell sees us four miles on the road.

Hic finis longæ chartæque, viæque,—as the Divine Flaccus hath it.

The poor ambassadors are reduced to the rank of private individuals—*Sic transit gloria mundi.*

P. P. and J. HUTTON.

November 7th. Dinner at Doyle's. Eighteen present, Tandy, Jones, Drennan, Pollock, McKenna, MacNeven, McCormick, P. P., and Mr. Hutton, &c. All quiet at first. Tandy says that Grattan is certainly with us ; also, the Duke of Leinster almost as certain. Read the declaration of the Catholic Society for constitutional information ; very much admired, and justly. Jones begins to broach opinions ; thinks the question involved and complicated unnecessarily by mixing the question of reform with the Catholic business ; get the last first, and the other will follow of course. Jones opposed by Mr. Hutton, on the ground that the mere right of the Catholics is not supported by sufficient strength to induce the Protestants to come forward, and therefore a common interest must call forth common exertions. If a compact be once established between the parties, it is of little import which part of the question comes first ; but absolutely necessary to hold out, on the one hand, reform to the Protestants, and, on the other, emancipation to the Catholics, by which the views and interests of both are inseparably consolidated and blended. Mr. Hutton very ingenious and persuasive on the occasion, and uses sundry other good arguments. Followed by Neilson, on the ground of past experience, that nothing can be done by disunited parties, and no secure bond of union but common interest ; instances the convention, and concludes with many compliments to Mr. Hutton. Neilson followed by Owen Roe (Pollock), who agrees in all that is laid down, and further states that it is nonsense to pretend to obviate opposition on the part of Government, by holding forth the Catholic question, and keeping back that of reform ; because they will immediately see their inseparable connection. The business wound up by Tandy, who coincides completely with Mr. Hutton, Neilson, and Owen Roe, to the great mortification of Jones, who can do nothing but exclaim, "Three millions! three millions!" Angry with P. P., who had said nothing. P. P. angry thereupon, but cooled by a bucketful of good advice, which was thrown upon his wrath by Neilson. All the Catholics with us to a man, except Dr. MacNeven, who has some doubts. Mr. Hutton agrees to breakfast, on Wednesday, with said Doctor. Many civilities on both sides. Good story of Major and Secretary Hobart being handcuffed in St. Ann's watch-house. Go to an ale-house with Neilson, P. P., and Belfast men. One, just come from England, says Dr. Priestley is delighted with the idea of union, and has begged six copies of a celebrated pamphlet (the *N. Whig*). Home at half-past eleven ; bed. *Mem.* Left P. P. getting very drunk, after all his fine resolutions. Bad ! bad !

[LETTERS TO MRS. TONE.]

(DUBLIN, *about the Summer of* 1791.]

DEAR LOVE,—I have nothing more to say, than that affairs are going on here swimmingly. We have got up a club of United Irishmen in Dublin, similar to that in Belfast, who have adopted our resolutions, with a short preface. We have pretty well secured all Connaught, and are fighting out the other two provinces. It is wonderful with what zeal, spirit, activity, and secrecy all things are conducted. I have dined with divers Papists, and, in particular, with Lord Dunsany, who lately reformed, but is still a good

Catholic in his heart. He begged the honour of my acquaintance, and I shall call on him to-morrow. My book is running like wild-fire. The castle has got hold of the story, but very imperfectly. All they know is that the disorder broke out in Belfast, and was carried there by one Toole, or Toomey, or some such name, a lawyer. I suppose they will endeavour to find out this Mr. Toole, or Toomey, or whatever his name is.

George Ponsonby is, on a sudden, grown vastly civil and attentive, . . . and so much for politics. I learn, and I am sorry, that you have got a return of the pain in your head. Willy is growing too strong for you, and therefore I beg you may wean him immediately. He is old enough now, and you must not injure your own health for that little monkey, especially when you know how precious your health is to me.

My stay in town is of such infinite consequence that I am sure you would not wish me to quit whilst things are in their present train. If you can get Mary down I shall be very happy ; I leave it to you, as I am with my head, hands, and heart so full of business, that I have scarcely time to subscribe myself, yours, &c.,

T. W. T.

BELFAST, October 20, 1791.

MY DEAREST LIFE AND SOUL,—I wrote a few posts since, just to let you know that I was alive and well. I did not tell you any news, as I journalise everything, and promise myself great pleasure from reading my papers over with you. I have christened Russell by the name of P. P., Clerk of this Parish, and he makes a very conspicuous figure in my memoirs. If you do not know who P. P. was, the joke will be lost on you. I find the people here extremely civil ; I have dined out every day since I came here, and have now more engagements than I can possibly fulfil. I did hope to get away on Sunday, but I fear I shall not be able to move before Thursday. You cannot conceive how much this short absence has endeared you to me. You think it is better for us to be always together, but I am sure, from my own experience, you are wrong; for I cannot leave you now, though but for one week, that I do not feel my heart cling to you and our dear little ones. I have no more to say, but to desire my love to all of you, and am, dearest love, ever yours. If you have not written before this you need not write ; I wish, however, I had one letter from you.

T. W. TONE.

P.S.—DEAR MATTY,—As to anything your wise husband may have said of me, I neither desire to know, nor do I care. It is sufficient, generally, "*I had a friend.*" I am at present composing a pretty moral treatise ·on temperance, and will dedicate it to myself, for I don't know who is likely to profit so much by it. Pray give my love to your virgin daughter and infant progeny. "God bless everybody."—Yours till death,   P. P.

P.S.—P. P. has been scribbling his bit of nonsense. He is a great fool, and I have much trouble to manage him. I assure you that you will be much amused by his exploits in my journal, which is a thousand times wittier than Swift's, as in justice it ought, for it is written for the amusement of one a thousand times more amiable than Stella. I conclude in the words of my friend P. P., God bless everybody.

P.S.—P. P. calls me "his friend Mr. John Hutton," but God knows the heart. He is writing a journal, but mine is worth fifty of it.

CHAPTER IV.

[BEFORE resuming Tone's story of his life (which in the pages immediately following deals with the struggle of the Catholics for the parliamentary franchise) it may be well to say, in a few words, what relaxations had been made in the penal code up to this time. In 1774 Catholics were allowed to take the oath of allegiance subject to making the declaration prescribed by law.[1] In 1778 Catholics were permitted to hold landed property on lease of 999 years. In 1782 the acts against celebrating or hearing mass, subjecting priests to the necessity of registration, making it penal for bishops or regular clergy to live in the country, enabling Protestants to appropriate the horse of a Catholic on offering the owner £5, and empowering grand juries to levy on Catholics damages for any loss inflicted by the privateers of an enemy, were repealed. Catholics were allowed to hold land in the same way as Protestants (unless the land was in a parliamentary borough), and to keep schools on obtaining licence from the ordinary of the diocese.[2] In 1792 Catholics were admitted to the outer bar, allowed to be attorneys, to intermarry with Protestants, to keep

[1] ["The Catholics who subscribed this declaration solemnly renounced all allegiance to the Stuarts, repudiated the opinion that heretics might be lawfully murdered, that faith need not be kept with them, and that excommunicated sovereigns may be deposed or murdered, and denied that the Pope had, or ought to have, ' any temporal or civil jurisdiction, power, superiority, or pre-eminence directly or indirectly ' within the realm" (Lecky, " History of Ireland in the Eighteenth Century," vol. ii. p. 196).—ED.]

[2] [Almost all good legislation for Ireland has been disfigured by fretful and worthless "guarantees." These concessions of 1782 were encumbered with restrictions, " re-affirming the provisions against proselytism, against perversion to Catholicism, against Catholics assuming ecclesiastical titles or rank, or

schools without the consent of the ordinary of the diocese, to send
their children abroad to be educated, and to have any number of
apprentices in trade.

With these concessions the Catholic aristocracy would probably
have been content for a long while. But the democratic members
of the Catholic Committee, led by Keogh, were resolved to give
the Government no breathing time, but to push forward for further
relief with vigour and persistence. They now claimed admission
to the parliamentary franchise. It had been the practice of the
aristocracy to approach Parliament with bated breath and whisper-
ing humbleness ; to come as suppliants craving a boon, as slaves
asking for mercy. Keogh took a different line. He came to the
front boldly, insisting on rights wrongfully withheld, and showing
a determination to secure them in defiance of the minister, if not in
spite of the law. He did not supplicate ; he demanded. He was
the first Irish Catholic who applied himself resolutely and fearlessly
to the work of combining the unenfranchised Catholic masses, and
of overawing Parliament by making their voices heard within and
without its walls. In Tone he found an intrepid ally ; a colleague
full of energy and of resource. There is not a more interesting
chapter in Irish history than the one which relates how the constitutional Catholic agitator and the Protestant rebel laboured
together to unite Irishmen of all religious persuasions for the
common good of their common country. What came of their
efforts Tone tells us in the pages of his diaries with characteristic
brightness and zest.—ED.]

1792.

July 4th. Waited on Mr. F.[1] by his desire, who told me that
Mr. Conolly was just returned from England, and that he was

wearing vestments outside the precincts of their chapels, against chapels having
steeples or bells, and against priests officiating anywhere except in their
accustomed places of worship " (Lecky, ibid. vol. ii. p. 312).—ED.]

[1] [Probably John Forbes, M.P., one of the founders of the Whig Club, an
intimate friend of Grattan, and a supporter of the Catholic claims.—ED.]

much better affected than they had expected, but some of Fitzgibbon's people had been endeavouring to frighten him with
Catholic insurrections, &c. That he was decidedly against the
conduct of the House of Commons, in rejecting the petition,
because, if the principles on which they justified that measure
were right, they should not have granted the Catholics anything,
not even Sir Hercules Langrishe's Bill.[1]   Mr. F. then said that Mr.
Conolly [2] was a man who liked attentions, and therefore he would
advise Byrne and Keogh, and some Kildare gentlemen (I mentioned Fitzgerald) to wait on him with the declaration,[3] and any
other papers; to prefer their earnest desire for the approbation and
support of so very respectable a character, and express their
apprehensions, lest pains might be taken to prejudice his mind
against them ; that, therefore, they took the first opportunity, after
his return to the kingdom, to wait on him with a fair statement of
their conduct and sentiments ; that if any part of the declaration
(particularly with regard to property) could be made stronger, they
were willing to adopt it ; and, finally, to profess their unalterable
attachment to the peace and good order and tranquillity of the
country, on which Mr. Conolly very much relies.   On leaving
Mr. F. I. met Mr. Grattan, who concurred exactly with him.   It
was agreed that Messrs. Byrne, Keogh, and Fitzgerald should go
to Castleton.

[1] [The Bill of 1792, *ante*, p. 92. Sir Hercules Langrishe (author of "Barataria," a
fictitious work dealing with the public characters of the period) was one of the
most brilliant members of the Irish Parliament. " The brightness of his mind
and the flashes of his wit," says the younger Grattan, "cast a lustre on all he
touched." Some of his witticisms are worth recording. "On one occasion,
when riding with the Lord Lieutenant in the Phœnix Park, his Excellency
complained of his predecessors, and asked why they had left the place in such
a wet and swampy state. Langrishe replied, ' They were too much occupied
in *draining* the rest of the kingdom.' On another occasion, being asked
where could be found the best history of Ireland, he answered, ' In the continuation of *Rapin* '" (author of "History of England to the Revolution,
with continuation by Tindal ").—Grattan, " Memoirs." Langrishe died in
1811.—ED.]

[2] [An influential member of the Irish Parliament.—ED.]

[3] [On the subject of the Catholic claims.—ED.]

Notes, letters, &c., of 1792. Journal of the Proceedings of Mr. John Hutton on his second embassy to Belfast; also his dealings with the Catholics, including his combinations with sundry dissenting Republicans, and his plan for a general system of Irish Jacobins.

Monday, July 9th.—Set out posting with the Keeper of the College Lions for Belfast (*Whitley Stokes*)—Breakfast at the Man-of-War; missed poor P. P. sadly. The Keeper dull. Proposed piquet; agreed to; played very fair; doubt that the Keeper is a blackleg. Nothing material until Dundalk; scored ten there for a man leading a pig in a string. Ditto at Loughbrickland; game at Banbridge; the Keeper 55, Mr. Hutton 95. Sleep at Banbridge.

10th. Set off early; see a cat before we come to the bridge; game.—The Keeper mortified. Very pretty amusement for a statesman and a philosopher. O Lord! O Lord!—On an average, about a cat and one-seventh of a cat per mile on the great northern road. Make no other remark of any importance or use on the journey.—Arrive at Belfast at one o'clock; learn that the first company is at exercise, and dine upon Waddel Cunningham. Unpack in a hurry, and dress in regimentals; run off to the field and leave the Keeper to fag. Meet everybody. Cunningham very civil; dine in the tent, at the right hand of the Captain. After dinner the whole company turn out and dance on the field; *vastly French;* march into town in the evening, "*all with magnanimity and benevolence.*" Sup with Neilson and the old set; very much tired after my journey. Bed at one o'clock.

11th. Rise with great headache; stupid as a mill-horse; call on Sinclair; read over the address. Agree to meet him and Dr. White,[1] with whom I learn I am appointed committeeman, the next morning at breakfast, and settle it finally. Call on the unfortunate Keeper, whom I have not seen Lord knows when; find that he gets on very well without me. Bring him to the

[1] [A leading United Irishman.—ED.]

Hypocrite and introduce him; the Hypocrite as gentle as ever; asks us to dine next day; agree thereto. All go to the Harper's at one; poor enough; ten performers; seven execrable, three good, one of them, Fanning, far the best. No new musical discovery; believe all the good Irish airs are already written. The company tired. See the Blue Company [1] march out to exercise; very fine front rank. Meet the Irish Slave, who is rejoiced to see me. Dine with Neilson and the old set; the Keeper comes late; conversation flat enough. More and more miss poor P. P. Bring the Keeper to the coterie. See an apparition of Jordan, who is in London; find, on speaking Latin to the said apparition, that it is Jordan himself; heartily glad to see him. Sup at the coterie; sup again at Neilson; the old set. Bed late. All this day dull as a post; no P. P. Sad! sad!

12th. Rise again with headache, resulting from late hours. Go out to the Draper at Lilliput. Meet Dr. White; settle the address; many alterations. Return to town again; do not know what to do; lounge to the Harper's; meet Vesey Knox, who shows me a letter from John,[2] with an account of their victory over the bloody tyrant. Dinner at the Hypocrite's, Joy, Williamson, Bryson,[3] A. Stewart, Renny Maxwell, the Keeper, &c. Williamson remembers the tossing he got from P. P. last October; calls P. P. the Socratic. Williamson clever, and says he is rather more a friend to the Catholics than he was; believe he is one of the time-to-time party. Go off at nine to meet the delegates at the Donegal Arms; fifteen present McTier in the chair. Read the address from the committee; Waddel Cunningham [4] opposes it, without assigning any reason. Neilson at him. At last out it comes. The coming down of Mr. Hutton has given great alarm, especially

---

[1] [Of Volunteers.—Ed.]

[2] [Knox, an officer in the British service, afterwards Brigadier-general. He commanded in Ireland in 1797. The "bloody tyrant" possibly refers to Tippoo Sahib, who was defeated at Seringapatam, May 15, 1791, and Feb. 6, 1792.—Ed.]

[3] [Minister of the Second Presbyterian Congregation, Belfast. "In consequence of some dissatisfaction on the part of some members of the congregation," he resigned in 1791 (Benn, "History of Belfast").—Ed.]

[4] Captain of Belfast Volunteers and member of the Irish House of Commons.

as he has brought with him some man from the college, whom no one knows. The company all laugh ; Cunningham goes off in a pet. The address read, paragraph by paragraph, and approved unanimously, except that part which relates to the Catholics, which had H. Joy's single negative. Address to the National Assembly read and approved in like manner. Broke up. Home. Bed as usual at half-past one. Damned bad hours !

13*th*. Rise again with a headache. Go to the Donegal Arms. No Catholics by the mail ; very odd. Saw them take places for last night. Will they come or not ? No letters. The Jacobin party up here; Lafayette down; think they are all wrong. Belfast not half so pleasant this time as the last. Politics just as good or better ; everything else worse. Grievous want of P. P. ; the Keeper not equal to him. By-the-bye, the Hypocrite made the Keeper drunk last night. Fine doings. Miss that unfortunate Digges. Weather bad. Afraid for to-morrow every way ; generally in low spirits. Hear that the Tribune, with his suite, is arrived ; go to the Donegal Arms and say *O* to him (*vide* " Robinson Crusoe"). The Harpers again. *Strum strum* and be hanged. Hear that several Catholics have been seen ; run to try ; find Magog, Weldon, and others, to a large amount. The hair of Dr. Haliday's [1] wig miraculously grows grey with fear of the Catholics. Several comets appear in the market-place. Walk the Catholics about to show them the lions. See a figure of Commerce at the insurance office ; the Catholics mistake it for an image, and kneel down, take out their beads, and say their prayers before it ; leave them at the Exchange, and go to dinner with Simms. The old set. Drink nothing. Go at seven to meet the Jacobins. The time-to-time people say with great gravity that Mr. Hutton is come to force seditious papers down their throats. Mr. Hutton a man of great consequence, as it seems. The Keeper, who is in the plot, a cunning hand ; all day out picking up clay, &c., the better to conceal his designs, but Waddel and Joy too knowing to be had in that manner. Mr. Hutton almost angry at all this nonsense, and very sorry that any man, woman, or child in Belfast should

[1] [A leading Belfast citizen, and secretary of the Northern Whig Club.—ED.]

listen to such trash. Expect a sharp opposition to-morrow. Some
of the country corps no better than Peep-of-day-boys. Antrim
folks, good ; Down, bad. Dress, and go to Gautherot's benefit ;
called out. Gog, but no McDonnell ! not like his namesake, who
was " *worthy to be a rebel.*" Good news from Munster : Gog
preaching for three days to six bishops, who are at last converted ;
so the returns will go on—*Ça ira !* Return to the concert.
Williamson very pleasant ; tells good stories of Lord Moira,[1] and
wants me to go there ; calls Mrs. O'Hara Caroline of Litchfield,
&c. Mr. Hutton envious, and endeavours to outshine, but can't.
Goes off, and falls upon A. Stewart, whom he attacks upon the
Catholic question, and mauls without remorse. Stewart very
shallow. The Draper tells Mr. Hutton that great exertions are
making to impress people with the idea that he is going to ram
something down their throats. Stuff, stuff ! The Draper moderate ; thinks it will be a work of time, &c., but still the cause gains
ground daily. All this not very encouraging. Come home in not
the most amiable temper. Get my belt, &c., for the review to-
morrow. Generally sulky. Want P. P. in order to advise him ;
just in a humour to give advice. Write a letter about the Catholic
committee, signed X. Y., for the *Northern Star.* Dull as a post,
but it cannot be helped. The Keeper dines this day in the country
with the Hypocrite and others ; suppose he will make a beast of
himself again. Bed. A plot ! a plot ! Neilson comes to my
bedside at one o'clock, with orders to prepare for battle in the
morning. Passing by a room in the inn, he heard Cunningham's
voice very loud ; the door being half open, he went in and found,
to his utter astonishment, delegates from the country corps, with
Waddel haranguing against the Catholics, and talking of some
sedition intended to be broached the next day. Waddel taken all
aback by this apparition of Neilson. Neilson abuses him and
reads the papers ; the company breaks up without coming to any
determination, but Neilson expects hot work in the morning.
Waddel a ——. Sleep at last, about two.

   14th July, era of the French Revolution ! Knocked up early by

----

[1] [Afterwards Governor-General of India and Marquis of Hastings.—ED.]

Neilson ; get on my regimentals, and go breakfast with the Catholics. McKenna arrived. Drums beating, colours flying, and all the honours of war. Brigade formed, and march off by ten ; 700 men, and make a tolerable appearance. First and second Belfast companies far the best in all particulars : Green company 102 ; Blue 90. Ride the Draper's mare. The review tolerably well. Some companies filled by little squads of six or eight men, who come in of their own motion, without officers. A council of war held in a potato field, adjacent to the review ground. Present, the Draper in the chair, the Tribune, his brother George, Dr. Crawford, of Lisburn ; Rev. Mr. Craig, Dr. McKenna, and Mr. Hutton : all fools except the first and last. Crawford and Tandy frightened out of their wits. We are undone ; shall be defeated ; all the country corps decidedly against us, from the report of some seditious paper (the old story) ; better to adopt something moderate, that shall include all parties ; danger of disunion ; risk of credit if we should even succeed by a small majority, which is the best that can be hoped ; the country folks afraid ; *da capo*, &c. McKenna very absurd ; takes upon him the man of influence ; says the Catholics are timid, and a repulse here would be fatal, and success of little consequence, as a declaration in favour of the Catholics was now useless, unless followed up by some strong step. Mr. Hutton at last breaks silence ; contradicts McKenna plump, as to the use of a declaration, in which the Draper concurs ; examines the question in three lights, as being carried by a small majority, or lost, or not proposed. In the first case, if we succeed by a small majority, it is still success and a majority, which is better than a defeat. In the second, if it be lost, let it go ; let us know the worst ; and not be afraid to look the question in the face, nor delude ourselves and the Catholics with the idea of support, where no support is to be found. As to the third idea, which seemed to prevail most in the council, of not proposing the address, that was, of all possible measures, the worst ; it carried in it all the evils of the other two, and many more ; it was cowardly and foolish, more ruinous than the worst defeat : for those men who had already spread so many lies about the address, would, if it was now kept back, utter a thousand more, and say it was so infamous that no man could be found hardy enough to propose it to the meeting ; that, in the Catholic question, not to advance was to recede, and if, after the strong measures of the last nine months, we were now to blink it, it would, at once, utterly destroy all hopes or prospect of union. Finally, it was more consonant to the spirit and decision of the Draper's character, to come fairly forward and let us see our friends and our enemies. Unanimity was a good thing in itself, but much more essentially so, as it was a means of promoting good principles ; if, however, the principle must be renounced, to procure unanimity, it was not worth buying at that price. Mr. Hutton, likewise, said that he did not see the question in so desperate a light ; he would hope it might be carried, even by a large majority, but, at all events, whether carried or not, he entreated the Draper to move it boldly, and leave the event to Providence. The Draper agrees ; the other members shrug up their shoulders, depart, and the council breaks up. The Draper and Mr. Hutton walk about the field, every man discouraging them, but all won't do. Both satisfied that half measures are no measures, and determined to hazard the event, let the worst come. The Draper, a fine resolute fellow. Mr. Hutton says nothing of the energy, spirit, and decision of his own character, especially when contrasted with the caution and *moderation* of the Lisburn men, and the bladdering stuff of McKenna. Moderation— nonsense ! March into town at three. Meet Haslitt and Neilson : take the word " Catholic " out, and put in the word " Irishmen " of every religious denomination. Procession. Meeting at the Linen Hall, astonishing full. Question moved by the Draper. Before the debate goes on five minutes, satisfied that we have it hollow ; the Lisburn men, and our good advisers in the field all mistaken. More and more satisfied that their *moderation* is nonsense and stuff. *Carry the question* with about five dissenting voices, among whom are Joy and Waddel Cunningham. All hollow. Could have carried anything. The business now fairly settled in Belfast and the neighbourhood. Huzza ! Huzza ! Dinner at the Donegal Arms. Everybody as happy as a king, but Waddel, who looks like the Devil himself ! Huzza ! God bless everybody ! Stanislas

Augustus, George Washington: *Beau-jour.* Who would have thought it this morning? Huzza! Generally drunk.—Broke my glass thumping the table. Home, God knows how or when. Huzza! God bless everybody again, generally.—Bed, with three times three. Sleep at last.

15*th, Sunday.* Rise and breakfast with the Hypocrite and the Keeper, who are both outrageously rejoiced at the events of yesterday. After breakfast take a long walk with Gog, who tells me that Lynch has been ripping up the old business of my appointment, and thinks that it would be better if a Protestant were not to interfere in their business. *That is wise!* Gog thinks that McKenna, whom he hates worse than hell, is at the bottom of all this. Not unlikely, but *I don't care.* (*See Tommy and Harry,* in the Spelling Book.) He likewise tells me of an odd manœuvre of the Tribune and McKenna, endeavouring yesterday to get him and the Catholics to express something of a wish that their affairs should not be introduced so as to risk disturbing the harmony of the meeting, or words to that effect, which he and the Catholics did very properly refuse to do, saying they could not dictate to any men ; but their wish was, that the question should be fairly tried, and if it was lost, let it be lost. Precisely Mr. Hutton's idea at the council of war, which more and more proves the great spirit, integrity, and understanding of that truly respectable gentleman. Gog takes great pains to turn Mr. Hutton's mind against McKenna ; very unnecessary, for Mr. Hutton sees the characters of both the parties already, and will not much believe what either says of the other, without collateral proof. Gog jealous of everybody, even of Magog. Leave him and go to dinner at Lilliput with the Draper. Conversation all upon banking. Blindman's-buff in the evening. Break my knee against a chair like a jackanapes. Drowned in the rain coming home at one in the morning, as usual. Fine doings. The Keeper, of the company. Bed.

16*th.* Rise and go to breakfast with Will Simms at the Grove all the Catholics from Dublin there. Council of war in the garden, Gog, Robert Simms, and Mr. Hutton. Gog expounds the plan of organising the Catholic body. Mr. Hutton takes the opportunity

to press an idea started by P. P. several months back, for organising, in a similar manner, the Dissenting interest.   All agree that if
that could be accomplished, the business would be done.   Query,
How?   Simms satisfied that we have already a great majority of
the thinking men through the North with us; says, however,
that if Government attack the Catholic Committee under the new
system in *two months* the North will not be *ready to support them.*
Mr. Hutton explains that we are not ready to call on any one yet
for more than good wishes, and asks Simms, who is indeed a
Tanner, and shall for the future be so called, what he thinks of the
next 14th of July.   The Tanner looks extremely wise and significant.   Gog, Mr. Hutton, and he worship each other, and *sign an
article with their blood ; flourish their hands three times in a most
graceful manner* (see Goldsmith's "Citizen of the World,") and
march off into town.   *Ho, but they are indeed most agreeable
creatures.*   (Do.)   Lounge till near dinner.   Go to the Donegal
Arms, and meet all the Catholics.   McKenna comes in, and
confesses that his behaviour at the council of war on the 14th was
indefensible, and that he is sorry, &c.   Frivolous in the extreme.
Mr. Hutton takes the opportunity to state his reasons for relating
the conversation in the field, and appeals to Mr. Lube whether
he had not acted fair and honourable?   Mr. Lube compliments
him, and McKenna declares his satisfaction and conviction that
Mr. Hutton would be incapable of acting otherwise.   Short reckon-
ings make long friends.   All fair!   Gog and Mr. Hutton go downstairs and meet a certain set of the Belfast men.   State the new
plan of organisation.   All the Belfast men laud it.   A crowd comes
in and breaks off the discourse.   Dinner ; McTier in the chair.
Chequered at the head of the table, a Dissenter and a Catholic.
Delightful !   The four flags, America, France, Poland, Ireland, but
no England.   Bravo !   *Beau-jour !*   The Draper and I sit together
at the foot of the table.   Conversation regarding McKenna, who
has acted very strangely.   When he said in the council of war that
he, as a Catholic, thought that a declaration was useless, unless
Belfast was prepared to follow it up with something stronger, he
impressed the Draper with an idea that he meant violent measures

immediately. The Draper, therefore, bid him not calculate on immediate support from the North, but said, at the same time, that the progress of the cause was rapid, and must, finally, succeed. McKenna then, when arguing with the Catholics, to induce them to express their wish not to embarrass the question with their claims, mentioned, as an argument, that the Draper had told him in the field not to reckon upon any support from the North. This struck them all of a heap, knowing the Draper's decided character. By this it appears that, by his nonsense, to call it no worse, he led the Draper into giving an opinion, *subject to a condition*, and then quoted that opinion, without mentioning the condition ; by which he had like to throw a damp on the spirits of both parties, which might have had ugly consequences. All this very odd. Mr. Hutton explains the whole to the Draper, and puts him up to the real character of McKenna. The Draper very glad to be undeceived, as he had been a good deal struck with what he had said, supposing him to be a man of weight in his own party. Huzza! More toasts! Three times three. God bless everybody. Go upstairs with the Catholics. Tell them the discourse with the Draper, which at once explains what had staggered them relative to expecting no support from Belfast. Neilson joins us, and we all swear an alliance. McKenna properly abused by all parties. Home. Bed. Determine to set off to-morrow and see P. P. Go to sleep thinking of my journey. Keeper gone to Scotland.

17*th*. Waked by Neilson, to see Gog, and other Catholics, before they set off. Go to the inn. Much conversation about the Peep-of-day-boys and Defenders. My letter in the *Northern Star* approved of. Proposed by Neilson that the Catholics should go by Rathfriland, where the disturbances are, and meet some of the gentlemen of the neighbourhood, in order to try if anything can be done to restore peace. He offers, in that case, to go himself, and all parties request me to go too. Vexed to the very soul at having my *expiration* to Dungannon all blown up. Rot it—sink it—damn it—must go—cannot possibly help it. Poor P. P.—Well, *'tis but in vain for soldiers to complain*. Agree to set off in half an hour to Rathfriland. Hope our journey may do some good, as the restoration of tranquillity is to us of the last importance. Console myself with this hope for the disappointment of not seeing P. P., but vexed damnably for all that. Set off in a very middling temper with Neilson and his wife. Stop at Hillsborough, and drink tea at a Mr. Henderson's ; see his son, the author of "Colin Mountain," in the magazines. Set off, and arrive at ten at a Mr. Lowry's, near Rath-friland. Received with great politeness and hospitality. Supper. Sit up late, as usual. Bed at half-past one. Sad ! sad !

18*th.* Rise, and set off with Neilson and young Lowry, to Rathfriland. In about an hour the Catholics arrive from Down-patrick. Meet Mr. Tighe, the Parson, Sam. Barber, the Dissenting Minister, Mr. Derry, the Priest, and about eighteen gentlemen of the neighbourhood. Agreed on all hands that the Protestants were the aggressors. Several have been killed on both sides. Great offence taken at the Catholics marching about in military array, and firing shots at unseasonable times. The Catholics certainly wrong in that, and must, if possible be stopped. The majority think that if that were accomplished, the disturbances would soon die away. Some bigots think that their arms should be taken from the Catholics. God forbid ! besides, the thing is in its nature impossible. A magistrate present ; a Captain Rowan tells one or two swinging lies. First, that information has been lodged with the Commissioners of the Revenue that a ship laden with arms was expected in a bay at the back of Mourne, and was to be escorted by a French frigate ; and that these arms were intended for the Catholics. Also, that orders had been sent to every port in the kingdom, to seize and detain all arms imported, until further orders. Mr. Hutton breaks out in a rage. As to the French sending over a ship load of arms, all the world knows that, at this moment, they are in the last distress for arms themselves, and buying them from England at any price. As to the other story, of the orders being sent to the ports, it was exactly like one of the tricks of our infamous Government, who are notoriously spreading the vilest calumnies and falsehoods, to exasperate the two sects against each other, that they may with the greater ease and security plunder both. The magistrate in a huff, and also

Parson Tighe, brother to Edward Tighe, the Hack. Mr. Hutton changes the discourse back to the business of the meeting. Proposes that the Catholics shall agree to desist from parading in bodies and firing, and the Dissenters shall declare that they will maintain the peace of the country against all who shall transgress, without *distinction of party or religion.* An amendment proposed by Neilson, that this declaration should be made by the volunteers. The idea unanimously approved, and three officers then present, Captain A. Lowry, Captain Cowen, and Captain Barber, engage for their respective companies. A refractory priest, of the name of Fitzsimons, much blamed ; the Catholics engage to have him removed. They, likewise, propose to have a pastoral letter from their bishop, and a circular one from the committee, to be read in every chapel, recommending peace and good order. All present highly satisfied with each other, except the magistrate, who looks glum. He was examined within these ten days at the Castle, on the subject of the riots : suppose he lied like the Devil. Earl Annesley much to blame in this business. No magistrate nearer than seven miles to Rathfriland. The Catholics always ready to make peace and keep it. Their adversaries uniformly the aggressors, by the admission of all present. Cannot, on the whole, learn that they do anything worse than meet in large bodies, and fire powder ; foolish certainly, but not wicked. They break open no houses, nor ever begin an attack. The Protestants, however, extremely alarmed at their meetings, which therefore must, if possible, be suppressed. The Catholic clergy have almost totally lost their influence, since the people have got arms, so fatal to superstition and priestcraft is even the smallest degree of liberty. The Catholics and Mr. Hutton receive the thanks of the meeting for their public spirit in coming down on the occasion. All part on excellent terms. Mr. Hutton meditates attempting an excursion to Dungannon. Finds, on calculation, that P. P. would, most probably, be in Belfast about the time he could reach there. Gives up his scheme in a pet, and sets off with the Catholics for Newry, on his way to Dublin. Gog converts a bishop at Newry, another at Downpatrick. Arrive at Dundalk. Gog insufferably vain, and fishing for compliments, of which Mr. Hutton at first is rather sparing. Gog then praises Mr. Hutton, who relents thereupon, and lays it on in return pretty thick. Nothing too gross. A great deal of wine. Bed, as usual, between one and two. Bad! Bad! Bad!

19th. Set off early, and ride twelve miles on a lame hack; pleasant and respectable. Get on to Drogheda, and find the Newry stage just setting off for Dublin. Leave Gog converting another bishop (the Catholic Primate), and drive off in the stage; no adventures; arrive in town at six in the evening. "Hic finis longæ chartæque, viæque."—*Hor.*

Addenda. Mr. Hutton, on several occasions, pressed his friends the Jacobins to try and extend their clubs through the North. The Draper highly approves the plan, also Haslitt, also the Tanner and his brother. The Irish Slave swears he will begin his operations immediately, as we have talked enough, and it is time to begin to act. Mr. Hutton to write a scurrilous letter for the said Slave, to John Foster.

N.B.—The meeting on the 14th like the old German meetings in the woods. All the people sitting, and the armed warriors in a ring standing round. Fine effect of the unanimous aye of the Assembly when passing the address. Mr. Hutton affected so that the tears stood in his eyes; sentimental and pretty.

Dublin, July 21st. Rode out with Gog to Grattan; entertained all the way with stories of Burke,[1] who is become most odious to Gog. Burke certainly scheming with the Catholics, either to get more money, or raise his value in England with the Minister, got 2,000 guineas for his expedition here last winter; foolish generosity in the Catholics, for he contrived to embroil them with everybody. He wants now to come over here, where he can be of no possible use, and leave England, where, by the bye, he is of just as little. A puppy, or worse. We arrive at Grattan's, and tell him of the state of things in the North and in the South, which he approves. Talk of next winter. He apprehends Government will make a blow at the Catholics by committing their chairman. Mr. Hutton

[1] [Richard.—ED.]

of opinion that the whole body should rise and go with him in that event. Grattan advises to let him go, and immediately elect another. If he be committed, elect another, and so on, but never to recede. If the House of Commons give words, let the General Committee do the same, and, if they be firm, the House will submit, because the one is an emanation from the people, the other not. Mr. Hutton asks for a committee to inquire, next session, into the state of the North, and the causes of the riots there. Grattan thinks it would do mischief, because the committee being, to a certainty, under the influence of the Castle, would misstate and garble facts, and draw conclusions which even these facts could not warrant. Mr. Hutton says that is very hard, which Grattan admits; but says the reason is obvious, that we have *no Parliament in Ireland.* Grattan seems angry. Mr. Hutton reads him the intended address to the Defenders, in which he suggests some alterations, but very much approves it generally. Say *O* to him and depart, having first promised to dine with him at Tinnehinch on Saturday next.

22*nd.* Meet the Sub-committee; read the address, which is approved, with a clause promising protection from the General Committee to all peaceable Catholics. Think this a capital stroke, as it gives such a hold of the *bas peuple,* of whom there are in this country above 3,000,000. Meet Gog in the evening, who is in a peck of troubles. Expects Burke over in Cork every day, notwithstanding all that has been done to prevent his coming. Burke pretends that he is come on his private affairs. *Private fiddlesticks !* Gog in a rage; determined to thwart him on all occasions, and put him down with the Catholics, which he most richly deserves for the great impropriety of his conduct in never communicating a syllable of information whilst acting as agent in England, though perpetually applied to for that purpose, and also for his now coming over (if he does come) against the inclination of every one concerned. Burke by far the most impudent, *opiniatre* fellow that ever I knew. Gog wants to have a Robin not to invite him to their houses. Believe, if he comes, he will be rumped. Does he want another 2,000 guineas?

23*rd*. Wrote an X. Y. for the *Northern Star* ; also a copy of a circular letter from the General Committee in answer to those conveying returns, recommending the permanency of the parochial electors, as a channel of communication, and the formation of committees of correspondence through each county, to consist of at least one gentleman for each barony. Also a sketch of a letter to Colonel Barry, on the present state of this country. Dined with Tom Braughall and Gog. Read a very long prancing letter from Burke, filled with nonsense about the French Revolution, on which he is as mad as his father. The issue is, that the Catholics will meet no support from ministry in England (who seemed to be bullied by ministry here) in their next application to Parliament ; they must, therefore, rely on their own force. And it seems pretty evident that England, if she will not interfere on their behalf, neither will she interfere against them ; so that the Catholics and the Protestant ascendency are left to fight it out, *propriis aribus (à la bonne heure)*. It should seem that Government here have gone so far as to menace stopping the mutiny bills and supplies, if they are not allowed the sole management of the Catholic affairs. What will be the issue of all this?

24*th*. In committee. Read over Burke's letter again, and receive orders to prepare an answer thereto, and also a letter to the Hon. Mr. Browne. Gave the address to the Defenders to Byrne, with orders to print 1,000 on large paper. Dined with Warren ; home early. Wrote the letter to Burke, giving him his congé, regretting that ministry in England had, by adopting a determined neutrality, rendered further application to them useless, and of course deprived the Catholics of the powerful aid of his talents, and giving him a remote prospect that he might again be employed on some future emergency. All very civil and indefinite ; not a bad letter. How will the Catholics like it? Wrote also to Mr. Browne. Spent a very pleasant evening at home. This day my appointment as Secretary to the sub-committee, until the rising of Parliament, was confirmed unanimously by the General Committee, with a stipend for that time of £200.

25*th.* Sub-committee. Letter to Burke read, and objected to by Mr. Fitzgerald, as being too pointed a dismissal. Long conversation thereupon, and alterations made. The majority of the sub-committee cowardly. Gog stout, but overruled. Letter to Mr. Browne agreed to. Dined at Warren's, and met Archdekin. Pleasant evening.

26*th.* Rode out to Grattan's, and dined there with Gog and Hardy. Little new; but the old ground beaten over again. Talking of the late Chief Baron Burgh,[1] Grattan said that he fell in love with daisies on his march; he stopped to pick them up, and twist them into a garland, which he flung about him, and so entered the field of battle, half a hero and half an opera dancer. Pretty! Captain Fitzgerald, Grattan's brother-in-law, a fine young fellow. Great deal of wine; Grattan keeps us to sup.

27*th.* Pleasant breakfast. Tell Grattan about Digges. Grattan eager to know him. Promise to send him Digges' letter on trade, &c. Ride into town with Gog. Dine with Warren and Archdekin again. No conversation. Wish to introduce Archdekin to Grattan on the subject of India, &c., &c.

28*th*, 29*th*, 30*th.* Sub-committee. Writing letters. Hear that Neilson is come to town. Dine with him at Braughall's. Nothing new. Introduced in form to the General Committee.

31*st.* Circular letter for the returns ready for signing. The

---

[1] [Walter Hussey Burgh (b. about 1742, d. 1783) was one of the most eloquent members of the Irish House of Commons. Though Prime Sergeant in 1779, he supported Grattan in his efforts to obtain Free Trade. It was during the debates on this question that he delivered a speech which electrified the House, and placed him in the first rank as an orator. Replying to some one who had said that Ireland was in a state of peace, and referring to the Volunteer force, he said, "Talk not to me of peace; it is not peace, but smothered war. England has sown her laws like dragons' teeth, and they have sprung up in armed men." Mr. Froude has graphically described the scene that followed. "Never yet had Grattan so moved the Irish House of Commons as it was moved at these words. From the floor the applause rose to the gallery. From the gallery it was thundered to the crowd at the door. From the door it rung through the city. As the tumult calmed down, Hussey Burgh rose again, and amidst a renewed burst of cheers declared that he resigned the office he held under the Crown." On the establishment of Legislative Independence, Burgh (1782) became Chief Baron of the Exchequer.—ED.]

Vintner comes in, and, after a long debate, refuses to sign. Cowardly! rascally! The fellow is worth £200,000. Gog in the horrors. Dine again with Warren and Archdekin. Sick all this day. Bed at nine o'clock.

August 1st. *Merry be the first of August!* Breakfast in college. Boswell shows us a loom of his invention, for weaving fishing nets, which executes it completely with the fisherman's knot. He sent a sample to the Society for Encouraging the Arts in London, which had offered sixty guineas premium for such an invention. Several others put in their claim, but his was the only one which answered. He would, in consequence, have got the reward, only it was luckily discovered, in time to prevent it, that he was an Irishman, for which reason only they did refuse him. *Wise* and *liberal.* Boswell gives us a yard of his net which he wove before us. Puts me in mind of Macabe and Pearce. This is the Broughsham review : What will the Volunteers do there ? No returns from Wexford : What is the meaning of that ?—Sub-committee. All abuse the Vintner for hanging back. Old cowardly slave ! Mr. Everhard, of Sligo, comes in ; gives a most melancholy account of the depression and insults under which the Catholics of that town labour ; every Protestant rascal breaks their heads and windows for his amusement, and no grand jury will find their bills, nor petit jury convict them. The Catholic spirit quite broken. They do not even beat one another. Sad! sad! Busy all day folding papers, &c., for the Munster bishops. Damn all bishops! Gog not quite well on that point. Thinks them a good thing. Nonsense. Dine at home with Neilson and McCracken.[1] Very pleasant. Rights of man. French Revolution. No bishops, &c., &c., &c.

---

[1] [Henry Joy McCracken, one of the United Irish leaders, was born in Belfast in 1767. Like so many United Irishmen he was engaged in business, at first in the linen trade, aftewards a cotton manufacturer. He threw himself heart and soul into the revolutionary movement. In 1796 he was arrested, but subsequently released on the recognisances of his cousin, Mr. (afterwards Chief Baron) Joy. In 1798 McCracken took the field, and attacked the town of Antrim. Successful in the first onset, and driving a troop of dragoons before him, he was ultimately repulsed and routed. Escaping from the field he was arrested, tried by court-martial, and sentenced to death. His sister has given a touching

August 2nd. Breakfast with Drennan and Neilson. Sub-committee. More papers. Gog not at all equal in steadiness to Magog, and as vain as the devil. Magog not a grain of a Papist, nor Warren; all the others so so enough. Meet J. Bramston just setting off for England. Dine at Sweetman's with a long set. All well. Half the county Down have returned their delegates. Bravo!

August 3rd. Sub-committee. Folding circular letters, &c. Wexford returns at last. Rent-roll of their delegates, £15,000 per annum. Bravo! This makes eight counties.

description of the last scene : "At 5 p.m. he was ordered to the place of execution—the old market-house, the ground of which had been given to the town by his great-great-grandfather. I took his arm, and we walked together to the place of execution, where I was told it was the general's orders I should leave him, which I peremptorily refused. Harry begged I would go. Clasping my hands round him (I did not weep till then), I said I could bear anything but leaving him. Three times he kissed me, and intreated I would go. . . . I suffered myself to be led away. . . . I was told afterwards that poor Harry stood where I left him, at the place of execution, and watched me until I was out of sight ; that he then attempted to speak to the people, but that the noise of the trampling of the horses was so great that it was impossible he should be heard ; that he then resigned himself to his fate, and the multitude who were present at that moment uttered cries which seemed more like one loud and long-continued shriek than the expression of grief or terror on similar occasions. He was buried in the old churchyard where St. George's Church now stands, and close to the corner of the school-house, where the door is." More than forty years afterwards she wrote : "Notwithstanding the grief that overcame every feeling for a time, and still lingers in my breast, connecting every passing event with the remembrance of former circumstances which recall some act or thought of his, I never once wished that my beloved brother had taken any other part than that which he did take."—Ed.]

CHAPTER V.

AMONG THE PEEP-OF-DAY-BOYS.

*Journal of the proceedings of John Hutton, Esq., on his third journey
to the North of Ireland, including his artful negotiations with
the Peep-of-day-boys, and sundry Peers of the realm ; also, his
valorous entry into, and famous retreat out of the city of
Rathfriland ; interspersed with sundry delectable adventures
and entertaining anecdotes.*—Vive le Roi.

August 7, 1792. Set out posting on my expedition among the
Peep-of-day-boys, with Gog and Neilson. Pleasant journey.
Arrive in Drogheda, and dine. Settle with Neilson to meet us
at Rathfriland. Go and drink tea with Mrs. Austin, an aunt of
Gog's, who insists on our lodging with her. Promise to dine
with Mr. Bird to-morrow. The 1st of last month kept here with
additional solemnity : "*July the first in Oldbridge Town there was a
grievous battle.*" Sick. Bed at eight o'clock.

8th. Go to the Coffee House. See the Derry Grand Jury resolutions, and the call of the county Wexford. In a horrible
rage. Sit down and write a paper for the *Northern Star*, signed
Vindex, abusing the resolutions, &c. Show Vindex to Gog, who
is as pleased as Punch ; tells me he has succeeded with the
bishops, and is to dine with them. Go to Bird's, and stay
amongst a parcel of girls all the evening. Puppy. Home late.

9th. Walk out with Gog, and plan counter-resolutions for
Derry : come home and write them. Gog takes them in his
pocket to the Primate. Bird and Hamill : propose to them to
offer a coalition to the Protestant ascendency, and that instead
of orange cockades, all parties should unite and wear green ones

on the next first of July. A good scheme, though it is my own.
They seem to think it could not be done. Let them try, how-
ever. Dinner with Dr. Reilly, the Primate, Plunket, Bishop of
Meath, Reilly, Bishop of Clogher, Cruise, Bishop of Ardagh
McMillan, Bishop of Down, Coyle, Bishop of Raphoe, M'Davit,
Bishop of Derry, and Lennon, Bishop of Dromore, all very
pleasant, sensible men. Dr. Plunket far the first ; think he would
be a credit to any situation. All well on the Catholic question.
The matter as to the North now settled. More and more admire
Dr. Plunket ; glad to find the Catholic prelates men of such manners and understanding : *beau-jour !* All very civil to me, and
complimentary about Vindex, and refuse to drink Lord Hillsborough. *Bon.* Home early. Bed.

10*th.* Travel with a third man, a Mr. Lynch, of Galway
Stupid. Newry. Introduced to Mr. O'Hanlon, Jun.: a clever
young man. Go early to bed.

11*th.* Breakfast at O'Hanlon's. Hear that Mr. Barber is of
opinion that we ought not to go to Rathfriland, and has desired
some one to write us word so to Dublin. It is surmised that his
reason is, lest we might be insulted by some of the bigots in that
town. Cannot help it : what must be, must be, and we must go
to Rathfriland. Buy powder and ball, and load our pistols, for
fear of accidents. My balls too little ; damn it ! Afraid of Capt.
Swan, who is a bloody Peep-of-day-boy : endeavour to make a pun
on his name : something about goose, but it won't do. "*When as
I sat in Babylon.*" Hear just now that if we go to Rathfriland
we shall be houghed : "*pleasant, but wrong.*" What is to be done?
This information we have from Mr. O'Neil, of Cabra : cowardly
enough, but dare say he heard it. Set off for Mr. O'Neil, of
Bannvale, on our way for Rathfriland. Arrive at length at that
flourishing seat of liberality and public virtue. "*I fear thee*, O
Rathfriland, *lest that thy girls with spits, and boys with stones,
in puny battle slay me.*" Stop at Murphy's Inn, six in number,
all valiant. Get paper, and begin to write to Dr. Tighe, Mr.
Barber, and Mr. A. Lowry. Stop short by the intelligence
that the Landlord will give us no accommodations ! Hey ! hey !

The fellow absolutely refuses. He has cold beef and lamb chops, and will give us neither, but turns off on his heel. Damned fine. Well, Mr. Murphy! The dog is a Quaker. What is to be done, now at past four? Agree to send Mr. O'Neil for Barber. He goes off. Send also for Mr. Linsey, about two miles off. Mr. Hutton offers to ride to Linen Hall for young Lowry. His horse wants a shoe. Damn it! Well. Too late now to get a messenger. Mr. O'Neil returns with news that Barber is out: all of a piece. A striking proof of the state of politics in this country, when a Landlord will not give accommodation for money to Catholics. Mr. Linsey has got a sore leg and cannot come. Get a Mr. Murphy at last, brother to our hospitable Landlord, and a decent man: explain the motives of our coming to him, and remind him of the conversation of 18th July last. He seems very much ashamed of the behaviour of his brother, and, in some degree, apprehensive of our meeting some insult ; which, however, he hopes may not happen. All stout. Some of us determined to make the boors of Rathfriland smoke for it, if they attack us, particularly McNally, who has ridden from Newry armed, merely to assist us in case of necessity ; manly and decided! The gentlemen of the town have learned, as we presume, that we are prepared, and therefore make no attempt to duck us, as they had lamented they did not do on our last visit. Leave Rathfriland in great force, the cavalry in the front. See about 150 Peep-of-day-boys exercising within a quarter of a mile of the town. Suppose if we had attempted to lie in the town, we should have had a battle. Arrive at Mr. O'Neil's and dine. Old gentry, and very hospitable and kind. Mr. O'Neil exceedingly hurt at being refused a dinner in Rathfriland, within sight of which he and his ancestors have lived for a century. Horrible thing, these religious discords, which are certainly fomented by the aristocrats of this country. Get off with great difficulty from O'Neil, and arrive at Newry about ten. Dismount with our four cases of pistols, very stout. "*Five pound for a Peep-of-day-boy.*" Huzza! Huzza! Generally glad that we are come back safe. Mug porter to a large amount. God bless everybody. Bed.

12*th.* This is the Prince of Wales's birthday. Waited on by sundry Defenders to know if I will go to Dundalk and conduct their defence next assizes. That may not be. Ask me whom I would recommend; tell them Chamberlaine, Saurin, and Jebb. See Vindex in print; incorrect enough; made out a quotation on Captain Swan: "If he had been saucy, we would have made him a rare bird on the earth, and very much like a black swan." Hit this off yesterday, as we were going into Rathfriland, when I was in a fright. Was I in a fright? The truth is, I was not, and yet I was not a jot sorry when it was bedtime, and all well, "All fair," as Mr. Breslaw hath it. Dine at O'Hanlon's. After dinner ride to Rosstrevor along shore. Beautiful! Mourne, the sea, &c. Sit up very late and talk treason. Sad!

13*th.* Breakfast at Mr. Fagan's; several Catholics; feuds in Newry. Advise them all to peace and unanimity. Agree to drink porter with them on our return, whither we mean to go to the Marquis of Downshire. How will his lordship receive us? Happy go lucky. Set off, and arrive at Hillsborough. Find that Lord Hillsborough is at Lord Annesley's, and will not be at home for two or three days. Agree to push on for Belfast, where we arrive and sup with Neilson and Simms. Neilson brings us home to lodge. Bed late.

14*th.* Walk out and see McCracken's new ship, the *Hibernia*. *Hibernia* has an English crown on her shield. We all roar at him. Dine at Neilson, with the old set. The county Down getting better every day on the Catholic question. Two of the new companies, commanded by Captains Cowan and Douglas, applied to be admitted in the Union regiment, commanded by Col. Sharman, and were refused, merely on the ground of their holding Peep-of-day-boy principles. *Bon.* Gog and Mr. Hutton called upon to give an account of the present state of Catholics. Mr. Hutton makes a long and accurate statement, which meets the unanimous approbation of all present. The Belfast men get warm with wine and patriotism. All stout; Gog valiant; also the Irish Slave; also the Tanner; also Mr. Hutton. The Catholics offer to find soldiers, if Belfast will provide officers. All fair. Lurgan green as usual. Something will come out of all this. Agree to talk the matter over to-morrow, when we are all cool. Huzza! Generally drunk. *Vive la nation!* Damn the Empress of Russia! Success to the Polish arms, with three times three. Huzzah! Generally very drunk. Bed. God knows how. To dine to-morrow with the Tanner. Huzzah! Huz—.

15*th*. Waken drunk. Breakfast with Neilson, the Jacobin, &c. Write a letter on the Grand Jury of Derry, signed a Derry Farmer; also a paragraph to the same purpose; also another on the report of the submission of the Poles (very bad news if it be true). Also another on the Derry Grand Jury. See Sinclair, and tell him of our expedition to Rathfriland. The Draper in a rage. More Volunteer companies springing up like mushrooms, nobody knows why. All the Antrim corps well. Please God, we shall furnish them with something to think of. This country will never be well until the Catholics are educated at home, and their clergy elective. Now a good time, because France will not receive their students, and the Catholics are afraid of the revolution, &c. Dinner at the Tanner's; all well. The Rev. T. Birch, of *Botany Bay*, tells us that he is just returned from a meeting of eighteen Dissenting clergymen from different parts of Ulster, and had the pleasure to find them *all* well disposed to Catholic liberty; he has no doubt but the cause is spreading most rapidly. His neighbour-hood, which is very populous, completely converted; some at-tempts made to prejudice his flock against him for the part he took on the 14th July, failed plump. He offered, in a very full congregation, to argue the point after meeting, with any man who differed from him, and was answered that there was no occasion, as all were satisfied. He thinks, what I fear is true, that the Catholic clergymen are bad friends to liberty. The priest of Saintfield preached against United Irishmen, and exhorted his people not to join such clubs, on which he was immediately rebuked in the chapel by one of his congregation. All this very good. It cannot be that the rabble of Rathfriland should stop the growing liberty of Ireland. Home. Bed early.

16*th*. The Tanner called on me to recommend two things:

first, to publish the plan alluded to by the Derry Grand Jury, to which we agree, as secrecy is no longer necessary ; and secondly, that the new committee should not meet so early as October, because the longer it is delayed, the more numerous our friends in the North will be, as every day produces converts, and therefore, if Government should attack the committee, we should have a stronger support. To this we answer that we are sure Government will not venture on any strong measure until Parliament is sitting to back them, and it will be advisable to have the country members assembled for some little time before the danger, if any can arise, that they may know each other, and be accustomed to stand fire. The Tanner acquiesces in this reasoning ; very glad to see him so anxious about us, and so eager to procure us *proper* support. Digges used to praise him and Getty ; also the Hypocrite thinks Macabe and him the two men in Belfast most to be depended upon. Set off for Hillsborough, accompanied by the Jacobin. Write to Lord Downshire, and request permission to wait upon him : he asks us to dinner, which we decline ; he then appoints seven o'clock in the evening, when we wait on him and Lord Hillsborough. Very long conversation on the subject of our mission. Lord Downshire's faculties quite gone. Lord Hillsborough's sharp enough ; a high aristocrat. Angry at the committee's interference. No notion of any mode of settling the disturbances but by a strong hand. Talks of more regiments of light horse, and calls the committee and the Defenders " Dublin Papists, and country Papists" ; says our going down has done great mischief, though our motives may be good ; abuses the men who formed the meeting at Rathfriland on the 18th July ; says there are four thousand stand of arms in the hands of the Defenders, and, if they will pile them up in one place, he will ensure their protection ; inveighs bitterly against the communications between the Catholics through the country, and against seditious publications, which he *explains* to signify Paine ; says the laws have been equally administered, for that six Protestants have been hanged for Peep-of-day-boy practices, and two of them on the spot where the burglary was committed. (*This a lie.*) In short, that he will see the laws execute themselves, without our interference. On the whole, his lordship was just civil, and no more. Fine fencing between his lordship and Mr. Hutton, who defends the Catholics with great address and ability; hits his lordship several times on the *riposte*. The ambassadors both bluff and respectful. State their case, and that they did not come until called upon; make a cut or two at the Protestant ascendency about Rathfriland. Admit the 4,000 stand of arms, but state that they have, in no one instance, been used offensively. Strike a little at the new corps; to the raising of which, and the spirit of the officers, we insinuate almost the whole of the present alarm may be attributed. Pin his lordship to the confession that the Catholics have never, in any case, begun the attack. As to their meeting in bodies, admit it is improper, but state that they have always dispersed without doing mischief. Finally, declare our convictions that, if the Catholics could see that they had equal protection with the Protestants, peace would be immediately restored. Part from their lordships, neither of us much pleased with the other. Set off, and arrive at Ballinahinch late. Introduced to M'Clokey, a proper man. That neighbourhood almost totally converted, though very bad some little time back. A new corps raised there on Peep-of-day-boy principles, converted by M'Clokey, who, in return, is chosen their lieutenant. All well. The Catholics and they are now on such good terms that the Catholics lend them their arms to learn their exercise, and walk to see them parade, and both parties now in high affection with each other, who were before ready to cut each other's throats. All this done in about two months, or less, and by the exertions of one obscure man. What might not be done by the aristocrats of the county Down if they were actuated by the same spirit? Damn them! Mug a quantity of mulled wine. Generally drunk. Union of Irishmen with three times three, &c. Bed late.

17th. Rise as sick as a dog. Walk out to Montalto and

meet Lord Moira. Breakfast with his lordship, the Abbé Berwick, and Williamson, of Lisburn. Apprise them of our expedition, and ask leave to introduce Gog, which he grants with much civility; his lordship well disposed, and the more so as Lords Hillsborough and Annesley are adverse. He abuses Lord Annesley, who is by all accounts a mere brute, and has a trick of knocking down the Catholics on the roads, or wherever he meets them for his amusement; scoundrel! Why do they not knock him down again and be hanged? Bring Gog up and introduce him; invited to dinner with his lordship, and promise accordingly. Walk off with Gog, the Abbé, and Williamson, to see Mr. Sharman; find him at the Spa, and state our case generally. Mr. Sharman extremely friendly, and condemns the conduct of the aristocrats and their dependents. He approves extremely of the address to the Defenders, which we show him; all this very well; great laughing with the Abbé on our return. The Abbé has "*a species of something like rationality.*" Williamson a sharp dog; has been tampering with the Union regiment to get addresses counter to the Belfast proceedings on the 14th July. Tried three different companies, and failed in every one; obliged to give it up, yet he prates about liberality and justice. Mr. Hutton half angry with him, but does not let him know it; flatters him between jest and earnest, but it won't do; the fellow is not to be depended upon. Dinner spoiled by the unexpected arrival of General Patterson and Colonel Marsh, on their way to England; stupid as the devil; the Abbé quite out of spirits. Mr. Hutton and Gog rise early and depart; leave Ballinahinch and travel in the dark to Banbridge; unpleasant enough; bad road; sleep at Banbridge.

18*th.* Arrive at Newry about eight. Meet O'Hanlon and some others; tell them of our journey; all agree that we should publish the address to the Defenders. Write to Lord Downshire, Lord Moira, Col. Sharman, Bishop McMullen, Bishop Lennon, and enclose copies of the address. Pat O'Hanlon engages to distribute the address through Mourne, and all other parts where the disturbances are, in the county Down. Propose to set off for Dublin ; prevailed upon to stay and endeavour to reconcile the Catholics of Newry, who have been bickering ; agree accordingly. Meet the contending parties in the evening at the inn. Gog makes a very lucid statement of the Catholic affairs ; never heard him half so well ; preaches up peace and union, and advises them to direct their animosities against the common enemy, the monopolists of the country. The whole company agree to bury all past feuds in oblivion ; rise and shake hands mutually. The chairman, by order of the meeting invites Gog and Mr. Hutton, who has played *Ripieno* all the evening, to dine with the Catholics of Newry next day, to commemorate the restoration of harmony, which they agree to though it breaks in on their system. Sit late, "*all with magnanimity and benevolence.*" *Beau-jour!* Good thing to have restored peace to the town. Gog proposes, and the Catholics agree, to form a society for the advancement of Catholic affairs ; Gog and Mr. Hutton admitted original members ; all present sign a paper, signifying their resolution to form a club, &c. Gog and Mr. Hutton "*flourish their hands in a most graceful manner and depart.*" Mr. Hutton *entre deux vins*, proposes a society of United Irishmen. The proposal much relished ; all this very good.

19*th, Sunday.* Go to mass ; foolish enough ; too much trumpery. *The king of France dethroned!!* Very glad of it, for now the people have fair play. What will the army do ? God send they may stand by the nation. Everything depends upon the line they take. *Our* success depends on things which some of us are such fools as not to see. Ride to Rosstrevor ; more and more in love with it ; dinner ; thirty people, many of them Protestants, invited on the occasion. Dr. Moody, the Dissenting minister, says grace ; bravo ! all very good ; toasts excellent. United Irishmen mentioned again, and the idea meets universal approbation ; hope it may do ; wonderful to see how rapidly the Catholic mind is rising, even in this Tory town, which is one of the worst spots in Ireland ; sit till nine ; set off for Dundalk, and arrive about twelve.

20*th*. Off very early, and breakfast in Drogheda ; get the people together, and put them up to everything; all stout. Set off for Dublin, and arrive at six in the evening ; a good deal fatigued. This has been, on the whole, a most excellent journey, and has done infinite good. We have put our adversaries in the North completely in the wrong, and of course ourselves in the right. We have materially contributed to restore peace in the county Down ; we have created a spirit in Newry which never existed there before ; we have reconciled their differences ; we have generally encouraged our friends, disheartened our enemies, and puzzled Lord Hillsborough. All very good.

> Hic finis longæ chartæque viæque.—*Hor.*
> Here our long journey and my paper ends.—*Francis.*

CHAPTER VI.

IN DUBLIN.

Dublin, 23rd *August*, 1792. Sub-committee. Letter from Dr. Esmonde, of Kildare. Mr. Conolly friendly in a great degree, and entirely condemns the Derry resolutions. Write an X. Y. containing an impartial account of our late journey, and reception in the North ; send it to Joy, for his paper, and write to Neilson to copy it, by which means we have the advantage of a double circulation. Will Joy be honest enough to print it ?

24*th*. Write a letter to O'Hanlon, in Newry, desiring him to collect facts relative to the disturbances in county Down ; and hints about the Catholic Society and United Irish, of Newry— good letter. Write a flourishing manifesto, on the part of the General Committee, in reply to a set of resolutions from the county Limerick ; certainly prepared by the Chancellor ; the resolutions very pert and saucy, and the manifesto not much behind them ; all the Catholics approve of it, and particularly the Vintner, who has recovered his spirits and is quite stout, which is partly owing to his being marked by name in the Chancellor's resolutions. Agreed that Gog and Mr. Hutton shall wait upon Grattan, and show him the manifesto, and also state to him the transactions in the North.

25*th*. Drive down to find Grattan ; Devereux, of county Wexford, accompanying me, Gog being hipped. Grattan not at home ; find him at last at Broome's, of Killmacud, and settle to call on him next day.

27*th*, *Sunday*. Tinnehinch. Read the manifesto to Grattan and Hardy ; Grattan thinks it too controversial and recommends moderation in language, and firmness in action. The manifesto taken to pieces, and at least three-fourths struck out ; many passages supplied by Grattan himself, Mr. Hutton taking them down from his dictation ; no man bears criticism half so well as Mr. Hutton. The manifesto, as amended, not to be published until all the grand juries have spoken out. Grattan desires Mr. Hutton to take *great pains* in incorporating the new with the original matter, so that the joining may not be perceived. Consultation, as to the conduct of the Catholic committee, on the subject of their petition. Mr. Hutton throws out the idea of the committee adjourning before the meeting of Parliament, which is eagerly adopted by the two members. Some months ago Mr. Hutton had mentioned it to Col. Hutchinson, who, in the true spirit of a soldier, rejected it ; gallant, but scarcely wise, though Hutchinson is a very clever man. The reasons which determine the question now, are—1st, It will make the new committeemen stout when they find themselves out of danger. 2nd, When the petition, &c., is prepared they can be of more use in the country than in town as mediums of information to the people. 3rd, It will remove the Chancellor's imputation of a Popish Congress sitting in the capital to overawe Parliament, and so put the friends to the cause in the House of Commons on strong ground, and of course cripple their adversaries. All very reasonable. Grattan takes Mr. Hutton aside, and tells him that, as the season for action is now approaching, it is the wish of himself and his friends that all communication between them and the Catholics should be through him, Mr. Hutton ; as, if they were to hold personal communication, Government would say they were agitators, inflaming the public mind, and that, instead of their being the organ of the Catholic sentiments, the Catholics were only instruments in their hands ; that the grievances of the Catholics would thereby be said not to be felt, but suggested by Grattan and his friends, to answer the purposes of a faction ; all which would entail a kind of responsibility on them, and embarrass and weaken them much in the operations of next winter. Mr. Hutton very much pleased with this ; and the more, as the party had absolutely refused to communicate with his great predecessor, *Burke*, and now refuse to communicate with the Catholics through any other medium than himself. Bravo! break the matter gently to Gog. Gog struck all of a heap—jealous as the devil; says he sees the cause is desperate, and that Grattan is going to give them up; no such thing. Argue with him, and satisfy him tolerably, but his vanity, of which he has plenty, has got a mortal blow—poor Gog! All this may not serve Mr. Hutton in the long run. Gog has not strength of mind to co-operate fairly; must do all, or seem to do all, himself. Has worked out *McKenna* first, and now *Burke*, both with sufficient appearance of reason; but the fact is a dirty personal jealousy, lest they might interfere with his own fame, is at the bottom of all. Little mind! paltry! Mr. Hutton will do *what is right, coûte que coûte.* Finds himself more and more necessary to the Catholics, which is his best chance; but if Gog sets his face against him, he must go down like the others: "'*Tis but in vain for soldiers to complain.*" No party will bear a minute inspection. Mr. Hutton advises Gog to keep this arrangement a secret from the Catholics, merely to let him down easy. Cunning! Mr. Hutton now established as the medium of communication between the Catholics and their friends in Parliament. How long will he remain so? Proud ground! Grattan considers the Catholic question as but a means of advancing the general good—Right! But do the Catholics consider it so? The devil a bit, except one or two of them. Gog says, if they get franchise we shall see all they will do for reform. God send; but I, for one, doubt it: however, I will go on—*their cause is just, independent of reform.*

28*th August.* Grattan again. Repeats his desire of communicating with the Catholics through Mr. Hutton only. He sails for England to-night. The Czar.[1] He cautions me not to lay myself under pecuniary obligations to Gog. See that he is right, and at any rate have no necessity for money just now.

29*th*, 30*th*, 31*st*. Nothing but ordinary business at the sub-committee. Burke expected. The Vintner quite stout.

[1] Peter Burrowes.

1st September, 1792. Dress myself in the Belfast uniform, and
go to dine at Dixon's. All the soldiers salute me as I pass, and
the sentries carry their arms ; pleased as Punch at this, and a great
fool for my pains. Suppose they take me for the Duke of Brunswick, or some foreign officer of distinction. Puppy !

3rd September. Burke is come. The Catholics all angry.
Fancy his reception will be mortifying enough.

5th. Agree that Gog shall go into a full exposition with Burke
of the grounds of the displeasure of the Catholics. Burke, a sad
impudent fellow, forcing himself upon these people. Gog thinks
he is coming over as a spy for Dundas. Rather think he has been
puffing his own weight among the Catholics with Ministers in
England, and finding himself civilly dismissed by letter, he is come
over, trusting to the powers of his effrontery, that the Catholics
will not have the spirit to maintain their letter *face* to *face*. Fancy
he will find himself in the wrong. They all seem exasperated
against him, and he richly deserves it. His impudence is beyond
all I have ever known. Sad dog ! Edmund Burke has Gog's
boys now on a visit at Beaconsfield, and writes him a letter in
their praise. The scheme of this obvious enough. He wants to
enlist Gog, on behalf of his son, but it won't do. Gog sees the
thing clear enough. Sad ! sad ! Edmund wants to get another
2,000 guineas for his son, if he can ; dirty work ! Edmund no
fool in money matters. Flattering Gog to carry his point. Is
that *sublime* or *beautiful ?* The Catholics will not be had, as I
judge, by the pitiful artifice of the father, or the determined impudence of the son.

6th. Gog has had his interview with Burke, and given him his
congé. Burke as mad as the devil, but can't help himself. He
deserves it all and more. Wait on Simon Butler with queries, for
his opinion on the circular letter signed E. Byrne. Plump in our
favour. Wait on Mr. Smith, who declines, and pleads privilege of
Parliament. Not quite fair. Burston. He reads the queries ;
gives a general opinion in our favour as to the principle, and
promises to consider the question as to the mode ; ten guineas
to him and Butler. Propose to disperse one hundred copies of the

circular letter among the Common Council, who are to meet on Tuesday next. Agreed to. Meet the Tribune and put him up to topics and arguments for that occasion. Find that the Union Club, of Newry, have printed our answer to an address. Silly enough; they should have warned us they meant to publish. Well it is no worse. " *'Tis but in vain for soldiers to complain.*"

7th. Breakfast with the Vintner and ride out with him to Burston, about the opinion, which he promises in less than a week. The Vintner a very sensible man. Excellent conversation. Sub-committee. Agree that Gog, McDonnell and T. Braughall shall call on Conolly on Sunday next, and that Mr. Hutton shall go down to-morrow to county Kildare, to secure Wogan Browne to introduce them. Dine with Gog. Rambling conversation about a noble marquis, the Knoxes, &c., change of ministry, &c., &c. Gog very obscure, but think I see light through it. May end in a jaunt to see my friend P. P., and converse with my friend George Knox. Foolish enough, as it strikes me, but can do no harm in the meantime, and if it only produces a journey to the North, no bad thing. The noble general expected in a day or two. Mr. Hutton sets off to-morrow, being Saturday, September 8th.

8th. County Kildare. Find my little boy grown a fine fellow. Dine at Rathcoffy ; Wogan Browne ; archery ; ride late and sleep at Clane.

9th, Sunday. Drive in Browne's carriage to Celbridge, and meet the Catholic Commissioners to the South ; agree to call first on the Duke of Leinster ; set off to Carton, and find Conolly there ; much conversation ; Gog very bad and diffuse ; T. B.[1] very well ; McDonnell excellent ; says more in *three* words than all the other commissioners ; Mr. Hutton almost silent ; Gog seeming determined to shine ; the Duke very friendly, and declares his approbation of the whole of the Catholic proceedings, and more especially of the plan. Conolly a strange rambling fool ; talked for near an hour, without the least connection, about a Union, the Regency, Mr. Fox, the Whig Club, the Catholics, a pension bill, a place bill, a Union, *Da capo*, &c., &c., &c. The Duke took much pains to

<hr>

[1] [Braughall.—ED.]

set and keep him right; has ten times the understanding of Conolly, the result was that we convinced him that we intended nothing violent or hostile, and then he declared himself satisfied. He condemned the grand juries extremely, and particularly his own county of Derry; told us, as a great discovery, that Government were at the bottom of all this. Lord help him! Shocking to think that such an ass should have influence anywhere; necessary to us, however; think we may count upon him next session. The Duke hollow with us. *Bon!* Conolly offers to go security his whole fortune on the good behaviour of the Catholics; all fair; the Duke asks us to dine, also Conolly: refuse both with many thanks, and go off to dine at Castle Browne with Rowan, &c. *Beau-jour.* Rowan a fine fellow, and Wogan Browne just as good. Drink—"The spirit of the French mob to the people of Ireland." Stout! All very pleasant and well; sleep at Rathcoffy.

10th and *11th.* Rathcoffy; archery; eating and drinking.

12th. Dublin in the boat; Captain Tone very ill (my uncle), fear he will not live through the winter; sorry for him; a gallant officer.

13th. Ride out with the Vintner to Burston for his opinion; plump with us; all fair; well done, Burston! Sub-committee; agree to publish the opinions in the papers, and also as a circular letter. Simon Butler asks me to dine, and meet Burke; returns from Cork; see the Protestant ascendency resolutions of the Common Council of Dublin; boobies! Please God we will try to pick a hole or two in them. Vindex has produced an imitator in the *Northern Star*, a Mr. Crito, a good kind of a man; not equal to the other; "*all fair, as Mr. Breslaw hath it.*" Dinner at Butler's; go away early; correct the press in the *Hibernian Journal.*

14th. Write to Dr. Toole about Capt. Tone; write to Devereux and advise him to have the opinions reprinted, either in the Wexford paper or in handbills, to distribute previous to the county meeting. Meet the Abbé; he tells me a friend of his (Lord Rawdon) is expected to-night; settle that he shall call on me to-morrow morning. The Abbé seems very eager to preoccupy that gentleman against false representations.

15th. The Abbé calls to tell me that his friend has turned back ; that his coming is fixed, but the time uncertain. Damn it ! Write a letter to the Corporation of Dublin on their resolutions against the Catholics, signed a Protestant Freeman. Dull enough ; very stupid all this day. Write a letter soliciting contributions from Irish Catholics, resident in foreign parts.

16th. Ride out with Tom Warren ; wet to the skin : broach a proposal to him of a general emigration to America, in case we fail in our present schemes. He approves of it highly, and thinks we should get Catholics enough to join us, and a vast property. A choice plan ! P. P. and his brother ; Whitley Stokes Principal of a College to be founded, &c. Warren and Mr. Hutton get drunk talking of their plan. *God bless everybody.*

17th. Gog's man has been dunning me for £20, I believe without orders, Gog being out on his mission. Give the man a short rebuke, but do not pay him. The devil to pay in Paris. The mob have broken open the prisons, and massacred all the prisoners, Montmorin, the Princess Lamballe, &c., with circumstances of great barbarity, but robbed no one, and were stopped from breaking into the Temple by a blue ribbon stretched across the street, reminding them that their magistrates were responsible for the King's safety. Strange mixture of cruelty and sentiment ! An Irish mob would have plundered, but shed no blood. A Parisian mob murders, but respects property ; which is best ? I lean to the Frenchman ; more manly. Our mob, very shabby fellows. Never would have stood as the Parisians did on the 10th of August. A Sergeant's Guard would drive the mob of Dublin.

18th. Pay Gog, and resolve to have no more to do with him in the money way. Receive a choice letter from the *Colonel* (Barry) in answer to one of mine written some time back. Hope to bring the *Noble General* (Lord Rawdon) round ; of the very last importance to Ireland to get *him.* He may, if he chooses, as I think, be one of the greatest men in Europe. Dine in the country with McDonnell : pleasant !

19th. The Galway Bishop, Egan, flinching. Hope Gog may be able to bring him round.

20th. Sick. Write an X. Y., abusing the Down grand jury, and send it to Neilson. Middling. Write a squib against all the foremen for one of the Dublin papers, signed " No Grand Juryman ;" poor enough. Write to Gog mysteriously on the subject of Lord Rawdon. God Almighty send we may be able to arrange that business.

September 21st. Burston angry that his opinion was published, and confesses that it is because he does not wish to offend the Chancellor. Shabby! Agree to publish that it was inserted without his knowledge. The Vintner dreads anything which may bring his name in question. Understand this apprehension arises from the consciousness of some peccadilloes in the way of trade, which he is apprehensive the Castle papers will lay hold on, and abuse him. Little enough. In great favour with the Vintner on account of "Vindex," which, he says, God knows why, has been the saving of him. Receive a letter from the Rev. Mr. Fleming, Vicar to Dr. Plunket, Bishop of Meath, whom I met at Drogheda, and admired so much. Plunket doing his business like a *man.* To send Fleming thirty sheets of parchment, thirty declarations, sixty plans, and one hundred and eighty opinions, for the counties of Meath and Westmeath. *Bravo!* We began to be afraid of those counties. *Ça ira!*

Sunday, 23rd. Write a second Protestant Freeman. The first has turned out better than I expected, or than in my own mind it deserved. I do not own them, nor will I, unless my vanity gets the better of me, own any newspaper thing hereafter. Read over a pamphlet which I wrote last winter, but which never was published. Very curious to see what pains I took to prove fifty things which are now received as axioms. Called at Moira House ; apprehend I am out of favour there for holding democratic principles. Cannot be helped. "'Tis but in vain," &c.

24th. Send off the parchments, &c., to Mr. Fleming. Write sundry letters, one to P. P. Very fond of P. P. after dinner. *I had dined.* Stayed at home all the evening like a virtuous man. Wrote a letter for the *Hibernian Journal,* signed *Senex.* Choice good I think ! also a squib at the Post Assembly, signed Q. Saucy enough. Call them dunces. " Vide *my Pamphlet, where*

I call my adversary Goose."   This morning introduced to an
aristocrat, the Earl of Granard. Seems a pleasant man. The
Abbé a good fellow, *toujours gai !* Lord Moira afraid of the
Papists. Fancy I am out there, though the Abbé will not tell me
so. However (sings), " 'Tis but in vain for soldiers to complain."
That is the six-and-fiftieth time I have quoted that line, and it is
quite fresh yet ; wears like steel ; learned it from P. P. as well as
sundry other good things. Pleased as Punch with Senex and Q.
" What will the learned world say to my paradoxes ? " The Protestant Freeman in to-day's paper, but I hear nobody praise it. Cruel !

25th.   Write an account of the Wexford meeting in consequence
of a letter from Devereux, and send it to the *Hibernian Journal.*
Determine to set off to-morrow and see the Translator. Sleep in
my clothes at an inn near the canal, to be off early.

26th, 27th, 28th.   At Ballybrittas. The Translator in very bad
spirits, and with great reason. Advise him to send his daughters
to a boarding school, and try his fortune for a few months in
London, as an author, for which I think him very well qualified.
He seems to approve of the plan.   His affairs in as bad a situation
as possible, and his temper badly adapted to recover them.   Wants
resolution and energy ; too much of the milk of human kindness.
Poor fellow !

29th.   Dublin. None of my late compositions in the *Hibernian
Journal !* Gog returned. Go to Mt. Jerome [1] and breakfast. All
well in Munster. Write resolutions for the Limerick Catholics.
Pretty good ; have brought on the Catholics to complain of being
taxed without being represented, and bound by laws to which they
do not consent ; *a great stride !* Gog's mode of considering the
question a good one. His way of putting it is, that for want of
the protection of the elective franchise, the poorer Catholics are
turned out of their little farms, at the expiration of their leases, to
make room for Protestant freeholders, who can assist their landlords by their votes. A good mode, but makes the question a
mere matter of convenience. My mode puts it on the broad basis
of right ; lucky that both are very compatible, and strongly sup-

[1] [Keogh's residence.—ED.]

port each other. In high favour with Gog. Much conversation about an *expiration* to Dungannon. Gog's plan is as follows: that I should go to George Knox, and suggest to him, that if Lord Abercorn would take up the cause of the Catholics, and assume the Lieutenancy of Ireland, he might make terms with Lord Shannon and his friends, and, if possible, with the Ponsonbys, keeping the negotiation *a profound secret* from the Beresford party. That the affairs of Ireland are in such a situation as must make them a considerable object of anxiety to the British Government; that our present administration, and particularly Fitzgibbon, are making things worse by their violence; that therefore the English Minister will naturally fall in with the men and measures which will keep this country quiet, and, consequently, we may reckon on his concurrence. That the Beresford party are very odious here and have little weight personally, but are supported by the patronage of Government, which, if removed, they would fall at once with the unanimous consent of the nation. That Lord Abercorn should, having previously made his terms, by direct bribery, with Lord Shannon, and being also sure of the support of the whole of the Catholics, and at least a part of the Protestants, propose to the Beresford party to grant the elective franchise, &c., to the Catholics, which they would, to a moral certainty, refuse to do; that he should then at once turn out the whole party, which would sink directly, being odious to the nation, and having little personal weight, and fill up their places with new men, Lord Shannon, the Knoxes, &c.; that this vast patronage falling into his hands at once, would enable him to make such terms as would carry everything easily: that, as to Lord Abercorn, it would make him the most popular Lord Lieutenant that ever was in Ireland, and secure him the strongest government: that, as to the Knoxes, it would make a short cut for them to arrive at power and honours, which, on the present system, they will but slowly, if ever, arrive at: that the mode itself is an honourable one, being the granting, or rather restoring, their just rights to three millions of people, &c. Such is the outline of Gog's system, in which he seems very sanguine. What do I think of it ? If I go to Dungannon, I will certainly put it as fairly and as strongly to George Knox as I can, but I confess I should be sorry to succeed. I feel myself bound in duty to do everything in my power to procure liberty to the Catholics of Ireland ; but this appears to me a bad scheme. In the first place, it is at once giving up the question of reform, or at least postponing it for an indefinite time, and is so far at once knocking up all that we have done, for this last twelvemonth, towards effecting an union between the Dissenters and the Catholics. Not that I think the former would have any right to complain, for they have not come forward in support of Catholic emancipation, *save only in Belfast ;* and the Catholics are not to renounce all separate measures for the sake of that one town. I believe if they were properly supported by the body of the Dissenters, they would keep faith ; but the fact is, they are not. In the next place, it would strengthen the hands of the English Government in this country for a considerable time to come. At present (1792) England, except in commercial regulations, where she buys us with our own money, has not a great deal of influence here ; on the contrary, administration rather holds them at defiance, and, in the present Catholic question, has actually, by bullying, prevented their interference ; which, by the by, is a circumstance in favour of Gog's plan : whereas, with the example of the great change intended, future Irish administrations would be more shy of opposing, much less of attempting to bully, the English Minister. In the third place, it would naturally, from gratitude, throw the whole Catholic interest into the support of a Government to which they would owe so much, and, I am unalterably satisfied, that the crown, as it is improperly said, but more truly the *oligarchy,* has already much too great a portion of power in our system ; which power I have never hitherto known them to exercise for any good purpose, and which they would be less likely, at least for a considerable time (if my judgment be right), to use for that end, inasmuch as I conceive English influence would be considerably increased. These objections occur to me on the moment, but I must consider the question much more maturely. One conversation with Knox will do more than twenty soliloquies. Admitting all my objections, if the scheme be practicable, *query*, is not the emancipating three millions of Catholics a great accession of strength, and even of liberty, to Ireland? and besides, though the immediate consequence would be an improper increase of strength to a vile Government, yet this could not continue for any great length of time. The Catholics having enjoyed a qualified degree of freedom for a few years, would come to think like other people, and especially from the information which would naturally accompany the prosperity consequent on their emancipation. Gratitude soon wears out, and when they were more advanced in prosperity, they would, besides being more capable of judging, actually feel the evils of a bad Government much more ; which looks like a paradox, but is very true. Mr. E. Byrne, besides being a better judge, *actually feels* the extended mischief of our vile system much more than one of his porters. Apply this idea. What is to be done on the whole? "6 *times* 12 *is* 72, 2 *and carry* 7, *how are we ruined?*" I believe if the Catholics were emancipated, no matter on what compact with Government, in a little time they would become like other people. At any rate they cannot bind their children by such compact (*vide* Thomas Paine). "*I am puzzled in mazes, and perplexed with errors.*" I abhor all capitulating with a bad Government if it could be helped. Natural enough that the Catholics should seek for and be glad to accept of liberty from any quarter. Oh, why are not those fellows in the North sufficiently enlightened to join heartily with us! Then, indeed, something might be done. Reform, liberty, and equality! The Catholics would, I think, join them ; yet I remember when I thought they were incurable Tories, and that is not eighteen months since. Live and learn. What if the Duke of Leinster was included? He is a friend to the Catholics, and no enemy to a good place. Suppose Grattan and Forbes secured by stipulating for one or two of their popular bills? Reform seems a good way off, and all this would be gaining ground in the meantime. It would be making something like a people of which something might be made. If these men come in, we should have a tolerably honest, I believe, but certainly a very strong Government.

What would become of Mr. Hutton in that case? and P. P.? "*I am lost in sensations of troubled emotions.*" What will Knox say to all this? Is it castle-building or not? A fine fellow I am to-night, not worth a groat, and planning the subversion of Ministers. Oh, Lord! Oh, Lord! I will go to bed. "*'Tis but in vain,*" &c., &c.

30th September, Sunday. Blank.

October 1, 1792. This day eighteen counties have completed the return of their delegates to the General Committee, and nine more are in progress, besides all the great towns. Correct the resolutions of the Roscommon and Leitrim Catholics. Middling enough. All that is good in them, borrowed from the Sligo resolutions, written by that able and steady friend to the interests of Ireland, Mr. John Hutton.

2nd. Dine with Gog. Talk over the plan of my Dungannon *expiration.* Find I have reported his ideas faithfully in my *Gurnal* of the 29th ult. Write a long letter to Colonel Barry, filled with important information on Catholic affairs; read it to Gog, who approves thereof. I fear, after all, Lord Rawdon will not have the sense to see what a great game he might play here. He would rather dangle at the tail of an English party, when, I think, he might be everything but King of Ireland. Mug with Gog, and walk home elevated with liquor. God bless everybody!

3rd. Call at Moira House, and see everybody. Most graciously received. Introduced to Lady Granard, who takes charge of my letter to Col. Barry. Dinner, and a great deal of wine. Frivolous day. Generally drunk. Fine doings twice running. Hear that the Duke of Brunswick has defeated the French under Dumourier, and cut the whole army in pieces. Hope it is a lie. If Dumourier fights, he will infallibly be beaten. Never fight an invading enemy. Keep on his flanks, and harass his convoys, &c., &c.

4th. Sick as a dog. Rode out to Gog. "Smoke the rhyme." Has had a letter from Myles Keon, requiring somebody of the committee to go to Ballinasloe to meet the Catholic gentry of Mayo and Galway. Denis Browne [1] playing tricks in the former county. Recommends a separate petition, and condemns the plan.

---

[1] [A member of the Irish House of Commons, and a moderate supporter of the Catholic claims.—ED.]

He is damned kind! Wishes, if he could, to act the patron to the
Catholics, that he might make a sale of 3,000,000 of clients at the
Castle. A blockhead, without parts or principles! But it won't
do. The Catholics here smoke him. Last winter they used to
stare at me for speaking contemptuously of him, a man who was
brother to a Lord, and a Member of Parliament. They have got
over all that now. Wonderful improvement in their sentiments.
Burke has disappeared these some days, and is gone no one knows
whither. To return to Mayo. Agreed that Tom Warren and I
shall go, and Randal McDonnell, if we can get him, to Ballinasloe
to-morrow, to convert the Catholic gentry of that county and of
Galway. Gog is afraid of *wet sheets*. Is that the real truth? No
matter, we will go without him. Call on McDonnell, but do not
find him. This jaunt knocks up one I had planned for Saturday
to Rathcoffy, where there are to be great doings. Rowan has
invited Mrs. Tone and me to meet Simon Butler and other *Sans
Culottes*. Cannot be helped. "'Tis but in vain," &c.; public business must take place of pleasure and vain delight. Settle with
Warren to leave town to-morrow at twelve. "This is the first time
that Mr. Hutton has been trusted on a separate negotiation." How
will he acquit himself? Gog has had a letter from the Jacobin,
praising Mr. Hutton to the skies. *Thereby hangs a tale*. A plot
between the Jacobin and Mr. Hutton, to raise the latter gentleman
in the eyes of the Catholics. Poor Gog falls in the snare. *All fair*.
Tea with Hamilton Rowan, who shows me a letter to Lord Abercorn, containing three-fourths of the plan as detailed in this *Gurnal*.
Very odd that Gog and he should coincide so exactly without communication. No confirmation of the defeat of Dumourier. Hope
in God it is a lie. Very sick!

 5*th*. Tom Warren cannot go to Ballinasloe, being detained by
his wife, who is just ready to lie in. All fair! Write resolutions
for Down and Louth. Tom Braughall, all of a sudden, offers to
go to Ballinasloe. Must go. Well, load my pistols, and pack up.
N.B.—For the miraculous events in that journey, see book——
wherein they are fully detailed, being "*moving accidents by flood
and field; how we were taken by the insolent foe, and sold to
slavery, and our redemption thence*," &c., &c.

CHAPTER VII.

VISIT TO CONNAUGHT.

*Journal of the proceedings of Mr. John Hutton, in his peregrination
to convert the natives of Connaught, and more especially of Galway and Mayo, to the true political faith.*

October 5, *Friday*, 1792. Left Dublin at eight in the evening in
a post-chaise, with Mr. Braughall, commonly called in this journal
T. B.   Loaded with good advice by Gog in the morning, who has
given me a broad hint to puff him in Connaught.   An adventure !
Stopped by three foot-pads near the park gate, who threaten to
exterminate the post-boy if he attempts to move ; T. B. valiant,
also Mr. Hutton.   Mr. Hutton uses menacing language to the said
foot-pads, and orders the post-boy, in an imperious tone of voice,
to drive on.   The *Voleurs,* after about three minutes' consideration,
give up the point, and the carriage proceeds.   If they had persisted, we should have shot some of them, being well armed.   Mr.
Hutton in a fuss ; his first emotion was to jump out and combat on
foot ; very odd ! but his fear always comes on *after the danger ;*
much more embarrassed in a quarter of an hour after than during
the dialogue ; generally stout, and would have fought, but had
rather let it alone ; glad we did not kill any of the villains, who
seemed to be soldiers.   Drive on to Kinnegad—another adventure !
The chaise breaks down at three in the morning ; obliged to get
out in the mud, and hold up the chaise with my body, whilst the
boy puts on the wheel ;   all grease and puddle ;   melancholy !
Arrive at Kinnegad at past four ; bad hours !

   6th.   Set off at eight ; sick for want of sleep ; meet Dr. French,
Catholic bishop of Elphin, at Athlone ; seems a spirited fellow, and

much the gentleman.   T. B. no great things in a post-chaise; arrive late at Ballinasloe, and get beds with great difficulty.   Meet Mr. Larking, the parish priest, a sad, vulgar booby, but very civil to the best of his knowledge.   Mr. Hutton falls asleep in company. Victuals bad; wine poisonous; bed execrable; generally badly off; fall asleep in spite of ten thousand noises; wish the gentleman over my head would leave off the bagpipes, and the gentlemen who are drinking in the next room would leave off singing, and the two gentlemen who are in bed together in the closet would leave off snoring; sad, sad.   All quiet at last, and be hanged!

7th, Sunday.   Find Mr. Larking has been so diligent that he has got nobody to meet us—dunce!   Send out ourselves for one or two gentlemen, whom T. B. knows, and who engage to get us some of the Mayo people, after twelve o'clock prayers.   Breakfast; the waiter brings us beefsteaks, fried with a great quantity of onions; nice feeding, but not to my taste.   Asked to dine with sundry Catholics; how will it turn out? "*'Tis but in vain,*" &c.   Walk out and meet Mr. Peter Lynch, and find him cool, or rather adverse. Denis Browne has been tampering with him; he seems disinclined to give us a meeting.   Meet Mr. Patrick Lynch, cool also; talk with him, and convert him.   He engages to get a meeting of the Mayo gentry to-morrow at three o'clock.   *Bon!* General O'Donnel; he knows nothing of politics.   James Plunket; bravo!   He engages to go among the Mayo people this evening, and bring them to-morrow; he also engages to convert Peter Lynch, who, it seems, is a great man amongst the Catholics.   He says the parochial electors of Mayo are already chosen.   Dinner with the Catholics; dull as ten thousand devils!   Dismal!   Dreary!   Bed at nine o'clock, in a crib about five feet square; damn these bagpipes.

8th.   Breakfast, more beefsteak and onions.   *Go gentle gales.* Fragrant and pretty.   Go and see the fair; great show of bullocks. The greatest cattle fair in Europe, except one in Hungary, as T. B. tells me.   Glad that I have seen it as matter of curiosity, but, on the whole, disappointed, as every man will be who expects extravagantly.   About 70,000 sheep sold.   This is a thin fair of cattle, but smart prices.   James Plunket seems to have found the Mayonians

slack; cannot be helped; "*'tis but in vain,*" &c. Go at three to
meet the gentlemen of Galway and Mayo; find a very respectable
number assembled. Sir Thomas French takes the chair; a fine
young fellow, and of consequence among the Catholics *de son
pays. Bon!* Braughall makes a very long, rambling, diffuse, bad
statement of the proceedings of the General Committee, and of the
objects of our mission. Followed by Mr. Hutton; not much
better. That gentleman no great orator at a set speech, though
he converses well enough. What is the reason? Because he is, in
fact, not only modest, but sheepish, which is a shame. Mr. Hutton
had probably better talents, and, to a moral certainty, better
education, and, beyond all question, more knowledge of the subject
than any of his hearers, yet, after all, he made but a poor exhibition. However, it passed, but by no means satisfied that truly
able gentleman. No speaking without much study and continual
practice; must try and mend, and get rid of that vicious modesty,
which obscures the great splendour and brilliancy of his natural
talents. Gog, in his digressive, rambling style, would have beat
Mr. Hutton all to nothing, which is a great shame to the latter
gentleman. Sir Thomas French states two objections, one to that
part of the circular letter which states that Lord Fingal approves
the plan, inasmuch as he has been well assured, on good authority
(the Bellews (*Rascals*) and Donellan of Bally Donellan, as we suppose), that such assertion arises from misconception, if not from
wilful misstatement; the other, that the committee had assumed to
themselves, in the new system, a power of expelling such members
as might prove refractory. These objections, stated by Sir Thomas
French with great perspicuity and candour, we replied to, the first
by stating the facts as they are; by mentioning the admission of
William Bellew before all the bishops on the 11th of September
last; by the letters of MM. Keon, Hay, and Devereux; and, finally,
by the testimony of Mr. James Plunket, then present, all supporting the veracity of the General Committee in their statement, and,
of course, discrediting the accusations thrown out by the Bellew
party against us. To the second point we show, by reference to
the plan, that the Committee has no such power of expulsion, but

that the constituents have a power of revoking their delegation.
Sir Thomas and all the gentlemen satisfied on both points, and fix
upon Saturday, the 20th next, and Glentane for the time and place
of choosing their delegates, of which Sir T. French will now be
one, a great point gained.   No Mayo men present, but Mr. James
Lynch, of Cullen.   Mr. Patrick Lynch, who engaged to meet us,
stays away, out of complaisance to his kinsman, Mr. Peter Lynch,
who is rich, and from whom he has expectations.   We apply to
Mr. James Lynch, who tells us the races at Castlebar begin on
Saturday next, where all the Catholic gentry of Mayo will meet,
and he has no doubt will elect delegates.   He seems very indignant
at the idea of Mr. Denis Browne, or Mr. Peter Lynch, or any one
man directing the whole county.   A good spirit which we endeavour
to aggravate.   The meeting breaks up, all parties well pleased.
Galway is now finally settled, and Mayo in a fair way.   They are
the two great Catholic counties in Ireland, and the cream and
flower of the Catholic gentry.   They have been, hitherto, rather
adverse to the General Committee, from the bad spirit of aristocracy, which has done the cause so much mischief by producing
disunion ; but we trust we have now fairly beat the Castle out of
Galway, and are pretty confident we have done the same in Mayo.
Ça ira.   Dinner very bad.   Retire early to my crib, and read
Chesterfield's Letters, which has been my great resource against
ennui.   His lordship a damned scoundrel ; he advises his son to
attack Madame De Blot, because she has been married a year and
loves her husband.   Damn his blood, the rascal!   I wish I was
kicking him !   I do not pretend to more virtue than other people,
but I have no notion of such cold-blooded villainy on deliberation.
Till I read this infamous letter I thought the character of Valmont,
in *Les liaisons dangereuses,* was a monstrous fiction, but I see now
that Lord Chesterfield had the inclination, though perhaps not the
talent, to be as great a scoundrel.   All this is for the edification of
P. P., and perhaps of my son, if he ever lives to be old enough to
read these memorandums.   He is now about a twelvemonth old,
and it is time for me to begin to think of forming his mind and
his principles.   I will never advise him to debauch his friend's

wife, only because she is such a fool as to love her husband. Base!
base! I lose my temper at it. It is the thirtieth of the letters,
second volume, wherein this precious paternal advice is communicated. I mention it particularly, because the fact is so unnatural that one would wish it could not be true. It is something
like the case of Sykes and Mrs. Parslow, another scoundrel.   I
have preached enough, and I will go to sleep. Indeed I have
preached more than enough, but what can I do better in this
vile inn?

9*th*. James Plunket will go to the meeting at Castlebar, and
take Lord Dillon in his way, with a view of converting his lordship, by exposing the game which Denis Browne is playing,
endeavouring to become the Padrone of the Mayo Catholics, and
establish thereby a strong interest in the county, which might
enable him hereafter to hold Lord Dillon at defiance. *Capot me,
but it wears a face!* At any rate, Plunket will attend the races
closely, and has very little doubt but that we shall have returns
from Mayo. *À la bonne heure!* T. B. writes a hundred letters to
different people ; Mr. Hutton not one, save one official to the sub-
committee. Our bill monstrous! A guinea for my crib, without
window or fireplace, for two nights. Oh Lord! Oh Lord! What
will this world come to? Oh, Miss Culahaun, Miss Culahaun,
where is your conscience? All will not do. *Il faut payer.* Well
(sings), "*'Tis but in vain for soldiers to complain.*" No letters from
Galway. If this mail brings us none from Dublin to change
our present intentions, we shall set off for Athlone at five this
evening. Mr. Hutton extremely sick of Ballinasloe in fair time.
It is, to be sure, a damned place. Dinner with James Plunket
and eight Galway bucks. All civil, but intolerably dull. Handi-
capping, wagers, horse-racing, swapping. Never saw such a scene
before, and hope sincerely I never may again. No chaise for
Dublin.

10*th*. No chaise yet. Our conscientious landlady, Miss Culahaun, asks twelve shillings for a buggy to Athlone. Jew! skin-
flint! Fear we must take it after all, but determine to wait till
twelve o'clock, and try for a place in the mail. Walk about the

town as a crutch to poor T. B., who is lame. Strange curiosity of T. B. to read all manner of handbills. Mr. Hutton something in the same way. The mail arrives empty. Take our places and set off. *No adventures.* Arrive in Dublin at nine in the morning.

CHAPTER VIII.

PREPARING FOR THE CATHOLIC CONVENTION.

October 11, 1792. The story of Dumourier a great lie. Huzza! huzza! Brunswick and his army dying of the flux and running out of France, with Dumourier pursuing him. Huzza! If the French had been beaten, it was all over with us. All safe now for this campaign. Huzza!

12*th*, 13*th*. Nothing done. More good news from France. Custine has taken 3,000 Germans and Spires—huzza.

14*th*. Dine with Magog: a good fellow; much better than Gog. Gog a Papist. " *Wine does wonders.*" Propose to revive Volunteers in this city. Magog thinks we may have 1,000 Catholics by the 17th March next. Agreed that he shall begin to canvass for recruits immediately, and continue through the winter. If he succeeds, he will resign his office of Secretary to the Catholic Committee, and commence a mere Volunteer. Bravo! All this looks well. Satisfied that volunteering will be once more the salvation of Ireland. A good thing to have 1,500 men in Dublin. Green uniforms, &c.

15*th*. Choice letters from Connaught. All well there. Galway and Mayo secure. A letter from P. P. He is envious of the laurels of Dumourier, and determined to go to France, and outdo that illustrious Democrat. Wants my advice, as he has made up his mind; and also to know if I can do anything by way of letters of recommendation. P. P. a gallant fellow, and quite right. If Mr. Hutton were a single man, he would go and supersede Kellerman. To try Kirwan for a letter to Condorcet; also Wogan Browne, Hamilton Rowan, and Ed. Byrne, the Vintner, for letters to Paris. Poor P. P.; a fine fellow. " *I have drank* medicines; the rogue hath given me medicines to make me love him." Sorry for P. P., but entirely approve his plan, and his spirit. Writes the best stuff of any man in the world. All his letters good.

15*th. Sub-Committee.* Read the reply to the grand juries. Many alterations suggested. Agreed to call an aggregate meeting of the Catholics of Dublin, proposed and pressed by Gog, who wants to shine. All fair! It will serve the cause. Gog's vanity sometimes, as in the present instance, of use. Emmet introduced to the sub-committee. All say O! to him, and he richly deserves their admiration. Emmet, the best of all the friends to Catholic emancipation, always excepting Mr. Hutton. Worth two of Stokes, and ten of Burrowes, and an hundred of Drennan. Dinner at M'Daniel's, the printer. A choice set, all United Irishmen. Sundry good toasts. Mr. Hutton *gris.* God bless everybody.

16*th.* Dr. Bellew, Catholic bishop of Killala, wants subscriptions to found a Catholic seminary in Connaught. Mr. Hutton suggests that it would be advisable to extend the plan, and educate all the Catholic clergy at home, an object which has long been a favourite with that gentleman. No doubt but many Protestants would subscribe for so wise and so benevolent a purpose; the university, United Irishmen, &c. Agreed that T. Braughall and Mr. Hutton shall wait on Kirwan, the philosopher, to talk over this plan. If a good system were devised, it would execute itself; that of the Catholic bishops a poor one, on a pitiful scale. Gog and Mr. Hutton have been talking over something of this kind already in their last expedition to the North; as may be seen in the journal of it. Gog then afraid that the clergy would be adverse; Mr. Hutton of opinion that the breaking up of the seminaries in France would oblige them to consent, and that in that light, as in ten thousand others, the Revolution was of infinite service to Ireland. Gog shied it; has a sneaking kindness for Catholic bishops and priests; pretends to Mr. Hutton that it is all out of policy, but there is a little superstition at the bottom. Magog and Warren have not a grain of this nonsense. *This* *education business appears to me of infinite importance, for a thousand reasons, which I shall detail hereafter.* Hope we may get Kirwan to make a sketch of the proposed plan. A strange letter from Burke, at Cork. He will be agent to the Catholics, whether they will or not, and absolutely commits a rape upon the committee. His impudence is beyond what I could have imagined, and his vanity greater. He has the modesty to say that the *existence* of Ireland depends on his enjoying the confidence of the Catholics, and many other sallies equally extraordinary. The Catholics, astonished and angry at all this persevering insolence, resolved that Gog shall write to him, and tell him that he *is not* the agent of the Catholics, and that, if he desires it, the committee will publish to that effect in the papers. I cannot help again expressing my admiration of his effrontery, which is consummate beyond all belief. He will not desist until he will compel the committee absolutely to advertise him, with a "warning that no one shall trust him, as," &c. He is, to be sure, a sad dog. — *Vide* this journal of August 3rd, 5th, and 6th.

18*th*. Spend the evening with Kirwan. Very pleasant, but no talk of our education plan. Hear that DD. Troy and Reilly, the Catholic archbishop of Dublin and Catholic primate, refuse to concur in a general system—Damn them ! ignorant bigots.

19*th*. Nothing done.

20*th*. Introduced to Captain Sweetman, of Wexford. He reads his speech to the sub-committee ; unanimously approved of, and requested to be printed. It is one of the best popular harangues I ever heard, and filled with choice animosity against the English. Sweetman has been a Catholic, and served in the Irish Brigade, Walsh's regiment, and is now a Protestant, and captain in the British service, and freeholder of county Wexford. Has been in America, the East Indies, &c.

21*st*, *Sunday*. Dine with the Vintner, and a large company. Extremely pleasant. The Vintner hates this Government most cordially. His daughters pleasant women. Mrs. Atkinson there. Mr. Hutton a puppy! . . . interesting, . . . &c. Mr. Hutton an egregious coxcomb! Stays late.

22*nd*. Dined with McDonnell. My son and heir come to town. Home early.

23*rd*. At work with Emmet, on the reply to the grand juries. Gog sick these three or four days, and no business done. Dine with Sweetman at the Green, and a long set. Nothing but dine with this Catholic and that Catholic ; very idle work. Mr. Hutton meditates leaving off the use of wine altogether. Stokes returned from Scotland. Had a narrow escape of being drowned, the ship he came in being wrecked on the northern coast. A million of pities if it had been so. Stokes one of the best heads and hearts that I know, and a man whom I regard as much as any other living.

24*th*. See the Galway resolutions. Two of them very bad, reflecting on the French. This Lynch's nonsense. Cannot he let the French alone, and be damned ? Breakfast with George Knox. Very long conversation on the subject of our proposal for a new ministry (*vide* this journal of September 27th). Knox seems a good deal struck with the proposition. Enters into all the articles minutely. Finally settled that Mr. Hutton shall tell Gog that he has conversed with Knox, that he, Knox, cannot immediately say anything definite on a subject of such magnitude, but in the meantime Gog nor his party shall lose nothing by communicating the idea to him. Dine with my father. Walk out in the evening in complete armour to Gog, and tell him the result of my conversation with Knox. Gog extravagantly delighted. Insists on my calling on Knox in the morning, and sending him to despatch Lord Abercorn to Pitt. Foolish enough of Gog. Proposes to obtain an audience of Knox. Mr. Hutton shies the same, and desires it may be submitted entirely to his discretion To which Gog submits. "*'Tis but in vain*," &c. Gog has been disgusted with Dr. Bellew, Catholic bishop of Killala, on the subject of a national college. The bishop wants to get money from the laity to endow it, and to exclude them from all share in the management. Damned kind ! Gog revolts like a fury, and tells Mr. Hutton he begins to see they (the Catholic bishops) are all scoundrels. *All fair*. Two or three things like this may cure Gog of his sneaking kindness for bishops, priests, and deacons (*vide* this journal of 17th inst.). Sleep at Gog's.

25th. This is the King's (God bless him!) accession. *How many more accessions shall we have?* Breakfast with George Knox. Walk round the Green and talk over our scheme. Knox appears to think seriously of it, but says, as the truth is, that the success thereof is very uncertain, as depending on so many events, any one of which failing would destroy the whole. Mr. Hutton presses all the arguments again, and dwells particularly on the strength of the Government, which would be formed in such event, viz., Lord Shannon and the Ponsonbys purchased by dint of money. The Duke of Leinster, who would, it is presumed, be glad to come in, *cum suis.* Grattan, and the two or three honest men who might be secured by agreeing to two or three popular bills, as the place, pension bills, &c., which would give *éclat* to administration, without depriving them of any degree of essential power. (In this assertion Knox completely concurs.) This, added to their own family interest, and the natural influence of the Castle, would form a very powerful Government. What would be the opposition? The Beresfords, &c., who, in losing their offices, would lose everything, for they are most odious to the people, and have no natural weight ; and the bigoted Protestant squire-archy of Ireland. Ridiculous to talk of such an opposition ! Who would listen to Marcus Beresford talking of the corruption of Government? Absurd ! The new administration would be *tolerated,* if not supported, by the North, for the sake of Grattan, and, coming in on popular grounds, and with two or three bills which are favourites, though, in fact, they signify nothing. This might be puffed so as to satisfy them ; and as for the Catholics, we should have them to a man on the ground of the elective franchise. Knox tells me he has written to the Marquis of Abercorn. That shows he has taken it up, for it was only broached to him yesterday. He refuses to see Gog, and asks, *Could Gog expect that he would open himself to him ?* Gog damned vain and absurd on some points. Always teases me to press Knox on the footing of *his* interest. Absurd ! Knox ambitious and proud, but not interested, *as I judge*. What will all this come to? Mr. Hutton is decidedly of opinion that the Government of Ireland must either alter their whole system, or be subverted by force, of which God knows the event. The Catholics are so totally changed, and so thoroughly roused, &c. Knox and he agree that there is no *immediate* danger of violence on the part of the people, but that there is forming a gradual mass of discontent, which will, at no short day, break out, and especially if a war should arise, and that this discontent is inflamed and accelerated by the gross petulance and indiscretion of Government here. This may probably be discussed without breaking, by such an arrangement as we meditate.—Sub-committee. Emmet reads an address, as from the Catholics of Dublin, in reply to that of the Corporation. Very good. This turns the scale in favour of the meeting of the Catholics, and Gog will now be gratified with an opportunity of making a speech. "Hurry durry! Nicky nacky!" (See *Venice Preserved*.) Write an opinion for the Catholics of Down, as from the sub-committee, exhorting them to thank the people of Belfast, &c.

26th. Denis Browne has been playing the rascal in Mayo. Procured a meeting on the 16th, and knocked up our plan by securing the measure of a separate petition from that county. Damn him! Yet he talks of his love for the cause, &c. The Catholics here in a horrible rage. More and more losing their respect for the brothers of Lords and Members of Parliament.

27th. Randal McDonnell has had a letter from the Secretary of the Mayo Catholics at the late meeting, by which it appears possible that we may yet have delegates from that county. Write a letter from the sub-committee, exhorting them to that measure. Good letter! Meet the parochial delegates in the evening, and settle everything for the aggregate meeting of the Catholics of Dublin. Mr. Hutton reads the Citizen Emmet's paper, which meets the unanimous approbation of the meeting. No wonder! It is a most excellent paper, and better than Mr. Hutton's intended reply to the grand juries. "*The dog has taken some of the very best strokes in my tragedy, and put them into his own comedy.*"

28th. The town has been filled these three or four days with reports of some seditious paper said to be circulated among the soldiers of the garrison. I do not believe it. One officer, Colonel of the Royal Irish Artillery, is said to have been so wise as to draw up the regiment on the parade, and harangue them, exhorting them to obedience, and warning them against "The Rights of Man," &c. Dunce! Blockhead! Could not take a readier way to create the mischief against which he wished to guard. Another report is, that the artillery and all the cavalry are to be ordered to England and replaced by English troops. I hope this is a lie too. These reports, however, show the agitation of the public mind.

29th. Advertisements are this day handed about, ordering a general illumination on account of the expulsion of the German armies from France. I don't know what to think. The illumination is good, but it may be made a handle for rioting, and if so, very mischievous, for Government would rejoice at anything which would give them an excuse to let the dragoons loose on the people. The illumination set on foot by Oliver Bond and James Tandy. We shall know all about it to-morrow. In the meantime, "*God send we may all be the better for it this day three months.*" Write a letter to the Draper, with resolutions for the Northern Whig Club, at their next meeting, in favour of the Catholics. Suppose he will not be able to carry them, but good to try. Write resolutions for the meeting on Wednesday next, thanking the people of Belfast, Cork, &c.

30th. The illumination has gone off quietly, notwithstanding the Lord Mayor issued a proclamation forbidding it, and threatening very hard, &c. The horse and foot were out in great force. It should seem, by their being called out so frequently, that Government are determined to accustom the people to see them in the streets. Emmet and I read over the Catholic address for the last time, and make corrections. N.B.—The said Emmet henceforward to be called "The Pismire."—*S. Committee;* a very full meeting to settle the plan for to-morrow. Agreed that D. T. O'Brien shall take the chair; said O'Brien refuses; cowardly! The chair offered to J. Ball; he refuses also; cowardly! What would the Belfast people say if they saw this? Fixed that old Bernard O'Neil shall be in the chair, and that Simon Maguire shall be secretary. Mr. Hutton reads the address. D. T. O'Brien objects to the resolution thanking the Volunteers of Ulster, because it may look like cultivating the friendship of *armed men.* Nobody seconds him. R. McDonnell wishes we had 100,000 of them to thank. Well done! All embrace and depart. Divers Protestants summoned to the meeting to-morrow, Butler, Rowan, Tandy, the Pismire, Mr. Hutton, &c. Gog at home all day rehearsing. All fair. This meeting will do good. The Pismire has written the address, Mr. Hutton the resolutions, and settled the plan of operations; but the world knows nothing of that. It will look well in the columns of the *Dublin Evening Post,* and encourage all the Catholics in the kingdom: besides, the publications will be infinitely better than those of the Corporation, to which they are intended to be an answer. Bravo! N.B.—All the good publications on the Catholic side, almost, are written by Protestants. Mr. Hutton chooses, for reasons which he does not wish to explain, to insert here the names of the present sub-committee of the Catholics of Ireland.

Thomas Fitzgerald,	Martin F. Lynch,
John Keogh,	Richard McCormick,
Thomas Braughall,	Hugh Hamill,
Edward Byrne,	Dennis Thomas O'Brien,
Randal McDonnell,	Thomas Warren,
Thomas Ryan, M.D.,	John Sweetman, *Secretary.*

October 31*st.* The grand day. A full and respectable meeting 640 summonses taken at the door, besides many who came in without any. Dr. Ryan's speech the best. Gog mortified thereat; consults Mr. Hutton whether he shall venture to speak after the Doctor. Fishing! Mr. Hutton advises him to speak by all means, and throws in sundry compliments, whereat Gog rises. All fair! Gog's speech rambling and confused, but full of matter Dine and crack nuts at my father's.

November 1st. Dinner at Warren's. A long set of the chief United Irishmen. All very pleasant and good. Mr. Hutton endeavours, being *entre deux vins*, to delude the gentlemen present into forming a volunteer company on good principles, civil and military. A. H. Rowan rises thereat, also Magog. Mr. Hutton a little mad on the subject of volunteering; would be a great Martinet "Army, damn me!" Talk a great deal of tactics and treason. Mr. Hutton grows warm with the subject; very much surprised, on looking down to the table, to see two glasses before him; finds, on looking at Hamilton Rowan, that he has got four eyes; various other phenomena in optics equally curious. Mr. Hutton, like the sun in the centre of the system, fixed, but everything about him moving in a rapid rotation; perfectly sober, but perceives that every one else is getting very drunk; essays to walk across the room, but finds it impossible to move rectilineally, proceeding entirely from his having taken a sprig of watercresses with his bread at dinner. "God bless everybody." Sundry excellent toasts. A round of citizens; that coming into fashion; trifling as it is, it is a symptom. All embrace and depart at twelve. Fine doings! fine doings!

2nd. Sick as Demogorgon; purpose to leave off watercresses with my bread. Dinner at John Sweetman's. Capt. Sweetman there. Has a great deal of the old school of popery in politics about him. Mr. Hutton and he argue for three hours, by Shrewsbury clock. Mr. Hutton victorious in the opinion of himself and all present, save his adversary. Huzza! Bed early.

3rd. Go out to Gog to prepare his speech. Correct it abundantly. Dine with Gog, who fishes for compliments with the old bait; civilities to Mr. Hutton on his excellent pamphlet, &c. Mr. Hutton rises and throws a bucket full of flattery in Gog's face, who receives it with great affability. Mr. Hutton tells him that Dr. Ryan is a schoolboy to him, which Gog believes religiously. Vain as the devil. Gog goes into a critical investigation of the merits of both speeches, and modestly insinuates the superiority of his own, to all which Mr. Hutton agrees. All fair! Mr. Hutton comes into town and writes twelve letters to different persons, enclosing copies of the proceedings of the 31st ; all well written, and done very speedily. Mr. Hutton would make a good private secretary. Apropos! On the 31st, Mr. Hutton being at breakfast with the Honourable George Knox, and talking with great asperity and vehemence, according to his custom, against the folly and wickedness of the Government, the following dialogue ensued :

Mr. Hutton. I wish to God, Knox, you were secretary here.

Knox. I wish I was ; will you be my private secretary ?

Mr. Hutton. That I will, most willingly.

Knox. Very well, remember.

Mr. Hutton. Remember.—*Exit Mr. Hutton.*

November 4th, Sunday. Dine at McDonnell's with United Irishmen. Tandy tells me the Volunteers refused to parade round King William's statue, this being the birthday of that monarch ; they have also abolished orange cockades. Bravo! A few of them met to-day as at an ordinary parade, and wore national (green) cockades. This is a striking proof of the change of men's sentiments, when "Our Glorious Deliverer" is so neglected. This is the first time the day has passd uncommemorated since the institution of Volunteers. Huzza! Union and the people for ever! Another thing—Sall and Potter, two of the most violent champions of Protestant ascendancy in the corporation of Dublin, and most active in carrying the late manifesto of that body against the Catholics, have lost their election ; notwithstanding Mr. Sall brought in a copy of the said manifesto in a gilt frame, and displayed it to the Cyclops of his corporation. What is more, the man who comes in in his room is a United Irishman, one Binns. This is a very remarkable circumstance, for the Smith's corporation is one of the most bigoted in the city. Mr. Hutton exercised his franchise this week by voting for common councilmen among the Sadlers. Mr. Hutton a free Sadler, and invited to dine with the candidates, which he respectfully declines.

5th. Gunpowder Treason !

> " This is the day, I speak it with sorrow,
> That we were all to've been blown up to-morrow."—*Rochester.*

Mr. Hutton, on his return from the post-office this evening, where he had been to put in a letter to P. P., is startled by a vision of Guy Vaux, which appears to him at Alderman Hart's door. Mr. Hutton speaks Latin to the said vision, on which it proves to be a policeman. Mr. Hutton diligently inspects the pantry, lest the Catholics might have conveyed combustibles therein, and so burn him and his innocent family in their beds. Wishes to have a fire-engine in his bedchamber, for fear of accidents from these bloody, barbarous, and inhuman Papists.

9th November. At court. Wonderful to see the rapid change in the minds of the Bar on the Catholic question; almost everybody favourable. Some for an immediate abolition of all penal laws; certainly the most magnanimous mode, and the wisest. All sorts of men, and especially lawyer Plunket,[1] take a pleasure in girding at Mr. Hutton, "*who takes at once all their seven points in his buckler, thus.*" Exceeding good laughing. Mr. Hutton called *Marat.* Sundry barristers apply to him for protection in the approaching rebellion. Lawyer Plunket applies for Carton, which Mr. Hutton refuses, inasmuch as the Duke of Leinster is his friend, but offers him Curraghmore, the seat of the Marquis of Waterford. This Mr. Hutton does to have a rise out of Marcus Beresford, who is at his elbow listening. Great laughter thereat. The Committee charged with causing the non-consumption agreement against Bellingham beer. Mr. Hutton, at the risk of his life, asserts the said charge to be a falsehood. Valiant! All declare their satisfaction thereat. Everything looks as well as possible. Huzza! Dine at home with Stokes, &c. Very pleasant and sober.

10th. Hear that Government is very much embarrassed to know what to do. Toler has been sounding D. T. O'Brien, a rich and timid Catholic, of some consequence in the party; wished to frighten him, but failed in his attempt. *Bon!* Sir F. Blacquiere has been with T. Braughall, on the same plan with the same success. Also, an anonymous personage with J. Sweetman. The Chancellor, we hear, talks big. If he attempts to use violent measures, I believe a war will be the inevitable consequence. My

---

[1] [Afterwards Lord Plunket.—ED.]

own conviction is that Government must *concede*. Gog, Magog, and Warren, three leading Catholics, had rather be refused this session, in order thoroughly to rouse the spirit of the people. Right! I rely very much on the folly and intemperance of Government for the complete emancipation of the country. Early and moderate concessions to the just demands of the nation may prevent mischief, but that is a degree of wisdom which Fitzgibbon never will be able to reach. My advice has been for the Catholics, at every refusal, to rise in their demands, like the ancient Sibyl; which they seem determined to do. *No want of spirit apparent yet.* The Committee, under the new organisation, is called for the 3rd December. We have this day returns from twenty-five counties and all the great cities of Ireland, with a strong confidence that we shall have the remainder before the day of meeting. The circumstance of the time being fixed will probably bring in the out-lyers. We have got Kerry, in spite of Lord Kenmare. Mayo has been off and on three or four times, owing to the manœuvres of that rascal, Denis Browne (*vide* this Journal of Oct. 26th, 27th); now they seem stout again. The Connaught gentry, more valiant than wise, easily led, especially by a great man, or a great man's man. Bad! But they will mend of all that. Hope we shall have returns from Mayo after all. If we do, a great victory! The Northern Whig Club have adopted the resolutions, which I sent to Sinclair on the 29th ult. Halliday the only dissentient. I did not expect they would have passed; this is another proof of the gradual change of the public mind. Custine is said to have advanced so far in Flanders, that his retreat is cut off. A lie, I hope, like that about Dumourier. *Right or wrong, success to the French; they are fighting our battles, and if they fail, adieu to liberty in Ireland for one century!* Apropos of fighting! Mr. Hutton has bought a fine sword, of which he is as vain as the devil; intends to sleep on it to-night. *Query,* May he not wear it in the court of chancery, with his wig and gown, to edify Lord Fitzgibbon? Mr. Hutton proposes to make it the pattern sword for his regiment, when he has one.

11*th, Sunday.* George Knox shows me a memorandum or

abstract of Lord Abercorn's answer to his letter on the subject of Gog's famous plan for turning out the Ministers here (*vide* Journal, &c.). Lord Abercorn quite wild; his idea is that the Catholics should renounce their present system, for the *chance* of what he would do for them. Damned kind! Mr. Hutton observes, coolly, that his lordship does not bid high enough, and so the negotiation ends; Knox declaring himself of Mr. Hutton's opinion.

12*th*. At Gog's to prepare papers, viz., petition to the King, petition to Parliament, address to the nation, &c. Hear a report that Foster is afraid of being assassinated. The rascal deserves it, if anything can justify assassination. Hard at work.

13*th*. A plot in Lower Ormond against the committee. The Tolers, Pretties, and other great landholders there, are compelling their tenants to sign some paper adverse to the Catholic claims. One priest, Mr. White, has the courage to refuse. Write a letter from the sub-committee, applauding him. Major and Secretary Hobart has sent for Dr. Troy,[1] to pump him; talks a great deal of stuff, that Government is determined to resist all violence; that Government in England will support them; that we have not the North, save only Belfast, &c. Sad stuff! By laying such stress upon the North, he is exposing his own weak side, and, of course, pointing out the best place for us to direct our batteries. Please God, the hint shall not be lost. We may work the major yet. Busy at the petition, &c.

14*th*. All the morning at work. Dine in town, at R. Dillon's. After dinner, turn the discourse to the probability of raising a new corps of Volunteers. Resolve that the party shall meet on Saturday next, to devise a plan. All provoked at an unnecessary affront the Dublin corps received last Sunday; an officer of the regulars took away a drummer, belonging to his regiment, whom the Volunteers had hired for the day, and the poor fellow has been sentenced to receive two hundred lashes. Strange policy of Government, in such a time as this, to choose to pick a quarrel with the Volunteers! Trifling as this circumstance is, it will assist in laying the foundation for a corps, which may vex Government hereafter. Return to

[1] [Catholic Archbishop of Dublin.—ED.]

Mount Jerome. Propose to Gog to go to some expense in fitting up the room for the meeting of the committee, as it will give the country delegates a high idea of their own consequence, and the importance of the business, when they see everything respectable and handsome prepared for their reception. All fair!

15*th*. Hear to-day that Ponsonby is come over. If it be so, a great point. Hard at work.

16*th*. Hear that the Castle-men say that our address to the King, if we persist in that idea, will embarrass his Majesty. The devil it will! And who doubts it, or who cares? We will address him, please God, and let him refuse it, if he pleases. Better that his Sacred Majesty should be embarrassed than a nation kept in slavery. More and more at work.

17*th*. In town, at the sub-committee. Read the intended address to the King. Very much liked, even by some of our timid people. Mr. Hutton very well pleased thereat. Gog also pleased. Compliments Mr. Hutton, and says that he (Mr. Hutton) has given the tone to all the Catholic politics; which Mr. Hutton, with all that amiable modesty which eminently adorns him, and gives a beautiful gloss to all his splendid actions, denies, and says, with a becoming diffidence, that if he has any merit, it was only in seeing their true interest a little earlier than some of themselves, and that it is their own good understandings, and not his arguments, that have set them on the right scent. This is partly true; and, at any rate, it is pretty in Mr. Hutton. It would not be for that gentleman's advantage to be thought wiser than Gog. Much better to stand behind the curtain and advise him. Mr. Hutton not anxious to appear on the canvas, provided the business be done, and if anything serious should ensue, he will find his own level. If he deserves to rise, he will probably rise; if not, he cannot help it: " *'Tis but in vain for soldiers to complain.*" Spend the evening at home, with my innocent family. After all, home is home.—I had like to forget. Attended a meeting, for the purpose of raising a Volunteer corps: Present, Rowan, chairman; Tandy, James Tandy, Dowling, Bacon, Bond, Warren, Magog, and Mr. Hutton, Secretary. Vote 1,000 men in ten companies; cheap

uniform, of coarse blue cloth, ticken trousers, and felt hats.   Not
to meddle with the existing corps, unless they choose to join us,
in which case they must adopt our plan, principles, and regimentals.   If this takes, it will vex the Castle, and they may not like to
come and take our drum from us.   Bond thinks the *ci-devant*
Merchant Corps will present us with two field pieces.   Huzza!
Huzza!

18*th, Sunday.*   Mt. Jerome again.   Dinner with J. Plunket, of
Roscommon, and J. Jos. Macdonnell, of Mayo.   Conversation right
good.   The country Catholics I think will *stand fire*.   All seem
stout.   Mayo has returned, in spite of Denis Browne, who is as
vexed as the devil, and cannot help himself.   Huzza!   Drink like
a fish till past twelve.   *God bless everybody*.   Embrace the Connaught men, and go to bed as drunk as a lord.   It is downright
scandalous to see in this, and other journals, how often that
occurrence takes place, yet I call myself a sober man!

19*th.*   R. Burke at Mt. Jerome; stays five hours; very foolish.
Proposes that the Committee, when they meet, shall not petition,
but address the King, to complain of the *Grand Juries*.   Nonsense!
What can the King do to the Grand Juries?   Makes a poke at Gog
relative to his being continued agent to the Catholics.   No beating
him out of that ground.   Gog maintains an obstinate silence.
Burke very superficial; affects great mystery and reserve; says
Grattan is only trained to local politics, but he himself is trained
to general politics, &c.   Modest and pretty!

20*th November.*   Mr. O'Beirne, of county Leitrim, a sensible
man.   Gog takes great pains to put him up to Catholic affairs,
and does it extremely well.   Gog lucky to-day; never lets an
opportunity pass to convert a country delegate—which answers
two ends: it informs them, and gives him an influence over the
country gentlemen.   O'Beirne says the common people are up in
high spirits, and anxious for the event.   Bravo!   Better have the
peasantry of one county than twenty members of Parliament.
Gog seems to-day disposed for all manner of treason and mischief;
separation of the countries, &c.; a republic, &c.; is of opinion this
will not end without blows, and says he for one is ready.   Is he?

Mr. Hutton quite prepared, having nothing to lose. Hard at work on the appeal to the people ; some strong attacks on the Grand Juries, &c. Dumourier has beaten the Austrians at Jemmape, and Mons and Tournay are the fruits of his victory. Bravo ! Come to town to meet the committee for framing the new corps. The whole evening spent in settling the uniform, which is at last fixed to be that of the—*Garde Nationale.* Is that quite wise ? Who cares ? The parties do not seem quite hearty in the business, and it is likely, after all, the corps will come to nothing. This night fifty-four members proposed ; the Protestants huffed that Mr. Byrne's sons are not of the number ; the Catholics that more of Napper Tandy's friends do not come forward. This does not look very well. Mr. Hutton a little disgusted. No body universally, and at all times right, except that truly spirited and patriotic character. . . .

CHAPTER IX.

THE CATHOLIC CONVENTION.

[IN December, 1792, the first representative gathering of Irish Catholics, which had been called together since the Parliament of James II., met in Tailor's Hall, Back Lane, Dublin, to concert measures for securing the admission of the Catholics to the parliamentary franchise. The best account which we have of the proceedings of this assembly is from the pen of Tone.—ED.]

Account of the proceedings of the General Committee of the Catholics of Ireland ; and of the delegation which presented their petition to the King.

The Catholics were thus once more, after a dreary interval of 104 years of slavery, fully and fairly represented by members of their own persuasion. The last Catholic assembly which Ireland had seen was the Parliament summoned by James II. in 1688, a body of men whose wisdom, spirit, and patriotism reflect no discredit on their country or their sect. The great object of this Parliament was national supremacy. By an act of navigation they wisely guarded the commerce, and, by a declaration of rights, boldly asserted the independence of their native land, both scandalously betrayed to the monopoly and the pride of England, by their immediate successors, the Protestant Parliament of William. The patriots of the present day found their best claim to public regard on maintaining principles first advanced by an assembly to whose merits no historian has yet ventured to do justice, but whose memory, when passion and prejudice are no more, will be perpetuated in the hearts of their grateful countrymen.

The proceedings of the General Committee fully justified the foresight, and far surpassed the hopes, of those who had devised the measure. On the first moment of their meeting, when they looked round and reviewed their numbers and their strength, they at once discarded the unworthy habits of deference and submission which their unhappy situation had so long compelled them to assume. They felt and acted with the decision of men who deserved to be free, and with the dignity becoming the representatives of 3,000,000 of people. The spirit of liberty ran like the electric fire through every link of their chains, and before they were an hour convened the question of their emancipation was, in fact, decided.

The first act of the assembly was, unanimously, to call to the chair Mr. Edward Byrne—a mark of distinction equally honourable to him and to themselves. In their cause he had exposed himself to every species of calumny and abuse ; his name had been held up as a target, against which the arrows of prejudice, falsehood, and corruption had been unceasingly discharged, and, after a persecution of many months, he had come forth unhurt. The General Committee, by thus placing him at their head, as their first President, at once discharged a debt of gratitude they had incurred, and marked their utter contempt for the impotent malice of those who had vilified and abused him only for his eminent services in the public cause.

The attempts which had been made, and which have been already mentioned, to introduce members who, under the old constitution, had an undubitable right to attend, rendered it necessary for the General Committee to close the question. They therefore resolved that the meeting, as then constituted, with the Peers and Prelates, were the only organ competent to speak the sense of the Catholic body—a measure which wisdom and, indeed, necessity impelled them to adopt. A faint attempt was made to oppose it (vide *debates of 3rd December, speeches of Lynch, McKenna*) on the ground that the circular letter, under which the meeting was convened, had stated that the rights of no person, then a member of the committee, were intended to be abridged ; and it was proposed, by a nice distinction, to say that the meeting was " *competent*," and not " *only competent*," to speak the sense of the people at large. But it was answered to this by Captain Sweetman, of Wexford, that the sub-committee could not, by their act, tie up the hands of the great body of the Catholics, then present by their representatives, who were alone empowered to determine this question ; and that admitting a confusion of personal and representative rights was but to lay a foundation for future dissension, since it might so happen, that, on a division, all those of one description might secede, and thereby enable the enemies of the Catholics to take shelter behind a specious pretence, of which, as they had formerly seized it with avidity, they would be glad again to avail themselves. These arguments appeared conclusive ; the opposition was withdrawn, and the motion passed unanimously. Thus, by a material change in the constitution of the General Committee, all future claims, grounded on personal rights, were extinguished ; the right of representation was established, and the strength of the whole Catholic people consolidated into one great and indivisible mass. The wisdom of the measure was justified by the event.

The General Committee next resolved that a petition be prepared to his Majesty, stating the grievances of the Catholics of Ireland, and praying relief, and the members of the sub-committee were ordered to bring in the same forthwith, which, being done, and the petition read in the usual forms, it was again read, paragraph by paragraph, each passing unanimously, until the last. A spirited and intelligent member (*Luke Teeling, Esq., of Lisburn,*[1] *county Antrim*), who represented a great northern county, then rose, and said, " That he must object to this paragraph, on the ground of its being limited in its demand. His instructions from his constituents were to require

[1] [A leading United Irishman.—ED.]

nothing short of total emancipation ; and it was not consistent with the dignity of this meeting, and much less of the great body whom it represented, to sanction, by anything which could be construed into acquiescence on their part, one fragment of that unjust and abominable system, the penal code. It lay with the paternal wisdom of the Sovereign to ascertain what he thought fit to be granted, but it was the duty of this meeting to put him fully and unequivocally in possession of the wants and wishes of his people." He therefore moved, "that, in place of the paragraph then read, one should be inserted, praying that the Catholics might be restored to the equal enjoyment of the blessings of the constitution."

It is not easy to describe the effect which that speech had on the assembly. It was received with the most extravagant applause. A member of great respectability, and who had ever been remarked for a cautious and prudent system in his public conduct (*D. T. O'Brien, Esq., of Cork*), rose to declare his entire and hearty concurrence in the spirit of the motion. "Let us not," said he, "deceive our Sovereign and our constituents, nor approach the throne with a suppression of the truth. Now is our time to speak. The whole Catholic people are not to be called forth to acquiesce in the demand of partial relief." The question would now have been carried by acclamation, but for the interposition of a member, to whose opinion, from his past services and the active part he had ever taken, the committee were disposed to pay every respect (*J. Keogh*). He said, "that he entirely agreed with the spirit of the motion, and he was satisfied that they had but to ask and they should receive. But the meeting had already despatched a great deal of business, the hour was now late, and the question was of the very last importance." "Have you," said the speaker, "considered the magnitude of your demand and the power of your enemies? have you considered the disgrace and the consequences of a refusal, and are you prepared to support your claim?" The whole assembly rose as one man, and, raising their right hands, answered, "WE ARE." It was a sublime spectacle. "Then," continued he, " I honour and rejoice in a spirit which must render your success infallible ; but let it not be said that you took up a resolution of this infinite magnitude in a fit of enthusiasm. Let us agree to retire. We meet again to-morrow. We will consider this question in the meantime, and, whatever be the determination of the morning, it will not be accused of want of temperance or consideration." This argument prevailed, and the meeting adjourned.

But the business of the day was, perhaps, not less effectually promoted by the convivial parties which followed, than by the serious debates which occupied the sitting of the committee. Those members resident in Dublin, whom it had been the policy of the enemies to Catholic emancipation to grossly malign and misrepresent in the remote parts of the kingdom, had taken care to offer the rites of hospitality to the delegates from the country. And, in unreserved communication, both parties compared their common grievances, and mutually entered into each other's sentiments. All distrust was banished at once, and a comparison of ideas satisfied them that their interests were one and the same, and that the only enemy to be dreaded was disunion among themselves. The delegate from Antrim, who sat beside the delegate from Kerry, at the board of their brother in the capital, needed but little argument to convince him, that as the old maxim, " divide and conquer," had been the uniform rule of conduct with their common enemies, so mutual confidence and union among themselves were the infallible presage and most certain means of securing their approaching emancipation. The attrition of parties, thus collected from every district of the kingdom, demolished in one evening the barriers of prejudice which art and industry, and the monopolising spirit of corruption, had, by falsehood and soothing, by misrepresentation and menaces, been labouring for years, and but too successfully, to establish between them.

In this spirit the assembly met on the next day. The business was opened by the same member (*L. Teeling*) who had introduced the amendment. He stated that it was the duty of the Catholics not to wrong themselves by asking less than complete emancipation. That it was also the idea of their friends in the province from whence he came, and this coincidence of sentiments would establish that union, from which the Catholic cause had already derived such essential benefit, and which had been found so formidable to their enemies. Something had been insinuated about danger; he saw none: violence was not the interest nor the wish of the meeting. "But," continued he, "we have been asked, what we will do in case of a refusal? I will not, when I look round me, suppose a refusal. But, if such an event should take place, our duty is obvious. We are to tell our constituents; and they, not we, are to determine. We will take the sense of the whole people, and see what *they* will have done." Similar sentiments were avowed by every member who followed him; and, on the question being put, the amendment, praying for complete restitution of the rights of the Catholics, was carried by the unanimous acclamation of the whole assembly.

It was not to be supposed that perfect secrecy could be preserved in so numerous a meeting, or that the industry of the enemies to Catholic freedom should not be exerted in so important a crisis, and on so material a question as that which was now determined with such unanimity. On the morning of the day it was whispered, that, if the prayer for complete emancipation was persisted in, a large number of the most respectable country delegates would instantly quit the meeting, and publish their dissent. Whether such a measure was ever seriously intended or not, is not accurately known. Certainly, had it been carried into execution, a secession of so formidable a nature would have extremely embarrassed, if not totally destroyed, a system which had cost so much time and labour to bring to its present state. Be that as it may, such was the force of virtuous example, so powerful the effect of public spirit in an assembly, uncontaminated with places or pensions, and freely chosen by the people, that not a murmur of dissent was heard; and a day which opened with circumstances of considerable doubt and anxiety terminated in the unanimous adoption of the great principle which, whilst it asserted, secured the emancipation of the Catholics.

The prayer of the petition having been thus agreed upon, it was proposed (*by Mr. Fitzgerald*) that the signatures of the delegates should not be affixed until the mode of transmission should be first determined. The object of this motion was, obviously, to embarrass, and, if possible, to prevent, a measure which, from the spirit of the meeting, it was more than suspected would be tried. Apprehensions were entertained that the usual form in presenting petitions would be broken through, and that, by a direct application to the throne, a very pointed mark of disapprobation would be attached on the government of this country. If to prevent administration from being exposed to such an insult was the object of the motion, it failed completely. The committee decreed that the signing the petition should precede all debate as to the mode of transmission. And not only so, but it was unanimously resolved (on the motion of *Mr. Edward Sweetman, of Wexford*) that every delegate should instantly pledge himself to support, with his hand and signature, the sense of the majority—an engagement which was immediately and solemnly taken by the whole assembly.

The petition having been thus agreed upon, and signed, the important question arose as to the mode of presenting it to his Majesty. The usual method had been, to deliver all former addresses to the Lord Lieutenant, who transmitted them to the King ; and, certainly, to break through a custom invariably continued from the first establishment of the General Committee, was marking, in the most decided manner, that the Catholics had lost all confidence in the administration of this country. But, strong as this measure was, it was now to be tried. The petition having been read for the last time, a spirited young member (*Christopher Dillon Bellew, Esq., of Galway*), whose property gave him much, and his talents and virtues still more, influence in the assembly, and who represented a county, perhaps the first in Ireland for Catholic property and independence, rose, and moved, without preface, that the petition should be sent to the foot of the throne by a deputation to be chosen from the General Committee. He was seconded by a delegate from a county adjacent to his own (*J. J. Macdonnell, of Mayo*).

A blow of this nature, striking so directly at the character, and almost at the existence of the administration, could scarcely be let to pass without some effort on their part to prevent it. As the attack had been foreseen, some kind of a negotiation had been attempted with individuals who were given to understand, that if the petition was sent through the usual channel, administration would instantly despatch it by express, and back it with the strongest recommendations. The negotiation was not yet concluded when the dreaded motion was made, and, with some difficulty, the assembly agreed to wait *half an hour* for the result of one more interview. There can hardly be imagined a revolution more curious and unexpected than that which was occurring in the General Committee. The very men who a few months before could not obtain an answer at the Castle, sat with their watches in their hands, *minuting* that Government which had repelled them with disdain. At length the result of the interview was made known, and it appeared that the parties had either mistaken each other, or their powers, or the intentions of the administration, for it was stated by the member (*Mr. Keogh*) who reported it, that what had been supposed to be offered was merely a conversation between a very respectable individual and himself, but he had *nothing to communicate from any authority.* This, which the majority of the assembly considered, whether justly or not, as an instance of duplicity in administration, and as trifling with their own time and dignity, determined them to stigmatise, as far as in them lay, a Government which they now looked upon as having added insult to injury. " Will you," cried the orator (*Keogh*), " trust your petition with such men ? " The assembly answered with an unanimous, repeated, and indignant negative—" No ! "

Yet still a few individuals were found who started at the idea of fixing so gross an insult on administration (*MM. McKenna, Fitzgerald, D. T. O'Brien*). It was suggested rather than argued, that it was not perhaps respectful, even to majesty itself, to pass over

with such marked contempt his representative in Ireland, and that
the usual mode was the most constitutional, or at least the most
conciliatory. But the spirit of the meeting was now above stoop-
ing to conciliate the favour of those whom they neither respected
nor feared. The member who moved the question (*Mr. C. Bellew*)
again rose to support it. He said he did not ground his motion
merely on the insults which the Catholics, through their delegates,
had so often received, but on this, that he had no confidence in men
who kept no faith with Catholics, and the attempt of the present
day had satisfied his mind. Faith had been broken, even with
those gentlemen (*Lord Kenmare and the sixty-eight*) who, in
support of administration, had seceded from their own body. The
engagement entered into with them had been mutilated and
curtailed. "It has been said," continued he, "my plan is disrespectful to administration. I answer, it is intended to be so.
It is time for us to speak out like men We will not, like
African slaves, petition our task-masters. Our Sovereign will
never consider it disrespectful that we lay before his throne the
dutiful and humble petition of 3,000,000 of loyal and suffering
subjects. For my part, I know I speak the sentiments of my
county. I wish my constituents may know my conduct; and
the measure which I have now proposed I am ready to justify
in any way." These were strong expressions ; they were followed
by others no less energetic. "We have not come thus far," said
a delegate from the west of Ireland (*Mr. M'Dermott, of Sligo*), " to
stop short in our career. Gentlemen tell us of the wounded pride
of the administration. I believe it will be wounded, but I care
not ; I consider only the pride of the Catholics of Ireland." The
last attempt was now made to postpone the further consideration
of the question until the next day, but this was immediately and
powerfully resisted. "We will stay all night, if necessary," cried a
spirited young member (*P. Russell, of Louth*), "but this question
must be decided before we part. If it go abroad that you waver,
you are undone." "Let us mark," cried another (*J. Edw. Devereux,
Esq., of Wexford*), "our abhorrence of the measures of our enemies,
for they are the enemies of Ireland. The present administration

has not the confidence of the people." The whole assembly confirmed his words by a general exclamation, No! No! "Our allegiance and attachment are to King, Lords, and Commons, not to a bad ministry, who have calumniated and reviled us through the kingdom." His assertions were ratified by repeated and universal plaudits.

The question on the original motion was at length unanimously decided in the affirmative. By passing over the administration of their country, in a studied and deliberate manner, and on solemn debate, the General Committee published to all the world that his Majesty's ministers in Ireland had so far lost the confidence of no less than 3,000,000 of his subjects, that they were not even to be entrusted with the delivery of their petition. A stigma more severe it has not been the fortune of many administrations to receive.

The General Committee (Dec. 7th) proceeded to choose, by ballot, five of their body, who should present their petition to his Majesty in person, and the gentlemen appointed were Edward Byrne, John Keogh, Christopher Dillon Bellew, James Edward Devereux, and Sir Thomas French. The only instruction they received was to adhere strictly to the spirit of the petition, and to admit nothing derogatory to the union, which is the strength of Ireland. And this instruction, for greater solemnity, was delivered to them, engrossed on vellum, signed by the Chairman, and counter-signed by the Secretary of the meeting.

The petition being thus disposed of, the next measure which occupied the attention of the General Committee was to prepare a vindication of the Catholic body from the many foul imputations which had lately been thrown out against their principles and their conduct. For many months, patiently listening to the calumnies and falsehoods, which affected terror and real corruption had un-remittently vented, and attending only to the great measure, the universal election of their delegates, they had not suffered them-selves to be entrapped in the snares of political controversy. They had, consequently, made no defence against the torrent of abuse which poured upon them from all quarters. They were not seduced, even by the glory of a contest with great names or high authorities, but proceeded in their march right onward, slowly and steadily, alike unmoved at the turbulent attacks of the numerous county meetings, the well-feigned alarms of the selected grand juries, and dictated and loyal fears of the obedient corporations. But now success had afforded them leisure, and the present opportunity was seized to give one general replication to all the invectives thrown out against them. They therefore framed and published their vindication, which was intended as a commentary on their petition, a defence of their own conduct, and a refutation of the malicious and unfounded charges of their adversaries.

On the principle of this vindication the assembly was unanimous; but, as to one or two particular passages, a doubt arose in the minds of certain of the delegates. Among the number of the enemies to their emancipation were to be found personages of the most exalted political situation, some of whom had presided, and others assisted at meetings, whence publications had issued of the most violent hostility to the Catholic cause. In replying to these publications it was hardly possible to avoid statements and expressions which must be directly offensive to the exalted characters concerned; for, as the attacks were not merely political, but from their extreme acrimony partook of somewhat of a personal feeling, so the nature of the defence, and, indeed, the nature of man suggested, and in a manner enforced, a language which in a controversy of a milder kind could not have arisen. It was not to be wondered at if men felt some degree of caution at committing themselves in this species of warfare with such grave and high authorities. The question, therefore, on those parts of the vindication which remotely alluded to or directly named the most potent of their adversaries (*the Lord Chancellor Fitzgibbon*), was very fully debated and maturely considered.

The conduct of the personages under deliberation could not be defended on any principle in an assembly of Catholics. Those, therefore, who doubted on the propriety of thus repelling force by force (*Messrs. Fitzgerald, Daly, Lynch*, &c.), contented themselves with the commonplace topics of the necessary respect to high station, and the danger of speaking evil of dignities. But these were arguments to which the great majority of the assembly was now very little disposed to pay any respect. Feeling their own strength and unanimity, and galled by the remembrance of the wanton abuse which had been so profusely lavished upon them, they determined not to let pass an opportunity which fortune and their own wise and spirited conduct had put into their hands, and to mark their adversaries in their turn. Almost every man was eager to express his contempt and abhorrence of those whom the assembly now considered as fallen tyrants, and the feeble attempt to rescue them from a public stigma was drowned in a universal outcry of disapprobation. " What," said they (*Capt. Edward Sweetman and J. E. Devereux, of Wexford*), " are we to spare one man (*Mr. Foster*), who smells of the blood of our peasantry ? or another who made it his public and profligate boast that he would prostrate the chapels of the Catholics ? We know that man (*Lord Fitzgibbon*) ; the road to his favour is through his fears. Let us become formidable to him and we shall be respected. He is the calumniator of the people, and therefore he has our hatred and our contempt. Loyalty itself becomes stupidity and vice where there is no protection ; and are we to tender a gratuitous submission to men who have held, and would hold us in fetters, and in mockery, and in scorn ? What have we to fear but our own disunion ? Let us boldly acknowledge our friends, and mark our enemies. Let us respect ourselves, and the world will respect us ; and, above all, let us not disgrace our cause, or the great body which we represent, by indecision, or temporising, or equivocation." The assembly then unanimously decreed that the passages which had been objected to should remain unaltered.

The great and important business for which the General Committee had been summoned was now in effect terminated, at least as far as their labours could advance it. What remained of their time was occupied in discharging the debt of gratitude to their friends, and forming an arrangement for their future assembling. They voted their unanimous thanks to the citizens of Belfast, " to whom," said a delegate, "we owe that we meet here in safety ; they stand sentinels at our doors ; they support you, Mr. President, in that chair" (*L. Teeling, Esq.*). A sentiment which was received with acclamation by the whole meeting. They voted their thanks to those illustrious members who had supported the cause of the Catholics in Parliament. They thanked those patriotic characters who had devoted their time and talents to forwarding the emancipation of their brethren. They thanked their officers ; they thanked their sub-committee. They empowered that body to act for them in the intervals between their rising and their next meeting ; but they made a material alteration in its constitution by associating to the twelve members who then formed it, the whole of the country delegates, each of whom was henceforward to be, *ipso facto*, a member thereof. They then resolved unanimously that they would re-assemble when duly summoned by the sub-committee, who were invested with powers for that purpose. "We will attend," cried a member from a remote county, "if we are summoned to meet across the Atlantic" (*O'Gorman, of Mayo*).

One occurrence deserves to be particularly noted. It had been the policy of the enemies of the Catholic cause for a long time to foment and continue divisions between the clergy and laity, and in some instances their acts had so far succeeded as, perhaps, nearly to produce a difference between the pastor and the flock. It has already been mentioned that it was not without difficulty that some of the prelates had been induced to concur with the General Committee in the plan for the electing of delegates—a circumstance not to be wondered at when we consider the peculiar delicacy and responsibility of their situation, and the uncommon diligence and art which were used to deter them from any interference. But, whatever might at first have been their doubts and diffidence, when they saw the great body of the laity come forward and unanimously demand their rights, they manfully cast away all reserve, and declared their determination to rise or fall with their flocks—a wise and patriotic resolution which was signified to the General Committee by two venerable prelates, Dr. Troy, Archbishop of Dublin, and Dr. Moylan, Bishop of Cork, who assisted at the meeting, and signed the petition in the name and on behalf of the great body of the Catholic clergy of Ireland. They were received by the assembly with the utmost deference and respect, due not less to their sacred functions and private virtues than to the great and useful accession of strength which they brought to the common cause.

The members of the General Committee having returned to their counties, the delivery of their petition to the King became the immediate and urgent business of the gentlemen delegated to that honourable duty. It so happened that there was no packet boat ready in the harbour, and the wind was contrary. They therefore determined to go by a route longer, it is true, but less subject to accidental delays. To go by Scotland, it was necessary to pass through the north of Ireland, and especially through Belfast. On their arrival in that town they were met by a number of the most active and intelligent inhabitants, who had distinguished themselves in the abolition of prejudice, and the conciliation of the public mind in Ulster to the claims of the Catholics. On their departure their horses were taken off, and they were drawn along with loud acclamations by the people, among whom were numbers of an appearance and rank very different from what are usually seen on such occasions. To the honour of the populace of Belfast, it should be mentioned that they refused a liberal donation which was offered by the Catholic delegates ; and, having escorted them beyond the precincts of the town, and cordially wished them success in their embassy, they dismissed them with three cheers.

Trifling as this circumstance may appear, it was the subject of much observation. By some it was considered as throwing additional difficulties on a measure already supposed to be sufficiently unpalatable to the British minister, by avowing a connection with men notoriously obnoxious to him. By others it was applauded, on the ground of strengthening that union of the great sects the beneficial effects of which had already begun to operate in the elevation of the Catholic mind—an advantage which was thought to carry an intrinsic weight and power far beyond the uncertain favour of any minister. Whatever effect it might have on the negotiation in England, it certainly tended to raise and confirm the hopes of the Catholics at home. " Let our delegates," said they, " if they are refused, return by the same route." To those who looked beyond the surface it was an interesting spectacle, and pregnant with material consequences, to see the Dissenter of the North drawing, with his own hands, the Catholic of the South in triumph through what may be denominated the capital of Presbyterianism. However repugnant it might be to the wishes of the British minister, it was a wholesome suggestion to his prudence, and when he scanned the whole business in his mind was probably not dismissed from his contemplation.

On the arrival of the delegates in London, their first business was to apprise the Secretary for the Home Department (*the Hon. H. Dundas*) that they were deputed to present to the King the humble petition of the Catholics of Ireland, and they requested to know at what time they should attend him with a copy for his Majesty's perusal. The minister having appointed a day, the delegates met him, and in a long conversation very fully detailed the situation and wishes of the Catholic body. It is not to be supposed that the minister, on his part, was equally communicative, but he heard them with particular attention, and dismissed them with respectful politeness. His object was to procure the petition to be delivered through his hands ; that of the delegates to deliver it to the King himself in person. Some dexterity was exhibited on both sides in negotiating this point, but the minister was at length obliged to concede, and the firmness of the delegates prevailed.

It is but justice to the merit of an illustrious character to state here the obligation which the Catholics of Ireland owe to their countryman, the Earl of Moira, at that time Lord Rawdon. He had, immediately on the arrival of the delegates in London, waited on them, and offered them the hospitality of his mansion, and the command of his household ; he entertained them repeatedly in a style of splendid magnificence ; and, if the dignity of their mission could have received lustre from the support of an individual, they would have found it in the zeal and friendship of the Earl of Moira.

But his services were not confined to acts of hospitality and politeness. He assisted in their councils, and, in a manner, committed his public character with their cause, for, on the emergency, when the minister was dallying with the earnestness of the delegates to procure admission to their Sovereign, and probably presumed that they would not readily find another channel of access, Lord Moira came forward and told them, that, if it became necessary, *he* would, as a Peer, demand an audience of his Majesty, and be himself their introducer ; adding, at the same time, with the frankness and candour of his profession and character, that, flattering as such a distinction would be to himself, it was his wish that the minister should rather have the honour, inasmuch as he thought it would better serve their cause. As an Irishman and a military man, continued he, it might be esteemed to wear, perhaps, too peremptory an appearance, were I to introduce you, and when the minister finds that you are, in all events, secure of admission, he will probably be less reluctant to have the credit of it himself. If, however, he should persist in his refusal, you may then command me. The event justified his prediction ; the minister relaxed ; and Wednesday, the 2nd of January, was fixed as the day of their introduction. On that day the delegates were introduced at St. James's in the usual forms by Mr. Dundas, and, agreeably to their instructions, delivered into the King's own hands the petition of his Catholic subjects of Ireland. Their appearance was splendid, and they met with, what is called in the language of courts, a most gracious reception ; that is, his Majesty was pleased to say a few words to each of the delegates in his turn. In those colloquies the matter is generally of little interest, the manner is all ; and with the manner of the Sovereign the delegates had every reason to be content.

Thus had the Catholics, at length, through innumerable difficulties, fought their way to the foot of the throne ; the King had, in the most solemn manner, received their petition, and his ministers were in full possession of their situation, their wants, and their wishes. Their delegates had now executed their mission, and began to prepare for their return. After allowing a decent interval of a few days, they attended on the minister, for the last time, to learn, if they could, his determination, and to take what may be called their audience of leave. In this conversation, as in every former one, the claims of the Catholics were powerfully enforced and impressed on the mind of the minister in language stronger than is often used to men in his high station, and which would most probably have shocked the delicacy of a gentleman usher. He was given to understand, in terms that were scarcely equivocal that the peace of Ireland, or, in other words, the submission of the Catholics, depended on the measures which Government might adopt on their behalf. Yet the cool and guarded temper of the minister was not to be disturbed, and, though he heard them with attention, and, apparently, at times, with emotion, he was not to be driven from the diplomatic caution, behind which he had carefully intrenched himself. After much of that general language, which is vernacular in official stations, the delegates were told that his Majesty was sensible of their loyalty and attachment to the principles of the constitution ; that, in consequence, they should be recommended in the speech from the throne at the opening of the impending session, and that ministers in England desired approbation and support from them only in proportion to the measure of relief afforded. If the elasticity of this answer, which would dilate or compress to any magnitude, did not appear entirely satisfactory to the plain and uncourtly understandings of the delegates, they were told, and probably with some truth, that the minister had gone farther than custom in similar circumstances would warrant ; and that, preserving the decorum due to the independent government and legislature in Ireland, more could not, with propriety, be said on the one hand, or required on the other. With this answer they were forced to be content, and they satisfied themselves in the reflection that nothing on their part had been left undone to procure one more definite.

It now became necessary to consider of the report which should be made to their constituents in Ireland. The expressions of the minister, according to all received rules of construction, were to be taken most strongly against himself ; the King was sensible of their loyalty ; they were to be liberally recommended, and their gratitude was to be commensurable with their relief. Combining these expressions with the general behaviour of the minister, and the effect produced on their minds in the various conferences, and making allowance for the delicacy of his station, which did not permit him to be more explicit, they resolved that the answer of the minister was satisfactory, and satisfaction to Catholic minds then inferred the idea of *complete relief*—a construction which they founded, not on this or on that expression, but adopted as a general impression, resulting from the whole tenor of Mr. Dundas's conduct, from the commencement to the termination of their negotiation.

In pursuance of this principle, as the session had already opened, two of their body were instantly despatched to state to the sub-committee all that had been done, and what the deputation did conceive to be the sentiments of ministry in England. The other members followed more leisurely, and in the course of a few days the deputation was collected, save one gentleman, Mr. Devereux, of Wexford, who remained in London as a kind of *Chargé d'Affaires.*[1]

---

[1] [This Convention led to the passing of the famous Convention Act, prohibiting delegated or representative assemblies outside Parliament. This Act was only repealed in our own day.—ED.]

[In the original edition Chapters IX. and XI. of the present edition formed one continuous statement. I have divided this statement into two chapters, inserting between them (so as to preserve the chronological order) Tone's diaries for January and February, 1793, making Chapter X.—ED.]

AFTER THE CONVENTION.

January 21*st.* I find it very hard to keep those journals regularly. I have an arrear on my hands since the week before I left London. I wish I could bring myself to set apart some certain time for journalising ; but, as that would be something approaching to system, I despair of ever reaching it.

In the sub-committee, Sir T. French, Byrne, Keogh, and McDonnell despatched to Hobart to apprise him that nothing short of unlimited emancipation will satisfy the Catholics. They return, in about an hour, extremely dissatisfied with each other, and, after diverse mutual recriminations, it appears, by the confession of all parties, that, so far from discharging their commission, they had done directly the reverse ; for the result of their conversation with the Secretary was, that he had declared explicitly against the whole measure, and they had given him reason, in consequence, to think that the Catholics would acquiesce contentedly in a half one. Sad, sad! I am surprised at Sir T. French, for, as for merchants, I begin to see they are no great hands at revolutions. And so Gog's puffing is come to this: I always thought, when the crisis arrived, that he would be shy, and I am more and more confirmed in that idea by every new incident. Agreed by the S. C. that a letter should be written to Hobart to rectify this mistake, which is done accordingly, after many alterations. It is not well done after all ; for, instead of putting the question on the true ground, it only says that his Majesty's gracious intentions towards the Catholics cannot be fulfilled, unless by the repeal of the penal laws. I wanted to express it a great deal stronger, and to hint at the danger of trifling, but was over-

powered. Magog, the single man who was up to the business
properly : H. Hamill next best. Gog damped them by puffing
his readiness for one to face any danger which might ensue from
a strong representation. Owen O'Connor asserted that he was
ready too, upon which Gog asked him, Was he prepared to enter
the tented field ? He answered " He was." Now the fact is, the
question was put to frighten Ned Byrne ; and another fact is, that
O'Connor was ready, and Gog was not. He is a sad fellow after
all. I see, if ever the business is done, it will be by the country
gentlemen. In the evening wrote three official letters to Devereux,
Chargé d'Affaires at the Court of London.—*Mauvais jour.*

January 22nd. Called on Sir Thomas French. A council of war.
The Baronet, James Plunket, Edward Sweetman, P. P., and Mr.
Hutton agreed unanimously that the cause has gone back
materially, from the conversation of yesterday ; that a sneaking
spirit of compromise seems creeping in, which, if not immediately
checked, may be fatal. Agreed that Sweetman shall prepare
a strong address to the nation, to show Ministers that we are as
resolute as ever. Agreed that, if all be given except the two
houses, the gentry of the Catholics will be the only disfranchised
body in the nation. All the country gentlemen present in a rage
thereat, which Mr. Hutton and P. P. aggravate to an extreme
degree.

January 23rd. Sweetman produces his paper at the Sub-committee, which is very strong and good. Mr. Hutton produces an
amendment in the shape of a most virulent attack on the Lord
Chancellor (Fitzgibbon). The Sub-committee staggered thereat.
The whole referred to a Committee, viz., Hamill, McDonnell,
Sweetman, Bellew, Dr. Ryan, and Mr. Hutton, to report next day.
Dine with T. Braughall, and a long set. In committee in the
evening : divers alterations in the paper, principally on the suggestion of Hamill, who is a very clever man, and far the first that
I have seen of the Catholic mercantile interest. Agreed to the
paper, which is very good. Will they pass it ?

January 24th. Sir T. French opens the business by a strong
attack on the meeting for the lukewarm spirit which they have

manifested for these last few days. I am very glad of this step, which indeed I put the Baronet upon. It will give them a fillip which they want. The paper read and received coldly enough. This is hard! They have now a noble opportunity of punishing their old enemy Fitzgibbon, and I am afraid they will let it slip. It is objected to on two grounds: 1st, as an attack on the privileges of Parliament; and 2nd, inasmuch as being below their dignity, to enter into an altercation with the Chancellor. The last is most insisted upon, the first appearing to savour a little of timidity. The fact is they *are* afraid, which is damned bad. They were much stouter three months ago, when they were, beyond all comparison, weaker. Now they have, I may say, the whole North, the sanction of the King's name, and their own party in the highest spirits, and most anxious expectations, and all of a sudden they are gone unaccountably backward. *This is vile.* It will give our execrable Government time to recollect themselves. They are now rocking to their very foundation, and they are still more frightened than hurt. We are going to take them very kindly out of this panic, and, by the fluctuation and indecision of our councils, to show them that they have nothing to fear from us. What does Gog want them to do this morning? Only to alter the prayer of the petition to Parliament, by striking out the part which mentions, in terms, a repeal of the penal laws, and to leave it general, according to the form of that presented to the King; and this wise and valiant proposal comes after we have put Hobart in possession of a copy of our intended petition. The Sub-committee unanimously reject the proposition. Gog is losing ground fast, and, if he does not take care, he will go down totally. He certainly wants either talents, integrity, or courage, to conduct the affairs of the Catholics in their present state. The intended paper is at length got rid of, by referring it to those who are called our *Parliamentary friends.* I never knew good come through that channel: but, however, "*'tis but in vain for soldiers to complain.*"

January 25th. Gog comes into town, and makes a most amazing flourish. He has found out that he is losing ground on the score of courage, and therefore he proposes to the Sub-committee to send proper persons to Dungannon, to propose to the convention which is to meet there on the 15th February, that the Catholics will accept of no relief, unless a reform be granted, provided the Dissenters will accept of no reform which shall not include the Catholics on a footing of equality. All this a rhodomontade. Gog knows very well that the Sub-committee will not agree to such a proposal, which, in the present state of the business, would be foolish ; and that, if they were disposed to do so, they have no authority or power. He just means to make a dash, and have to say that he proposed a measure which was too bold for the Sub-committee to adopt.

January 26th to 31st. The Sub-committee is infected more and more with Gog's timidity, which is now, to all intents, as ruinous as downright treachery. T. Fitzgerald, who behaved infamously in the convention, and was most odious to Gog, is in town, and they have formed a most unnatural coalition. They have poisoned T. Warren between them. The Vintner is cowardly, and, besides, is under Gog's influence ; McDonnell is perpetually wavering. The country delegates do not step out. Altogether, everything looks ill. A deputation has been with Hobart again, as to the presenting the petition. He objects to the prayer as being too specific. He is asked if it be altered to the very words of that presented to the King, will he then present and support it. This he declines, but says, if they choose to give it to any of their own friends, it will make no alteration in his conduct relative to the extent of the measures which he will support. This is a good opening, if the Catholics have the grace to avail themselves of it, for the Minister is bound by the King's recommendation, and opposition will be bound, as bringing in the petition. The only use of Hobart's bringing it in, is, that it may pledge him to the whole measure.

Sub-committee. After sundry debates for two or three days, the prayer of the petition is altered to Gog's mind. I am clear he is wrong. If the form now agreed upon were the best, which I doubt, there should not be allowed the least alteration, for no form of words that was not downright offensive to Parliament can do such mischief as this appearance of fluctuations and indecision in our councils. This is very bad ; not that the alteration is very material, but that it betrays a sad decay in our spirit. Three or four days ago the Sub-committee rejected the idea of alteration unanimously, and with some appearance of resentment. To-day the same alteration is unanimously and very quietly adopted. Sad ! sad !

A scuffle between MM. Gog and Hutton. In the last debate on the alteration Mr. Hutton mentioned some expressions which he had heard out of doors. Gog, in his reply, remarked, in a very pointed manner, "that the Sub-committee were not to be influenced in their decisions by reports of *conversations with persons whom they knew nothing about.*" And in another part, "that they were not to attend to conversations that were *held in corners.*" Mr. Hutton taketh fire thereat, as the insinuation is too strong and pointed to be overlooked. He riseth in great heat. T. Warren adviseth him not to speak, but he sweareth with vehemence that he will. In the meantime Edward Sweetman addresses the chair, and pronounces a handsome eulogium on Mr. Hutton, which a little abates the choler of that illustrious patriot, and also gives him a moment's time to recollect himself. He determines to make the apology to Gog as easy as possible, that he may have no reason to accuse himself. He, therefore, fixing his eyes on Gog, says, with great *mildness,* " that he is sure that gentleman did not intend to cast any imputation on him, but as, unluckily, the words he had used might be construed so as to bear a bad sense, he thought it but right to give him an opportunity to explain them. That he (Mr. Hutton) had never had a conversation with any man on Catholic affairs, that he would not hold before every man in the room ; nor done any action, in a corner or elsewhere, which he would not repeat at the Royal Exchange at noonday. That he had no *secret,* and, consequently, no fear. That he mentioned this, in justice to Gog, to induce him to give a proper explanation, *for he would not suffer himself to suppose that Gog could intend to convey the smallest imputation upon his conduct.*"

These last words brought up Gog in a fuss. He payeth Mr.

Hutton sundry compliments, and appeals to the Sub-committee whether he had not always expressed the obligations which the Catholic cause owed to his exertions and talents, and whether he had not always said that the Catholics were bound, in honour, not only to *reward him, but to raise his fortune.* That he thought his (Mr. Hutton's) measures for the last few days, alluding to the business of the petition, had tended too much to commit the Catholics with Parliament, but was satisfied, at the same time, of the perfect purity of his intentions; that, as to the expressions himself had used, he never intended by them to convey the smallest imputation on Mr. Hutton, and, particularly, as to what he had said about "corners," which he now saw was equivocal; he was sorry it had escaped him, and begged to recall it; he added sundry civil things, to all which Mr. Hutton answered by a low bow, and so the affair ended.

Now the fact is, Gog knew very well what he was saying, and did intend to attach an oblique censure on Mr. Hutton, which would have stuck to that gentleman, if he had not immediately resented it. Another fact is, *that Gog is not a firm man,* which is so much the better for Mr. Hutton, who has, thereby, a claw upon the said Gog. If he had not apologised, Mr. Hutton would have sent a certain officer, of the name of Edward Sweetman (who is indeed delegate for Wexford, and does not much love Gog), with a message, which would, as is presumed, have speedily brought him to a proper sense of his duty. *The fellow will ruin me yet with the Catholics, if he can : let him, but I will do, at all risks, what I feel to be my duty.*

The paper, with the attack on the Chancellor, seems universally given up. Nobody mentions it. A long despatch from Devereux, containing an account of a conversation which he had with Dundas, wherein, after pressing him very hard, he had driven him to confess that they did not intend to go beyond partial relief. The Sub-committee puzzled to know what to say to this. Devereux is several notes above their present key. Gog, at length, makes a very artful and insidious attack on Devereux, under colour of excusing his warmth and inexperience, and, in the course of his harangue, he twice *hoped the S. C. would not dishonour their deputy.* Edward Sweetman flames out, being indeed cousin and bosom friend to Devereux ; he seizes the word "*dishonour*," and says his kinsman is not to be dishonoured by any man. Gog finds, to his great mortification, that this won't do, and that he has a chance of being very roughly handled by Sweetman. He immediately begins to apologise with great earnestness and vehemence, and to express his great respect and affection for Devereux. The S. C. all at once declare their assent to this, and say that no man could possibly intend disrespect to Mr. Devereux ; so, at length, with some difficulty, Sweetman is pacified, and Gog got out of what, at first, appeared to be an ugly scrape. Gog has managed his matters poorly enough, to be obliged to apologise twice in one week ; he hates Sir Thomas French, Sweetman, and Mr. Hutton worse than the devil, *and for a good reason.*

My own opinion is, that Devereux did not act like a trained politician in this business, but he did like a good Irishman, and a man of high spirit ; at any rate, no bad consequence has resulted, for the ultimatum was despatched to Ireland before this conversation.

The King of France was beheaded on the 21st—*I am sorry it was necessary.* Another interview with Hobart ; he agrees to present the petition as altered, but takes care to protest against his being thereby committed to the whole measure. He says he will go so far as he is supported by the House, and the Catholics give him the petition to present, saying they hope his conduct will be such as to entitle him to the gratitude, and his Majesty's Government to the support, of the Catholics. They are all wrong in my judgment. They should give it to some independent man, for Hobart is bound already to do what he can by the speech from the throne, and this imposes no additional tie, whilst it cripples opposition ; besides, he did not appear any way anxious to present it, and they in a manner forced it upon him, which is very bad, as it betrays a want of confidence in themselves and their friends. I am not much in love with their proceedings for some time back. They have totally lost the spirit which they seemed to have in England.

February 1st. Debate on the late business with the Goldsmith's corps. A few days ago they paraded, when they were informed by Alderman Warren, that if they attempted to march, he would take the officers into custody ; on which, after some consideration, it was agreed to disperse. The reason of this was, that some individuals threatened to resist, by force, and it was not thought advisable to commit the Volunteers with Government just now. There are about 250 Volunteers in Dublin, and the garrison is not less than 2,500, so that resistance is out of the question for the present. Do Government mean to carry the principle on with other corps? Will they go on and disarm us all? I hope not.

February 4th. Hobart presented the petition, and moved for leave to bring in a bill, which is granted. The measure of relief intended, as chalked out by him, is as follows : The elective franchise. Magistracies. Right of endowing schools. Admissibility to corporations. Right of carrying arms, subject to modification. Civil offices, subject also to modification ; but we shall see more when the bill is introduced, and still more when it is carried. The points withheld are : The two Houses of Parliament. The Bench, and the Board of Commissioners of the Revenue. The last two are nonsense. There is no need of an Act of Parliament to do what the King can do of himself, and it establishes a principle of exclusion, which ought to be kept out of sight as much as possible. Will the Catholics be satisfied with this bill? I believe they will, and be damned! I am losing ground amongst them, I see, hourly, owing to my friend Gog, who, I know, will work me out. He does not like to have me close enough to inspect his actions, and I am much afraid he has some foul negotiation on foot. I know no more of their plans for the last week than the man in the moon.

February 5th. Gog has exhibited a master-stroke! He moved this day, when only nine gentlemen were present, " that, in order to unite secrecy and despatch, the gentlemen who have been appointed to wait on the Minister be requested to continue their applications, in order to carry into effect the object of the petition." This seems innocent enough, but what does it mean? It is a delegation of the whole power of the Catholic body to seven men who have no definite instructions, who are not bound to report their proceedings, and who have no responsibility. The Sub-committee is thus adjourned *sine die*, and the Catholic body is governed by a Septemvirate, Gog being Dictator. This is all damned fine, but it won't do. What makes it more curious, is, that, of the nine men who voted this wise measure, *five* were of the deputation. Magog, Mr. Hutton, and everybody else are fairly excluded from all knowledge of or interference in Catholic affairs, and that without the least bustle or noise. This scheme will never do. We must have a counter-revolution, or an open meeting. Gog is as deep as a draw-well. Mr. Hutton informs Magog of this unexpected change. Magog in a rage ; swears he will take Gog off his stilts. Goes off to inflame the citizens against the Septemviri. Their reign, I see clearly, will be very brief. It is, to be sure, a damned impudent attempt, and a very artful one of Gog.

February 6th. A meeting of malcontents : Present, Magog, Capt. Sweetman, P. P., and Mr. Hutton. Much railing against the new Dictator ; a formal conspiracy against his authority. Magog has poisoned the whole city. Agree to call the Sub-committee, and rescind the vote appointing the *Septemviri ;* if defeated in the Sub-committee, to call the General Committee. Gog's new authority tottering already. Mr. Hutton and P. P. walk together ; much laughing at Mr. Hutton, who is indeed an ex-minister, and no longer possesses the confidence of the Catholics. All this will soon be rectified. As the Septemviri will soon be abolished, it is thought proper here to insert a list of their names : Sir Thomas French, John Keogh, Thomas Fitzgerald, Randal McDonnell, Christopher Bellew, Edward Byrne, and Dennis Thomas O'Brien.

February 7th. Magog is ready, and has summoned the Sub-committee for to-morrow.

February 8th. A complete counter-revolution effected, and the Septemviri removed without tumult or disturbance. Magog moved, that the order of the 5th be rescinded, which, after a feeble opposition from the Dictator, who is once more indeed become plain Gog, is carried *una voce*. Gog lays down the fasces, and walks forth a private citizen—Huzza! huzza! Mr. Hutton restored, also Magog, also all good Catholics. Huzza! that business is over, and the Dictatorate at an end, after an existence of three days. May all unjust power have as speedy a termination ! The deputation report that they were sent for this morning by Hobart, to tell them "that nothing could be done in the business of the bill for the relief of the Catholics, unless he should be enabled to say that they would be satisfied with the measures at present intended ; that, by being satisfied, is meant, that the public mind should not be irritated in the manner it has been for some time past ; that it is not meant to say that future applications may not be made, but that if they (the Catholics) will not for the present be satisfied, it is better to make a stand here than to concede, and thereby to give them strength by which they might be able further to embarrass Administration, perhaps next session." This is pretty stout language of the Secretary. It is observable that last night 20,000 army and 16,000 militia were voted by the House of Commons, and that Opposition, and particularly Grattan, were as earnest in the measure as the Treasury Bench. They are a fine set, to be sure, altogether. Grattan dreads the people as much as Monck Mason. A long conversation amongst the Catholics on the point of declaring themselves satisfied, or not, with Hobart's bill. For satisfaction, Sir Thomas French, Bellew, Byrne, O'Connor, and Keogh ; against it, O'Gorman, Sweetman, McCormick, and James Plunket. This is as important a crisis as any which has occurred in Catholic affairs.

For satisfaction, it is said that the people out of doors would disown us if we were, after bringing the question thus far prosperously, now to refuse purchasing the present bill at so cheap a price ; that the Secretary did not say that we were to acquiesce for *ever* under the measures intended, but only that the public mind should not be irritated ; that every accession of strength enabled us the better to secure the remainder ; that we might take what was now offered, and in a year or two apply for what was withheld ; that the present bill would give substantial relief ; that the numbers who would suffer by what was withheld were very few, in comparison with those who would be satisfied by what was granted ; that, as to the Bench, few Catholic lawyers could be, even in point of standing, fit for that station for many years, before which time it was hoped all distinctions would be done away ; that, as to seats in Parliament, if all were this moment granted, no Catholic gentleman is prepared, by freeholders or otherwise, for an immediate contest, so that in case of a General Election immediately, the Protestant gentry must come in without opposition ; that a few years would alter this, and enable the Catholics to make their arrangements, so as to engage in the contest on equal terms. It was again and again pressed, that the people would not be with us, and, finally, it was asked, were we prepared for the consequences of a refusal ? that is, in plain English, were we ready to take the field ? An argument which seemed to have its due weight with divers of the assembly.

On the other hand, it was said, that what had been determined by the general will of the Catholics of Ireland assembled, could not be reversed by the persons appointed to carry that will into execution ; that the Sub-committee had not even the power of discussing the Minister's propositions ; that if the Catholics were still to be kept from an equal share of the benefits of the Consti- tution, they should not sanction the exclusion by concurring in it ; that it would ill become them now to ask less, when they had obtained the royal approbation of their claims, when they had the support of the entire North, and so many respectable county meetings of their Protestant brethren joined to their own united strength, than they had done at a time when so many fortunate circumstances had not yet concurred in their favour ; that the proposal originated with men who had always been their enemies, and therefore was brought forward evidently with a view to distract and divide them ; that the people were with the Sub- committee, as appeared by the universal satisfaction which the resolution of the Grand Committee, to go for complete emancipation, had given to all ranks and descriptions of Catholics ; that they were unable to cope with their enemies in the arts of negotiation ; that if the Minister desired that expression of satisfaction, which the Sub-committee neither could nor ought to give, the Grand Committee might be summoned, the bare mention of which would deter him from pressing it farther ; that, as to the "tented field," such language was not to be held out to an unarmed people, pursuing their just rights, and using, and desiring to use, no other weapons than a "sulky, unaccommodating, complaining, constitutional loyalty." Finally, it was again pressed, and insisted upon, that the Grand Committee having already decided in favour of the whole measure, no body nor individual among the Catholics had power to sanction any measure short of complete relief.

After much altercation and repetition of the above arguments, on both sides, the Sub-committee broke up, without coming to any determination. *I see the whole measure is decidedly lost.*

CHAPTER XI.

THE FRANCHISE ACT.

THE opening of the session of 1793 was, perhaps, as critical a period as had occurred for a century in Ireland. In consequence of the regulation above mentioned, every country gentleman delegated for either county or city was now a member of the Sub-committee, and the anxiety which they felt for the event of a question, in which their dearest interests and warmest hopes were so deeply involved, had detained a number of the most active, spirited, and intelligent of the Catholic gentry in town during the whole period of the absence of their deputation. On their return the Sub-committee was, in consequence, very diligently attended, and the process of the measures intended for the relief of the Catholics was very fully investigated, and, on several material points, debated in crowded meetings and with considerable heat.

At the adjournment of the General Committee, in December, and for some time after, administration in Ireland was in a state of deplorable depression and dismay. Already stunned with the rude shock received from the Catholics, the Minister, at the opening of the session, was a perfect model of conciliatory concession. To the astonishment of the nation, the principle of parliamentary reform was asserted unanimously by the House of Commons, and admitted without a struggle, almost without a sigh, by administration. The people seemed to have but to demand and to obtain their long withheld rights, and sanguine men began to indulge the hope that the constitution of their country would, at length, be restored to its theoretical simplicity and justice, and all its impurities be purged away. But this vision, so bright in the perspective, was soon dispelled, and the nation, in the course of a few short weeks, awakened from its fancied triumph over inveterate corruption to a very solid and substantial system of coercion. To follow in detail many of the measures which materially contributed to this sudden and unexpected change would now be, at best, useless, perhaps prejudicial ; yet truth requires that some of them should be developed ; the investigation of past errors, if it cannot recall lost opportunity, may at least prevent their repetition in similar circumstances, should such ever recur again.

The solid strength of the people was their union. In December the Catholics had thundered out their demands, the imperious, because unanimous, requisition of 3,000,000 of men ; they were supported by all the spirit and intelligence of the Dissenters. Dumourier was in Brabant, Holland was prostrate before him ; even London, to the impetuous ardour of the French, did not appear at an immeasurable distance ; the stocks were trembling ; war seemed inevitable ; the Minister was embarrassed ; and, under those circumstances, it was idle to think that he would risk the domestic peace of Ireland to maintain a system of monopoly, utterly useless to his views. The Catholics well knew this ; they well knew their own strength and the weakness of their enemies ; and therefore it was that the Sub-committee derided the empty bluster of the Grand Juries, and did not fear, in the moment that they stigmatised the administration, to approach their Sovereign with a demand of unlimited emancipation. Happy had the same decided spirit continued to actuate their councils. But it would be fruitless to deny what it is impossible to conceal. From whatever cause the system was changed, the simple universality of demand was subjected to discussion, and from the moment of the first interview with the Minister of Ireland the popular mind became retrograde, the confidence of administration and their strength returned, and the same session which afforded a mutilated, though important relief to the Catholics, carries on its records a militia bill, a gunpowder act, and an act for the suppression of tumultuous assemblies. These bills are now the law of the land. In times like the present it is not safe to descant on their merits ; they will be appreciated by the fair and impartial judgment of posterity. But, though a critical investigation of their excellencies, however curious or interesting, be, for the present, denied to him who feels himself indignantly bound by their extensive operation, it is not yet, perhaps, criminal to relate historically, in a work like the present, the progress of measures so closely connected with the Catholic question, or to conjecture at the probable views of those who planned, those who supported, and those who connived at those famous statutes.

The General Committee had framed their demand for total emancipation ; their instructions to the deputation had been to adhere to the spirit of the petition. These instructions had been faithfully observed, perhaps exceeded, in every interview with the British Minister. Even in the unimportant circumstance of the day of their introduction they had refused to consult his convenience or his caprice, and they parted from him with a reiteration of the principle which in every conversation they had maintained, that nothing short of total emancipation would be esteemed satisfactory by the Catholics of Ireland. But, when they had returned, having executed the object of their mission, certain it is that this unaccommodating spirit relaxed, and something of a more conciliatory nature, and a system of less extensive demand, appeared to pervade the councils of the Catholics. In the first interview with the Irish Minister the two Houses of Parliament were at once given up, but the question began to be, not how much must be conceded, but how much might be withheld. So striking a change did not escape the vigilance of administration ; they instantly recovered from the panic which had led them into such indiscreet and, as it now appeared, unnecessary concessions at the opening of Parliament ; they dexterously seduced the Catholics into the strong ground of negotiation, so well known to themselves, so little to their adversaries ; they procrastinated, and they distinguished, they started doubts, they pleaded difficulties ; the measure of relief was gradually curtailed, and during the tedious and anxious progress of discussion, whilst the Catholic mind, their hopes and fears, were unremittingly intent on the process of their bill, which was obviously and designedly suspended, the acts already commemorated were driven through both houses with the utmost impetuosity, and, with the most cordial and unanimous concurrence of all parties, received the royal assent.

This negotiation, however, did not proceed without serious opposition amongst the Catholics themselves. Many warm debates occurred in the Sub-committee, and several of the members strenuously resisted the idea of compromising the general demand. It is not necessary, nor could it now be useful to detail these various combats, in which the same ground was fought over again and again, with equal obstinacy and the same success. It may suffice to give the substance of one debate as a specimen.

During the progress of the bill, the Minister having sent for the gentlemen appointed to communicate with him, informed them that he could not pretend to answer for the success of the bill unless he was enabled, from authority, to reply to a question proposed to him by a noble lord in debate, " Whether the Catholics would be satisfied with the measure of relief intended ? " By " satisfied " he meant that the public mind should not be irritated in the manner it had been for some time back ; he did not mean to say that future applications might not be made ; but if they, the Catholics, would not, for the present, be satisfied, it were better to make a stand here than to concede, and thereby to give them strength, by which they might be able farther to embarrass administration—perhaps next session. This was pretty strong language from the Minister (Secretary Hobart), and very unlike what he had held at the opening of the session, but the aspect of the political hemisphere had been materially altered in that short space. The very night before this interview the House of Commons had voted an army of 20,000, and a militia of 16,000 men, a measure in which the opposition party had outrun the hopes and almost the wishes of administration. Every measure for strengthening the hands of government was adopted by one party with even more eagerness than it was proposed by the other ; the nation was submitted implicitly to the good pleasure of the Minister, and the leader of opposition was contented, in *terms*,

to implore the gratuitous clemency of the man to whom he could
have dictated the law—a mode of proceeding that seems to have
been more sentimental than wise, as the subsequent measures of
the administration abundantly verified. Government was invested
with dictatorial powers; to what purpose they were exerted,
posterity may safely, and will impartially, determine. But to
return.

The deputation having reported the speech of the Secretary, a
very warm debate ensued in the Sub-committee, which, it may be
necessary to repeat, then comprised a great portion of the spirit
and ability of the General Committee. The question was,
" Whether they would accede to the wish of the Minister, and, by
admitting their satisfaction at the present bill, sanction a measure
short of complete emancipation ? "

Those who argued in the affirmative stated that the people out
of doors would disown them if they were, after bringing the question thus far prosperously, now to refuse purchasing a bill conveying such solid benefits at so cheap a price. That the Minister did
not say the Catholics were to acquiesce for ever under the measures
intended, but only that the public mind should not be irritated ;
that every accession of strength enabled them the better to secure
the remainder ; that what was now offered might be accepted, and,
under the terms of the stipulation, application might, in two or
three years, be made for what was withheld ; that no man could
deny that the present bill afforded substantial relief ; that the
members who might suffer by what was refused were very few, in
comparison with those who would be satisfied with what was
granted ; that, taking the bench as an example, few Catholic
lawyers could be, even in point of standing, fit for that station in
many years, long before which time, it was presumed, all distinctions would be done away ; that as to seats in Parliament, if all
distinctions between the sects were at that moment abolished, no
Catholic gentleman was prepared, by freeholders or otherwise, for
an immediate contest ; so that, in case of a general election
immediately, the Protestant gentry must come in without opposition ; that a few years would alter this, and enable the Catholics

to make their arrangements so as to engage in the contest on equal terms ; that what was given by the bill, and particularly the right of elective franchise, was an infallible means of obtaining all that remained behind ; it was again and again pressed, and relied on, that the people would not be with them who would reject it ; and finally, it was asked, under those circumstances, were they prepared for the consequences of a refusal—that is," Were they ready to take the tented field ? "

To these arguments, which were certainly of great cogency, it was replied, " That what had been once determined by the general will of the Catholics of Ireland assembled, could not be reversed by persons merely appointed to carry that will into execution ; that the Sub-committee had not even the power of discussing the Minister's proposition ; that, if the Catholics were still to be kept from an equal share of the benefits of the constitution, it was not for them to sanction the exclusion by concurring themselves in the principle ; that it would ill become them now, when they had obtained the royal approbation of their claims, when they had the support of the entire North, and so many respectable meetings of their Protestant brethren, joined to their own united and compact strength, to ask less than they had unanimously done in December last, when so many fortunate circumstances had not yet concurred in their favour ; that the proposal under debate had originated with men who had ever been enemies to the Catholics, and was now brought forward evidently with a view to distract and divide them ; that the people would support the Sub-committee, which might be inferred from the universal approbation which the resolution of the General Committee to go for complete emancipation had given to all ranks and descriptions of Catholics ; that they were unable to cope with their enemies in the intricate arts of negotiation ; but that, if the Minister persisted in desiring that expression of satisfaction which the Sub-committee neither could nor ought to give, he should be told that the General Committee would be summoned, the mention of which would probably deter him from pressing it further ; that, as to 'taking the tented field,' such language was not to be held out to an unarmed people.

pursuing their just rights, and using, and desiring to use, no other weapons than a sulky, unaccommodating, complaining, constitutional loyalty." Finally, it was again pressed and insisted on, that the General Committee having already decided in favour of the whole measure, no body nor individuals among the Catholics had power to sanction any measure short of absolute and complete relief.

The result of these arguments, which brought conviction to neither side, was a compromise. The deputation again saw the Minister, and, with a nice distinction, they refused, in the name of the body, to express the wished-for satisfaction; they refused to express it officially as members of the Sub-committee, but, as individuals of the Catholic body, they admitted that the bill did contain *substantial relief*, and even this admission was guarded with a stipulation that it should not be quoted in debate. But the Minister had ascertained all that he wished to know by the proposal; he saw that the Catholics would acquiesce in a measure short of complete relief, and he inferred that they would not risk the safety of their bill by opposition to any measures, however repugnant to their own feelings or subversive of the general interest, and the whole process of the session justified his sagacity. The expression of satisfaction was therefore no longer required, and the bill proceeded in the usual forms.

But while it was in progress through the House of Commons a very serious blow was struck at the hopes of the Catholics and the honour of the Sub-committee in the House of Lords. A noble peer (*Lord Fitzgibbon*), high in legal station, and to whom not envy herself can deny the praise of consistency on the subject of Catholic emancipation, had, early in the session, declared his opposition in terms of the bitterest invective. Very shortly after, advantage was taken of the riotous and tumultuous outrages committed by the rabble in certain counties, and a committee of secrecy was appointed by the Lords to inquire into the causes of the disorders and disturbances which prevailed in several parts of the kingdom. In due time this committee published a report, whose object was two-fold : to attach a suspicion on the most active members of the

Sub-committee of having fomented those disturbances, and to convey a charge little short of high treason on certain corps of Volunteers, particularly in Belfast, preparatory to disarming or otherwise suppressing that formidable body. In the first of these schemes the authors of the measure completely failed ; in the last they were but too successful.

On the merits of that report I am, with deep reluctance, compelled to refrain. The examples which I have seen of victims to the unforgiving revenge of offended privilege, force me to bury in silence the ardent spirit of resentment which I feel. What single man will again be found to encounter the strong hand of power for a country that would suffer him to rot in a dungeon ? When I reflect on that publication a thousand ideas crowd at once into my mind, and struggle for a vent. Perhaps a time may come——

The Sub-committee could not overlook an attack of so very serious a nature, containing charges which, if established, would subject them to penalties of the severest kind. Their Secretary (*Richard McCormick, Esq.*), a man universally respected in public and in private life, was more peculiarly marked out, and though it might be thought that such charges, if at all founded, should be instantly followed by criminal prosecution, and that, where no such prosecution did ensue, it was probable that no foundation existed for the imputation ; yet the Sub-committee, knowing, in the pending state of the Catholic bill, how severely a stigma like that conveyed in the report might affect their dearest hopes, and conjecturing that such was the object of the framers of that paper, determined to give it an immediate answer, disclaiming, in the most solemn manner, every article of the charges alleged against them, and tendering themselves, their publications, and their accounts, to the most severe and public scrutiny that the malice of their enemies could devise. Their Secretary likewise published a separate defence, in which he very fully explained those circumstances which, were they not contained in a report of a Committee of the House of Lords, might be said to be grossly and wilfully misstated. Yet the defence of the Sub-committee, and the vindication of the Secretary, were languid compared with

former publications. The body and the individual were confined
to a defensive war, and obliged to parry, without returning the
blow: a situation more severe to an honourable mind cannot well
be imagined. The felon in the dock has his irons knocked off,
that his mind may be free for his defence. The Sub-committee
were arraigned at the bar of their country with their hands
manacled, their feet shackled, and the halter of undefined privileges dangling on their necks.

Fortunately, however, the measure of Catholic relief had now
taken such deep root that it was not to be subverted even by this
storm. The bill, after a long and tedious discussion of several
weeks, at length passed the House of Commons, and was transmitted to the Lords. Through that House it also passed, without
alteration, receiving, however, in its transit, one more severe
philippic from the exalted character who had, with undeviating
consistency, condemned the measures intended for Catholic relief
in this and the preceding session; and, finally, on the 9th day of
April, 1793, it received, with the usual solemnities, the royal assent.

It would, in a work like the present, be impossible to do justice
to the talents displayed in support of the Catholic claims by all
their advocates in Parliament. It would be invidious, perhaps, to
make a selection, yet the self-love of none amongst them will be
wounded by the acknowledgment of the superior talents manifested
by Mr. Grattan. He was the early, the steady, and the inde-
fatigable friend of Catholic emancipation. The splendour of his
talents reflected a light upon their cause in the darkest moments
of its depression. To that great object he bent the undivided
powers of his mind, and did not scruple to hazard his popularity
by a manly declaration in their favour, at a time when the tide of
popular clamour ran most strongly against them, and when his own
constituents were foremost in the cry. He saw that clamour subside at his feet; the voice of truth and reason prevailed over the
storm, and the same man had the rare and unexampled good
fortune to be foremost in restoring a people to the constitution, as
he had been in restoring a constitution to the people.

A copy of the bill is subjoined. By one comprehensive clause all penalties, forfeitures, disabilities, and incapacities are removed; the property of the Catholic is completely discharged from the restraints and limitations of the penal laws, and their liberty, in a great measure, restored by the restoration of the right of elective franchise, so long withheld, so ardently pursued. The right of self-defence is established by the restoration of the privilege to carry arms, subject to a restraint, which does not seem unreasonable, as excluding none but the very lowest orders. The unjust and unreasonable distinctions affecting Catholics, as to service on grand and petty juries, are done away; the army, navy, and all offices and places of trust are opened to them, subject to exceptions hereafter mentioned. Catholics may be masters or fellows of any college hereafter to be founded, subject to two conditions: that such college be a member of the University, and that it be not founded exclusively for the education of Catholics. They may be members of any lay body corporate, except Trinity College, any law, statute, or bye-law of such corporation to the contrary notwithstanding. They may obtain degrees in the University of Dublin. These, and some lesser immunities and privileges, constitute the grant of the bill, the value of which will be best ascertained by referring to the petition. From comparison, it will appear that every complaint *recited* has been attended to; every grievance *specified* has been removed. Yet the prayer of the petition was for *general* relief. The bill is not coextensive with the prayer. The measure of redress must, however, be estimated by the extent of the previous suffering and degradation of the Catholics set forth by themselves, and, in this point of view, the bill will undoubtedly justify those who admitted that it afforded *solid and substantial relief.*

But, though many and most important privileges were now secured to the Catholics, it will appear that much has been withheld, and withheld in the manner most offensive to their feelings, because the bill, admitting the lower orders of the Catholic people to all the advantages of the constitution which they are competent to enjoy, excludes the whole body of their gentry from those functions which they are naturally entitled to fill. A strange inconsistency! During the whole progress of the Catholic question a

favourite and plausible topic with their enemies was the ignorance
and bigotry of the multitude, which rendered them incompetent to
exercise the functions of free men. That ignorance and bigotry are
now admitted into the bosom of the constitution, whilst all the
learning and liberality, the rank and the fortune, the pride and pre-
eminence of the Catholics, are degraded from their station, and
stigmatised by Act of Parliament.

"A Catholic may not be "—(See Act of 9th April, 1793, from
page 23, line 4, to page 26, line 1).[1]

Of this bead roll of disqualifications, many are unnecessary, doing
that by Act of Parliament which his Majesty is already competent
to do by his royal discretion. The exclusion is the more invidious
from the utter improbability of any Irish Catholic being called to
fill the stations of Lord Lieutenant, Lord Deputy, Lord High
Chancellor, which are formally excepted in the bill, merely, as it
should seem, to affix on them a mark of distrust and inferiority.
But these are exceptions offensive only to the pride ; there are
others directly trenching on their interests.

By their exclusion from the two Houses of Parliament the whole
body of the Catholic gentry of Ireland, a high-spirited race of men,
are insulted and disgraced, thrown down from the level of their
fortune and their talents, and branded with a mark of subjugation,
the last relic of interested bigotry. This is the radical defect of
the bill. If the Catholics deserved what has been granted, they
deserved what has been withheld ; if they did not deserve what has
been withheld, what has been granted should have been refused.
There is an inconsistency, not to be explained on any principle of
reason or justice, in admitting the alleged ignorance and bigotry
and numbers of the Catholics into the pale of the constitution, and
excluding all the birth, rank, property, and talents. By granting
the franchise, and withholding seats in Parliament, the Catholic
gentry are at once compelled and enabled to act with effect as a

---

[1] [Catholics were still excluded from Parliament, the Privy Council, and
Judicial Bench ; and (*inter alia*) from the offices of Lord Lieutenant, Lord
Chancellor, Chancellor of the Exchequer, Secretary of State, Commander-in-
Chief, Attorney or Solicitor-General, Sheriff or Sub-Sheriff, or Lord Lieutenant
of a County (33 Geo. III., c. 21, s. 9).—Ed.]

distinct body and a separate interest. They receive a benefit with one hand and a blow with the other, and their rising gratitude is checked by their just resentment—a resentment which in the same moment they obtain the means and the provocation to justify. If it was not intended to emancipate *them* also, they should have been debarred of all share of political power. Will they not say that they have received just so much liberty as will enable them to serve the interests of others? to be useful freeholders and convenient voters, artificers of the greatness and power in which they must not share, subaltern instruments in the elevation of those who their honest pride tells them are in no respect better than themselves? A mortifying state of degradation to men of ardent spirit and generous feelings! As the law now stands, a Catholic gentleman of the first rank and fortune is, in a political point of view, inferior to the meanest of his tenants ; combining their situation and their feelings, *they* are fully emancipated, *he* drags along an unseemly and galling link of his ancient chain.

An attempt was made to do justice to the Catholics, to preserve the consistency of Parliament, and to carry into execution his Majesty's paternal wish for the complete union of all his subjects in support of the established constitution. On the day of the committal of the bill in the House of Commons the Hon. George Knox, member for Dungannon, moved that the committee be empowered to receive a clause to make it lawful for Catholics to sit and vote in Parliament. The justice and magnanimity of the principle were supported by the spirit and ability of the mover, who, in a strain of eloquence, unanswered because unanswerable, enforced the wisdom of the measure and the claims of the Catholics by arguments drawn, not merely from local or temporary topics, but from the principles of good government and the feelings and nature of man. What, said he, is the object of this bill? To admit the Catholics to some degree of civil liberty. On what principle then, with what object have you singled out that portion which you are about to concede? (Vide *Hibernian Journal*, March 18, 1793, 2nd col., 2nd paragraph.) It will not much impeach the abilities of the opposers of the motion to say, that to these arguments they were unable to reply. It does not, however, always happen that the weight of argument concurs with the weight of members. Notwithstanding the powerful exertions of the friends to Catholic emancipation, and the talents they are known to possess, and which were never displayed in greater lustre, the motion was lost by a very large majority, seventy-one members voting in the affirmative, and no less than one hundred and sixty-five in the negative.[1] Yet even this defeat, compared with the last session of Parliament, was a victory. But —— men could then be found to vote for receiving a petition which, in effect, asked for nothing ; now seventy-one members, constituting a great portion of the character, the property, and, above all, the talents of the House, voted for the complete admission of the Catholics to the privileges of the constitution.

The denial of the right to sit and vote in Parliament is now, undoubtedly, the chief grievance of the Catholics of Ireland. Another function, from which they are excluded, is of material import. They may not be high sheriffs nor sub-sheriffs—an exception which diminishes extremely the value of the concessions whereby they are admitted to serve on grand juries. When it is considered that the office is never conferred but on gentlemen of property and figure, it is not easy to see any good reason for the exclusion of a man, in all other respects unexceptionable, merely because he is a Catholic. Every argument which can be used for their admission to Parliament applies with much greater force to their filling the office of sheriff ; and the danger, if danger can be apprehended, ought surely to vanish in the reflection, that the appointment to that office appertains to the Crown, whose discretion and whose advisers may, in this prerogative, be safely trusted. Excluding Catholics by law, therefore, is at best an unnecessary precaution, and every such precaution, as springing from a principle of distrust and suspicion, is for so much an insult, and an insult solely on the men of family, property, and education.

From another function, and of considerable importance, Catholics

---

[1] [The figures generally given are 163 and 69. The Tellers are, probably, counted by Tone, but not by the other authorities. The slight discrepancy may, perhaps, be explained in this way.—ED.]

are yet excluded in fact, though not in express terms. By the bill "they may be members of any lay body corporate, any rule or bye-law to the contrary notwithstanding." But this is, in effect, a nugatory license. There are but three ways of obtaining freedom of corporations—by birth, by service, or by special grace. From the first Catholics are excluded, for their fathers, for generations back, have been slaves. From the second they are excluded, because it has been hitherto a part of the oath of a freeman that he would take as an apprentice no bondman's son—a clause which effectually shuts out the Catholics. The third door may be opened by the liberality of Protestant corporators; but in this instance our laws have outrun our manners. In the metropolis the vigilant bigotry of the corporation of the city has been successfully exerted to effect and, as far as in them lay, to perpetuate the exclusion of Catholics, and this unworthy spirit has been manifested in the refusal of their freedom to some who have passed through the ordeal of their respective guilds, among whom are men of character and respectability, equal to any, not merely in the corporation, but in the community. The unbounded influence which administration is known to possess in that body renders this conduct in this instance the more paradoxical, and it certainly wears a great appearance of insincerity to grant the Catholics a valuable privilege, and, in the very same moment, to render them incapable to avail themselves of its benefits.

It is not my wish to aggravate discontent by dwelling on those parts of the bill which have disappointed the Catholic hope. Some of them are above, and some of them below, the general contemplation. Those parts which I have selected are, in form, offensive to the feelings, and, in substance, subversive of the interests of the Catholic body. But the radical and fundamental defect of the bill is, that it still tends to perpetuate distinctions, and, by consequence, disunion amongst the people. While a single fibre of the old penal code, that cancer in the bosom of the country, is permitted to exist, the mischief is but suspended, not removed, the principle of contamination remains behind and propagates itself. Palliatives may, for a while, keep the disease at bay, but a sound and firm constitution can only be restored by its total extirpation.

CHAPTER XII

JACKSON'S MISSION.

[TONE was much dissatisfied with the conduct of the Catholics in not pressing forward their demands for complete emancipation in 1793.[1] He believed that they could have obtained it then ; or if they failed he, doubtless, felt that renewed agitation would advance the cause of separation from England which was nearest and dearest to his heart. After their partial success the Catholics for a time rested, and were thankful. But Tone did not pause in his onward course. Watchful, eager, determined, bent on seizing every opportunity to further his aims, and confident of success, he neither relaxed his efforts, nor suspended his plans. An incident soon occurred which brought him prominently under the notice of the Government. In 1794 the Rev. William Jackson, an Anglican clergyman, visited Ireland. Jackson (who was of Irish descent) had begun life as a tutor in London. Afterwards he entered the Church, obtained some distinction as a popular preacher, and finally became the friend and chaplain of the Duchess of Kingston. In 1790 he went to Paris, interested himself in French politics, and formed relations with the Government. In 1794 he was sent to Ireland by the Committee of Public Safety to communicate with the United Irish leaders, and to bring back an account of the condition of the country. Passing through London he renewed his acquaintance with an old friend—Cockayne, who had been solicitor to the Duchess of Kingston. He told Cockayne all about his projected mission to Ireland. Cockayne immediately put Pitt in

---

[1] [It has already been stated that Tone's friend, George Knox, moved an amendment to the Franchise Bill in favour of the admission of Catholics to Parliament. But it was negatived by 163 to 69.—ED.]

possession of the whole story. Pitt desired him to keep quiet, to accompany Jackson to Ireland, to watch his movements, and to report everything to the Government. Cockayne and Jackson set out together, and reached Ireland in the spring of the year. They soon met Tone, under circumstances which he himself has detailed.—ED.]

Some days previous to the Drogheda Assizes I was informed by A. — [1] that there was a gentleman in town who was very recently arrived from France, and who, he suspected, was in the confidence of the *Comité de Salut public.* I was very desirous to see him, in order to hear some account of the state of France, which might be depended on. A. — accordingly wrote a note, which he gave me to deliver, stating that he could not have the pleasure of seeing the gentleman next day, being Sunday, but would be glad he would call any other time ; and, I believe, added, that the bearer was his particular friend. *I did not then, nor since, ask A. — how he became acquainted with the gentleman, nor do I yet know who introduced him.* I went with this note, and saw the gentleman and another person [2] at the hotel, where they lodged. I stayed about half an hour, and the conversation was either on mere general politics, or the want of accommodation for travellers in Ireland ; the superiority of England in that respect, &c. On my rising to depart, the gentleman asked me to dine with him on Wednesday subsequent, which I accordingly agreed to do. On the Monday after, as I recollect, I paid a visit to A. —, which I was in the habit of doing, daily, for some time back ; and, while I was there, the gentleman above mentioned and his friend came in together ; and, after some time, he and A. — entered into close conversation, and his friend and I retired to a distant part of the room, where we talked of the mode of travelling in Ireland, and amused ourselves looking over Taylor's map for about half an hour. *Neither of us heard, nor could hear, the conversation between A. — and the gentleman.* A. —, at length, beckoned me over, and I went. He then said they had been

---

[1] [Leonard McNally, an Irish barrister, who afterwards became an infamous informer. For particulars about him, see Mr. Fitzpatrick's " Secret Service under Pitt."—ED.]   [2] Cockayne.

talking of the state of the country ; that I knew what that state was as well as anybody, and that it was that gentleman's opinion, that if it were made fully known to people in France, they would, to a certainty, afford every assistance to enable the Irish to assert their independence. I said, that it would be a most severe and grievous remedy for our abuses, but that I saw no other ; for that liberty was shackled in Ireland by such a variety of ways, that the people had no way left to expose their sentiments but by open resistance. That, in the alternative between that and unconditional submission, many would differ ; but that I was one of those who, seeing all the danger and horror of a contest, still thought the independence of the country an object worth risking all to obtain, satisfied as I was, that, until that were secured, Ireland would never attain to her natural state of power, and opulence, and glory. In these sentiments A. — concurred, and the gentleman, as I recollect, again said, " *If this were known in France assistance might certainly be obtained.*" The conversation, at that time, went no farther. I had a latent suspicion he might possibly be an emissary of the British Minister, and therefore to mortify him, if that were the case, I spoke with the greatest asperity of the English nation, and of their unjust influence on the government of Ireland. His friend sat at a distance during this conversation, and I am sure could have heard no part of it, neither *did I inquire, nor do I know*, what conversation A. — and the gentleman had previous to their beckoning me over ; and the reason I did not inquire was, that, not knowing how the affair might terminate, and especially not knowing but this person might be an English spy, I determined I would know as little of other people's secrets as I could, consistent with my taking any part in the business.

The next day, I think, I saw A. — again. He showed me a paper, admirably drawn up, in my judgment, which he said he had got from the gentleman above mentioned. The paper went to show the political state of England, and the deduction was, that an invasion there would only tend to unite all parties against the French. I said the state of Ireland was totally different, and that it would be easy, in the same compass, to explain that on paper

He bid me try, and I agreed to do so. I do not recollect that we had any further conversation at that time. I went home, and that evening made a sketch of the state of Ireland, as it appeared to me, and the inference of my paper was, that circumstances in Ireland were favourable to a French invasion. I made no copy.

On Wednesday morning, the day I had fixed to dine with the gentleman and his friend, I found myself called upon to go down to Drogheda immediately, to arrange matters preparatory to the trial of MM. Bird and Hamill, &c. I therefore wrote, and sent an apology, stating the fact. I then went, as usual, to call on Mr. A. —, and showed him the paper. Shortly after, the gentleman and his friend came in. After a short general conversation of regret at the disappointment, &c., A. —, the gentleman, and I retired to a window at one end of the room, and his friend took up a book and retired to the other end. The conversation between us was carried on in a very low voice, so that he could not possibly hear us. I then said I had seen the English paper, and had attempted a similar sketch as to Ireland, which I read. As I understand some copy of that paper has been found, I refer to that for the *general outline* only, as A. — assured me that several alterations had been made in it, some, I believe, softening, and others aggravating the matter contained. *When I had done, the gentleman asked me, " Would I intrust the paper to him ? "　I gave it without hesitation, but, immediately after, I saw I had been guilty of a gross indiscretion, to call it no worse, in delivering such a paper to a person whom I hardly knew, and without my knowing to what purposes he might apply it. I therefore, in about five minutes, demanded it back again ; he returned it immediately, having neither opened nor read it, nor any part of it.* I then gave it to A. —, and, I believe, the precise words I used, but certainly the purport of them, was, " that if he had a mind, he might make a copy, in which case I desired him to burn the one I gave him. The conversation then turned, as before, on the state of Ireland, the necessity of seeking aid from France, and her readiness and ability to afford it, if a proper person could be found who would go over, and lay the situation of things here before the *Comité de Salut public.* But I do not recollect that either A. —, the gentleman, or I came to the definite point of myself being that proper person. I went away, leaving the paper, as I said, in the hands of A. —, and set off directly for Drogheda.

On Saturday morning I received a letter from A. — (a circumstance which I had forgotten until my sitting down to write, and referring to dates for greater accuracy, revived it in my memory) expressing an earnest desire to see me immediately on indispensable business. In consequence I set off instantly, posted up to town, and called directly on A. —. He told me that the gentleman was in a great hurry to be off, and wanted to see me of all things. I could not, however, learn that any new matter had occurred, and therefore was a little vexed at being hurried up to town for nothing. I said, however, I could call on the gentleman the next morning (Sunday) at nine, which I was, however, determined not to do, and, in consequence, instead of calling on him, set off for Drogheda at six o'clock. On Thursday I returned to town, and received a rebuke from A. — for breaking my engagement. He then told me, to my unspeakable astonishment and vexation, that he had given two or three copies of the paper I had left with him to the gentleman, with several alterations, but that he had burned my copy, as I had desired him. Finding the thing done, and past recalling, I determined to find no fault, but to withdraw myself as soon as I could from a business wherein I saw such grievous indiscretion. I am not sure whether it was on that, or on the next morning, that the gentleman and his *friend* came in. But, after some time, the conversation was taken up on the usual topics, and for the first time, to my knowledge, the gentleman's friend made one. Before that he seemed to me to avoid it. I then took an opportunity, on the difficulty of a proper person being found to go to France being stated, and it being mentioned (*I cannot precisely recollect by whom of the party*) that no one was, in all respects, so fit as myself, to recapitulate pretty nearly what I had said in all the preceding conversations on the general state of the country ; and I then added, that, with regard to my going to France, I was a man of no fortune, that my sole dependence was on a profession ; that I had a wife and three children, whom I dearly loved, solely depending on me for support ; that I could not go and leave them totally unprovided for, and trusting to the mercy of Providence for existence ; and that, consequently, with regard to me, the going to France was a thing totally impossible. They all agreed that what I said was reasonable, but there *was no offer of money or pecuniary assistance of any kind held out to induce me to change my determination*—a circumstance which I mention merely because I understand it is believed that some such was made.

The gentleman before mentioned was about to point out certain circumstances, which would facilitate such an expedition, if a person could be found, but I stopped him, adding that, as I could make no use of the information, I did not desire to become the depositary of secrets useless to me, and which might be dangerous to him. I think it was at this conversation, the last I was at, previous to the gentleman's being arrested, that some one, I cannot at all ascertain whom, mentioned a letter being put into the post office, containing the papers before mentioned, and directed to some person at some neutral port, but I am utterly ignorant how, or when, or to whom the letter was addressed, or what were its contents, other than as I have now stated ; and the reason of my not knowing is, that I studiously avoided burthening my mind with secrets which I might afterwards be forced to betray, or submit to very severe inconveniences.

[Jackson was arrested in April. We have already seen that, on his arrest, Hamilton Rowan (who had also been in communication with him) escaped from prison, and fled to France.[1] But Tone held his ground, anxious to await the development of events.—ED.]

At the time of Mr. Jackson's arrest, and Mr. Rowan's escape, and Dr. Reynolds's emigration, my situation was a very critical one. I felt the necessity of taking immediate and decided measures to extricate myself. I therefore went to a gentleman, high in confidence with the then administration, and told him at once fairly every step I had taken. I told him, also, that I knew how far I was in danger ; that my life was safe, unless it were

[1] [*Ante*, p. 57.]

unfairly practised against, which I did not at all apprehend, but that it was certainly in the power of the Government, if they pleased, to ruin me as effectually as they possibly could by my death ; that on two points I had made up my mind. The first was that I would not fly ; the other, that I would never open my lips, as a witness, either against Mr. Rowan, to whom I felt myself bound by the strongest ties of esteem and regard ; or against Mr. Jackson, who, in whatever conversations he had held in my presence, must have supposed he was speaking to a man who would not betray him ; that I had no claim whatsoever on the Government, nor should I murmur at any course they might please to adopt. What I had done I had done, and if necessary I must pay the penalty ; but, as my ruin might not be an object to them, I was ready, if I were allowed, and could at all accomplish it, to go to America. In the meantime here I was, ready to submit to my fate, whatever that might be, but inflexibly determined on the two points which I have mentioned above, and from which I would sacrifice my life a thousand times rather than recede. The gentleman to whom I addressed myself, after a short time, assured me that I should not be attacked as a principal, nor summoned as a witness ; which assurance he repeated to me afterwards on another occasion, and it has been very faithfully kept.

[After twelve months' imprisonment Jackson was put on his trial for high treason. He was defended by Curran. The only witness for the Crown was Cockayne. Jackson was found guilty. On April 30, 1795, he was brought up for sentence. On entering the dock he looked pale and worn. Asked if he had anything to say why sentence should not be passed upon him, he pointed to his counsel. A technical objection was raised, but while the argument was proceeding the prisoner fell forward against the bar. The attendants gathered around him. He was dead. That morning he had taken a dose of arsenic in his tea at breakfast. "We have deceived the Senate," he is reported to have whispered to one of his counsel on entering the dock.

Indiscreet and even reckless, a worse ambassador than Jackson could not have been employed on a revolutionary mission. But, at least, he bore himself honourably to the end, keeping faith with his friends, and seeking to involve no man in his fall.

Ten days after Jackson's death, and about six weeks after the recall of Lord Fitzwilliam [1] had proved the hopelessness of constitutional agitation, arrangements were completed for reorganising the United Irish Society on a rebellious basis.[2] A month later

---

[1] [Lord Fitzwilliam had been sent to emancipate the Catholics, but was recalled, leaving the work undone. "I was decidedly of opinion," said Lord Fitzwilliam, "that not only 'sound' policy, but justice required, on the part of Great Britain, that the work which was left imperfect in 1793 ought to be completed, and the Catholics relieved from every remaining disqualification. In this opinion the Duke of Portland uniformly concurred with me ; and when this question came under discussion previous to my departure for Ireland, I found the Cabinet, with Mr. Pitt at their head, strongly impressed with the same conviction. Had I found it otherwise I never would have undertaken the Government."—ED.]

[2] [" In 1794 the violence of the language, and the publicity with which the daring proceedings of the United Irishmen were carried on, brought the vengeance of Government on their society. On the 4th of May their ordinary place of meeting, the Tailors' Hall in Back Lane, was attacked by the police, their meeting dispersed, and their papers seized. The leaders had been successively prosecuted and imprisoned ; many of the timid and more prudent part of the members seceded from the society ; the more determined and indignant, and especially the republican portion of the body, remained, and in 1795 gave a new character to the association, still called the ' Society of United Irishmen.' The original test of the society was changed into an oath of secrecy and fidelity ; its original objects—reform and emancipation— were now merged in aims amounting to revolution, and the establishment of a Republican Government. These designs, however, were not ostensibly set forth, for a great number of the members, and even of the leaders, were not prepared to travel beyond the Hounslow of reformation. The proceedings of the society, however, ceased to be of a public nature ; the wording of its declaration was so altered as to embrace the views both of reformers and republicans, and the original explanation of its grand aim and end—*the equal representation of the people in Parliament*—was now changed into the phrase, ' a full representation of all the people of Ireland' ; thus adding the word ' all ' and omitting the word ' Parliament.' The civil organisation of the society was likewise modified ; the arrangement was perfected of committees, called baronial, county, and provincial. The inferior societies originally were composed of thirty-six members ; in the new organisation each association was limited to twelve, including a secretary and treasurer. The secretaries of five of these societies formed a lower baronial committee, and had the immediate direction of the five societies from which they had been taken. From each lower baronial committee one member was delegated to an upper baronial committee, which had the superintendence and direction of all the

Tone left Ireland bent on new schemes for advancing the cause of national independence.

In the following chapters he tells the story of his fortunes in other lands with increasing interest and animation.—ED.]

lower baronial ones in the several counties. In each of the four provinces there was a subordinate directory, composed of two or three members of the society delegated to a provincial committee, which had the general superintendence of the several committees of that province. In the capital the executive directory was composed of five persons, balloted for and elected by the provincial directories. The knowledge of the persons elected for the executive directory was confined to the secretaries of the provincial committees, and not reported to the electors ; and the executive directory, thus composed, exercised the supreme and uncontrolled command of the whole body of the Union. The orders of the executive were communicated to one member only of each provincial committee, and so on in succession to the secretary of each upper and lower baronial committee of the subordinate societies, by whom they eventually were given to the general body of the society. . . . The new organisation of the Society of United Irishmen was completed on the 10th of May, 1795. Separation and a Republican Government became the fixed objects of its principal leaders, but not the avowed ones till a little later, when, at the conclusion of every meeting, the chairman was obliged to inform the members of each society, 'they had undertaken no light matter,' and he was directed to ask every delegate present what were his views, and his understanding of those of his society, and each individual was expected to reply, ' A Republican Government and a separation from England'" (Madden, *United Irishmen*, vol. i. pp. 143, 145, and 153).

The test of the reorganised society ran : " I, A. B., do voluntarily declare that I will persevere in endeavouring to form a brotherhood of affection among Irishmen of every religious persuasion, and that I will also persevere in my endeavours to obtain an equal, full, and adequate representation of all the people of Ireland. I do further declare that neither hopes, fears, rewards, nor punishments shall ever induce me, directly or indirectly, to inform on, or give evidence, directly or indirectly, against any member or members of this or similar societies for any act or expression of theirs, done or made collectively or individually, in or out of this society, in pursuance of the spirit of this obligation " (Madden, vol. ii. p. 312). After 1794 a candidate for admission "was sworn either by individuals or in the presence of several members in a separate room from that in which the meeting was held " (Madden, vol. ii. p. 372). " The military organisation was engrafted on the civil, and originated in Ulster about the latter end of 1796, and in Leinster at the beginning of 1797 " (Madden, vol. i. p. 168).—ED.]

CHAPTER XIII.

TONE LEAVES IRELAND.[1]

I HASTEN to the period when, in consequence of the conviction
of William Jackson, for high treason, I was obliged to quit my
country, and go into exile in America. A short time before
my departure, my friend Russell being in town, he and I walked
out together, to Rathfarnham, to see Emmet, who has a charming villa there. He showed us a little study, of an elliptical
form, which he was building at the bottom of the lawn, and
which he said he would consecrate to our meetings, if ever
we lived to see our country emancipated. I begged of him,
if he intended Russell should be of the party, in addition to
the books and maps it would naturally contain, to fit up a
small cellaret, which should contain a few dozens of his best
old claret. He showed me that he had not omitted that circumstance, which he acknowledged to be essential, and we both rallied
Russell with considerable success. I mention this trifling anecdote
because I love the men, and because it seems now at least possible
that we may yet meet again in Emmet's study. As we walked
together into town I opened my plan to them both. I told them
that I considered my compromise with Government to extend no
further than the banks of the Delaware, and that the moment I
landed I was free to follow any plan which might suggest itself to
me, for the emancipation of my country; that, undoubtedly. I
was guilty of a great offence against the existing Government;
that, in consequence, I was going into exile; and that I considered
that exile as a full expiation for the offence, and consequently
felt myself at liberty, having made that sacrifice, to begin again on

---

[1] [This chapter was written at Rennes, September, 1796.—ED.]

a fresh score. They both agreed with me in those principles, and I then proceeded to tell them that my intention was, immediately on my arrival in Philadelphia, to wait on the French Minister, to detail to him, fully, the situation of affairs in Ireland, to endeavour to obtain a recommendation to the French Government, and, if I succeeded so far, to leave my family in America, and to set off instantly for Paris, and apply, in the name of my country, for the assistance of France, to enable us to assert our independence. It is unnecessary, I believe, to say that this plan met with the warmest approbation and support from both Russell and Emmet ; we shook hands, and, having repeated our professions of unalterable regard and esteem for each other, we parted ; and this was the last interview which I was so happy as to have with those two invaluable friends together. I remember it was in a little triangular field that this conversation took place ; and Emmet remarked to us that it was in one exactly like it in Switzerland, where William Tell and his associates planned the downfall of the tyranny of Austria. The next day Russell returned to Belfast.

As I was determined not to appear to leave Ireland clandestinely, whatever might be the hazard, I took care, on the day of Jackson's trial, to walk up and down in the most public streets in Dublin, and to go, contrary to my usual custom, into several of the most frequented coffee houses, and to my bookseller's, which was still more frequented. In this last place I was seen by Lord Mountjoy, who gave himself the pains to call on the Attorney General [1] the next day, and inform him that I was to be found, for that he had seen me in *Archer's* the day before. The Attorney General gave him, however, no thanks for his pains, and so the affair ended ; my obligation, however, to his lordship is not the less for his good intentions. Having made this sacrifice to appearances, I set, with all diligence, to prepare for my departure ; I sold off all my little property of every kind, reserving only my books, of which I had a very good selection of about six hundred volumes, and I determined to take leave of nobody. I also resolved not to call on any of my friends, not even Knox or

[1] [Wolfe, afterwards Lord Kilwarden.—Ed.]

Emmet, for, as I knew the part I had taken in Jackson's affair had raised a violent outcry against me, with a very numerous and powerful party, I resolved not to implicate any of those I regarded in the difficulties of my situation. Satisfied as I was of the rectitude of my own conduct, and of the purity of my motives, I believe I should have had fortitude to bear the desertion of my best friends; but, to their honour be it spoken, I was not put to so severe a trial. I did not lose the countenance and support of any one man whom I esteemed; and I believe that I secured the continuance of their regard by the firmness I had shown all along through this most arduous and painful trial; and, especially, by my repeated declarations that I was ready to sacrifice my life, if necessary, but that I would never degrade myself by giving testimony against a man who had spoken to me in the confidence that I would not betray him. I have said that after Jackson's death I visited nobody; but all my friends made it, I believe, a point to call on me; so that for the short time I remained in Dublin after, we were never an hour alone. My friends McCormick and Keogh, who had both interested themselves extremely, all along, on my behalf, and had been principally instrumental in passing the vote for granting me the sum of £300, in addition to the arrears due me by the Catholics, were, of course, amongst the foremost. It was hardly necessary, to men of their foresight, and who knew me perfectly, to mention my plans; however, for greater certainty, I consulted them both, and I received, as I expected, their most cordial approbation, and they both laid the most positive injunctions upon me to leave nothing unattempted on my part to force my way to France, and lay our situation before the Government there, observing, at the same time that if I succeeded, there was nothing in the power of my country to bestow to which I might not fairly pretend. It has often astonished me, and them, also, that the Government, knowing there was a French Minister at Philadelphia, ever suffered me to go thither, at least without exacting some positive assurance on my part that I should hold no communication with him, direct or indirect; so it was, however, that, either despising my efforts, or looking on themselves as too firmly established to dread anything from France, they suffered me to depart, without demanding any satisfaction whatsoever on that topic—a circumstance of which I was most sincerely glad : for had I been obliged to give my parole, I should have been exceedingly distracted between opposite duties.   Luckily, however, I was spared the difficulty ; for they suffered me to depart without any stipulation whatsoever. Perhaps it would have been better for them if they had adhered to their first proposal of sending me out to India ; but as to that, the event will determine.

Having paid all my debts, and settled with everybody, I set off from Dublin for Belfast on the 20th May, 1795, with my wife, sister, and three children, leaving, as may well be supposed, my father and mother in a very sincere affliction. My whole property consisted in our clothes, my books, and about £700 in money and bills on Philadelphia. We kept our spirits admirably. The great attention manifested to us, the conviction that we were suffering in the best of causes, the hurry attending so great a change, and, perhaps, a little vanity in showing ourselves superior to fortune, supported us under what was certainly a trial of the severest kind. But if our friends in Dublin were kind and affectionate, those in Belfast, if possible, were still more so. During near a month that we remained there, we were every day engaged by one or other ; even those who scarcely knew me were eager to entertain us ; parties and excursions were planned for our amusements ; and certainly the whole of our deportment and reception at Belfast very little resembled those of a man who escaped with his life only by miracle, and who was driven into exile to avoid a more disgraceful fate. I remember, particularly, two days that we passed on the Cave hill. On the first, Russell, Neilson, Simms, McCracken, and one or two more of us, on the summit of M'Art's fort, took a solemn obligation—which, I think I may say I have, on my part, endeavoured to fulfil—never to desist in our efforts until we had subverted the authority of England over our country, and asserted our independence. Another day we had the tent of the first regiment pitched in the Deer Park, and a company of thirty of us, including the family of the Simms, Neilsons, McCrackens, and my own, dined and spent the day together deliciously. But the most agreeable day we passed during our stay, and one of the most agreeable of our lives, was in an excursion we made with the Simmses, Neilson, and Russell, to Ram's Island, a beautiful and romantic spot in Loch Neagh. Nothing can be imagined more delightful, and we agreed, in whatever quarter we might find ourselves, respectively, to commemorate the anniversary of that day, the 11th of June. At length the hour of our departure arrived. On the 13th of June we embarked on board the "Cincinnatus" of Wilmington, Capt. James Robinson, and I flatter myself we carried with us the regret of all who knew us. Even some of my former friends, who had long since deserted me, returned on this reverse of my fortune, struck, I believe, with the steadiness with which we all looked it into the face. Our friends at Belfast loaded us with presents on our departure, and filled our little cabin with sea stores, fresh provisions, sweetmeats, and everything they could devise for the comfort of my wife and children. Never, whilst I live, will I forget the affectionate kindness of their behaviour. Before my departure I explained to Simms, Neilson, and C. G. Teeling my intentions with regard to my conduct in America, and I had the satisfaction to find it met, in all respects, with their perfect approbation ; and I now looked upon myself as competent to speak fully and with confidence for the Catholics, for the Dissenters, and for the Defenders of Ireland.

We were now at sea, and at leisure to examine our situation. I had hired a state room, which was about eight feet by six, in which we had fitted up three berths ; my wife and our youngest little boy occupied one, my sister and my little girl the second, and our eldest boy and myself the third. It was at first grievously inconvenient, but necessity and custom by degrees reconciled us to our situation ; our greatest suffering was want of good water under which we laboured the whole passage, and which we found it impossible to replace by wine, porter, or spirits, of which we had abundance. The captain was tolerably civil, the vessel was stout, and we had good weather almost the whole of our voyage. But we were 300 passengers on board of a ship of 230 tons, and of

course crowded to a degree not to be conceived by those who have
not been on board a passenger ship. The slaves who are carried
from the coast of Africa have much more room allowed them than
the miserable emigrants who pass from Ireland to America; for
the avarice of the captains in that trade is such, that they think
they never can load their vessels sufficiently, and they trouble their
heads in general no more about the accommodation and stowage
of their passengers than of any other lumber aboard. I laboured,
and with some success, to introduce something like a police, and a
certain degree, though a very imperfect one, of cleanliness among
them. Certainly the air of the sea must be wonderfully wholesome; for, if the same number of wretches of us had been shut
up in the same space ashore, with so much inconvenience of every
kind about us, two-thirds of us would have died in the time of our
voyage. As it was, in spite of everything, we were tolerably
healthy; we lost but one passenger, a woman; we had some sick
aboard, and the friendship of James McDonnell, of Belfast, having
supplied me with a small medicine chest and written directions, I
took on myself the office of physician. I prescribed and administered accordingly, and I had the satisfaction to land all my
patients safe and sound. As we distributed liberally the surplus
of our sea stores, of which we had a great abundance, and especially
as we gave, from time to time, wine and porter to the sick and
aged, we soon became very popular aboard, and I am sure there
was no sacrifice to our ease or convenience, in the power of our
poor fellow-passengers to make, that we might not have commanded. Thirty days of our voyage had now passed over without any event, save the ordinary ones of seeing now a shoal of
porpoises, now a shark, now a set of dolphins, the peacocks of the
sea, playing about, and once or twice a whale. We had, indeed,
been brought to, when about a week at sea, by the *William Pitt*,
Indiaman, which was returning to Europe with about twenty
other ships, under convoy of four or five men-of-war; but on
examining our papers they suffered us to proceed. At length,
about the 20th of July, some time after we had cleared the banks
of Newfoundland, we were stopped by three British frigates, the

Thetis, Captain Lord Cochrane, the *Hussar*, Captain Rose, and the *Esperance*, Captain Wood, who boarded us, and after treating us with the greatest insolence, both officers and sailors, they pressed every one of our hands, save one, and near fifty of my unfortunate fellow-passengers, who were most of them flying to America to avoid the tyranny of a bad government at home, and who thus most unexpectedly fell under the severest tyranny, one of them at least, which exists. As I was in a jacket and trousers, one of the lieutenants ordered me into the boat, as a fit man to serve the king, and it was only the screams of my wife and sister which induced him to desist. It would have been a pretty termination to my adventures if I had been pressed and sent on board a man-of-war. The insolence of these tyrants, as well to myself as to my poor fellow-passengers, in whose fate a fellowship in misfortune had interested me, I have not since forgotten, and I never will. At length, after detaining us two days, during which they rummaged us at least twenty times, they suffered us to proceed.

On the 30th of July we made Cape Henlopen; the 31st we ran up the Delaware, and the 1st of August we landed safe at Wilmington, not one of us providentially having been for an hour indisposed on the passage, nor even sea-sick. Those only who have had their wives, their children, and all, in short, that is dear to them, floating for seven or eight weeks at the mercy of the winds and waves, can conceive the transport I felt at seeing my wife and our darling babies ashore once again in health and in safety. We set up at the principal tavern, kept by an Irishman, one Captain O'Byrne O'Flynn (I think), for all the taverns in America are kept by majors and captains, either of militia or continentals, and in a few days we had entirely recruited our strength and spirits, and totally forgotten the fatigues of the voyage.

During our stay in Wilmington we formed an acquaintance, which was of some service and a great deal of pleasure to us, with a General Humpton, an old continental officer. He was an Englishman, born in Yorkshire, and had been a major in the 25th regiment, but, on the breaking out of the American War, he resigned his commission, and offered his services to Congress, who immediately gave him a regiment, from which he rose by degrees to his present rank. He was a beautiful, hale, stout old man, of near seventy, perfectly the soldier and the gentleman, and he took a great liking to us, as we did to him on our part. On our removal to Philadelphia he found us a lodging with one of his acquaintance, and rendered all the little services and attentions that our situation as strangers required, which indeed he continued without remission during the whole of my stay in America, and I doubt not equally since my departure. I have a sincere and grateful sense of the kindness of this worthy veteran.

Immediately on my arrival in Philadelphia, which was about the 7th or 8th of August, I found out my old friend and brother exile, Dr. Reynolds, who seemed, to my very great satisfaction, very comfortably settled. From him I learned that Hamilton Rowan had arrived about six weeks before me from France, and that same evening we all three met. It was a singular *rencontre*, and our several escapes from an ignominious death seemed little short of a miracle. We communicated respectively our several adventures since our last interview, which took place in the gaol of Newgate in Dublin, fourteen months before. In Reynolds' adventures there was nothing very extraordinary. Rowan had been seized and thrown into prison immediately on his landing near Brest, from whence he was rescued by the interference of a young man named Sullivan, an Irishman, in the service of the Republic, and sent on to Paris to the Committee of Public Safety, by Prieur de la Marne, the Deputy on Mission. On his arrival he was seized with a most dangerous fever, from which he narrowly escaped with his life ; when he recovered, as well as during his illness, he was maintained by the French Government ; he gave in some memorials on the state of Ireland, and began, from the reception he met with, to conceive some hopes of success, but immediately after came on the famous 9th Thermidor the downfall of Robespierre, and the dissolution of the Committee of Public Safety. The total change which this produced in the politics of France, and the attention of every man being occupied by his own immediate personal safety, were the cause that Rowan and his plans were forgotten in the confusion. After remaining, therefore, several months, and seeing no likelihood of bringing matters to any favourable issue, he yielded to the solicitude of his family and friends, and embarked at Havre for New York, where he arrived about the middle of June, 1795, after a tedious passage of eleven weeks.

It is unnecessary to detail again my adventures, which I related to them at full length, as well as everything relating to the state of politics in Ireland, about which, it may be well supposed, their curiosity and anxiety were extreme. I then proceeded to tell them my designs, and that I intended waiting the next day on the French Minister with such credentials as I had brought with me, which were the two votes of thanks of the Catholics, and my certificate of admission into the Belfast Volunteers, engrossed on vellum, and signed by the chairman and secretaries ; and I added, that I would refer to them both for my credibility in case the Minister had any doubts. Rowan offered to come with me and introduce me to the Minister, Citizen Adet, whom he had known in Paris ; but I observed to him that as there were English agents without number in Philadelphia he was most probably watched, and consequently his being seen to go with me to Adet might materially prejudice his interests in Ireland. I therefore declined his offer, but I requested of him a letter of introduction, which he gave me accordingly, and the next day I waited on the Minister, who received me very politely. He spoke English very imperfectly, and I French a great deal worse ; however, we made a shift to understand one another ; he read my certificates and Rowan's letter, and he begged me to throw on paper, in the form of a memorial, all I had to communicate on the subject of Ireland. This I accordingly did in the course of two or three days, though with great difficulty, on account of the burning heat of the climate, so different from what I had been used to, the thermometer varying between ninety and ninety-seven. At length, however, I finished my memorial, such as it was, and brought it to Adet, and I offered him, at the same time, if he thought it would forward the business, to embark in the first vessel which sailed for France ; but the Minister, for some reason, seemed not much to desire this, and he eluded my offer by reminding me of the great risk I ran, as the British stopped and carried into their ports indiscriminately all American vessels bound for France ; he assured me, however, I might rely on my memorial being transmitted to the French Government, and backed with his strongest recommendations ; and he also promised to write particularly to procure the enlargement of my brother Matthew, who was then in prison at Guise : all which I have since found he faithfully performed.

I had now discharged my conscience as to my duty to my country ; and it was with the sincerest and deepest contristation of mind that I saw this, my last effort, likely to be of so little effect. It was barely possible, but I did not much expect that the French Government might take notice of my memorial, and if they did not there was an end of all my hopes. I now began to endeavour to bend my mind to my situation, but to no purpose. I moved my family first to Westchester and then to Downingstown, both in the State of Pennsylvania, about thirty miles from Philadelphia, and I began to look about for a small plantation, such as might suit the shattered state of my finances, on which the enormous expense of living in Philadelphia, three times as dear as at Paris, or even London, was beginning to make a sensible inroad. While they remained there, in the neighbourhood of our friend General Humpton, whose kindness and attention continued unabated, I made divers excursions on foot and in the stage-waggons in quest of a farm. The situation of Princeton, in New Jersey, struck me, for a variety of reasons, and I determined, if possible, to settle in that neighbourhood. I accordingly agreed with a Dutch farmer for a plantation of one hundred acres, with a small wooden house, which would have suited me well enough, for which I was to pay £750 of that currency ; but the fellow was too covetous, and after all was, I thought, finished, he retracted, and wanted to screw more out of me, on which I broke off the treaty in a rage, and he began to repent, but I was obstinate. At length I agreed with a Captain Leonard for a plantation of 180 acres, beautifully situated within two miles of Princeton, and half of it under timber. I was to pay £1,180 currency, and I believe it was worth the money. I moved, in consequence, my family to Princeton, where I hired a small house for the winter, which I furnished frugally and decently. I fitted up my study, and began to think my lot was cast to be an American farmer.

In this frame of mind I continued for some time, waiting for the lawyer who was employed to draw the deeds, and expecting next spring to remove to my purchase and to begin farming at last, when one day I was roused from my lethargy by the receipt of letters from Keogh, Russell, and the two Simmses, wherein, after professions of the warmest and sincerest regard, they proceeded to acquaint me that the state of the public mind in Ireland was advancing to republicanism faster than even I could believe; and they pressed me, in the strongest manner, to fulfil the engagement I had made with them at my departure, and to move heaven and earth to force my way to the French Government in order to supplicate their assistance. Wm. Simms, at the end of a most friendly and affection-ate letter, desired me to draw upon him for £200 sterling, and that my bill should be punctually paid, an offer, at the liberality of which, well as I knew the man, I confess I was surprised. I immediately handed the letters to my wife and sister, and desired their opinion, which I foresaw would be that I should immediately, if possible, set out for France. My wife, especially, whose courage and whose zeal for my honour and interests were not in the least abated by all her past sufferings, supplicated me to let no consideration of her or our children stand for a moment in the way of my engagements to our friends and my duty to my country, adding, that she would answer for our family during my absence, and that the same Providence which had so often, as it were, miraculously preserved us, would, she was confident, not desert us now. My sister joined her in those in-treaties, and it may well be supposed I required no great supplica-tion to induce me to make one more attempt in a cause to which I had been so long devoted. I set off, accordingly, the next morning (it being this time about the end of November) for Philadelphia, and went, immediately on my arrival, to Adet, to whom I showed the letters I had just received, and I referred him to Rowan, who was then in town, for the character of the writers. I had the satisfac-tion, contrary to my expectations. to find Adet as willing to forward and assist my design now, as he seemed, to me at least, lukewarm when I saw him before, in August. He told me immediately that he would give me letters to the French Government, recommending me in the strongest manner, and also money to bear my expenses, if necessary. I thanked him most sincerely for the letters, but I declined accepting any pecuniary assistance. Having thus far surmounted my difficulties, I wrote for my brother Arthur, who was at Princeton, to come to me immediately, and I fitted him out with all expedition for sea. Having entrusted him with my determination of sailing for France in the first vessel, I ordered him to communicate this immediately on his arrival in Ireland to Neilson, Simms, and Russell in Belfast, and to Keogh and McCormick only in Dublin. To every one else, including especially my father and mother, I desired him to say that I had purchased and was settled upon my farm, near Princeton. Having fully instructed him, I put him on board the *Susanna*, Captain Baird, bound for Belfast, and on the 10th of December, 1795, he sailed from Philadelphia, and I presume he arrived safe, but as yet I have had no opportunity of hearing of him. Having despatched him, I settled all my affairs as speedily as possible. I drew on Simms for £200, agreeable to his letter, £150 sterling of which I devoted to my voyage; my friend Reynolds procured me Louis d'ors at the bank for £100 sterling worth of silver. I converted the remainder of my little property into bank stock, and having signed a general power of attorney to my wife, I waited finally on Adet, who gave me a letter in cypher directed to the *Comité de Salut public*, the only credential which I intended to bring with me to France. I spent one day in Philadelphia with Reynolds, Rowan, and my old friend and fellow-sufferer, James Napper Tandy, who, after a long concealment and many adventures, was recently arrived from Hamburgh, and, at length, on the 13th December, at night, I arrived at Princeton, whither Rowan accompanied me, bringing with me a few presents for my wife, sister, and our dear little babies. That night we supped together in high spirits, and Rowan retiring immediately after, my wife, sister, and I sat together till very late, engaged in that kind of animated and enthusiastic conversation which our characters and the

nature of the enterprise I was embarked in may be supposed to give
rise to. The courage and firmness of the women supported me, and
them too, beyond my expectations; we had neither tears nor lamen-
tations, but, on the contrary, the most ardent hope and the most
steady resolution. At length, at four the next morning, I embraced them both for the last time, and we parted with a steadiness
which astonished me. On the 16th December I arrived in New
York, and took my passage on board the ship *Jersey*, Capt. George
Barons.   I remained in New York for ten days, during which time
I wrote continually to my family, and a day or two before my departure I received a letter from my wife informing me that she was
with child, a circumstance which she had concealed so far, I am
sure, lest it might have had some influence on my determination.
On the 1st January, 1796, I sailed from Sandy Hook with nine
fellow-passengers, all French, bound for Havre de Grace. Our
voyage lasted exactly one month, during the most part of which
we had heavy blowing weather ; five times we had such gales of
wind as obliged us to lie under a close-reefed mizen stay-sail ; however, our ship was stout. We had plenty of provisions, wine,
brandy, and especially, what I thought more of, remembering my
last voyage, excellent water, so that I had no reason to complain of
my passage. We did not meet a single vessel of force, either
French or English ; we passed three or four Americans bound
mostly, like ourselves, to France. On the 27th we were in sound-
ings at 85 fathoms ; on the 28th we made the Lizard, and, at length,
on the 1st of February, we landed in safety at Havre de Grace,
having met with not the smallest accident during our voyage. My
adventures, from this date, are fully detailed in the Diary which I
have kept regularly since my arrival in France.

CHAPTER XIV.

ARRIVES IN FRANCE.

February 2, 1796. I landed at Havre de Grace yesterday, after a rough winter passage from New York of thirty-one days. The town ugly and dirty, with several good houses in alleys, where it is impossible to see them. Lodged at the Hôtel de Paix, formerly the Hotel of the Intendant, but reduced to its present state by the Revolution. " My landlord is civil, but dear as the devil." Slept in a superb crimson damask bed; great luxury, after being a month without having my clothes off.

February 3rd. Rose early ; difficult to get breakfast ; get it at last ; excellent coffee, and very coarse brown bread, but, as it happens, I like brown bread. Walked out to see the lions ; none to see. Mass celebrating in the church ; many people present, especially women ; went into divers coffee-houses; plenty of coffee, but no papers. *No bread* in two of the coffee-houses ; but pastry ; singular enough ! Dinner ; and here, as matter of curiosity, follows our bill of fare, which proves clearly that France is in a starving situation. An excellent soup ; a dish of fish, fresh from the harbour ; a fore-quarter of delicate small mutton, like the Welsh ; a superb turkey, and a pair of ducks roasted ; pastry, cheese, and fruit after dinner, with wine *ad libitum*, but still the *pain bis;* provoked with the Frenchmen grumbling at the bread ; made a saying : *Vive le pain bis et la liberté !* I forgot the vegetables, which were excellent ; very glad to see such unequivocal proofs of famine. Went to the Comédie in the evening ; a neat theatre, and a very tolerable company ; twenty performers in the orchestra ; house full ; several officers, very fine-looking fellows ; the audience just as gay as if there was no such thing as war and brown bread in the world.　Supper just like our dinner, with wine, &c.　N.B.—*Finances.*　The louis worth 5,000 livres, or about two hundred times its value in assignats ; the six-franc-piece in proportion.　My bill *per diem*, for such entertainment as above-mentioned, is six francs (five shillings), and my crimson damask bed, 20 sols, or tenpence ; coffee in the morning, 12 sols, or sixpence ; so that I am starving in the manner I have described for the enormous sum of 6s. 4d. a day ; sad ! sad !　Paid for my seat at the theatre, in the box next to that of the Municipalité, 80 livres in assignats, or about fourpence sterling.　Be it remembered, I lodge at the principal hotel in Havre, and I doubt not but I might retrench, perhaps one-half, by changing my situation ; but hang saving.

February 4th.　A swindler in the hotel ; wishes to take me in ; wants to travel with me to Paris ; says he is an American, and calls me Captain ; is sure he has seen me somewhere.　Tell him perhaps it was in Spain.　"*A close man, but warm ;*" it won't do.　He tries his wily arts on an old Frenchman, and, to my great surprise, tricks him of about one guinea.　The Frenchman finds it out, and is in a rage ; going to beat the *aventurier*, who is forced to refund. This is our first adventure.　My friend was no American, which I very soon found out : for "*there is no halting before cripples,*" as poor Richard says.

February 5th.　A new arrangement with my landlord ; I now pay 5s. a day for everything, including my crimson damask bed ; walk out ; every third man a soldier, or with something of the military costume about him.　In the evening the Comédie ; *Blaise and Babet*, and the *Rigueurs du Cloître*, a revolutionary piece ; applauses and honourable mention.　I can account for the favourable reception of the latter piece, but the former is as great a favourite, though the fable is as simple as possible.　Two lovers fall out about a nosegay and a ribbon, and, after squabbling through two acts, are reconciled at last, and marry.　The sentiments and the music are pretty and pastoral, but what puzzles me is to reconcile the impression which the piece, such as I have described it, seemed to make on the audience with the sanguinary and ferocious character attributed to the French.

February 6th. It is very singular, but I have had several occasions already to observe that there is more difficulty in passing silver than paper. I have seen money refused where assignats have been taken currently. This is a phenomenon I cannot understand, especially when the depreciation is considered. The republican silver is received with great suspicion. People have got it into their heads that it is adulterated, but, even so, surely it is worth, intrinsically, more than a bit of paper. So it is, however, that assignats are more current. The Comédie again. The Marseillaise Hymn sung every night, and the verse, " *Tremblez Tyrans*," always received with applause. The behaviour of the young men extremely decorous and proper, very unlike the riotous and drunken exhibitions I have been witness to in other countries. The women ugly, and some most grotesque head-dresses. Supper, as usual, excellent; the servants at the hotel remarkably civil, attentive, and humble, which I mention, because I have been so often tormented with blockheads arguing against liberty and equality as subversive of all subordination. I have nowhere met with more respectful attendance than here, nor better entertainment, and all for five shillings a day.

February 7th, Sunday. I was curious to observe how this day would be kept in France. I believe nobody worked; the shops were half open, half shut, as I have seen them on holidays in other countries; everybody walking the streets. A vessel from Boston was wrecked last night within twenty yards of the Basin, and an unfortunate French woman lost, with two little children. She had fled to America early in the Revolution, and was now returning to her husband on the restoration of tranquillity. God Almighty help him! She might have been saved alone, but preferred to perish with her infants : it is too horrible to think of. Oh, my babies, my babies, if your little bodies were sunk in the ocean, what should I do? But you are safe, thank God! Well, no more of that. Comédie again ; house quite full, being Sunday ; Mad. Rousselois principal singer ; just such another in person, age, manner, and voice, as the late Mrs. Kennedy, but a much better actress.

February 8th. An arrangement for Paris at last. An American has a hired coach, a very good one, and we, viz., D'Aucourt, my fellow-traveller, and I, are to pay one louis apiece for our seats, and bear two-thirds of the travelling expenses, post-horses, &c. This is very comfortable, cheaper, and much better than any public carriage. We are to set off early on Wednesday; I have now waited eight days on my companion, who, by the by, does not improve on acquaintance; he is as proud as Lucifer, and as mean as avarice can make him. I foresee that we shall not live long together at Paris, but at first he will be absolutely necessary to me. "*Damn it, and sink it, and rot it for me,*" that I cannot speak French. "*Rues they call them here.*" "*Oh that I had given that time to the tongues that I have spent in fencing and bear-baiting.*" Well, "*'tis but in vain,*" &c. With God's blessing, my little boys shall speak French. Comédie in the evening, as usual.

February 9th. My lover, the swindler, has been too cunning for us; he has engaged the fourth place in the coach, so we shall have the pleasure of his company on to Paris. He certainly has some designs on our pockets, but I hope he will find himself defeated. Wrote to my family and to Dr. Reynolds of Philadelphia, and gave the letters to Captain Baron. Tired of Havre, which is dreadfully *monotonous*, and D'Aucourt's peevishness, proceeding partly from ill-health, makes him not the pleasantest company in the world. Got our passports; engaged post-horses, &c. I do not bear the separation from my family well, yet I certainly do not wish them at present in France. If I can make out my brother Matthew, I shall be better off. Poor P. P.! I shall never meet with such another agreeable companion in a post-chaise. Well, hang sorrow! But I am dreadfully low-spirited : "*Croker is a rhyme for joker.*" "*Poor Dick !*" Comédie as usual; sad trash this evening; a boy of fifteen in love and married; introduced to his spouse by his nurse; confined to his room by his papa, and let out in order to be married; much fitter to peg a top or play marbles; yet the audience did not seem to feel any incongruity, though, to heighten the absurdity, his lover was Madame Rousselois, a fat woman of forty. It was excessively ridiculous to see her and the "*Amoureux de quinze ans*" together, and to hear her singing "*Lindor a su me plaire.*" She was easily pleased. The dresses at the theatre of Havre are handsomer and better appointed than I have seen anywhere, except at London, which is wonderful, considering it is but a small seaport town, and more so when one reflects on the price of admission. I suspect the Government must assist them, or I am sure they could not live on the receipts; if so, it is an additional trait in the resemblance of character between the French and Athenians, which is most striking.

February 10*th.* Up at five o'clock ; a choice carriage lined with blue velvet; five horses; a French postillion, a most grotesque figure—cocked hat and jacket, two great wisps of straw tied on his thighs, and a pair of jack-boots, as big as two American churns. "*Their horses (chevauxes they call them) ben't quite so nimble as our'n.*" Set off for Paris. Huzza! The country flat and amazingly populous ; the houses of the peasantry scattered as thick as they can lie, about a mean between an English cottage and an Irish cabin, or hovel; but if the house be inferior, there is an appearance in the spot of ground about far beyond what I have seen in England. Every cottage stands in the middle of a parallelogram of perhaps an acre or two, which is planted with trees, and I suppose includes their potagerie, &c. ; the quantity of wood thus scattered over the face of the country is immense, and has a beautiful effect; every foot of ground seems to me under cultivation, so there will be no starving, please God, this year. France, D'Aucourt says, in a good year, grows one-third more than she consumes. No enclosures, but all the country open ; excepting that circumstance, not unlike Yorkshire, which I look upon as the finest part of England ; an orchard to every cottage, besides rows of apple trees, without intermission, by the roadside. Why might it not be so in *other* countries whose climate differs but very little from that of Normandy? *Think of this.* The country still flat as a bowling green, but as interesting as much wood and the most perfect cultivation can make it. Again and again delighted with the prospect of the abundant harvest which a few months will produce. No streams nor meadows, but all tilled ; roads excellent. Arrive at Rouen at two hours after nightfall ; a beautiful approach to the

town through a noble avenue of trees, I believe, "*for it was so dark,
Hal, thou couldst not see thy hand.*" Lodge at the Hôtel d'Égalité.

February 11th. Set off at ten o'clock. A hill immediately over
Rouen of immense height, and so steep that the road is cut in
traverses. When at the top, a most magnificent prospect to look
back over Normandy, with Rouen at your feet, and the Seine winding beautifully through the landscape. The face of the country
pretty much as yesterday, except that the cottages are not so much
detached, but rather collected in small hamlets; a mean appearance, and far inferior in all respects. The little plantations around
the cottages set them off and hide all defects; but here they are
grouped together and completely exposed; yet still they are far
beyond the cottages I have been used to see. Very few towns,
and those of a sombre appearance; the manufacturing towns of
England beyond all comparison superior. The beauty of France
is in the country. Pass two or three *châteaux*, which are very thinly
scattered; all shut up and deserted, their masters having been
either guillotined or being now on the right (viz., the wrong) bank
of the Rhine. In general they are in a bad taste; no improvements around them, as in England, but built close on the road, and
generally a dirty little hamlet annexed, the wretched habitation of
the slaves of the feudal system. Well! all those things are past
and gone, just as if they had never been. I can see the genius of
the French noblesse was not adapted to the country. In England,
I suppose the seats of the gentry, in the same kind of country,
would be as one hundred to one. Pass a beautiful valley, with a
stream, the first I have seen, winding through it, and mount a
second hill almost as high as that above Rouen. Table-land cultivated as before, that is to say, without one foot of ground wasted.
To my utter astonishment, a large flock of sheep! What, sheep
in France! I suppose they must have swam over from England.
Another flock—another: "*They scar mine eyeballs.*" I could wish
John Bull were here for one half hour, just to look at the fields of
wheat that I am passing. It is impossible to conceive higher
cultivation: I have seen nothing of a corn country like it in
England. The road this day but middling. Sleep at Magny.

February 12*th.* A most blistering bill for supper, &c. In great indignation, and the more so, because I could not scold in French. Passion is eloquent, but all my figures of speech were lost on the landlord. If this extortion resulted from any scarcity, I would submit in silence ; but it is downright villainy. Well, "*'Tis but in vain,*" literally. Set off in a very ill humour, but soon reconciled to my losses by the smiling appearance of the country. Still flat, and richly cultivated. Breakfast at Pontoise. The serenity of my temper, which I had just recovered, ruffled completely by a second bill. "*Landlords have flinty hearts ; no tears can move them.*" This comes of riding in fine carriages, with velvet linings! We are downright *Milords Anglais*, and they certainly make us pay for our titles. Several vineyards, the first I have met with. An uninterrupted succession of corn, vines, and orchards, as far as the eye can reach, rich and *riant* beyond description. I see now clearly that John Bull will be able to starve France. *St. Denys*—The building for washing the royal linen turned into an arsenal, and a palace into a barrack for the Gendarmerie : a church, with the inscription —"*Le peuple Français reconnait l'être Suprême, et l'immortalité de l'âme.*" *Groscaillou*—Several windmills turning, as if they were grinding corn, but, to be sure, they have none to grind : an artful fetch to deceive the worthy Mr. Bull, and make him believe there is still some bread in France. In sight of Paris at last. Huzza ! Huzza !

I have now travelled one hundred and fifty miles in France, and I do not think I have seen one hundred and fifty acres uncultivated, the very orchards are under grain. All the mills I have seen were at work, and all the *châteaux* shut up, without exception. *Paris*— Stop at the *Hôtel des Étrangers, Rue Vivienne*, a magnificent house, but, I foresee, as dear as the devil ; my apartment in the third story very handsomely furnished, &c., for fifty francs per month, and so in proportion for a shorter time ; much cheaper than the Adelphi and other hotels in London ; but I will not stay here for all that— I must get into private lodgings. At six o'clock, dinner with D'Aucourt at the *Restaurateur's* in the *Maison Égalité*, formerly the Palais Royal, which is within fifty yards of our hotel. The bill of fare printed, as large as a play bill, with the price of everything marked. I am ashamed to say so much on the subject of eating, but I have been so often bored with the famine in France, that it is, in some degree, necessary to dwell upon it. Our dinner was a soup, roast fowl, fried carp, salads of two kinds, a bottle of Burgundy, coffee after dinner, and a glass of liqueur, with excellent bread—(I forgot, we had cauliflowers and sauce)—and our bill for the whole, wine and all, was 1,500 livres, in assignats, which, at the present rate (the Louis being 6,500 livres), is exactly 4s. 7 $\frac{1}{10}$d. sterling. What would I have given to have had P. P. with me! Indeed we would have discussed another bottle of the Burgundy, or, by'r Lady, some two or three.—" *The rogue has given me medicines to make me love him. Yes! I have drank medicines.*" I wish to God our bill of fare was posted on the Royal Exchange, for John Bull's edification. I do not think he would dine much better for the money, even at the London Tavern, especially if he drank such Burgundy as we did. The saloon in which we dined was magnificent, illuminated with patent lamps, and looking-glasses of immense size; the company of a fashionable appearance, full as much as ever I have seen at the Bedford Coffee House ; in short, everything wore a complete appearance of opulence and luxury. Walked round the Palais Royal, but too dark to see anything. Ascend a shop kept by J. B. Louvet.[1] Coffee houses all full as they can hold, but did not go into one of them. D'Aucourt grumbling at the appearance of things not being half so brilliant as formerly : believe he is fibbing a little. Bed !

February 13*th.* Capt. Sisson, with whom we travelled up, called to breakfast. Settled our account of expenses. From Havre to Paris is 160 miles, or thereabouts. We lay two nights on the road. We were charged once or twice extravagantly. We were driven with four, five, and, during two stages, with six horses, and yet our expense for the whole was but sixty crowns, or £15 sterling, which was £5 apiece. In England, to travel the same distance, with four horses, would have cost us, at the very lowest, double the money. So much for the relative expense of the two countries, which I am

[1] [Celebrated author of *Faublas.*—Ed.]

fond of comparing, and I think I know England pretty well. Council of war with D'Aucourt. Agree to keep close for a day or two, until we get French clothes made, and then pay my first visit to Monroe (the American Ambassador), and deliver my letters. In the meantime to make inquiries. The *Directoire Exécutif* have presented General Jourdan with six horses, magnificently caparisoned, a sword, and a case of pistols. What a present for a Republican General! I observe they have given nothing to Pichegru. It looks odd that he should be passed over. Do they intend to fix the public attention on Jourdan? *Mind this.* I should be sorry if Pichegru were thrown into the shade. In the evening, at the *Grand Opéra, Théâtre des Arts, Iphigénie.* The theatre magnificent, and, I should judge, about one hundred performers in the orchestra. The dresses most beautiful, and a scrupulous attention to the costume in all the decorations, which I have never seen in London. The performers were completely Grecian statues animated, and I never saw so manifestly the superiority of the taste of the ancients in dress, especially the women. Iphigénie (*La citoyenne Cheron*) was dressed entirely in white, without the least ornament, and nothing can be imagined more truly elegant and picturesque. The acting admirable, but the singing very inferior to that of the Haymarket. The French cannot sing like the Italians. Agamemnon excellent. Clytemnestra still better. Achilles abominable, and more applauded than either of them. Sung in the old French style, which is most detestable, shaking and warbling on every note; vile! vile! vile! The others sung in a style sufficiently correct. The ballet, *L'Offrande à la Liberté*, most superb. In the centre of the stage was the statue of Liberty, with an altar blazing before her. She was surrounded by the characters in the opera, in their beautiful Grecian habits. The civic air, " *Veillons au salut de l'Empire*," was sung by a powerful bass, and received with transport by the audience. Whenever the word " *esclavage* " was uttered, it operated like an electric shock. The Marseillaise Hymn was next sung, and produced still greater enthusiasm. At the word, " *Aux armes citoyens!* " all the performers drew their swords, and the females turned to them as encouraging them. Before the last verse there was a short pause, the time of the music was changed to a very slow movement, and supported only by the flutes and oboes; a beautiful procession entered; first little children like cherubs, with baskets of flowers; these were followed by boys, a little more advanced, with white javelins (the *Hasta pura* of the ancients) in their hands. Then came two beautiful female figures, moving like the graces themselves, with torches blazing; these were followed by four negroes, characteristically dressed, and carrying two tripods between them, which they placed respectfully on each side of the altar; next came as many Americans, in the picturesque dress of Mexico, and these were followed by an immense crowd of other performers, variously habited, who ranged themselves on both sides of the stage. The little children then approached the altar with their baskets of flowers, which they laid before the goddess; the rest in their turn succeeded, and hung the altar and the base of the statue with garlands and wreaths of roses; the two females with the torches approached the tripods, and, just touching them with the fire, they kindled into a blaze. The whole then knelt down, and all of this was executed in cadence to the music, and with a grace beyond description. The first part of the last verse, " *Amour sacré de la patrie*," was then sung slowly and solemnly, and the words " *Liberté, Liberté, chérie*," with an emphasis which affected me most powerfully. All this was at once pathetic and sublime, beyond what I had ever seen, or could almost imagine; but it was followed by an incident which crowned the whole, and rendered it indeed a spectacle worthy of a free republic : At the words, ' *Aux armes, citoyens !*" the music changed again to a martial style, the performers sprung on their feet, and in an instant the stage was filled with National Guards, who rushed in with bayonets fixed, their sabres drawn, and their tricolour flag flying. It would be impossible to describe the effect of this. I never knew what enthusiasm was before, and what heightened it beyond all conception was, that the men I saw before me were not hirelings, acting a part ; they were what they seemed, French citizens flying to arms, to rescue their country from slavery. They were the men who had precipitated Cobourg into the Sambre, and driven Clairfait over the Rhine, and were, at this very moment, on the eve of again hurrying to the frontiers, to encounter fresh dangers and gain fresh glory. This was what made the spectacle interesting beyond all description. I would willingly sail again from New York to enjoy again what I felt at that moment. *Set the ballets of the Haymarket beside this!* This sublime spectacle concluded the ballet; but why must I give it so poor a name? It was followed by a ballet, which one might call so, but even this was totally different from what they used to be. The National Guards were introduced again, and instead of dancing, at least three-fourths of the exhibition were military evolutions, which, it should seem, are more now to the French taste than allemandes and minuets and *pas de deux.* *So best!* It is curious now to consider at what rate one may see all this. I paid for my seat in the boxes 150 livres, in assignats, which, at the present rate, is very nearly sixpence sterling. The highest price seats were but 200 livres, which is eightpence. I mention this principally to introduce a conjecture which struck me at Havre, but which seems much more probable here, that the Government supports the theatres privately. And in France it is excellent policy, where the people are so much addicted to spectacles, of which there are now about twenty in Paris, and all full every night. What would my dearest love have felt at the "*Offrande à la liberté*"?

February 14*th.* Dined at a tavern in a room covered with gilding and looking-glasses down to the floor. Superb beyond anything I had seen. It was the Hotel of the Chancellor to the Duke of Orleans. There went much misery of the people to the painting and ornamenting of that room, and now it is open to any one to dine for three shillings. "*Make aristocracy laugh at that.*" But Paris now yields so many thousand instances of a similar complexion that nobody minds them. Comédie, ballet (improperly so called), *Le chant du départ.* A battalion under arms, with their knapsacks at their backs, ready to march with their officers and a representative of the people (whom P. P. would call a tyrant) at their head. On one side of the stage a group of venerable figures, representing the parents of the warriors. On the other, a band of females, who, I can venture to say, were not selected for their ugliness, appeared as their wives and lovers, and a number of beautiful children were scattered over the stage. The representative began the song, which was answered by the soldiers ; the next verse was sung by the women, and I leave it to any man with a soul capable of feeling, what the effect of such a song from such beautiful beings must have been. The next was sung by the old men, and, at the end of it, the little boys and girls ran in amongst the soldiery, who caught them up in their arms and caressed them. Some of the little fellows pulled off the grenadiers' caps, and put them on their own heads, whilst others were strutting about with great sabres longer than themselves. At length the battalion was formed again and filed off, the representative and officers saluting the audience as they passed, whilst the women and children were placed on an eminence, and waved their hands to them as they passed along. Nothing could exceed the peals of applause when the ensign passed with the tricolour flag displayed. *Here was no fiction*, and that it was which gave it an interest, that drew the tears irresistibly into my eyes. N.B.—From all this it is evident that the French are a nation of cannibals, incapable of human feeling, and that John Bull will just begin at the banks of the Wahal, and never stop till he has driven them into the Mediterranean.

February 15*th*. Went to Monroe's, the Ambassador, and delivered in my passport and letters. Received very politely by Monroe, who inquired a great deal into the state of the public mind in America, which I answered as well as I could, and in a manner to satisfy him pretty well as to my own sentiments. I inquired of him where I was to deliver my despatches. He informed me, at the Minister for Foreign Affairs, and gave me his address. I then rose and told him that when he had read B——'s letter (which was in cypher), he would, I hope, find me excused in taking the liberty to call again. He answered, he would be happy at all times to see me, and, after he had inquired about Hamilton Rowan, how he liked America, &c. I took my leave, and returned to his office for my passport. The Secretary smoked me for an Irishman directly. *À la bonne heure.* Went at three o'clock to the Minister for Foreign Affairs, Rue du Bacq, 471. Delivered my passport, and inquired for some one who spoke English. Introduced immediately to the Chef de Bureau, Lamare, a man of an exceedingly plain appearance. I showed my letter, and told him I wished for an opportunity to deliver it into the Minister's hands. He asked me, "would it not do if he took charge of it?" I answered, he undoubtedly knew the official form best, but if it was not irregular, I should consider myself much obliged by being allowed to deliver it in person. He then brought me into a magnificent antechamber, where a general officer and another person were writing, and, after a few minutes delay, I was introduced to the Minister, Charles de la Croix, and delivered my letter, which he opened, and seeing it in cypher, he told me, in French, he was much obliged to me for the trouble I had taken, and that the Secretary would give me a receipt, acknowledging the delivery. I then made my bow and retired with the Secretary, the Minister seeing us to the door. He is a respectable-looking man ; I should judge him near sixty, and has very much the air of a bishop. The Secretary has given me a receipt, of which the following is a translation : "I have received from Mr. James Smith, a letter addressed to the Committee of Public Safety, and which he tells me comes from the citizen Adet, Minister Plenipotentiary of the French Republic at Philadelphia, Paris, 26th Pluviose, third year of the French Republic. The Secretary General of Foreign Affairs, Lamare." I have thus broken the ice. In a day or two I shall return for my passport.

I am perfectly pleased with my reception at Monroe's and at the Minister's, but can form no possible conjecture as to the event. The letter being in cypher, he could form no guess as to who I might be, or what might be my business. All I can say is, that I found no difficulty in obtaining access to him ; that his behaviour was extremely affable and polite, and, in a word, that if I have no ground to augur anything good, neither have I reason to expect anything bad. All is *in equilibrio*. I have now a day or two to attend to my private affairs, and the first must be that of Mr. W. Browne (my brother Matthew). Opera in the evening. The "*Chant du départ*" again. I lose three-fourths of the pleasure I should otherwise feel, for the want of my dear love, or my friend

P. P. to share it with. How they would glory in Paris just now! And then the Burgundy every day at the restaurateurs. Poor P. P.! he is the only possible bearable companion, except the boys. Well, "*'Tis but in vain,*" &c.

February 16th. Walked out alone to see sights. The *Tuileries,* the *Louvre, Pontneuf, &c.,* superb. Paris a thousand times more magnificent than London, but less convenient for those who go afoot. Saw two companies of grenadiers in the garden of the Tuileries, the first I have met. All very fine fellows, but without the *air militaire* of private sentinels ; many in the ranks have the appearance of gentlemen in soldiers' coats, and, on the whole, they exactly resembled two companies of Irish Volunteers, as I have seen them in that country, in the days of my youth and innocence. These are the youth of the first requisition. Their uniform blue, faced white, red cape and cuffs, red shoulder knots, and plumes in their hats, white belts, vest and breeches, black stocks and gaiters. I think them equal in figure to any men I have ever seen of their number. The women! only to think what a thing fashion is! The French women have been always remarkable for fine hair, and therefore at present they all prefer to wear wigs. They actually roll and pin up their own beautiful tresses, so that they become invisible, and over them they put a little shock periwig. Damn their wigs! I wish they were all burnt; but it is the fashion, and that is a solution for every absurdity. In the evening walked to the Palais Royal ; filled with the military, most of them superb figures. I do not mean as to dress, but air, manners, and gait. I now perceive the full import of the expression, an armed nation, and I think I know a country that, for its extent and population, could produce as many and as fine fellows as France. Well, all in good time. It will be absolutely necessary to adopt measures similar to those which have raised and cherished this spirit here, if ever God Almighty is pleased, in His goodness, to enable us to shake off our chains. I think Ireland would be formidable as an armed nation.

CHAPTER XV.

February 17th. Went at one o'clock to the Minister's bureau for my passport. A clerk tells me that a person called yesterday in my name and got it. I assured him I knew nobody in Paris, and had not sent any one to demand it, and reminded him that it was on this day he had desired me to call. He looked very blank at this, and just then the principal Secretary coming up, I informed him of what had happened. He recollected me immediately, and told me the Minister wished to see me, and had sent to the Ambassador to learn my *address.* I answered I should attend him whenever he pleased ; he replied, " instantly," and accordingly I followed him into the Minister's cabinet, who received me very politely. He told me, in French, that he had had the letter I brought deciphered, and laid instantly before the Directoire Executif, who considered the contents as of the greatest importance ; that their intentions were that I should go immediately to a gentleman, whom he would give me a letter to, and, as he spoke both languages perfectly and was confidential, that I should explain myself to him without reserve ; that his name was Madgett. I answered that I knew him by reputation, and had a letter of introduction to him, but did not consider myself at liberty to make myself known to any person without his approbation. He answered that I might communicate with Madgett[1] without the least reserve ; sat down and wrote a note to him, which he gave me ; I then took my leave, the Minister seeing me to the door. I mention these minute circumstances of my reception, not that I am a man to be too much elevated by the attentions of any man in any station, at

[1] [An Irishman in the French Foreign Office.—ED.]

least I hope so, but that I consider the respect shown to me by De la Croix as really shown to my mission, and of course the readiness of access, and the extreme civility of reception that I experience, I feel as so many favourable presages. I have been at the bureau twice, and both times have been admitted to the Minister's cabinet without a minute's delay. Surely all this looks well. The costume of the Minister was singular; I have said already that he had the presence of a bishop. He was dressed to-day in a grey silk *robe de chambre*, under which he wore a kind of scarlet cassock of satin, with rose-coloured silk stockings, and scarlet ribands in his shoes. I believe he has as much the manners of a gentleman as Lord Grenville. I mention these little circumstances because I know they will be interesting to her whom I prize above my life ten thousand times. There are about six persons in the world who will read these detached memorandums with pleasure; to every one else they would appear sad stuff. But they are only for the women of my family, for the boys, if ever we meet again, and for my friend P. P. Would to God he were here just now. Well, "*if wishes were horses, beggars would ride.*" And there is another curious quotation, equally applicable, on the subject of wishing, which I scorn to make. Set off for Madgett's and delivered my letter. Madgett delighted to see me, tells me he has the greatest expectation our business will be taken up in the most serious manner; that the attention of the French Government is now turned to Ireland, and that the stability and form it had assumed gave him the strongest hopes of success; that he had written to Hamilton Rowan about a month since, to request I might come over instantly, in order to confer with the French Government, and determine on the necessary arrangements, and that he had done this by order of the French Executive. He then asked me had I brought any papers or credentials; I answered that I only brought the letter of Adet to the Executive, and one to the American Ambassador, that I had destroyed a few others on the passage, including one from Mr. Rowan to himself, as we were chased by a Bermudian; that, as to credentials, the only ones I had, or that the nature of the case would permit, I had shown to Adet on my first arrival in Philadelphia, in August last. That these were the vote of thanks of the General Committee of the Catholics of Ireland for my services as their agent, signed by Mr. Edward Byrne and the two secretaries, Richard McCormick and John Sweetman, and dated in April, 1793. A second vote of thanks from the Catholics of Dublin, signed by the Chairman and Secretary, and the resolution of the Belfast regiment of Volunteers, electing me an honorary member, in testimony of their confidence, and signed by the officers of the regiment. These I had offered to Adet to bring with me to France, but he said it was sufficient that I satisfied him, and, as they were large papers, it would be running an unnecessary risk of discovery, in case we were stopped by British cruisers. That he would satisfy the French Executive, and that the fewer papers of any kind I carried the better, and, consequently, that I had brought only those I mentioned. Madgett then said that was enough, especially as he had the newspapers containing the resolutions I mentioned, and that the French Executive were already fully apprised who I was. He then added that we should have ten sail of the line, any quantity of arms that were wanted, and such money as was indispensable, but that this last was to be used discreetly, as the demands for it on all quarters were so numerous and urgent, and that he thought a beginning might be made through America, so as to serve both Ireland and France. That is to say, that military stores might be sent through this channel from France to Ireland, purchased there by proper persons, and provisions, leather, &c., returned in neutral bottoms. I answered this last measure was impracticable, on account of the vigilance of the Irish Government, and the operation of the Gunpowder Act, which I explained to him; I then gave him a very short sketch of what I considered the state of Ireland, laying it down as a *positum* that nothing effectual could be done there unless by a landing; that a French army was indispensably necessary as a *point de ralliement,* and I explained to him the grounds of my opinion. He then told me it was necessary we should arrange all the information we possessed, and, for that purpose, fixed me to breakfast with him to-morrow, when we could go at length into the business, and so we parted. N.B.—I shall, in all my negotiations here, press upon them the necessity of a landing being effectuated. If it is not, the people will never move, but to the destruction of a few wretches, and we have had already but too much of that in Ireland. A French army, with a general of established reputation at their head, is a *sine quâ non ;* Pichegru to choose, but, if not, Jourdan. Their names are known in Ireland, and that is of great consequence.

February 18*th.* Breakfast at Madgett's. Long account, on my part, of the state of Ireland when I left it, which will be found substantially in such memoirs as I may prepare. Madgett assures me again that the Government here have their attention turned most seriously to Irish affairs ; that they feel that unless they can separate Ireland from England, the latter is invulnerable ; that they are willing to conclude a treaty offensive and defensive with Ireland, and a treaty of commerce on a footing of reciprocal advantage; that they will supply ten sail of the line, arms, and money, as he told me yesterday ; and that they were already making arrangements in Spain and Holland for that purpose. He asked me, did I think anything would be done in Ireland by her spontaneous efforts. I told him most certainly not ; that if a landing were once effected, everything would follow instantly, but that that was indispensable ; and I begged him to state this as my opinion to such persons in power as he might communicate with ; that if 20,000 French were in Ireland, we should in a month have an army of 100,000, 200,000, or, if necessary, 300,000 men, but that the *point d'appui* was indispensable. He said it appeared so to him also. He then returned to the scheme of importing stores, &c., through the medium of America. I again mentioned the difficulty from the Gunpowder Act, and the risk of alarming the Irish Government. He said he still thought it would be possible, and mentioned as a reason, that eighteen brass cannon had, to his knowledge, lately been smuggled to Ireland through Belfast. If this be true it surprises me not a little, but I rather judge Madgett is misinformed. I answered that if the landing were once effected, the measure would be unnecessary ; as, in that event, we should soon have all the stores of the kingdom in our hands ; and, if it was not effected, the people would not move, unless in local riots and insurrections, which would end in the destruction of the ringleaders. He seemed struck with this, and said he saw that part of the scheme was useless. I then mentioned the necessity of having a man of reputation at the head of the French forces, and mentioned Pichegru or Jourdan, both of whom are well known by character in Ireland. He told me there was a kind of coolness between the Executive and Pichegru (this I suspected before), but that, if the measures were adopted, he might still be the General ; adding that he was a man of more talents than Jourdan. I answered, "either would do." He then desired me to prepare a memorial in form for the French Executive as soon as possible, which he would translate and have delivered in without delay. We fixed to dine together at his lodgings, and so parted. There is one thing here I wish to observe : Madgett showed me the Minister's note, which appeared to me completely confidential, and in which he mentions his own desire to forward the business as much as possible, as a friend to liberty and to humanity. The Minister also desired me to explain myself to Madgett without reserve. Am I too sanguine in believing what I so passionately wish, that the French Executive will seriously assist us ?

February 18*th*, 19*th*, 20*th*. At work in the morning at my memorial. Call on Madgett once a day to confer with him. He says there will be sent a person to Ireland immediately, with whom I shall have a conference ; and that it would be desirable he should bring back an appointment of Minister Plenipotentiary for me, in order to conclude an alliance offensive and defensive with the Republic ; in which case I should be acknowledged as such by the French Government. Certainly nothing could be more flattering to me ; however, I answered that such an appointment could not be had without communicating with so many persons as might endanger the betraying of the secret to the Irish Government ; that I only desired credit with the Directoire Exécutif, so far as they should find my assertions supported by indisputable facts ; that the information I brought was the essential part, and the credential, though highly gratifying to my private feelings, would be, in fact, but matter of form. That when a government was formed in Ireland it would be time enough to talk of embassies ; and then, if my country thought me worthy, I should be the happiest and proudest man living to accept the office of Ambassador from Ireland. So there was an end to my appointment. I must wait till the war at least is commenced, if ever it commences, or perhaps until it is over, if I am not knocked on the head meantime. I should like very well to be the first Irish Ambassador ; and if I succeed in my present business, I think I will have some claim to the office. "*Oh, Paris is a fine town and a very charming city.*" If Ireland were independent I could spend three years here with my family, especially my dearest love, very happily. I dare say P. P. would have no objection to a few months in the year *à l'hôtel d'Irlande.* He is a dog. Indeed, we would discuss several bottles of diplomatic Burgundy. But all this is building castles in the air ; let me finish my memorials, which Madgett tells me this day, the 20th, the Minister has written to him about. I am glad of that impatience. He, Madgett, says if we succeed, it is part of the plan, but I believe he means *his own* plan, to demand Jamaica for Ireland, by way of indemnity. I wish we had Ireland without Jamaica. My memorial filled with choice facts. Dine alone every day ; D'Aucourt leaving me very much to myself, of which I am glad. Military in the Palais Royal, superb figures (but this I said already). Many fine lads of twenty, who have sacrificed an arm or a leg to the liberty of their country. I could worship them. "*The Baronet can ca' for aught he needs, but he is not yet quite maister o' the accent.*" Very wise memorandums for a Minister Plenipotentiary planning a revolution. Oh Lord ! Oh Lord ! Well, "*'Tis but in vain,*" &c.

February 21st. Bought the *Constitution Française* at the shop of J. B. Louvet, in the Palais Royal, and received it from the hands of his wife, so celebrated under the name of Lodoïska. I like her countenance very much. She is not handsome, but very interesting. Louvet is one of those who escaped the 31st May, and after a long concealment and a thousand perils, in which

Lodoïska conducted herself like a heroine, returned on the fall of Robespierre, whom he had been the first to denounce, and resume his place in the Convention. He is now a distinguished member of the *Conseil des Cinq Cent;* supports a newspaper *La Sentinelle*, and keeps a bookseller's shop in the Palais Royal. I am glad I have seen Lodoïska : I wish my dearest love could see her. I think she would behave as well in similar circumstances. Her courage and her affection have been tried in some, very nearly as critical. Well! I must go finish my memorial. N.B.—Stone has been acquitted in England, I believe very justly. He will never set the Thames in a blaze.

February 22nd. Finished my memorial, and delivered a fair copy, signed, to Madgett for the Minister of Foreign Relations. Madgett in the horrors. He tells me he has had a discourse yesterday for two hours with the Minister, and that the succours he expected will fall very short of what he thought. That the marine of France is in such a state that Government will not hazard a large fleet ; and, consequently, that we must be content to steal a march. That they will give 2,000 of their best troops, and arms for 20,000 ; that they cannot spare Pichegru nor Jourdan ; that they will give any quantity of artillery; and, I think he added, what money might be necessary. He also said they would first send proper persons among the Irish prisoners of war, to sound them, and exchange them on the first opportunity. To all this, at which I am not disappointed, I answered, that as to 2,000 men, they might as well send 20. That with regard to myself, I would go if they would send but a corporal's guard, but that my opinion was, that 5,000 was as little as could be landed with any prospect of success, and that that number would leave the matter doubtful ; that if there could be an imposing force sent in the first instance, it would overbear all opposition, the nation would be unanimous, and an immense effusion of blood and treasure would be spared ; the law of opinion would at once operate in favour of the Government, which, in that case, would be instantly formed ; and I pressed particularly the advantages resulting from that circumstance. He seemed perfectly satisfied of all this, but equally satisfied that it would not, or rather could not be done. I bid him then remember that my plan was built on the supposition of a powerful support in the first instance; that I had particularly specified so in my memorial; and begged him to apprise the Minister that my opinion was so; that, nevertheless, with 5,000 men, the business might be attempted, and I did believe would succeed; but that, in that case, we must fight hard for it; that, though I was satisfied how the militia and army would act in case of a powerful invasion, I could not venture to say what might be their conduct under the circumstances he mentioned; that, if they stood by the Government, which it was possible they might, we should have hot work of it; that, if 5,000 men were sent, they should be the very flower of the French troops, and a considerable proportion of them artillerymen, with the best General they could spare. He interrupted me to ask who was known in Ireland after Pichegru and Jourdan. I answered, Hoche, especially since his affair at Quiberon.[1] He said he was sure we might have Hoche. I also mentioned, that if they sent but 5,000 men, they should send a greater quantity of arms, as in that case we could not command, at once, all the arms of the nation, as we should if they were able to send 20,000 or even 15,000. I added, that as to the prisoners of war, my advice was to send proper persons among them, but not to part with a man of them, until the landing was effected, and then exchange them as fast as possible. He promised to represent all this, and that he hoped we would get 5,000 men at least, and a greater quantity of arms. We then parted. Now what is to be my plan? Suppose we get 5,000 men, and 30,000 or even 20,000 stand of arms and a train of artillery: I conceive, in the first place, the embarkation must be from Holland, but in all events the landing must be in the North, as near Belfast as possible. Had we 20,000, or even 15,000 in the first instance, we should begin by the capital, the seizing of which would secure everything; but, as it is, if we cannot go large

---

[1] [Quiberon taken by French Royalists in English pay, July 3, 1795; retaken by Hoche, July 21st.—ED.]

we must go close-hauled,' as the saying is. With 5,000 we must proceed entirely on a revolutionary plan, I fear (that is to say, reckon only on the Sans-culottes) ; and, if necessary, put every man, horse, guinea, and potato in Ireland in requisition. I should also conceive that it would be our policy at first to avoid an action, supposing the Irish army stuck to the Government. Every day would strengthen and discipline us, and give us opportunities to work upon them. I doubt whether we could, until we had obtained some advantage in the field, frame any body that would venture to call itself the Irish Government, but if we could, it would be of the last importance. *Hang those who talk of fear!* With 5,000 men, and very strong measures, we should ultimately succeed. The only difference between that number and 20,000, is that, with the latter, there would be no fighting, and with this, we may have some hard knocks. " *Ten thousand hearts are great within my bosom.*" I think I will find a dozen men who will figure as soldiers. O good God, good God! what would I give to-night that we were safely landed, and encamped on the Cave Hill! If we can find our way so far, I think we shall puzzle John Bull to work us out. Surely we can do as much as the Chouans or people of La Vendee.

February 23rd. Looked over Paine's " Age of Reason, second part." Damned trash! His wit is, without exception, the very worst I ever saw. He is discontented with the human figure, which he seems to think is not well constructed for enjoyment. He lies like a dog. Ask P. P. whether it is not possible to be most exquisitely happy, even under the incumbrance of that shape so awkward in Mr. Paine's eyes? I beg the gentleman may speak for himself. I suppose he includes the female shape also. He seems to have some hopes that he shall enjoy immortality in the shape of a butterfly. " *Say, little foolish fluttering thing.*" Damn his nonsense! I wish he was a butterfly with all my soul. He has also discovered that a spider can hang from the ceiling by her web, and that a man cannot ; and this is *Philosophy.* I think Paine begins to dote ; but damn his trash, as I said with great eloquence already, and let me mind my business. I must

now write my own credentials to the French Government.
Awkward enough for a man to trumpet himself, however, it must
be, and so " *'Tis but in vain,*" &c.   This is an invaluable quotation,
and wears like steel ; for it, amongst other obligations, I am
indebted to the witty and ingenious lucubrations of my friend
P. P. Apropos ! I never wanted the society, assistance, advice,
comfort, and direction of the said P. P. half so much as at this
moment. I have a pretty serious business on my hands, with a
grand responsibility, and here I am, alone, in the midst of Paris,
without a single soul to advise or consult with, and nothing in
fact to support me but a good intention. Sad ! sad ! well, hang
fear, " *'Tis but in vain for soldiers to complain.*" *Da capo.* A busy
day ! Called on Madgett in order to explain to him that all I had
said relative to the support to be expected from the people in
Ireland, and the conduct of the army, was on the supposition of a
considerable force being landed in the first instance. This I had
pressed upon him yesterday, but I cannot make it too clear for my
own credit. My theory, in three words, is this : With twenty
thousand men there would be no possibility of resistance for an
hour, and we should begin by the capital ; with five thousand I
would have no doubt of success, but then we should expect some
fighting, and we should begin near Belfast ; with two thousand I
think the business utterly desperate, for, let them land where they
would, they would be utterly defeated before any one could join
them, or, in fact, before the bulk of the people could know that
they were come. This would be a mere Quiberon business in
Ireland, and would operate but as a snare for the lives of my brave
and unfortunate countrymen, to whose destruction I do not wish,
God knows, to be accessory. Nevertheless, I concluded, that if
they sent but a sergeant and twelve men, I would go, but wished
them to be fully apprised of my opinion, that, in case of a failure,
they might not accuse me of having deceived them. He agreed
with me in every word of the statement, and desired me to insert
part of it in my letter to the Minister. He also promised
positively, to have a letter written from the proper office to Guise,
to inquire after Mr. William Browne (my brother Matthew), though

he assures me the order for his liberation was expedited about the first of May last. If we can find the said Mr. Browne, he may be very serviceable amongst the prisoners of war, both soldiers and seamen being Irish. I have not pressed my inquiries about him, as my wishes prompt, lest I should appear to prefer the dearest affections of my heart, which God and my dearest love know I do not, to the public business with which I am charged. Quit Madgett, whom I believe *honest*, and whom I feel *weak*; go to Monroe; received very favourably. He has had my letter deciphered, and dropped all reserve. I told him I felt his situation was one of considerable delicacy, and therefore I did not wish to press upon him any information, relative either to myself or to my business, farther than he might desire. He answered that the letters had satisfied him, particularly that from H. R.,[1] of whom he spoke in terms of great respect, and that, as he was not responsible for what he might hear, but for what he might do, I might speak freely. I then opened myself to him, without the least reserve, and gave him such details as I was able, of the actual state of things, and of the grounds of my knowledge from my situation. I also informed him of what I had done thus far. He then addressed me in substance thus : " You must change your plan; I have no doubt whatsoever of the integrity and sincerity of the Minister De la Croix, nor even of Madgett, whom I believe to be honest. But, in the first place, it is a subaltern way of doing business, and, in the next, the vanity of Madgett will be very likely to lead him, in order to raise his importance in the eyes of some of his countrymen, who are here as patriots, and of whom I have, by no means, the same good opinion as to integrity that I have of him, to drop some hint of what is going forward. Go at once to the Directoire Exécutif, and demand an audience ; explain yourself to them, and, as to me, you may go so far as to refer to me for the authenticity of what you may advance, and you may add that you have reason to think that I am, in a degree, apprised of the outline of your business." I mentioned Carnot, of whose reputation we had been long apprised, and who, I understood, spoke

---

[1] Hamilton Rowan.

English. He said, "nobody fitter, and that La Reveilliere Lepaux also spoke English; that either would do." I then expressed a doubt whether, as I was already in the hands of Charles de la Croix, there might not be some indelicacy in my going directly to the Directoire Exécutif, and, if so, whether it might not be of disservice. He answered, "By no means; that in his own functions the proper person for him to communicate with was De la Croix, but that nevertheless, when he had any business of consequence, he went at once to the fountain head." He then proceeded to mention that, in all the changes which had taken place in France, there never was an abler or purer set of men at the head of affairs than at present; that they were sincere friends to liberty and justice, and in no wise actuated by a spirit of conquest; that, consequently, if they took up the business of Ireland on my motion, I would find them perfectly fair and candid; that not only the Government, but the whole people were most violently exasperated against England, and that there was no one thing that would at once command the warmest support of all parties, so much as any measure which promised a reduction of her power. He then examined me pretty closely on the state of Ireland; on which I gave him complete information, as far as I was able, and we concluded by agreeing that to-morrow I should go boldly to the Luxembourg and demand an audience of Carnot or La Reveilliere Lepaux. Monroe tells me that Barére (for I inquired) is yet in France, and he thought would not quit it. I told him Barére would be very acceptable in Ireland, as a deputy with the army. He answered that he did not at all doubt but it might so happen; that he would not advise me to begin by bolting out the name of Barére, but that I might take an opportunity to mention him. I remarked that it had fallen to Barére's lot to make some of the most splendid reports in the Convention, which made him well known to us, and that the people were used, in a degree, to associate the ideas of Barére and victory, which, trifling as it was, was of some consequence. On the whole, I am glad to find my lover Barére, as I hope, in no danger. It would be a most extraordinary thing if I should happen to be an instrument in restoring

his talents to the cause of liberty. I have always had a good
opinion of him. M. tells me the ground of the coolness between
Pichegru and the Government is, that he is supposed to be attached
too much to the party of the Modérés. I am glad of this, not that
there is a coolness, but that the Government is not of that party.
We talked of the resources of France and England. I mentioned
that, in my judgment, France had one measure, which sooner or
later she must adopt, and the sooner the better, and that was a
bankruptcy : that she would then start forth with her immense
resources against England, staggering under 400,000,000 of debt.
Monroe took me by the hand and said, " You have hit it ; and
I will tell you that it is a thing decided upon." If it be so, look to
yourself, Mr. John Bull. " Look to *your house, your daughter, and
your ducats.*" Take my leave of Monroe with whom I am extremely pleased. There is a true republican frankness about him,
which is extremely interesting. And now am not I a pretty fellow
to go to the Directoire Exécutif? It is very singular that so
obscure an individual should be thrown into such a situation. I
presume I do not write those memorandums to flatter myself, and
I here solemnly call God to witness the purity of my motives, and
the uprightness with which I shall endeavour to carry myself
through this most arduous and critical situation. I hope I may
not ruin a noble cause by any weakness or indiscretion of mine.
As to my integrity, I can answer for myself. What shall I do for
the want of P. P.? I am in unspeakable difficulty for the want
of his advice and consolation. Well, if ever we meet again, it will
amuse him to read those hints, but he is a dog, and so "*'Tis but
in vain,*" &c.

CHAPTER XVI.

CARNOT.

February 24th. Went at twelve o'clock, in a fright, to the Luxembourg ; conning speeches in execrable French, all the way : What shall I say to Carnot ? Well, "*whatsoever the Lord putteth in my mouth, that surely shall I utter.*" Plucked up a spirit as I drew near the palace, and mounted the stairs like a lion. Went into the first bureau that I found open, and demanded at once to see Carnot. The clerks stared a little, but I repeated my demand with a courage truly heroic ; on which they instantly submitted, and sent a person to conduct me. This happened to be his day for giving audience, which each member of the Executive Directory does in his turn. Introduced by my guide into the antechamber, which was filled with people ; the officers of state, all in their new costume. Write a line in English and delivered it to one of the Huissiers, stating that a stranger just arrived from America wished to speak to citizen Carnot on an affair of consequence. He brought me an answer in two minutes that I should have an audience. The folding doors were now thrown open, a bell being previously rung to give notice to the people, that all who had business might present themselves, and citizen Carnot appeared, in the *petit costume of* white satin with crimson robe, richly embroidered. It is very elegant, and resembles almost exactly the draperies of Van Dyke. He went round the room receiving papers and answering those who addressed him. I told my friend the Huissier, in marvellous French, that my business was too important to be transacted there, and that I would return on another day, when it would not be Carnot's turn to give audience, and when I should hope to find him at leisure. He mentioned this to Carnot, who ordered me

instantly to be shown into an inner apartment, and that he would
see me as soon as the audience was over. That I thought looked
well, and began accordingly to con my speech again. In the
apartment were five or six personages, who being, like myself, of
great distinction, were admitted to a private audience. I allowed
them all precedence, as I wished to have my will of Carnot, and
while they were in their turns speaking with him, I could not help
reflecting how often I had wished for the opportunity I then
enjoyed; what schemes I had laid, what hazards I had run; when
I looked round and saw myself actually in the cabinet of the
Executive Directory, *vis-à-vis* citizen Carnot, the *organiser of
victory*, I could hardly believe my own senses, and felt as if it were
all a dream. However, I was not in the least degree disconcerted,
and when I presented myself, after the rest were dismissed, I had
all my faculties, such as they were, as well at my command as on
any occasion in my life. Why do I mention those trifling circumstances? It is because they will not be trifling in her eyes, for
whom they were written. I began the discourse by saying, in
horrible French, that I had been informed he spoke English. " A
little, sir, but I perceive you speak French, and if you please, we
will converse in that language." I answered, still in my jargon,
that if he could have the patience to endure me, I would endeavour,
and only prayed him to stop me whenever I did not make myself
understood. I then told him I was an Irishman; that I had been
Secretary and Agent to the Catholics of that country, who were
about 3,000,000 of people; that I was also in perfect possession of
the sentiments of the Dissenters, who were at least 900,000, and
that I wished to communicate with him on the actual state of
Ireland. He stopped me here to express a doubt as to the
numbers being so great as I represented. I answered a calculation
had been made within these few years, grounded on the number of
houses, which was ascertained for purposes of revenue; that, by
that calculation, the people of Ireland amounted to 4,100,000, and
it was acknowledged to be considerably under the truth. He seemed
a little surprised at this, and I proceeded to state that the sentiments of all those people were unanimous in favour of France,

and eager to throw off the yoke of England. He asked me then “What they wanted.” I said, “An armed force in the commencement, for a *point d'appui*, until they could organise themselves, and undoubtedly a supply of arms and some money.” I added that I had already delivered in a memorial on the subject to the Minister of Foreign Relations, and that I was preparing another, which would explain to him, in detail, all that I knew on the subject, better than I could in conversation. He then said, “We shall see those memorials.” The Organiser of Victory proceeded to ask me, “Were there not some strong places in Ireland?” I answered I knew of none, but some works to defend the harbour of Cork. He stopped me here, saying, “Aye, Cork! But may it not be necessary to land there?” By which I had perceived he had been *organising* a little already, in his own mind. I answered, I thought not. That if a landing in *force* were attempted, it would be better near the capital, for obvious reasons ; if with a small army, it should be in the North, rather than the South of Ireland, for reasons which he would find in my memorials. He then asked me, “Might there not be some danger or delay in a longer navigation?” I answered, it would not make a difference of two days, which was nothing in comparison of the advantages. I then told him that I came to France by direction and concurrence of the men, who (and here I was at a loss for a French word, with which, seeing my embarrassment, he supplied me) *guided* the two great parties I had mentioned. This satisfied me clearly that he attended to and understood me. I added, that I had presented myself in August last, in Philadelphia, to citizen Adet, and delivered to him such credentials as I had with me ; that he did not at that juncture think it advisable for me to come in person, but offered to transmit a memorial, which I accordingly delivered to him. That about the end of November last, I received letters from my friends in Ireland, repeating their instructions in the strongest manner, that I should, if possible, force my way to France, and lay the situation of Ireland before its Government. That, in consequence, I had again waited on citizen Adet, who seemed eager to assist me, and offered me a letter to the Directoire Exécutif, which I accepted with gratitude

That I sailed from America in the very first vessel, and was arrived about a fortnight; that I had delivered my letter to the Minister for Foreign Affairs, who had ordered me to explain myself without reserve to citizen Madgett, which I had accordingly done. That by his advice I had prepared and delivered one memorial, on the actual state of Ireland, and was then at work on another, which would comprise the whole of the subject. That I had the highest respect for the Minister, and that as to Madgett, I had no reason whatsoever to doubt him, but, nevertheless, must be permitted to say that, in my mind, it was a business of too great importance to be transacted with a mere *Commis.* That I should not think I had discharged my duty, either to France or Ireland, if I left any measure unattempted which might draw the attention of the Directory to the situation of the latter country; and that, in consequence, I had presumed to present myself to him, and to implore his attention to the facts contained in my two memorials. That I would also presume to request that, if any doubt or difficulty arose in his mind on any of those facts, he would have the goodness to permit me to explain. I concluded by saying that I looked upon it as a favourable omen that I had been allowed to communicate with him, as he was already perfectly well known by reputation in Ireland, and was the very man of whom my friends had spoken. He shook his head and smiled, as if he doubted me a little. I assured him the fact was so; and, as a proof, told him that in Ireland we all knew, three years ago, that he could speak English; at which he did not seem displeased. I then rose, and after the usual apologies, took my leave; but I had not cleared the antechamber, when I recollected a very material circumstance, which was, that I had not told him, in fact, *who*, but merely *what* I was; I was, therefore, returning on my steps, when I was stopped by the sentry, demanding my card; but from this dilemma I was extricated by my lover the Huissier, and again admitted. I then told Carnot that, as to my situation, credit, and the station I had filled in Ireland, I begged leave to refer him to James Monroe, the American Ambassador. He seemed struck with this, and then for the first time asked my name. I told him, in fact, I had two names, my real one and that under which I travelled and was described in my passport. I then took a slip of paper, and wrote the name "James Smith, citoyen Americain," and under it, "Theobald Wolfe Tone," which I handed him, adding that my real name was the undermost. He took the paper, and looking over it, said, "Ha! Theobald Wolfe Tone," with the expression of one who has just recollected a circumstance, from which little movement I augur good things. I then told him I would finish my memorial as soon as possible, and hoped he would permit me, in the course of a few days after, to present myself again to him; to which he answered, "By all means"; and so I again took my leave. Here is a full and true account of my first audience of the Executive Directory of France, in the person of citizen Carnot, the organiser of victory. I think I came off very clear. What am I to think of all this? As yet I have met no difficulty nor check, nothing to discourage me, but I wish with such extravagant passion for the emancipation of my country, and I do so abhor and detest the very name of England, that I doubt my own judgment, lest I see things in too favourable a light. I hope I am doing my duty. It is a bold measure; after all if it should succeed, and my visions be realised—Huzza! *Vive la République!* I am a pretty fellow to negotiate with the Directory of France, pull down a monarchy and establish a republic; to break a connection of 600 years' standing and contract a fresh alliance with another country. "*By'r Lakin, a parlous fear.*" What would my old friend Fitzgibbon say if he was to read those memorandums? "*He called me dog before he had a cause.*" I remember he used to say that I was a viper in the bosom of Ireland. Now that I am in Paris, I will venture to say that he lies, and that I am a better Irishman than he and his whole gang of rascals, as well as the gang who are opposing him *as it were.* But this is all castle-building. Let me finish my memorial, and deliver it to the Minister.—Nothing but *Minister and Directoires Exécutif and revolutionary memorials.* Well, my friend Plunket (but I sincerely forgive him), and my friend Magee, whom I have not yet forgiven, would not speak to me in Ireland, because I was a Republican. Sink or swim, I stand to-day on as high ground as either of them. My venerable friend, old Captain Russell, always had hopes of me in the worst of times. Huzza! I would give five louis d'ors for one day's conversation with P. P. What shall I do for want of his advice and assistance? Not but what I think I am doing pretty well, considering I am quite alone, with no papers, no one to consult or advise with, and shocking all Christian ears with the horrible jargon which I speak, and which is properly no language. I see I have grand diplomatic talents, and by and by I hope to have an opportunity of displaying my military ones, and showing that I am equally great in the cabinet and the field. This is sad stuff! except for my love, who will laugh at it, or P. P., who will enjoy it. I have to add to this day's journal, that I saw yesterday at the Luxembourg, besides my friend Carnot, the citizens Letourneur, the President, Barras, and La Reveilliere Lepaux. Barras looks like a soldier, and put me something in mind of James Bramston. La Reveilliere is extremely like Dr. Kearney. Mem.: I saw two *poissardes* admitted to speak to Carnot, who gave them money, whilst a general officer in his uniform was obliged to wait for his turn. Oh Lord! Oh Lord! shall I ever get to finish my memorial? But when I begin to write those ingenious memorandums, I feel just as if I were chatting with my dearest love, and know not when to leave off. By the by, there is a good deal of vanity in this day's journal. No matter, there is no one to know it, and I believe that wiser men, if they would speak the truth, would feel a little elevated in my situation; hunted from my own country as a traitor, living obscurely in America as an exile, and received in France, by the Executive Directory, almost as an Ambassador! Well, murder will out. I am as vain as the devil; and one thing which makes me wish so often for P. P. (not to mention the benefit of his advice) is to communicate with him the pleasure I feel at my present situation. I know how sincerely he would enjoy it, and also how he would plume himself on his own discernment, for he always foretold great things. So he did, sure enough; but will they be verified? Well, if all this be not vanity, I should be glad to know what is. But nobody is the wiser, and so I will go finish my memorial. Sings, "*Allons, enfants de la patrie*," &c.

February 25th. Finish the draft of my second memorial, and read it over with Madgett.

February 26th. This morning finished an awkward business, that is to say, wrote a long letter to the Minister, all about myself; very proper in an ambassador to frame his own credentials. My *commission was large, for I made it myself.* Read it over carefully ; every word true and not exaggerated. Resolved to go at once to the Minister and deliver my letter, like a true Irishman, with my own hands. Went to his bureau and saw Lamare, the Secretary, whom I sent in to demand an audience. Lamare returned with word that the Minister was just engaged with Neri Corsini, Ambassador from the Grand Duke of Tuscany, and would see me the moment he was at leisure. Waited accordingly in the antechamber. A person came in, and after reconnoitring for some time, pulled out an English newspaper and began to read it. Looked at him with the most interesting indifference, as if he was reading a chapter in the Koran. Did the fellow think I would rise at such a bait as that? Neri Corsini being departed, I was introduced, leaving my friend in the antechamber to study his newspaper. I began with telling the Minister, that though I spoke execrable French, I would, with his permission, put his patience to a short trial. (Once for all, I am thus minute for the sake of my wife, whom I love ten thousand times more than all the universe, and who will consider every circumstance, even the most trifling, which relates to me, of consequence.) I then told him, that, in obedience to his orders, I had finished a memorial on the actual state of Ireland, which I had delivered to Madgett; that I had finished the draft of another, which I would deliver to-morrow, on the means necessary to accomplish the great object of my mission, the separation of Ireland from England, and her establishment as an independent Republic in alliance with France. De la Croix interrupted me here by saying that I might count upon it, there was no object nearer the heart of the Executive Directory ; that they had that business, at that very moment, before them, and would leave no means, consistent with their utmost capacity, untried to accomplish it. And he repeated again, with earnestness, "that I might count upon it." These are strong expressions from a man in his station. I then said that this information gave me the most sincere pleasure, not only on account of my own country, but of France, to whom the independence of Ireland was scarcely less an object than to Ireland itself. He answered, "We know that perfectly; and, for myself, I can assure you, that for the sake of both countries, as well as for the sake of liberty and humanity, you may depend on my most sincere and hearty co-operation in every measure likely to accomplish that end." I then returned to the business which brought me to him, that is to say, my credentials. I told him, in as few words as possible, the station I had filled in Ireland, and added that I had thrown a few facts relative to myself on paper, which I deliverrd to him, and that as to my credit or veracity I could refer him to James Monroe, who had allowed me to mention his name as a voucher for my integrity. He said it was unnecessary, and as to applying to Monroe, he would not wish to take any step relating to the business which could in the least by possibility take wind; that Madgett was the only person whatsoever to whom he confided the affair; that his principal Secretary, and those who were most confidential with him, knew nothing of it; and he recommended to me to be equally cautious. I assured him, as the fact was, that I kept the most rigid guard on myself; that I did not know a soul in Paris, nor desire to know any one; that I formed no connections, nor intended to form any; and that, in short, I kept myself purposely in solitude, that I might escape notice as much as possible. He said I was very right, and asked me, did I know the person I saw in the antechamber. I answered, I did not. He said he was an Irish patriot, named Duchet,[1] as he pronounced it, who

---

[1] [Duckett, an Irish rebel agent. Tone suspected him of being a spy, and Dr. Madden shared this view. But Mr. Fitzpatrick's more recent researches tend to show that both Tone and Dr. Madden were mistaken. Mr. Fitzpatrick says that Duckett was employed by the French Government to stir up disaffection in the English fleet, and that the mutiny of the Nore was "largely" his work ("Secret Service under Pitt," chap. x.—ED.]

was persecuted into exile for some writing under the signature of *Junius Redivivus.* I said it might be so, but that I knew nothing of him, or of the writings, and that if such an event had taken place, it must have been since June last, when I left Ireland. I then mentioned the circumstance of his pulling out an English newspaper, and setting a trap for me therewith, and how I avoided falling into his snare. The Minister said again I was quite right, but that that person had delivered in several memorials on the state of Ireland. This is very odd! I never saw the man in my life, and yet I rather imagine he knew my person. Who the devil is Junius Redivivus? or who is Duchet, if his name be Duchet? I must talk a little to Madgett of this resurrection of Junius, of whom, to speak the truth, I have no good opinion. The Minister then asked me what we wanted in Ireland? I answered, that we wanted a force to begin with, arms, ammunition, and money. He asked me, what quantities of each would I think sufficient? I did not wish to go just then into the detail, as I judged, from Madgett's discourse, that the Minister's plan was on a smaller scale than mine, and I did not desire to shock him too much in the outset. I therefore took advantage of my bad French, and mentioned that I doubted my being able sufficiently to explain myself in conversation, but that he would find my opinions at length in the two memorials I had prepared; and when he had considered them, I hoped he would allow me to wait on him, and explain any point which might not be sufficiently clear. He then proceeded to give me his own ideas, which were, as I suspected, upon a small scale. He said he understood Ireland was very populous and the people warlike, so as soon to be made soldiers, and that they were already in some degree armed. I answered, not so much was to be calculated upon in estimating the quantity of arms wanted, as most of the guns which they had were but fowling-pieces. He then said he knew they had no artillery nor cannoniers, and that, consequently, it would be necessary to supply them with both; that field pieces would be sufficient, as we had no strong places; that we should have thirty pieces of cannon (*une trentaine*), half eight-pounders, and half sixteen-pounders, properly manned and officered, and twenty thousand stand of arms. I interrupted him, to say, twenty thousand at least, as the only limitation to the numbers we could raise would be the quantity of arms we might have to put into their hands. He then went on to say, that these should be landed near Belfast, where he supposed they would be most likely to meet with early support. I answered, " Certainly, as that province was the most populous and warlike in the kingdom." He then produced a map of Ireland, and we looked over it together. I took this advantage to slide in some of my own ideas, by saying that if we were able to begin in considerable force, we should commence as near the capital as possible, the possession of which, if once obtained, would, I thought, decide the whole business ; but, if we began with a smaller force, we should commence as near Belfast as we could, and then push forward, so as to secure the mountains of Mourne and the Fews, by means of which and of Lough Erne we could cover the entire province of Ulster, and maintain ourselves until we had collected our friends in sufficient force to penetrate to Dublin. He liked my plan extremely, which certainly appears to be the only feasible one, in case of a small force being landed. He then mentioned the Irishmen serving in the British navy, and asked me what I thought of sending proper persons amongst them to insinuate the duty they owed to their country ; and whether, in such case, they would act against us or not? This is Madgett's scheme ; and, if it is not followed by very different measures, is nonsense. I answered, that undoubtedly the measure was a good one, if accompanied properly ; but, to give it full effect, it was absolutely necessary there should be a Government established in Ireland, for reasons which he would find detailed in my memorials, and of which I gave him an imperfect abstract. I think he seemed satisfied on that head. I added, that great caution ought to be used in sending these persons, lest it might take wind in some shape, and alarm the British Government. On the whole, I fancy the scheme of sending apostles among the Irish seamen will be given up ; for, certainly, if there be once a Government established in Ireland, it would, in my mind, be unnecessary, and if there be not, it would be useless. The Minister then repeated, in the plainest and most unequivocal terms, his former assurances, as well of his personal support, as of the positive and serious determination of the Executive Directory, to take up the business of Ireland in the strongest manner that circumstances would possibly admit. He added, that he hoped if France made the sacrifices she was inclined to do of men and money, to enable us to establish our freedom, and even delayed to make peace on our account, we would, in return, manifest more gratitude and principle than other nations had done in similar cases ; and desired me, as to any part of the business whose preparations might rest with me, not to lose a minute. He also desired me to press Madgett to expedite the translations as much as possible, and, on the whole, certainly appeared to be nearly as earnest and anxious in the business as myself. I then took my leave. The result of this conversation, the principal circumstances of which I have substantially related, is, that the Executive Directory at present are determined to take us up, but on a small scale ; that they will give us thirty pieces of cannon, properly manned, and twenty thousand stand of arms, with some money, of course, to begin with ; but I did not collect from the Minister that they had an idea of any definite number of troops, at least he mentioned none, and I did not press him on that head, as I wish they should first read and consider my memorials ; perhaps what is said in them may induce them to reconsider the subject ; and, if so, I shall have done a most important service both to France and Ireland. If they act on the plan mentioned to me by De la Croix, as above related, I, for one, am ready and willing, most cheerfully, to stake my life on the hazard : but the measure is against my judgment ; not from any doubt of the people at large, but from the difficulty, perhaps the impossibility, of having a proper organised Government. Do I say, therefore, that the measure ought not to be attempted on the present scale ? By no means : I am clear it ought. As to

France, it is but the risk of the outfit, which is nothing ; and, as to Ireland, she is in that situation that she ought to hazard everything on the chance of bettering her condition. I speak of the people at large, and not of the aristocracy. For one, then, I am decided. We have, at all events, the strength of numbers, and if our lever be too short, we must only apply the greater power. If the landing be effected on the present plan we must instantly have recourse to the strongest revolutionary measures, and put, if necessary, man, woman, and child, money, horses, and arms, stores and provisions, in requisition : " *The King shall eat, though all mankind be starved.*" No consideration must be permitted to stand a moment against the establishment of our independence. I do not wish for all this, if it can be avoided, but liberty must be purchased at any price; so " *Lay on, Macduff, and damned be he who first cries—Hold, enough.*" We must strike the ball hard, and take the chance of the tables. I think P. P. will shine in the character of a youth of the first requisition. I should have observed, that in the course of the conversation, De la Croix mentioned that, on the receipt of Adet's letter enclosing the memorial which I delivered to him on my arrival in Philadelphia in August last, he had written to him that the subject was too important to be discussed at 3,000 miles distance, and therefore desired I should come over. I was very glad to hear this, and answered, I was happy to have anticipated his desire. So, it seems, I was written for, as Madgett said. I should be glad to see that memorial now, for I remember it was written in the burning summer of Pennsylvania, when my head was extremely deranged by the heat. Bad as I dare say it was, it caught the attention of people here. Well—vanity again !

February 27th. At work at my memorial, which begins to look very spruce on paper.

February 28th. Went to Monroe's about my passport, and had an hour's conversation with him ; I like him very much ; he speaks like a sincere republican ; he praises the Executive Directory to the skies, and Charles De la Croix ; all for the better.

Carnot, he tells me, is a military man, and one of the first engineers of Europe. (*Vide* my observation touching his organising about Cork harbour.) Le Tourneur is also a military man, so that, with Barras, there are three soldiers in the Directoire. I am very glad of that.

February 29th. Finished my second memorial, and delivered it to Madgett for translation. Madgett has the slowness of age, and at present of the gout about him. Judge! O ye Gods, how that suits with my impatience! Well, the Minister gave me directions to expedite him, so, please God, I will levee him at least once a day. We have not a minute to spare, for in a little time the channel fleet will probably be at sea, and the camps formed in Ireland, and of course the Government there will have the advantage of a force ready concentred and prepared to act instantly, and perhaps they may happen to take the wrong side, which would be very bad. (Mem. To *insense* Carnot on this head.) I must allow two or three days for translation, and two or three more for reflection on the subject of my memorials, before I go again to the Luxembourg. It is very singular! In cool blood I can hardly frame a single sentence in French, and both with Carnot and De la Croix, I run on without the least difficulty. I screw my mind up, and I do not know how it is, but expressions flow upon me; I dare say I give them abundance of bad language, but no matter for that; they understand me, and that is the main point. I have now six days before me, and nothing to do; huzza! Dine every day at Beauvilliers for about half-a-crown, including a bottle of choice Burgundy, which I finish regularly. Beauvilliers has a dead bargain of me for water; I do not think I consume a spoonful in a week. A bottle of Burgundy is too much, and I resolve every morning regularly to drink but the half, and every evening regularly I break my resolution. I wish I had P. P. to drink the other half, and then perhaps I should live more soberly. Oh Lord! Oh Lord! Soberly. Yes, we should be a sober pair; patriots, as Matty says. Well, "*It is the squire's custom every afternoon, as soon as he is drunk,*" to begin thinking of his wife and family. I have to be sure sometimes most delightful reveries. If I succeed in my business here, and ever return to Ireland, and am not knocked on the head, there will not be on earth so happy a circle as round my fireside. Well, huzza! "*I hope to see a battle yet before I die.*" The French have an abominable custom of adulterating their Burgundy with water. (*Mem. Mr. Nisby's opinion thereon.*) I cannot but respect the generous indignation which P. P. would feel at such a vile deterioration of that noble liquor, and the glorious example he would hold up for their imitation. He would teach them how and in what quantities generous Burgundy ought to be drank ; I would gladly pay his reckoning to-day *en numéraire*, which would be no small sum, for the pleasure of his company. Well, "*'tis but in vain.*" I think it right for my credit to mention that all these wise reflections are written before dinner. So now I will go to Beauvilliers. (Sings, "*when generous wine,*" &c.).

March 1st. This day I got an English newspaper from Madgett, dated the 2nd of last month, in which there is a paragraph alluding to the death of the late unfortunate Major Sweetman, in a duel. I do not think I ever received such a shock in my life! Good God! if it should be my friend! The only chance I have is, that there may be another person of that name, but I fear the worst. I had the sincerest and most affectionate regard for him ; a better and a braver heart blood never warmed ; I have passed some of the pleasantest hours of my life in his society. If he be gone, my loss is unspeakable, but his country will have a much severer one ; he was a sincere Irishman, and if ever an exertion was to be made for our emancipation, he would have been in the very foremost rank ; I had counted upon his military talents, and had amused myself often in making him a General ; poor fellow ! If he be gone, there is a chasm in my short list of friends that I will not find it easy to fill. After all, it may be another, but I fear, I fear. I cannot bear to think of it.

March 6th. I have not had spirits since the news of poor

Sweetman's death to go on with my memorandums. As it happens, I have no serious business, and I am glad of it, for my mind has been a good deal engaged on that subject. It seems the quarrel arose about treading on a lady's gown in coming out of the opera—a worthy cause for two brave men to fight about! They fought at four yards' distance, which was Sweetman's choice; they were both desperately wounded, but Capt. Watson (an Irishman also) is likely to recover; my poor friend is gone. When he received the shot, which went through his body, he cried out to Watson, "Are you wounded?" "Yes," replied the other, "I believe mortally." "And so am I," replied Sweetman; he fell instantly. I certainly did not think I could have been so much affected on his account as I have been. Independently of my personal regard for him, I reckoned much upon his assistance, in case of the French Government affording us any aid. His courage, his eloquence, his popular talents, his sincere affection for his country, would have made him eminently serviceable; all that is now lost; we must supply his place as we can. I will write no more about him, but shall ever remember him with the most sincere regret.

Madgett has not 'yet finished the translation; hell! hell! However, he tells me he has written to the Minister on the subject of Bournonville's being appointed to the command, in case the expedition takes place. I have been reading the report of Camus, and it has satisfied me that I could not have wished for a General fitter for the station; I hope we may get him. One thing I see; Madgett must appear to do everything himself; he pleases himself with the idea that it was he who thought of Bournonville. *A la bonne heure.* I am sure at present I care little who has the credit of proposing any measure, provided the business be done; but the truth and fact is, that it was I who mentioned him. Madgett has lost two or three days in hunting for maps of Ireland; certainly maps are indispensable, but not in this stage of the business. He had been much better employed in translating; his slowness provokes me excessively, but I keep it all to myself; this day, however, he promises me he will have finished, and given in my last memorial to the Minister; if he does, I will see De la Croix the day after to-morrow, and Carnot, if possible, the day after that. In the meantime I am idle. I have been at the Museum, where there is, I suppose, the first collection of paintings in the world; all France and Flanders have been ransacked to furnish it. It is a school where the artists are permitted to go and copy the best works of the best masters. The day I called, it was not open to the public, but when the porter perceived I was a foreigner, he admitted me directly; it would not be so in England. I like the works of Guido best; there are some portraits incomparably executed by Van Dyke, Rubens, Rembrandt, and Raphael; but the Magdalen of Le Brun is, in my mind, worth the whole collection. I never saw anything in the way of painting that came near to it; I am no artist, but it requires no previous instruction to be struck with the numberless beauties of this most enchanting picture. It is a production of consummate genius. I have been likewise at the Hôtel des Invalides, where I had the pleasure of seeing the veterans at their dinner; they are very well accommodated, and it was a spectacle which interested me very much. It put me in mind of the Royal Hospital and my old friend Captain Russell, and that brought a thousand other ideas to my mind. Well, I hope I shall get back to Ireland yet. *Utinam.*

March 7th. Spent this day with *Dupetit Thouars*, an ex-lieutenant of the marine, who came over with me in the *Jersey*, and Roussillon, an ex-lieutenant also; they are both of the *ci-devant noblesse.* Dupetit Thouars is a great original; he has a good deal of talent and still more humour, and is the most complete practical philosopher I ever saw: nothing can ruffle him; but it is his *temperament.* Roussillon is a young man of very elegant manners, and adversity, I am sure, has improved him. It is a pity they should be aristocrats; yet I can hardly be angry with them. Aristocracy has been most terribly humbled in France, and this reverse of fortune is too much for them. It is not only their own downfall, but the exaltation of others, whom they were accustomed to despise, which mortifies them. But when I come to analyse their complaints, there is so much fanciful grievance mixed with severe actual suffering, that it abates a good deal of the compassion I should otherwise feel for them ; and I must add, that much of what they regret, they are deprived of most meritoriously, and many of the pleasures they have lost were the pleasures of the most depraved luxury: splendid, indeed, but most abominably vicious. It is not fair, however, to judge too hardly of them, now they are down ; but I confess I should be most sincerely sorry to be a witness of their resurrection : there is, however, no great danger of that, and they seem to be sufficiently sensible of it. They had quit the service some time back, I dare say in great disdain, and are now suing unsuccessfully to be readmitted. I cannot blame the Republic for being doubtful of the ancient marine, since the affair at Toulon. Apropos ! Roussillon tells me that Trogoff, the Admiral who betrayed the French fleet, and delivered it into the hands of Lord Hood, died in an hospital at Leghorn, where the English generously paid *one shilling* a day for his maintenance. The scoundrel ! it was just one shilling too much. And Dumourier, an exile on the face of the earth, ordered to quit England in six hours after his arrival, expelled from Brabant by the Emperor, whom he had served, or endeavoured to serve, by his treachery. If men had common sense, not to say common honesty, they would not be traitors to their country, with such examples before their eyes. But, I am preaching about aristocracy, and God knows what ! To return : I pity, sincerely, my two *ci-devant* lieutenants, for " *Cot knows I have had afflictions and trouples enough upon my own pack, and as for a gentleman in distress, I lofe him as I lofe my own powels.*" We spent the day in seeing sights, viz., the Pantheon, which will be most superb when it is finished, but far inferior to St. Paul's, either in size or magnificence. We descended into the catacombs where were the cenotaphs of Voltaire, Rousseau, and, what interested me much more, of Dampierre, who was killed at Famars. Certainly nothing can be imagined more likely to create a great spirit in a nation than a depository of the kind, sacred to everything that is sublime, illustrious, and patriotic. The French

have, however, a little overshot the mark ; for they have had
occasion already to displace two at least of their mighty dead ; I
mean Marat, whom I believe to have been a sincere enthusiast,
incapable of feeling or remorse, and Mirabeau, whom I look upon
to have been a most consummate scoundrel. If we have a
Republic in Ireland, we must build a Pantheon, but we must not,
like the French, be in too great a hurry to people it. We have
already a few to begin with : Roger O'Moore, Molyneux, Swift,
and Dr. Lucas, all good Irishmen.[1] Mounted to the top of the
Pantheon, from whence we could see all Paris, as in a ground plan,
together with the country for several leagues round. It was the
most singular spectacle I had ever seen. Went from thence to the
Botanic Garden, where there was not much vegetation to be seen,
there being a foot deep of snow upon the ground : walked, however,
through the green-houses, where there is a vast collection of
curious exotics. I felt my ancient propensities begin to revive,
for I love botany, though I do not understand it. It reminded me
of my walks round Chateauboue,[2] with my dearest love and our
little babies, when I used to be gathering my *vetches.* Well, I hope
I shall be there yet before I die. Crossed the Seine, and saw the
Place Royale, formerly the principal square of Paris, and built by
Richelieu ; his hotel is on one side of the quadrangle : it is now a
park of artillery for the Republic, and filled with cannon. Saw the
spot where the Bastille once stood and where there is now a statue
of Liberty. Traversed that great lyceum of French politics, the

---

[1] [Roger O'Moore (whose ancestors were well-nigh exterminated by the
English plantation of the Queen's County) took a foremost part in the
Rebellion of 1641. Molyneux (b. 1656, d. 1698) and Lucas (b. 1713, d. 1771)
were famous advocates of Irish Legislative Independence. The former is
well known as the author of " The Case of Ireland, being Bound by Acts of
Parliament made in England, Stated." The latter founded the *Freeman's
Journal.* Grattan's allusion to Molyneux in moving the " Declaration of
Rights," in 1782, is familiar to the students of Irish history : " I found Ireland
on her knees ; I watched over her with an eternal solicitude ; I have traced
her progress from injuries to arms, and from arms to liberty. Spirit of Swift !
Spirit of Molyneux ! your genius has prevailed ! Ireland is now a nation ! In
that new character I hail her ! and bowing in her august presence, I say, *Esto
perpetua.*"—ED.]

[2] [Tone's cottage in county Kildare.—ED.]

Faubourg St. Antoine; arrived at the Temple, where Louis XVI. was imprisoned, from whence Marie Antoinette was led to execution, and where Louis XVII., if I may so call him, died. Nothing can be imagined more gloomy than the appearance of this prison. It made me melancholy to look at it.

March 8th. Went to Madgett, in consequence of a report which I saw in the papers relative to a general peace. He assures me there is nothing in it : a peace would ruin all. He tells me also that he has finished and delivered yesterday my second memorial to the Minister, who had read the first with great attention, and was extremely edified thereby, as may well be imagined. Madgett assures me that De la Croix assures him that the Executive Directory are determined on the measure ; that is to say, on the principle of it. All that is very good, but, please God, I will have it from the Minister's own mouth ; after which I will indulge myself with a short interview with Carnot. I have not seen him since February 24th, a fortnight ago, but that has not been my fault, and the time has been employed in writing, copying, and translating my memorials. The day after to-morrow I will go to the Minister, and the day after that to the Luxembourg. Madgett tells me Bournonville is appointed to the command of the army in Holland. That is bad ; nevertheless, from the idea I have formed of his character, I should hope that, if he was properly *insensed* on the subject of Irish affairs, he would prefer that command, supposing the expedition to be once undertaken. There would be glory, and, if we succeeded, which I cannot for a moment doubt, the Irish are a generous people, even to a fault, and would reward his services most liberally. Desired Madgett, if he had an opportunity, and could do it with security as to secrecy, to explain all this to Bournonville. Dined at the Restaurateur, with Roussillon, whom I like very much. In the evening, the Théâtre Italien—saw Lodoïska, &c.

March 9th, 10th. Strolling about : the Museum again, and the inimitable Magdalen of Le Brun : spent near an hour looking at it.

March 11th. Went to the Minister, De la Croix, and had a long conversation. He began by saying, that he had read my two

memorials carefully, and that I seemed to insist on a considerable
force, as necessary to the success of the measure ; that, as to that,
there were considerable difficulties to be surmounted, arising from
the superiority of the English fleet.   That, as to 20,000 men, they
could not possibly be transported, unless the French were masters
of the channel, in which case they could as easily send 40,000, or
60,000, and march at once to London.   (N.B.—In this De la
Croix is much mistaken.   It would be, in my mind, just as impossible for France to conquer England as for England to conquer
France.   He does not know what it is to carry on war in a country
where every man's hand is against you, and yet his own country
might have given him a lesson ; however, it was not my business to
contest the point with him, so I let him go on.)   As to 20,000
men, it was thus out of the question.   As to 5,000, there would be
great difficulties ; they would require, for example, 20 ships to
convey them ; it would not be easy to equip 20 sail in a French
port, without the English having some notice, and, in that case,
they would instantly block up the port with a force double of any
that could be sent against them.   To this I answered that I was
but too sensible of the difficulty he mentioned ; that, however, all
great enterprises were attended with great difficulties, and I
besought him to consider the magnitude of the object.   That, as
to 5,000, when I mentioned that number, it was not that I thought
it necessary for the people at large, but for those men of some property, whose assistance was so essential in framing a government
in Ireland, without loss of time, and who might be deterred from
coming forward at first, if they saw but an inconsiderable force to
support them ; that I begged leave to refer to my second memorial,
where he would find my reasons on this subject detailed at length ;
that I had written those memorials under a strong sense of duty,
not with a view to flatter or mislead him, or to say what might be
agreeable to the French Government, but to give them such
information as I thought essential for them to know ; that, as to
the truth of the facts contained in them, I was willing to stake my
head on their accuracy.—He answered, he had no doubt as to
that ; that he saw as well as I the convenience of an immediate

government, but was it not feasible on a smaller scale than I had mentioned ? For example, if they gave us a General of established reputation, an État-Major, thirty pieces of artillery, with cannoniers, and 20,000 stand of arms, would not the people join them, and, if so, might we not call the clubs that I had mentioned in my memorials (meaning the Catholic Committee and the United Irishmen of Belfast), and frame of them a provisory government, until the national convention could be organised.—I answered, that, as to the people joining them, I never had the least doubt ; that my only fear was lest the men who composed the clubs of which he spoke, might be at first backward, from a doubt of the sufficiency of the force ; that I hoped they would act with spirit, and as became them, but that I could not venture to commit my credit with him, on any fact of whose certainty I was not positively ascertained.   " Well, then," replied he, " supposing your patriots should not act at first with spirit ; you say you are sure of the people.   In that case you must only choose delegates from the army, and let them act provisorily, until you have acquired such a consistency as will give courage to the men of whom you make mention."   I answered, that, by that means, we might undoubtedly act with success ; that a sort of military government was not, however, what I should prefer to commence with, if I saw any other, but that the necessity of the case must justify us in adopting so strong a measure in the first instance. (N.B.—In this I lied a little, for my wishes are in favour of a very strong, or, in other words, a military government in the outset, and if I had any share or influence in such government, I think I would not abuse it, but I see the handle it might give to demagogues, if we had any such among us. It is unnecessary here to write an essay on the subject, but the result of my meditations is, that the advantages, all circumstances considered, outweigh the inconveniences and hazard, and I, for one, am ready to take my share of the danger and the responsibility ; I was, consequently, glad when De la Croix proposed the measure.) I added, that the means which he then mentioned undoubtedly weakened my argument, as to the necessity of numbers, considerably. He then said, that from Madgett's representations he had been induced to think that men were not at all wanting. I answered, that was very compatible with my theory, for that certainly, if there were any idea of national resistance, 5,000 might be said to be no force at all for a conquest. I then shifted the discourse by saying, that, as to the embarkation, on whatever scale it was made, it might be worth consideration whether it could not be best effected from Holland; that their harbours were, I believed, less closely watched than the French, and that, at any rate, England had no ports for ships of war to the northward of Portsmouth; so, that even if she had a fleet off the coasts of Holland, it must return occasionally to refit, and, during one of these intervals, the expedition might take place. He asked me, "Was I sure England had no port to the northward of Portsmouth?" I said, "Certainly." "Not in Scotland?" I referred him to the map. (I was a little surprised that he did not know this.) This brought on the old subject of debauching the Irish seamen in the British navy, which seems a favourite scheme of De la Croix, and is, in my mind, flat nonsense. He questioned me as before, whether, by preparing a few of them, and suffering them to escape, they might not rouse the patriotism of the Irish seamen, and cause a powerful revulsion in the navy of England. I answered, as I had done already, that the measure was undoubtedly good, if properly followed up, at the same time that there was great hazard of alarming the British Government; that he would find my plan on the subject in my second memorial, where he would see that an Irish government was, in my mind, an indispensable requisite; that I did not build on the patriotism of the Irish seamen, but on their passions and interests; that we could offer them the whole English commerce as a bribe, whilst England has nothing to oppose in return but the mere force of discipline; and I pressed this as strongly on the Minister as my execrable French would permit. He then mentioned that it would be necessary to send proper persons to Ireland to give notice to the people there of what was intended. I answered, one person was sufficient. He asked me, "Did I know one Duckett?" (the fellow who pulled out the English newspaper to decoy me). I answered, I knew nothing at all about him. He then asked me,

"Did I know one Simon, a priest?" I answered, I had some recollection of one Fitzsimon, a priest, in Ireland, but that I was not personally acquainted with him. I also added that I had a strong objection to letting priests into the business at all; that most of them were enemies to the French Revolution, and, if it were possible to find a military man, he would be the properest person; the more so, as it would encourage those to whom he might address himself, by showing that the French Government were serious in their intentions. He then said he would look out for such a person. I took this occasion to observe that there was not an hour to lose, that the season was approaching fast when the British Channel fleet would be at sea, and the various encampments formed in Ireland, which generally took place about the middle of May or beginning of June. He said the necessary preparations, on the smallest scale, could not be ready sooner than one month. I replied that one month would be time enough, but added again, that there was not a minute to lose. I then took my leave, having been closeted nearly one hour and an half. On the whole, I do not much glory in this day's conversation. If I have not lost confidence I certainly have not gained any. I see the Minister is rooted in his narrow scheme, and I am sorry for it. Perhaps imperious circumstances will not permit him to be otherwise; but, if the French Government have the power effectually to assist us, and do not, they are miserable politicians. It is now one hundred and three years since Louis XIV. neglected a similar opportunity of separating Ireland from England, and France has had reason to lament it ever since. He, too, went upon the short-sighted policy of merely embarrassing England, and leaving Ireland to shift as she might. I hope the Republic will act on nobler motives, and with more extended views. At all events, I have done my duty in submitting the truth to them, and I shall continue so to do, and to press it upon them in all possible modes that I can compass. If they will give us 5,000 men, so. If not, "*Let the sheriff enter, if I become not the gallows as well as another, a plague o' my bringing up.*"

Seriously. I would attempt it with *one hundred* men. My life is of little consequence, and I should hope not to lose it neither. " *Please* God, *the dogs shall not have any poor blood to lick.*" In that case, as I have pleasantly said already, if our lever be short we must apply the greater power. Requisition! Requisition! Our independence must be had at all hazards. If the men of property will not support us, they must fall ; we can support ourselves by the aid of that numerous and respectable class of the community, *the men of no property.*

March 12*th.* Called on Madgett. He tells me that the business is going forward, but that the French Government is in the greatest difficulty for the want of money ; that the Executive Directory was, within these few days, on the point of resigning, and that they had signified to the Legislature that they would do so if they were not properly supported. I should be sincerely sorry if this were the case, as well for the sake of France as of Ireland, for I believe they are both able and honest. Madgett told me further, that he expected we were on the eve of some considerable change, not of measures, but of men ; that the party who wanted to come in were throwing difficulties in the way of the present administration, in order to force them to resign ; that if the change took place, it would not extend to the Directors, but to the Ministers ; that with regard to the affairs of Ireland, they would be bettered rather than injured by the alteration : that it was the Jacobin party who expected to come in, not the terrorists, but the true original Jacobins who had begun the Revolution ; that if they were in power, he was sure they would give us 10,000 men ; that, however, as to Bournonville, he was obnoxious to them, and of course would not be appointed to the command. If there is to be any change, I confess I should be glad the Jacobins were to come again into play, for I think a little more energy just now would do the French Government no harm On the whole, I am not much delighted with our present prospects.

March 13*th.* Went as usual to the opera. *Serment de la liberté.* The scene represented the Champ de Mars, on the day of the con- federation. As usual, the spectacle all military. In the procession was a band of young men in regimentals, but without arms. At

a particular verse of the hymn, which was chanted before the
altar of liberty, they approached the grenadiers, who were under
arms, and received from them their firelocks, which they shouldered,
and took their places in the line ; several evolutions, and the
manual exercise, were then performed by the whole body, for, as I
have already remarked, these are the ballets of the French nation
at present.   At the conclusion a band of beautiful young women,
equal in number to the young men, entered, carrying drawn sabres
in their hands, and ranged themselves on one side of the stage ;
the young men being drawn up in a line on the other.   Each of the
youths advanced in his turn to the centre of the stage, when he was
met by his mistress, who presented him with his sabre with one
hand, and with the other pointed to the altar of liberty ; the youth
kissed the hilt of the sabre, and returned it to the scabbard ; they
then fell back into their places, and were succeeded by the next
pair, until they had all received their arms and saluted their
mistresses.   The whole then joined in a grand chorus, and the
soldiery filed off as for the frontiers, the women being placed on
an eminence to view them as they passed.   I do not know what
Mr. Burke may think, but I humbly conceive, from the effect all
this had on the audience, that the age of chivalry is not gone
in France.   I can imagine nothing more suited to strike the
imagination of a young Frenchman than such a spectacle as this,
and indeed, though I am no Frenchman, nor at present over and
above young, it affected me extremely.   I am sure nothing on
earth has such an influence on me as my wife's opinion ; every
action of my life has a reference more or less to that, and in the
very business I am now engaged in, if I succeed, I look for, and
shall find the reward dearest to my heart, in her commendation.
It is inconceivable (I lie, I lie, it is not at all inconceivable) the effect
which the admiration or contempt of a woman has on the spirit of
a man.   Hector, when he is balancing in his mind whether he
shall stand or fly before Achilles, is determined by the consideration of what the Trojan ladies will say of him.   " *Troy's proud
dames, whose garments sweep the ground.*"   From which I infer
that human nature is pretty much now what it was three thousand

years ago, and that Homer knew it well, so did Shakespeare, and
so did Fielding, who has hit off the same point admirably when
Lady Bellaston is working upon Lord Fellamar. To return, I owe
so much to my wife for her incomparable behaviour on ten thousand different occasions, that I feel myself bound irresistibly to
make every effort to place her and her dear little babies in a
situation in some degree worthy of her merit, and suitable to my
sense of it. I am not without ambition or vanity, God knows ; I
love fame, and I suppose I should like power ; but I declare here
most solemnly that I prefer my wife's commendations to those of
the whole world. Well, if I succeed here, I shall stand on high
ground, and I must be allowed to say, I shall deserve it, and then
she will be proud of me, as I am of her, and with that sentiment I
conclude this day's journal.

CHAPTER XVII

GENERAL CLARKE.

March 14th. Went this day to the Luxembourg ; I have the luck of going on the days that Carnot gives audience, and of course is most occupied ; waited, however, to the last, when only one person remained besides myself. Carnot then called me over, and said, ' You are an Irishman." I answered I was. " Then," said he, " here is almost a countryman of yours, who speaks English perfectly. He has the confidence of Government : go with him and explain yourself without reserve." I did not much like this referring me over ; however, there was no remedy ; so I made my bow, and followed my new lover to his hotel. He told me on the way that he was General Clarke ; that his father was an Irishman ; that he had himself been in Ireland, and had many relations in that country ; he added (God forgive him if he exaggerated), that all the military arrangements of the Republic passed through his hands, and, in short, gave me to understand that he was at the head of the War Department. By this time we arrived at the hotel where he kept his bureau, and I observed in passing through the office to his cabinet an immense number of boxes labelled, Armée du Nord, Armée des Pyrennées, Armée du Rhin, &c., &c., so that I was pretty well satisfied that I was in the right track. When we entered the cabinet I told him in three words who and what I was, and then proceeded to detail, at considerable length, all I knew on the state of Ireland, which, as it is substantially contained in my two memorials, to which I referred him, I need not here recapitulate. This took up a considerable time, I suppose an hour and a half. He then began to interrogate me on some of the heads, in a manner which showed me that he was utterly unacquainted with the present state of affairs in Ireland, and particularly with the great internal changes which have taken place there within the last three or four years, which, however, is no impeachment of his judgment or talents; there were, however, other points on which he was radically wrong. For example, he asked me, would not the aristocracy of Ireland, some of which he mentioned, as the Earl of Ormond, concur in the attempt to establish the independence of their country? I answered, " Most certainly not," and begged him to remember that if the attempt were made, it would be by the people, and the people only; that he should calculate on all the opposition that the Irish aristocracy could give; that the French Revolution, which had given courage to the people, had, in the same proportion, alarmed the aristocracy, who trembled for their titles and estates; that this alarm was diligently fomented by the British Minister, who had been able to persuade every man of property that their only security was in supporting him implicitly in every measure calculated to oppose the progress of what were called French principles; that, consequently, in any system he might frame in his mind he should lay down the utmost opposition of the aristocracy as an essential point. At the same time, I added, that, in case of a landing being effected in Ireland, their opposition would be of very little significance, as their conduct had been such as to give them no claim on the affections of the people; that their own tenants and dependants would, I was satisfied, desert them, and they would become just so many helpless individuals, devoid of power and influence. He then mentioned that the Volunteer Convention in 1783 seemed to be an example against what I now advanced; the people then had acted through their leaders. I answered they certainly had, and as their leaders had betrayed them, that very convention was one reason why the people had for ever lost all confidence in what were called leaders. He then mentioned the confusion and bloodshed likely to result from a people such as I described, and he knew the Irish to be, breaking loose without proper heads to control and moderate their fury. I answered it was but too true; that I saw as well as he, that, in the first explosion, it was likely that many events would take place in their nature very shocking ; that revolutions were not made without much individual suffering ; that, however, in the present instance, supposing the worst, there would be a kind of retributive justice, as no body of men on earth were more tyrannical and oppressive in their nature than those who would be most likely to suffer in the event he alluded to ; that I had often in my own mind (and God knows the fact to be so) lamented the necessity of our situation, but that Ireland was so circumstanced that she had no alternative but unconditional submission to England, or a revolution, with a chance of all the concomitant sufferings, and that I was one of those who preferred difficulty and danger and distress to slavery, especially where I saw clearly there was no other means. " It is very true," replied he, " there is no making an *omelette* without breaking of eggs." He still seemed, however, to have a leaning towards the co-operation of our aristocracy, which is flat nonsense. He asked me was there no one man of that body that we could not make use of, and again mentioned, " for example, the Earl of Ormond." I answered, " Not one ; " that as to Lord Ormond, he was a drunken beast, without a character of any kind, but that of a blockhead ; that I did believe, speaking my own private opinion as an individual, that perhaps the Duke of Leinster might join the people, if the revolution was once begun, because I thought him a good Irishman ; but that for this opinion I had merely my own conjectures, and that, at any rate, if the beginning was once made, it would be of very little consequence what part any individual might take. I do not know how Fitzgibbon's name happened to come in here, but he asked me would it not be possible to make something of him. Any one who knows Ireland will readily believe that I did not find it easy to make a serious answer to this question. Yes, Fitzgibbon would be very likely, from his situation, his principles, his hopes, and his fears, his property, and the general tenor of his conduct, to begin a revolution in Ireland ! At last I believe I satisfied Clarke on the subject of the support to be expected from our aristocracy. He then asked me what I thought the revolution, if begun, would terminate in. I answered, undoubtedly, as I thought, in a Republic allied to France. He then said what security could I give that in twenty years after our independence we might not be found engaged as an ally of England against France? I thought the observation a very foolish one, and only answered that I could not venture to foretell what the combination of events for twenty years might produce; but that, in the present posture of affairs, there were few things which presented themselves to my view under a more improbable shape. He then came to the influence of the Catholic clergy over the minds of the people, and the apprehension that they might warp them against France. I assured him, as the fact is, that it was much more likely that France would turn the people against the clergy; that within these last few years, that is to say, since the French Revolution, an astonishing change, with regard to the influence of the priests, had taken place in Ireland. I mentioned to him the conduct of that body, pending the Catholic business, and how much and how justly they had lost character on that account. I told him the anecdote of the Pope's legate, who is also Archbishop of Dublin, being superseded in the actual management of his own chapel, of his endeavouring to prevent a political meeting therein, and of his being forced to submit and attend the meeting himself; but, particularly, I mentioned the circumstance of the clergy excommunicating all Defenders, and even refusing the sacraments to some of the poor fellows *in articulo mortis*, which to a Catholic is a very serious affair, and all to no purpose. This last circumstance seemed to strike him a good deal. He then said that I was not to augur anything either way, from anything that had passed on that day; that he would read and consider my memorials very attentively, but that I must see that a business of such magnitude could not be discussed in one conversation, and that the first; that I was not, however, to be discouraged because he did not at present communicate with me more openly. I answered I understood all that; that undoubtedly, on this occasion, it was my turn to speak, and his to hear, as I was not to get information, but to give it. I then fixed with him to return in six days (on the 1st of Germinal), and having requested him to get the original memorials, as he was perfect master of the English, and I could not answer for a translation which I had never seen, I took my leave.

I see clearly that all Clarke's ideas on Irish politics are at least thirty years behind those of the people, and I took pains to impress him with that conviction as delicately as I could. We should, according to his theory, have two blessed auxiliaries to begin with, the noblesse and the clergy. I hope, however, I have beat him a little out of that nonsense, and that, when he reads the memorials in cool blood, he will be satisfied of its absurdity. By-the-by, my memorials I find have never been laid before the Executive ; that is bad ; I trust they are now in train. When I mentioned that De la Croix had referred me to Madgett, I found, with some little surprise, that Clarke did not know Madgett. To hear the latter speak one would suppose it impossible that could be the case. This comes of being a stranger. I must grope my way here as well as I can. Carnot has positively referred me to Clarke, and if he be as confidential as he gives me to understand, I have no reason to complain ; but suppose he is not, where is my remedy ? and how am I to ascertain that fact ? I know nobody here of whom I can inquire. If I rest in the hands of subalterns, I risk the success of my plans, and I act against my wishes and my judgment. If I go back to the principals, I risk making an enemy of the subalterns, and there is no animal so mean but has the power to do mischief. I would rather stick to Carnot, but what can I do when he has handed me over to Clarke ? " *Suffolk, what remedy ?* " At any rate, I must let things go on in the present track until I see some open, or until I conceive myself neglected. As yet, I certainly have no reason to complain. " *A pize upon thee for a wicked La'yer, Tom Clarke,*" I would rather deal with your master, but that can't be for the present, and so " '*Tis but in vain,*" &c. We will see what the first of Germinal will produce, and, in the meantime, I will, as Matty says, " *let the world wag.*" It is unnecessary to observe that I only give the outlines of the various conversations related in these memorandums. There are a thousand collateral points which it is impossible to detail. The general tenor of my discourse was grounded on the facts contained in my two memorials, which I endeavoured to state and support in the strongest manner I could, dwelling particularly on the Defenders, the Dissenters, the recent union between the sects, which I mentioned as a circumstance of the last importance, the probable consequences to the naval power of England, and the effects to be hoped for from the proclamations mentioned in my second memorial, which seemed to strike Clarke very forcibly ; though he combated them at first, until I asked him how he would like to be an English admiral leaving Portsmouth under the circumstances I had described ; on which he submitted as became him. I do not detail all this, for in fact it would be but amplifying my memorials. One thing I must observe here : though I told Carnot that I had been with the Minister, I never told the Minister I had been with Carnot. In like manner, Clarke knows I have seen Madgett, but Madgett does not know I have ever been at the Luxembourg. There is something like duplicity in this ; if there be, my situation must excuse it. I am acting to the best of my judgment, and I have not a soul to advise with. P. P., P. P. what would I give that you were here to-day ! Mem. Beauvilliers' Burgundy, &c.

March 15*th.* Went to breakfast with Madgett, in consequence of a note which I received from him. Madgett in high spirits; tells me everything is going on as well as possible ; that our affair is before the Directory ; that it is determined to give us 50,000 stand of arms, artillery for an army of that force, 672 cannoniers, and a demi-brigade, which he tells me is from 3,000 to 4,000 men ; that the Minister desires my opinion in writing as to the place of landing. All this is very good and precise. I told him with that force we must land near Belfast, and push on immediately to get possession of the Fews Mountains, which cover the province of Ulster, until we could raise and arm our forces ; that, if possible, a second landing should be made in the Bay of Galway, which army should cover itself, as soon as possible, by the Shannon, breaking down most of the bridges, and fortifying the remainder ; that we should thus begin with the command of one half of the nation, and that the most discontented part : that, as to the port of embarkation, which the Minister had also mentioned, I suggested some of the Dutch ports, first, because I believed they were less watched than the French, and next, that England having no harbour, where she could refit a fleet, to the north of Portsmouth, even if she kept a fleet in the North Seas, it must return occasionally to refit, and the expedition might take place in the interval. If, however, the Dutch ports were too strongly watched, we might go from any of the French harbours on the ocean, and coast round by the West of Ireland into the Loch of Belfast. Madgett reduced this to writing in French, and we went together to the Minister, where he delivered it to him before my eyes. Madgett tells me that Prieur de la Marne is in the secret, and has recommended and guaranteed a Capuchin friar of the name of Fitzsimons, to go to Ireland. I told Madgett I had the most violent dislike to letting any priest into the business at all. He said he did not like it either, but that Prieur de la Marne had known this man for twenty years, and would stake his life on his honesty. I do not care for all that; I will give my opinion plump against his being sent. Madgett mentioned that the fellow had some notion of a resumption of the forfeited lands. That would be a pretty measure to begin with! Besides, he has been out of the country twenty or thirty years, and knows nothing about it, and I dare say hates a Presbyterian like the devil. No! no! If I can help it, he shan't go; if I can't, why I can't. I want a military man. I must see whoever is sent, I presume, and how can I commit the safety of my friends in Ireland to a man in whom I have no confidence myself? And, indeed, I have some doubts whether I have any right to commit the safety of any person but myself. However, the way that I answer that objection, is, that it is absolutely necessary; that I am acting by their own advice and direction, and with their concurrence; that I have not shrunk myself from any trouble, labour, or danger; that it is but just they should take their share, especially when it is essential for the success of the measure; and, finally, that I rely very much upon their discretion to avoid all unnecessary hazard, and conduct themselves properly through this arduous business. These reasons are, with me, of sufficient weight to decide me in giving the names of five or six men in Ireland, in order that, whoever is sent if any one is sent by the French Government, may see them. At the same time, I give my advice that the messenger see but one of them, and leave it to him to communicate with the others. And that one shall be P. P. I will put him in the post of danger and honour, though I love him like a brother. I wish Ireland to come under obligations to the said P. P. And now I must observe that it is very odd, if the business be as Madgett says, before the Directory, and so far advanced, that Clarke should know nothing about it. Carnot did not appear to me yesterday to have even seen my memorials, and I rather believe that to be the case. Madgett is much more sanguine than I am, for I preserve in all this business a phlegm which is truly admirable. I have resolved never to believe that the expedition will be undertaken till I see the troops on board, nor that it will succeed until I have slept one night under canvas in Ireland. Then I shall have hopes. At present I keep my mind under a strict regimen, and, without affectation, I think it must be an extraordinary circumstance which would much elevate or depress me. All which is truly edifying and extremely philosophical. Madgett tells me that Rewbell is the member of the Directory who is the most sanguine and earnest in support of the measure. Well! The first of Germinal, I suppose, I shall know more of the matter. Clarke, after all, must be better authority than Madgett. One thing I see, that Madgett wishes to keep me out of sight as much as possible, which is very natural, and I am sure I am not angry with him for it. Nevertheless, I will smuggle an odd visit now and then to the Luxembourg, "just to see things a little." "*Wheels within wheels?*" "*Business, business, says I, Mr. Secretary, must be done.*" Wise memorandums. I had like to have forgotten, I have not neglected Mr. Wm. Browne's (my brother Matthew's) affair. Lamare has written to Guise by this day's post on that subject, having received no answer to a letter which he wrote on the same head about a fortnight since. I wish the said Mr. Browne were here, for a vast multiplicity of reasons.

March 16th. Blank. Dined alone in the Champs Elysées. A most delicious walk. The French know how to be happy, or at least to be gay, better than all the world besides. The Irish come near them, but the Irish all drink more or less (except P. P., who never drinks), and the French are very sober. I live very soberly at present, having retrenched my quantity of wine one-half; I fear, however, that if I had the pleasure of P. P.'s company to-morrow, being St. Patrick's day, we should, indeed, "*take a sprig of watercresses with our bread.*" Yes, we should make a pretty sober meal of it. Oh Lord! Oh Lord!

March 17th. St. Patrick's day. Dined *alone* in the Champs Elysées. Sad! Sad!

March 18th. Blank! Theatre in the evening.

March 19th. Madgett called on me this morning to tell me the Directory had resolved to give us an entire brigade (viz., 8,000 men instead of 4,000.) He told me, also, that the Minister had asked him whether I had ever been to the Directory, and that he had said he was sure I had not. (*Mem.* I rather believe that honesty is always the best policy in every affair, public and private ; for though I am sure it was from the purest motives that I had not told Madgett of my visits to the Luxembourg, yet I felt very awkward at the question.) I answered, that, in consequence of the extreme anxiety which I felt for the success of the business, as well as in pursuance of the directions I had received to omit nothing likely to bring the state of Ireland before the French Government, I had thought it my duty to go, in person, to the Executive, and obtain, if possible, an audience ; the more so, as Carnot, who is now one of the Directory, was well known by reputation in Ireland ; and I was particularly charged, if possible, to find him out. Madgett seemed quite satisfied at this, and, having fixed to breakfast with him to-morrow, we parted.

March 20th. Breakfast with Madgett. The Minister wants to know our plan of conduct, supposing the landing effected. This has been already detailed in my memorial, but it is necessary to go over the same ground again and again. "*Put it to him in other words*," viz., the Catholic Committee is already a complete representation of that body, and the Dissenters are so prepared that they can immediately choose delegates. That those two bodies, when joined, will represent, numerically, nine-tenths of the people, and, of course, under existing circumstances, are the best Government we can form at the moment. This Madgett reduced to writing, but I have no copy, which is of the less consequence, as the paper is only a paraphrase of part of my last memorial. Desired Madgett to explain to the Minister that my visit to the Luxembourg was in consequence of positive directions I had to communicate with Carnot, whether in or out of power; that I had the highest respect for the Minister's talents and patriotism, and, if there was any irregularity in my applying to Carnot, it was merely an error in judgment, as he must be convinced that, circumstanced as I was, I could never dream of doing anything which might be disagreeable to a person in his station, &c. I believe this will satisfy De la Croix; but I fancy, between friends, that Madgett, rather than the Minister, is a little piqued; for, with great sincerity, and, I am sure, an honest anxiety for the success of the measure, I can see a little desire in his mind of doing everything himself; for which, as I have already said, with a laudable magnanimity, I am not at all angry with him; nevertheless, I shall take the liberty, under the rose, to follow my own plan a little: I do not think I have made a blunder yet, unless (which I do not think) my going to Carnot, without informing the Minister, was one. Took a delightful walk in the Champs Elysées, and dined alone, as usual, at a very retired Restaurateur. I live here in Paris, absolutely like a hermit.

March 21st. Went, by appointment (this being the 1st Germinal) to the Luxembourg, to General Clarke; "*damn it and rot it for me*"—he has not yet got my memorials; only think how provoking. I told him I would make him a fair copy, as I had the rough draft by me. He answered it was unnecessary, as he had given in a memorandum, in writing, to Carnot, to send for the originals, and would certainly have them before I could make the copy. We then went into the subject as before, but nothing new occurred. He dwelt a little on the nobles and clergy, and I replied as I had done in the former conversation: he said he was satisfied that nothing was to be expected from either, and I answered that he might expect all the opposition they could give, if they had the power to give any, but that happily, if the landing were once effected, their opinion would be of little consequence. He then asked me, as before, what form of Government I thought would be likely to take place in Ireland, in case of the separation being effected, adding that, as to France, though she would certainly prefer a Republic, yet her great object was the independence of Ireland under any form? I answered, I had no doubt whatever that, if we succeeded, we would establish a Republic, adding that it was my own wish, as well as that of *all* the men with whom I co-operated. He then talked of the necessity of sending some person to Ireland to examine into the state of things there, adding, "You would not go yourself." I answered, certainly not; that, in the first place, I had already given in all the information I was possessed of, and for me to add anything to that, would be, in fact, only supporting my credit by my own declaration; that he would find, even in the English papers, and I was sure much more in the Irish, if he had them, sufficient evidence of the state of the country to support every word I had advanced, and evidence of the most unexceptionable nature, as it came out of the mouths of those who were interested to conceal it, and would conceal it, if they could; that, for me to be found in Ireland now, would be a certain sacrifice of my life to no purpose; that, if the expedition was undertaken, I would go in any station; that I was not only ready and willing, but should most earnestly supplicate and entreat the French Government to permit me to take a part, even as a private volunteer, with a firelock on my shoulder, and that I thought I could be of use to both countries. He answered, "As to that, there could be no difficulty or doubt on the part of the

French Government." He then expressed his regret at the delay of the memorials, and assured me he would use all diligence in procuring them, and would not lose a moment after they came to his hands. I entreated him to consider that the season was now advancing fast when the channel fleet would be at sea, and the camps in Ireland formed, and, of course, that every hour was precious, which he admitted. I then took my leave, having fixed to return in five days, on the 6th Germinal. I apologised for pressing him thus, which I assured him I should not do in a business of my own private concern, and so we parted. And now is it not extremely provoking that, in a business of such magnitude, seven days have been lost? The papers are lying in the Minister's hands, ready and finished, and nothing to do but to send for them, yet they are not got. Well, if ever I get to be a Citizen Director, or a Citizen Minister, I hope I shall do better than that: I am in a rage; hell! hell! *"Fury, revenge, disdain, and indignation tear my swollen breast, whilst passions, like the winds, rise up to heaven, and put out all the stars."* As I have nothing to add more outrageous I will here change the subject.

Went to see *Othello*; not translated, but only taken from the English. Poor Shakespeare! I felt for him. The French tragedy is a pitiful performance, filled with false sentiment; the Moor whines most abominably, and Iago is a person of a very pretty morality; the author apologises for softening the villainy of the latter character, as well as for saving the life of Desdemona, and substituting a happy termination in place of the sublime and terrible conclusion of the English tragedy, by saying that the humanity of the French nation, and their morality would be shocked by such exhibitions: *"Marry come up, indeed! People's ears are sometimes the nicest part about them."* I admire a nation that will guillotine sixty people a day for months, men, women, and children, and cannot bear the catastrophe of a dramatic exhibition! Yet, certainly the author knows best, and I have had occasion repeatedly to observe, that the French are more struck with any little incident of tenderness on the stage, a thousand times, than the English, which is strange. In short, the French *are* a humane people when they are not mad, and I like them with all their faults, and the guillotine at the head of them, better, a thousand times, than the English. And I like the Irish better than either, and as no one can doubt my impartiality, I expect my opinion will be received with proper respect and deference by all whom it may concern. I have nothing to add. Upon further recollection, I have something to add. In the course of the conversation, when I desired Clarke to count upon all the opposition which the Irish aristocracy, whether Protestant or Catholic, could give, he said he believed I was in the right ; for that, since he saw me last, he had read over a variety of memorials on the subject of Irish affairs, which had been given in to the French Government for forty years back, and they all supported my opinion as to that point. I answered, I was glad of it, but begged him not to build much on any papers, above a very recent date ; that the changes, even in France, were not much greater than in Ireland since 1789 ; that what was true of her ten or seven years ago, was not true now ; of which there could not be a stronger instance than this, that if the French had landed during the last war, the Dissenters, to a man, and even the Catholics, would have opposed them ; but then France was under the yoke, which she had since broken ; that all the changes in the sentiment of the Irish people flowed from the Revolution in France, which they had watched very diligently, and that being the case, he would I hope, find reason to believe that my opinion on the influence of the nobles and clergy was founded in fact. I then went on to observe, that, about one hundred years ago, Louis XIV. had an opportunity of separating Ireland from England during the war between James II. and William III. ; that, partly by his own miserable policy, and partly by the interested views of his Minister, Louvois, he contented himself with feeding the war by little and little, until the opportunity was lost, and that France had reason to regret it ever since ; for, if Ireland had been made independent then, the navy of England would never have grown to what it is at this day. He said, "that was very true ;" and added, "that even in the last war, when the Volunteers were in force, and a rupture between England and Ireland seemed likely, it was proposed in the French Council to offer assistance to Ireland, and overruled by the interest of Count De Vergennes, then Prime Minister, who received for that service a considerable bribe from England, and that he was informed of this by a principal agent in paying the money." So, it seems, we had a narrow escape of obtaining our independence fifteen years ago. It is better as it is, for then we were not united amongst ourselves, and I am not clear that the first use we should have made of our liberty would not have been to have begun cutting each other's throats : so out of evil comes good. I do not like this story of Vergennes, of the truth of which I do not doubt. How, if the devil should put it into any one's head here to serve us so this time ! Pitt is as cunning as hell, and he has money enough, and we have nothing here but assignats ; I do not like it at all. However, it is idle speculating on what I cannot prevent. I can answer for myself, at least, I will do my duty. But, to return : Clarke asked me had I thought of subsisting the French troops after the landing, in case the Executive decided in favour of the measure. I answered, I had not thought in detail on the subject, but there was one infallible mode which presented itself, which was, requisition in kind of all things necessary ; adding, that he might be sure, whoever wanted, the army should not want, and especially our allies, if we were so fortunate as to obtain their assistance. He asked me, "might not that disgust the people of property in Ireland ? " I answered, the revolution was not to be made for the people of property ; but as to those of them who were our friends, the spirit of enthusiasm would induce them to much greater sacrifices ; and as to those who were our enemies, it was fit that they should suffer, and I referred him for a proof of what sacrifices the enthusiasm of a revolution would lead to, to his own experience of what had happened in France, and what I knew to have been the case in America, where, during the contest for their liberties, it was a scandal to enjoy the luxuries and almost the conveniences of life, insomuch that people of the first properties and situations went in old and tattered clothes. He admitted this, but observed that this enthusiasm would subside in time, and that this was already the case in France. I admitted that; but observed, that I hoped our revolution, if attempted, would be completed long before the spirit of enthusiasm had cooled. I do not recollect any other circumstances material in our conversation.

March 22nd. I have worked this day like a horse. In the morning I called on Madgett to tell him that Carnot wanted the memorials, and begged him to expedite them. He boggled a good deal, and I got almost angry; however, I am growing so much of a statesman, that I did not let him see it. It would be a most extraordinary thing, indeed, if one of the Executive Directory could not command a paper of this kind out of the pocket of citizen Madgett. I resolved, however, not to contest the point, but quietly make a copy of the two memorials, and give them myself to Clarke. It is only the trouble, and I have nothing else to do, and it is very good business for me, and I do not understand people being idle and giving themselves airs, and wanting to make revolutions, whilst they are grumbling at the trouble of writing a few sheets of paper. I therefore dropped the business of the memorials, and Madgett then told me that he sets off to-morrow, on a pilgrimage, to root out the Irish prisoners of war, and especially Mr. Wm. Browne, who is to be sent to Ireland if he can be found out, or if he has not long since been discharged; that he is to go to Versailles, Compiegne, Guise, and propagate the faith amongst the Irish soldiers and seamen. This is his favourite scheme, and is, in my mind, not to mince the matter, *damned* nonsense. What are five hundred or one thousand Irishmen, more or less, to the success of the business? Nothing. And then there is the risk of the business taking wind. I do not like it at all; but I surmise the real truth to be, that it is a small matter of job (*à l'Irlandaise*), and that there is some cash to be touched, &c. Madgett's scheme is just like my countryman's, that got on horseback in the packet in order to make more haste. He is always hunting for maps, and then he thinks he is making revolutions. I believe he is very sincere in the business, but he does, to be sure, at times, pester me confoundedly. With regard to Mr. William Browne (my brother Matthew), I wish to God, if he be still in France, that Madgett may be able to find him. And yet I dread his going to Ireland. If he be caught there, his life is gone ; and, though I am willing to hazard my own, I have some doubts as to his. If Madgett proposes it to him, he will go, *bon gré, mal gré.* Well, let him. If he escapes, and Ireland is freed, she will reward him, and he will deserve it. He would, certainly, be the fittest person to go from this, as he is known to all my confidential friends ; and I could communicate with him, and he with them, much better than any stranger whatsoever. On the whole, if he is found, he must go, and I hope God Almighty will protect him, poor fellow ; for I love him most affectionately. Perhaps, whilst I am writing this, he may be at Princeton, with Matty and the children. I have sent one brother already to Ireland on this business. It is pretty early to entrust a matter of high treason to a boy of fourteen. However, I have no doubt of him ; and, if we succeed, I hope to see him yet a flag officer in the Irish navy. Well, I have made great sacrifices in this business. But, to return. Madgett tells me that the Minister is quite satisfied as to my having seen Carnot, and that he would be very glad if I would take an opportunity to insinuate artfully to him that Prieur de la Marne would be a very acceptable person in Ireland (which I dare say he would, as his name is well known there), and which I may fairly do, as I am here the representative of the Irish people ; so I am accredited. I will certainly mention Prieur to Carnot, as the Minister desires it ; and I recollect Rowan told me in Philadelphia that when he was leaving Brest on his way to Paris, after his escape from Ireland, Prieur, who was then Deputy on Mission, shook hands with him, observing that he hoped that they would land in Ireland together. It is not impossible that they may meet there. So, I am to become an *intrigant,* I find, and to procure appointments for ex-deputies and I know not what. "*Hey day, what doings, what doings are here!*" It is very laughable to think of the Minister of Foreign Affairs desiring *me* to recommend a member of the National Convention to the Executive Directory of France.   Having done with Madgett, I returned home, and set doggedly to copying my two memorials ; finished the first, and made a practicable breach in the second ; then wrote the eight foregoing pages in my journal, and now it is ten o'clock at night and I am as tired as a dog, and my fingers are cramped, and I cannot see out of my eyes.   To-morrow I will finish my second memorial, I expect time enough to go to the Luxembourg and give it either to Carnot or Clarke.   "*Business, business, said I, Mr. Secretary, must be done.*"   I quoted that once already, but a good thing cannot be done too often, and it is a choice quotation, and I caught it from P. P., who quotes better than anybody, except my dearest love.   I am but a fool to them, only I make sometimes a lucky hit.   Oh Lord ! oh Lord ! what wise memorandums I am making, and I am as tired as a devil, for I have written nine hours to-day, which is more than I ever did in my life.   "*What do I not suffer, O Athenians, that you may speak well of me ?*"   Pretty and modest, comparing myself by craft to Alexander the Great !   Well, the vanity of some people is most unaccountable !   When I get into this track of witty and facetious soliloquy, I know not how to leave off, for I always think I am chatting to my dearest life and love and the light of my eyes. Well, I will not begin another page, and that is flat.—After all, I must begin another page, for, with my nonsense, I had like to forget the most important part of the business.   The Minister is in daily expectation of three millions of livres in specie, one million of which he destines for our expedition.   If this be so, it looks like business at last.   The moment he receives the money he will begin his preparations.   But then, Clarke, who is certainly at the head of the military correspondence, knows nothing of all this.   "*I am lost in sensations of troubled emotions.*"   What am I to think ? "*Hey ho, hey day ! I know not what to do, nor what to say !*"   I have made a very wise rule for myself, and I will keep it, that is, never to be elevated by appearances, and, indeed, to say the truth, I see as yet no great appearances to elevate me.   Well, I am blind with sleep, and yet I am bound in honour to finish this page as I have begun it.   Now for a quotation.

> " There's thirteen lines gone through, driblet by driblet,
>   'Tis done.   Count how you will, I warrant there's fourteen."

March 23rd.   Madgett sent for me this morning to tell me, as usual, that everything is going on well, but, for my part, I think everything is going on very slowly.   However, I did not say so, and he went on, that he was going express to look among the prisoners for Mr. Wm. Browne, by the Minister's directions, and, if he found him, he would be sent off instantly for Ireland, after I had given him his instructions.   So, that affair is settled, if Matthew is to be found.   It is a perilous business, but he must take his chance, and, as he will have no papers, I hope he may come off clear.   He then consulted me as to the old scheme (which I am more and more satisfied is some kind of a job) concerning debauching the Irish prisoners.   His idea is, they should be put aboard privateers, and landed in different parts of Ireland, to prepare the people, though neither they nor the people were to be in the secret.   How they are to communicate what they do not know, is not very clear ; however, let that pass.   I answered, I should be very glad to see them all in Ireland on a proper occasion, but conceived it would be hazarding the whole measure to part with one of them until the landing was effected, as the enemy might surmise something of the business, and take effectual measures to prevent it.   That, as to preparing the people, he might take my word that they were sufficiently prepared already.   This is the six-and-fiftieth time I have given my opinion on this head, yet he still returns to the charge.   I know the Irish a little.   The way to manage them is this : If they intend to use the Irish prisoners, let them be marched down under other pretences to the port from whence the embarkation is to be made.   When everything else is ready, let them send in a large quantity of wine and brandy, a fiddle and some French *filles*, and then, when Pat's heart is a little soft with love and wine, send in two or three proper persons in regimentals, and with green cockades in their hats, to speak to them, of whom I will very gladly be one. I think, in that case, it would not be very hard to persuade him to take a trip once more to Ireland, just to see his *people* a little. At least, I am sure if this scheme does not answer, that nothing will. It may also be right to make the first man who offers, a captain on the spot, and one or two more subalterns. To return. Madgett spoke to me again about Prieur, with great commendation, and I dare say justly, of his talents and patriotism, adding, that he had come out of power as poor as Job, and literally drank water to save the expense of wine, which he could not afford. This, in a member of the late *Comité de salut public,* is strong presumptive proof of his honesty. He added that Prieur was almost a stranger to him, but that it was the Minister's desire, and that I should use some little address in mentioning it to Carnot. I answered, I certainly would do my best, and if I succeeded, and that we went to Ireland together, I believed if Prieur continued to drink water it would be out of a preference for that liquor, for we would put him in a state to drink what he liked. I always keep up the idea, and, in fact, it is my opinion that liberal provision should be made, in case we succeed, for those Frenchmen who might be in high station in Ireland, as the Generals, Commissaires Civils, &c. I am sure it would be money well laid out, and agreeable to the native generosity of the Irish people. In fine, I should like Prieur very well from what I have heard of him, and will certainly push that affair as far as it will go. Madgett then told me the Minister desired I should draw up such a memorial as I thought the French commander ought to publish on landing. That is not quite so easy. I wished to evade it, by saying the style of French eloquence was so different from ours that I doubted my abilities to do it. He answered, it was precisely for that reason it was necessary I should write it ; that, when I had done, the Executive Directory would make such alterations and additions as they might see necessary ; but the groundwork must be mine. I then said I would try, and we parted. He is to be seven or eight days on his tour, apostolising among the Irish prisoners, which, once for all, as he is conducting it, I do not like. For the manifesto. I never in my life had less appetite for composition than just now. It is a serious business, and I have no assistance. I wish to God P. P. was here, or Gog.[1] What shall I do? I am in a damned fright. Well, to-morrow we will see. At present my idea is to make it as plain as a pikestaff, but how will the French like that? They love meta-phors, but I think, in the present case, I will stick to plain English. *"Well, if we must, we must, and since 'tis so, the less that's said the better."* Apropos! I should have observed that I finished the copies of my two memorials, and left them at Clarke's bureau, with a note that I would call the day after but one.

March 24*th*. Began my French manifesto. It drags a little heavy or so, but there is no remedy. I wish they would write it themselves.

March 25*th*. At work in the morning at my manifesto. I think it begins to clear up a little. I find a strong disposition to be scurrilous against the English Government, which I will not check. I will write on, pell-mell, and correct it in cool blood, if my blood will ever cool on that subject. Went, at one o'clock, to Clarke— Damn it, he has had my memorials, and never looked at them. Well, this is my first mortification: God knows I do not care if the memorials were sent to the devil, provided the business be once undertaken. It is not for the glory of General Clarke's admiration of my compositions that I am anxious. He apologised for the delay by alleging the multiplicity of other business, and perhaps he had reason, yet I think there are few affairs of more consequence than those of Ireland, if well understood. But how can they be understood if they will not read the information that is offered them?—Well, *"'Tis but in vain,"* &c. Clarke fixed with me to call on him the day but one after, at two o'clock. The delay, to be sure, is not great; nevertheless, I do not like it. There was something, too, in his manner, which was not quite to my taste, not but that he was extremely civil. Perhaps it is all fancy, or that I was out of humour. Well, the 27th I hope we shall see, and till then, let me work at my manifesto. Heigho! I have no great stomach for that business to-day; but it must be,

<hr>

[1] Another clear indication of where Keogh stood.

and so *allons*. But first I will go gingerly, and dine alone in the Elysian fields. It is inconceivable the solitude I live in here. Sometimes I am most dreadfully out of spirits, and it is no wonder. Losing the society of a family that I dote upon, and that loves me so dearly, and living in Paris, amongst utter strangers, like an absolute *Chartreux*. Well, "*Had honest Sam Crowe been within hail—but what signifies palavering?*" I will go to my dinner. Evening; did no good—"*I cannot write this selfsame manifesto, said I, despairingly.*" No opera. Went to bed at eight o'clock.

March 26th. At work at the manifesto like a vicious mule, kicking all the way. However, I am getting on, but I declare I know no more than my Lord Mayor whether what I am writing is good, bad, or indifferent : "*Fair and softly goes far in a day.*" I am going fair and softly, but I cannot say I go far in a day. I have been writing now five hours, without intermission, and I am surprised to find how little I have done ; but I write two lines, and blot out three, so it is easy to see how I get on. Well, now I think it is time to go to my dinner. I am to dine with my friend Dupetit Thouars, who has, I am heartily glad to find, re-entered the service. He has at present the rank of Commodore, and if the war continues some time longer, may probably become an Admiral. I hope and believe he will do his duty, though he is a damned Aristocrat ; but then he hates the English cordially, and that covers a multitude of sins. Evening : Dupetit Thouars prevented by business ; but, to make amends, left a very troublesome French boy, to keep me from being low-spirited, I suppose. Got rid of him as well as I could. At night sent for a bottle of Burgundy, intending to drink just one glass. Began to read (having opened my bottle) " Memoirs of the Reign of Louis XIV." After reading some time, found my passion at a particular circumstance kindled rather more than seemed necessary, as I flung the book from me with great indignation. Turned to my bottle, to take a glass to cool me—found, to my great astonishment, that it was empty—Oh ho !—Got up and put everything in its place, exactly—examined all my locks—saw that my door was fast, as there may be rogues in the hotel—peeped under my bed, lest the enemy should surprise me there. It is the part of a wise man to be cautious, and I found myself, just then, inclined to be extremely prudent. Having satisfied myself that all was safe, " *I mounted the wall of my castle, as I called it, and having pulled the ladder up after me, I lay down in my hammock and slept contentedly.*" This is vilely misquoted, but no matter for that ; it is just like one of P. P.'s quotations. Slept like a top all night.

CHAPTER XVIII.

MILITARY PLANS AND PROJECTS.

March 27th. On looking over my manifesto this morning, I begin to think it is damned trash God forgive me if I judge uncharitably, but it seems to me to be pitiful stuff; at any rate, it certainly is not a French manifesto at all, and I foresaw in the outset the difficulty of writing in the character of a French General. If I were to compose a manifesto for the Irish Convention, and had good advisers, I might get on ; but, as to this affair, I see that I shall have to give it up for hard work, as they say in Galway. Went at two o'clock to General Clarke, and had a long conversation. He told me he had read my two memorials, and without flattery could assure me they were extremely well done (that of course): that he had made, in consequence, a favourable report to Carnot, who endeavoured to read them also, but finding a difficulty in reading English manuscript, he (Clarke) was to translate them for him ; that all he could at present tell me was, that the Executive was determined to send a person directly to Ireland, and that he had in consequence written to an ex-officer of the Irish Brigade to know if he would go, but that he declined on the score of health. I told him I was sorry for that, as a military man, if one could be found proper in other respects, would be what I would prefer. He asked me, did I myself know any person fit to go? I answered, I did not, having no acquaintance, and industriously avoiding having any, in France ; that I did not know, however, but that at that moment I had a brother lying in the prison of Guise. I then gave him a short history of Mr. Wm. Browne's (my brother Matthew's) affair, concluding by saying that if he was yet in France, and no more proper person could

be found, he might do. At the same time, I did not at all like
to propose him ; first, because it was a service of danger, in which
I did not wish to hazard his life, and next, that I would avoid
recommending a person so nearly connected with me to the
French Government, lest I might appear to act on interested
views. Clarke then, after some civilities in reply, asked me what
I thought of some of the Irish priests yet remaining in France.
I answered, that he knew my opinion as to priests of all kinds ;
that in Ireland they had acted, all along, execrably; that they
hated the very name of the French Revolution, and that I feared,
and indeed was sure, that if one was sent from France, he would
immediately, from the *esprit de corps,* get in with his brethren in
Ireland, who would misrepresent everything to him ; and, of
course, that any information which he might collect would not
be worth a farthing. I added, that the state of Ireland might
be much better collected from the debates of their Parliament,
even mutilated as he would find them in the English newspapers
which I saw upon his table, than from the report of any individual
just peeping into the country and returning, supposing that he
was lucky enough to escape ; and I observed that these debates
furnished the very strongest evidence, because they were extorted
from the mouth of the enemy, who was so interested to conceal
the facts, and who would conceal them if he was able. (This
I had mentioned in a former conversation, but I thought it right
to press it, and it seemed to strike Clarke very forcibly.) I then
went on to observe, that I hoped, if the measure were adopted
by the French Executive, that they did not mean to delay it till
the return of this emissary, if one were sent, especially as his
business would be to give information in Ireland, not to bring any
thence. Clarke answered, supposing the measure to be adopted,
certainly not ; that all preparations would be going on in the
meantime ; but I must see it would be necessary to send a person
to apprise the people in Ireland. I replied, by all means, but that
whoever we sent, he must carry no papers, nor speak to above four
or five persons whom I would point out, for fear of hazarding a
discovery, which might blast all ; in which Clarke agreed. We

then fell into a discourse on the detail of the business, being in
fact a kind of commentary, *viva voce*, on the memorials. I began
by saying, that as I presumed the number of troops would not be
above five or six thousand men, I hoped and expected they would
be the best that France could spare us. Clarke replied, they
would undoubtedly be sufficiently disciplined. I answered, it was
not merely disciplined troops, but men who were accustomed to
stand fire, that we wanted, some of the old battalions from
Holland or the Rhine ; for as to raw troops, we should soon have
enough of them. Clarke answered, that he could not promise we
should have the pick and choice of the French army, but that,
if any were sent, they would be brave troops, that would run
on the enemy as soon as they saw them. I answered, as to the
courage of the French army, it was sufficiently known, and I would
venture to say, that wherever they would lead, the Irish would
follow. (I see that we shall not get veterans, if we get any, which
is bad, but we must do as we can.) I then said, at least as to the
cannoniers, of which we had none, it would be indispensable they
should be perfectly trained and disciplined ; in which he agreed.
I then came to the General, and said it would be of the greatest
consequence, if the thing were possible, that he should be an
officer of reputation, whose name might be known in Ireland,
where names were things of weight. He replied that it would not
be easy to get an officer such as I described to undertake the
enterprise with so small a force. (This I was all along afraid of.)
I replied, none would, unless some dashing fighting fellow, with
a good deal of enthusiasm in his character ; adding, that Bournonville, whom I only knew by reputation and Camus's report, seemed
to me to be precisely such a man as we wanted. Clarke replied,
as to Bournonville, he was already appointed to the army in
Holland, and it was not to be supposed he would quit the
command of sixty thousand men to go command six thousand.
I answered, he knew best, but my opinion was, there was more
glory to be acquired in Ireland, even with that force, and also
more profit, if profit were any object, as he must suppose the Irish
nation would amply reward those who were instrumental in

establishing their liberties, adding, that we were generous even
to prodigality. He said he was sure Bournonville would prefer
his present situation. (So there is an end of that expectation,
for which I am sorry.) Clarke then said there were some Irish
officers yet remaining in France who might go, and he mentioned
Jennings, who used to call himself Baron de Kilmaine, God knows
why. I answered that in Ireland we had no great confidence
in the officers of the old Irish Brigade, so many of them had either
deserted, or betrayed the French cause ; that, as to Jennings,
he had had the misfortune to command after Custine, and had
been obliged to break up the famous "*Camp de Cæsar ;*" that,
though this might probably have been no fault of his, it had made
an impression, and, as he was at any rate not a fortunate general,
I thought it would be better to have a Frenchman. This naturally
introduced the Irish Brigade, in which Clarke had served for two
years in Berwicks, and I gave him an account of the various slights
and mortifications they had undergone, both in England and
Ireland ; how they had been obliged to accept the King's pardon
for high treason, for having been in the French service ; how those
who were able, were obliged to pay the fees, and those who were
not, to accept it *in formâ pauperis*, a circumstance so excessively
degrading, that nothing could be worse ; how the Lord Lieutenant
had applied on their behalf to the Catholic Committee, and had
been refused ; how the very mob despised them, as an instance
of which I mentioned the anecdote of the Etat-Major intending
to go to mass on Christmas Day in grand costume, and how they
were obliged to give it up for fear of being hustled by the populace, who had given Dr. Troy warning that they would treat them
as crimps ; with all which Clarke was exceedingly delighted.
He spoke of O'Connell with respect, as a good parade officer to
prepare troops for service, but no extent of genius for command.
(He would do for us as Baron Steuben did in America, and if
matters go forward, I for one will be for his being employed, for
I know he hates England, and my poor friend Sweetman, whom
I shall ever deeply regret, had an excellent opinion of him.) He
also said that Colonel Moore was the best officer amongst them ;

and, as to all the others, they were to be sure brave men, but none of them of any reputation. We then returned to our own affairs. I said, we would want a few engineers. He asked me for what, since we had no fortifications. I replied, for field service, redoubts, &c. He replied, that was always done by the Adjutant Generals. I then observed I had one thing to mention entirely personal ; that I had exerted myself a good deal, risked my safety on more than one occasion, and had a very narrow escape for my life ; that if this business went forward, I hoped and expected the French Government would allow me to take a part in the execution, and that I was sure, if he would excuse the vanity of the assertion, that I could be of material service ; that I was willing to encounter danger as a soldier, but had a violent objection to being hanged as a traitor ; that, consequently, I desired a commission in the French army ; that, as to the rank, that was indifferent to me, my only object being a certainty of being treated as a soldier, in case the fortune of war should throw me into the hands of the enemy, who I knew would otherwise show me no mercy; and that I hoped, under all the circumstances of the case, that my request would not be considered unreasonable. He answered, that as to that, he could see no possibility of difficulty ; that, undoubtedly, I had a claim at the least for so much, and he was sure it would be done, and that in the manner most agreeable to my feelings. (So I am in hopes, if the business goes forward, that this affair will be settled.) We then began to chat, rather than talk seriously, and moot points of war. First, as to Dublin, I told him I did not expect, with the proposed force, that much could be done there at first ; that its garrison was always at least five thousand strong, and that the Government, taking advantage of the momentary success of the coalesced despots, had disarmed the people, taken their cannon, and passed the Gunpowder and Convention bills, whose nature and operation I explained to him ; that, however, if the landing were once effected, one of two things would happen : either the Government would retain the garrison for their security, in which case there would be five thousand men idle on the part of the enemy, or they would march them off to oppose us, in which case the people would rise and seize the capital ; and I added if they preferred the first measure, which I thought most likely, whenever we were strong enough to march southward, if we were, as I had no doubt we should be, superior in the field, we could starve Dublin in a week, without striking a blow. I then mentioned the great advantages which would result from a diversion in Connaught, if possible, from the discontents prevailing in that province, and the strong line of defence which the Shannon affords ; and this I pressed upon him as strongly as I could. He saw all the advantages of it as clearly as I did, for indeed they are self-evident, but I cannot say he gave me any violent hopes that it would be attempted in the first instance. (N.B.—What is to hinder our doing it ourselves in a week, by way of Sligo? Mind this, and examine the map.) We then spoke of Cork, of which I know nothing. He tells me the harbour is admirably situated for defence against any attack by sea, but if you are superior at land, you can, by taking possession of a hill that supplies the town with water, force it to surrender without striking a blow. I then mentioned my scheme, as to the Irish, now prisoners in France, and made him laugh immoderately at my mode of recruiting, which is, however, admirably adapted to the gentlemen whom I should have to address. Seeing that he was tickled with the business, I exerted myself, and made divers capital hits at the expense of poor Pat, concerning

> "Women and wine, which compare so well,
>   That they run in a perfect parallel,"

as the poet hath it. To be sure, it is in vain to deny it, but the poor fellow is a little exposed on those two sides, and the foul fiend, who knows it right well, always judiciously chooses one or the other, or sometimes both, to defeat him. God knows, I have been buffeted by Satan, as well as another, in my time :

> "With women and wine I defy every care."—(Sings.)

I would be glad to know what P. P. would say to my doctrine, concerning the fallibility of poor Pat's judgment, when

> "The wine looks red in the glass,
> And the bright eyes of beauty are beaming."

Yes! yes! he is proof to all that, and so is P. P., and another person that shall be nameless. Well, we are all men, and so let me say no more about the matter. Clarke asked me, might they not serve us as the French prisoners did the British at Quiberon? I answered, there was this most material difference, that the French were brought back to fight against their country, and the Irish would be brought back to fight, not against their country, but against the English; and that I had no doubt but they would do their duty. I then begged him to keep me in Carnot's recollection, and having fixed to call on him regularly once a week, to see how things were going on, I took my leave, his last words being, "I wish most sincerely, and I hope" (which he marked) "the business will be seriously taken up by the Executive."

I like this day's business very well. I see I was wrong the day before yesterday in thinking Clarke's manner cold. I fancy that it was myself that was out of temper, because, forsooth, he had not read my memorials. That was not unnatural on my side neither, but, indeed, it was much more my anxiety about the business, than my *amour propre*, or any attachment to my own compositions. I hope I am above that, for I have a very pretty opinion of the purity of my motives. I have protested again and again, in these memorandums, that I am acting to the best of my judgment, seeing that I have no advisers, which is a great loss, and on the very fairest principles. Have I no selfish motives? Yes, I have. If I succeed here, I feel I shall have strong claims on the gratitude of my country; and as I love her, and as I think I shall be able to serve her, I shall certainly hope for some honourable station, as a reward for the sacrifices I have already made, and the dangers I have incurred, and those which I am ready and shall have to make and incur in the course of the business. Why not? If it were the case of any other person I am sure I should have the same opinion. I hope (but I am not sure) my country is my first object, at least she is my second. If there be one before her, as I rather believe there is, it is my dearest life and love, the light of my eyes, and spirit of my existence. I wish more than for anything on earth to place her in a splendid situation. There is none so elevated that she would not adorn, and that she does not deserve, and I believe that not I only, but every one who knows her, will agree as to that. Truth is truth! she is my first object. But would I sacrifice the interests of Ireland to her elevation? No! that I would not, and if I would, she would despise me, and, if she were to despise me, I would go hang myself like Judas. Well, there is no regulator for the human heart like the certainty of possessing the affections of an amiable woman, and, if so, what unspeakable good fortune do I not enjoy? Well, I do love my wife dearly, and that is the God's truth of it, and she is a thousand times too good for me, and I am not very bad neither, but then she is so infinitely better that it throws my great merit into the shade. For all that I have said of her and myself here, I will be judged by Whitley Stokes, and Peter Burrowes, and P. P., who are three fair men ; and I now have done this day's journal, and shall only observe, on looking over it, that I think I am as pretty a negotiator as a man would wish to see of a summer's day. But then this damn'd manifesto sticks in my stomach. Well, " *'Tis but in vain,*" &c.

March 28th. Went to the opera, as usual, like a fine gentleman. I always go to that theatre, because, as yet, I understand music better than French. *Panurge.* Superb spectacle. Lays, the best singer of the men, Madame Maillard of the women, Madame Pontriel extremely pretty, with something foolish in the expression of her countenance ; Mademoiselle Gavaudan an excellent comic actress ; Dufresne an admirable actor and sings tolerably ; all the others middling enough. Dancers. Vestris certainly the first, then Nivelon, Deshayes, Goyon, &c. Females : Clotilde, a fine figure with an infinity of grace and execution, but wants, as the French tell me, the *aplomb,* as they call it, that is, immobility of posture after executing a difficult passage. For my part I did not observe it till it was pointed out to me, but now I am beginning to grow something of a judge myself ; Perignon and Chevigny admirable dancers, and of merit so exactly equal that I know not which to prefer. They are both ordinary both in face and figure, but manage themselves with such dexterity that nothing can appear more graceful than they do in all their movements. Duchemin pretty, and dances very well. Milliere as ugly as mortal sin, but a most charming dancer ; I believe I like her the best. The Parisians prefer Chevigny. Nothing could be executed with more taste, or I may say more classically, than the Pas Russe was to-night by Nivelon and Milliere. Once for all, the King's theatre in the Haymarket is no better than a barn of strollers beside the Théâtre des Arts, as to scenery, machinery, dresses, and decorations ; but in revenge, their singers (being Italians) are far before the French, who, on the other hand, excel the Italians, and all other nations, in their dances. It is impossible to conceive anything in its kind more perfect than a grand ballet at the Opera of Paris, and, indeed, in all their theatres there is an attention paid to the preservation of costume, even in the minutest points, very far beyond the English theatres, where, I have seen myself, Macbeth, a Scottish chief of eight centuries ago, dressed in a very spruce vest of scarlet regimentals, and a bag wig, in which he need not be ashamed to show his face at St. James's, and where, to this hour, Hamlet the Dane, the son of Horwendillus, is exhibited, even by Kemble, from whom I would expect better things, in a fine black velvet full-trimmed suit, with the ribbon of the order of the Elephant over his shoulder ; where King John is habited after the fashion of 1160, and his antagonist, King Philip, confronts him in a cocked hat and feather, and a coat and waistcoat of the last court fashion. These absurdities the eye is never shocked with in France, and they are as attentive to the appearance of the meanest domestic as of the hero of the piece. All the minutiæ of the scene are equally correct : for example, in a Grecian tragedy they would not introduce a pair of handsome plated candlesticks. They have carefully studied the antique, and whatever is graceful among the moderns, and profited accordingly. I believe I have now said enough of the opera, to which the French are devoted *à la folie*. All the theatres are as full every night as they can hold, and I have never seen an instance of what we call in England a bad or even a middling house.

March 29th. "*My time, oh ye Muses, was happily spent, when Phœbe went with me wherever I went.*" Am I not to be sincerely pitied here? I do not know a soul; I speak the language with great difficulty; I live in taverns, which I detest; I cannot be always reading, and I find, by experience, that, when one reads perforce, there is not much of either profit or pleasure in it, from which I infer, philosophically, that the nature of man is adapted to liberty, and that all restraint beyond what is necessary——. Oh Lord! oh Lord! metaphysics! I return to my apartment, which is, notwithstanding, a very neat one, as if I was returning to gaol, and finally I go to bed at night as if I was mounting the guillotine. I do lead a dog's life of it here, that is the truth of it; my sole resource is the opera.

March 30th. Went to-day to the Church of St. Roch, to the *Fête de la Jeunesse ;* all the youth of the district, who have attained the age of sixteen, were to present themselves before the municipality and receive their arms, and those who were arrived at twenty-one were to be enrolled in the list of citizens, in order to ascertain their right of voting in the assemblies. The Church was decorated with the national colours, and a statue of Liberty, with an altar blazing before her. At the foot of the statue the municipality were seated, and the sides of the Church were filled with a crowd of spectators, the parents and friends of the young men, leaving a space vacant in the centre of the procession. It consisted of the Etat-Major of the sections composing the district, of the National Guards under arms, of the officers of the sections, and, finally, of the young men who were to be presented. The guard was mounted by veterans of the troops of the line, and there was a great pile of muskets and of sabres before the municipality. When the procession arrived, the names of the two classes were enrolled, and, in the meantime, the veterans distributed the arms amongst the parents and friends and mistresses of the young men. When the enrolment was finished, an officer pronounced a short address to the youths of sixteen, on the duty which they owed to their country, and the honour of bearing arms in her defence, to which they were about to be admitted. They then ran amongst the crowd of spectators and received their firelocks and sabres, some from their fathers, some from their mothers, and many, I could observe, from their lovers. When they were armed, their parents and mistresses embraced them, and they returned to their station. It is impossible to conceive anything more interesting than the spectacle was at that moment ; the pride and pleasure in the countenance of the parents ; the *fierté* of the young soldiers, and, above all, the expression in the features of so many young females, many of them beautiful, and all interesting from the occasion. I was in an enthusiasm. I do not at all wonder at the miracles which the French army has wrought in the contest for their liberties. When I looked at the spectacle before me, and recalled to mind the gangs of wretched recruits I had seen in Ireland, marching in their fetters, and handcuffed, I was no longer surprised at anything ; yet the poor Irish are a brave people ; and I think it would not be impossible to bring them up to the enthusiasm of the French ; at least if we have an opportunity we will try. I am more and more satisfied of the powerful effect of public spectacles, properly directed, in the course of a revolution. I should have observed that, during the ceremony, all the civic hymns were chanted, accompanied by a full band, and joined in the choruses by the young men. I wish my dearest love had heard the burst of "*Aux armes, Citoyens.*" It is impossible to conceive the effect of that immortal hymn, unless by those who have heard it at a festival in France ; it is absolute enchantment. This was a good day.

March 31*st.* Blank ! Not knowing what to do, I stroll about the bookstalls, and pick up military books dog cheap. If I had money to spare, I could make up a famous French library for a trifle. There are very expensive editions just now, if one chooses to lay out money in fine types, paper, and binding, but there are also most excellent editions of excellent works for half nothing. The ordinary price I pay for a duodecimo, bound, is fifty francs, in assignats, which, at the present rates of the louis, is about twopence. Mary, I know, will laugh at my collection of États Militaires, as she calls them ; no matter for that: "*By Cot's* *providinch they may be yused some time or other.*" I laugh at them myself sometimes, but I am tempted because they are bargains, in spite of Poor Richard. *Never*, says he, *buy what you don't want, because it is a bargain. I have known many a man ruined by buying bargains.*

April 1st. Lounged about "*cheapening old authors at a stall.*" Saw a superb battalion of infantry, and a squadron of cavalry inspected at the Tuileries by a general officer. The French are very fine troops, such of them as I have seen ; they are all of the right military age, with scarcely any old men past service, or boys not grown up to it. They are not very correct in their evolutions, not near equal to the English, and much less, as I suppose, to the Germans. This has a little shaken my faith in the force of discipline, for they have certainly beaten both British and Germans like dogs ; but, after the spectacles which I see daily, why need I wonder at that ? The *Fête de la Jeunesse*, for example, of yesterday explains it at once. Discipline will not stand against such enthusiasm as I was a witness to, and, I may say, as I felt myself. I remember P. P. was always of that opinion too, though I doubted it, which shows the superiority of his judgment, and his more accurate knowledge of the human character. If we go on in Ireland, we must move heaven and earth to create the same spirit of enthusiasm which I see here ; and, from my observation of the Irish character, which so nearly resembles the French, I think it very possible. The devil of it is, that poor Pat is a little given to drink, and the French are very sober. We must rectify that as well as we can ; he is a good man that has no fault, and I have sort of sympathetic feeling which makes me the more indulgent on this score. Query : Would it have a good effect to explode corporal punishment altogether in the Irish army, and substitute a discharge with infamy for great faults, and confinement and hard diet for lesser ones ? I believe there is no corporal punishment in the French army, and I would wish to create a spirit in our soldiers, a high point of honour, like that of the French. When one of their Generals (Marshal Richelieu) was besieging a town, he was tormented with the drunkenness of his army. He gave out, in orders, that any soldier who was seen drunk should not be suffered to mount to the assault, and there was not a man to be seen in liquor afterwards. Drunkenness then induced a suspicion of cowardice, which kept them effectually sober. It is a choice anecdote, and pregnant with circumstances. To return. There is a great latitude in dress allowed both to the French officers and soldiers, which has demolished, or, at least, much circumscribed another of my prejudices; for I was, on that score, a great martinet. I fancy truth may lie between P. P.'s opinion and mine, so let us compound as follows : If there be a high point of honour, and a spirit of ardent enthusiasm, then discipline (I mean that discipline which makes men machines) may be, in a great degree, suffered to relax, and, *à fortiori*, the minutiæ of dress to be neglected ; but if that point of honour and spirit of enthusiasm do not exist, their absence must be supplied by the force of discipline, and then, as part of the system, even the article of dress becomes of some importance. The French cavalry are armed only with sabres and pistols, without carbines. I am glad of that, for I always thought carbines useless. The fire of infantry seems to me to have very little effect in comparison of the noise it makes, and the fire of cavalry I am sure is nonsense. The *arme blanche* is the system of the French, and I believe for the Irish, at least if our affair goes forward it will be what I shall recommend, for poor Pat is very furious and savage, and the tactics of every nation ought to be adapted to the national character. Platooning at forty yards' distance may answer very well to the English and German phlegm, but as we have rather more animal spirits, I vote for the bayonet. I do not love playing at long bullets. To conclude, I wish to study the character of the French soldiers, and, if possible, to create the same spirit in Ireland, and, in a word, to make the French army our model instead of the Prussian. I think P. P. will allow that this is candid in me, after all the disputes he and I have had on the subject of discipline. In the afternoon went, for the first time, to the Conseil des 500 (the French House of Commons). It is certainly the first assembly in Europe, and the worst accommodated ; the room is mean, dirty, and ill-contrived ; the system of speaking from a tribune in itself bad, and they have made it worse by placing it at the feet of the President (to whom the orator's back is turned) at one end of a very oblong room, so that those at the lower end cannot possibly hear half of what is said. They are likewise very disorderly, which I wonder at the more as they have had now six years' experience of public assemblies, but it is the same impetuosity that makes them redoubtable in the field, and disorderly in the Senate. As to their appearance, it was extremely plain. Nobody was what I would call dressed, many without powder, in pantaloons and boots. From the figure of the room, and the appearance of the assembly, they put me strongly in mind of my old masters, the General Committee, at their famous meetings in Back Lane. The resemblance was very striking, with this difference, that I must say the General Committee looked more like gentlemen, and were ten times more regular and orderly, or, in a word, like a legislative body. They were only on business of course, and, as I found nobody to point out to me the most celebrated members, I did not remain above half an hour. On the whole, they looked more like their countrymen who broke into the Roman Senate, than like the Senators assembled in their ivory chairs to receive them ; nor can I say, as the Ambassador of Pyrrhus did of the Senators of Rome, that they looked like an assembly of Demigods. But it is very little matter what they look like. They have humbled all Europe thus far, with their blue pantaloons and unpowdered locks, and that is the main point ; the rest is of little consequence.

April 2nd. Went to-day to Clarke, at the Luxembourg. He tells me he has been hunting in vain for a proper person to go to Ireland ; that he had a Frenchman tampered with, who was educated from a child in England, and spoke the language perfectly. That, at first, he agreed to go, but afterwards, on learning the penalties of the English law against high treason, his heart failed him and he declined. This is bad. However, there is no remedy. Clarke went on to tell me that if the measure were pursued (without saying whether it would or not) the Executive were determined to employ me in the French service in a military capacity ; and

that I might depend on finding everything of that kind settled to
my satisfaction.   I answered that, as to my own personal feelings,
I had nothing more to demand.   He then wished I would give
him a short plan for a system of *Chouannerie* in Ireland, particularly in Munster, for he would tell me frankly the Government had
a design before anything more serious was attempted, to turn in a
parcel of renegadoes (or, as he said, blackguards) into Ireland in
order to distress and embarrass the Government there, and distract
them in their motions.   I answered I was sorry to hear it.   That
if a measure of that kind was adopted with a view to prepare the
minds of the people it was unnecessary, for they were already sufficiently prepared.   That it would only produce local insurrections,
which would soon be suppressed, because the army (including the
militia) would, in that case, to a certainty, support the Government,
and every man, of any property, even those who wished for the
independence of their country would do the same, from the dread
of indiscriminate plunder, which would be but too likely to ensue
from such a measure as he described ; that there was another
thing very much to be apprehended in that case, and which, if I
was Minister of England, I should not hesitate one moment about,
and in which the Parliaments of both countries would instantly
concur, viz., to pass two acts, repealing those clauses which enact
that the militia shall only serve in their own country, and directly
to shift the militia of Ireland into England, and replace them by
the English militia, which would serve to awe both countries, and
most materially embarrass us.   That if all this was so, and those
insurrections suppressed, their inevitable effect, grounded upon all
historical experience, would be to strengthen the existing Government.   That England would take that opportunity to reduce Ireland again to that state of subjection, or even a worse one, that she
had been in before 1782, and would bind her, hand and foot, in
such a manner as to make all future exertion impossible ; in which
she would be supported by the whole Irish aristocracy, who
compose the Legislature, and who would sacrifice everything to
their own security.   That if France had nothing in view but to
distress England for the moment, undoubtedly what he mentioned,

however ruinous to Ireland, might have that effect ; but if the Republic went on more enlarged views, and sounder policy, she ought not, for a moment, to give consideration to the scheme. That if the main force were once landed, undoubtedly it would be right to set Ireland in a blaze at the four corners, and burn out the English Government, but that I was satisfied it would be ruinous to make the measure he described precede the landing. Finally, I added, that, as to myself, I was ready to be one of ten men, if the French Government were determined to send no more. I also begged him to remember that I gave this, with all due deference, as my fixed opinion on a point which I had considered, in consequence of an idea of the same kind having been stated to me by Madgett, from the Minister. Clarke began by saying that, as to my being sent, it was not the idea of the French Government to risk my safety in that stage of the business. That the objections I had urged were of considerable weight, and that he would give them serious consideration. He then desired to see me in four or five days, and, after demanding my address, which I gave him, I took my leave. (*Vide* Journal of February 2, and March 22 and 23, on this subject, which, I am sorry to see, has got ground amongst them.) This conversation explains what Madgett (who is returned from his mission) told me this morning : that he has got fifty-one Irish prisoners, who would fight, blood to the knees, against England, and that he thought it would be very serviceable if they were dispersed through the country. I referred him, for my opinion, to our former conversations on that head ; that I thought, undoubtedly, if the business were once begun, the wider the flame was spread, the better ; but that the grand blow of the landing near Belfast should precede all others, and that being once effected, as many more as he pleased. I see, clearly, that my opinion will not be followed ; and I fear it will be found to be so much the worse. I have, however, discharged my conscience. I cannot blame France for wishing to retaliate on England, the abomina-tions of La Vendee and the Chouans, but it is hard that it should be at the expense of poor Ireland. It will be she and not England that will suffer, and the English will be glad of it, for they hate us next to the French. If these ragamuffins are smuggled into the country, local insurrections will ensue, the militia will obey their officers, the bravest of our poor peasants will stand to be cut down, and of those who run away, numbers will be hanged, and many more sent aboard the fleet, to fight the battles of England, and the Government will be so much the stronger ; not to mention the mischief which will be unprofitably done, even to the aristocracy. I dislike all this very much if I could help myself, but I fear I shall not be able to prevent it. At all events, I have given my opinions honestly. Poor Pat ! I fear he is just now in a bad neighbourhood. Madgett tells me that Mr. W. Browne left Guise with his passport eight months ago. So there is an end of that business. I hope in God he is, by this, safe with the girls at Princeton. How happy shall we be if ever we have the good fortune to meet again ! I suffer a great deal in this business ; however, "*'Tis but in vain for soldiers to complain.*"

April 3rd. Called on Madgett this morning by appointment. He is always full of good news. He tells me the marine force will be seventeen ships of war, great and small, arms and artillery, &c., for 50,000 men ; that many of the officers are already named, but he believes not the general-in-chief. All this is very good, but " *Would I could see it, quoth blind Hugh.*" We then came to my commission in the service of the Republic. He asked me, as I was here the representative of the Irish people, would I not feel it beneath the dignity of that character to accept of a commission, for, as to the French Government, they would give me any rank I pleased to demand. I answered that I considered the station of a French officer was one that would reflect honour on any one who filled it ; that, consequently, on that score, I could have no possible objection ; that, besides, my object was to ensure protection, in case any of the infinite varieties of accidents incident to the fortune of war should throw me into the hands of the enemy ; that I was very willing to risk my life in the field, but not to be hanged up as a traitor ; that, as to rank, it was indifferent to me, as I did not doubt, but as soon as things were a little reduced into order in Ireland, I should obtain such a station in that service as they

might think I merited ; that, in the meantime, I should wish to be
of the family of the general-in-chief, as I could be of use there,
speaking a little French, to interpret between him and the natives ;
unless the Government here thought proper to raise a corps of the
Irish prisoners, in which case I hoped they would entrust me with
the command. Madgett asked me how many might be necessary
to form the *cadre* of a corps ? I answered if we could muster one
hundred and fifty it would be sufficient, and as soon as we got to
Ireland we would mount them as hussars. Just then we were
interrupted by the arrival of Fitzsimons, the priest, who has been
recommended by Prieur de la Marne to go to Ireland. Madgett
began to speak without reserve, but, for my part, I kept myself in
generals, because "*Dolus versatur in universalibus.*" I was soon
very glad I did so, for I see that he is a damned fool, not fit to
deliver a common message. He may be honest, for aught I know,
and may have the courage necessary, but he has not one grain of
talents. I never was more provoked in my life, and the fellow was
pinning himself on me, though my manner was as cold and dry as
possible, but he seems to have a reasonable assurance, resulting
partly from his extreme ignorance. Curse on him ! for a bladdering idiot ; what shall I do with him ? How can I explain myself
to such a damned dunce, or entrust the safety of my friends, not
to speak of the measure itself, to a blockhead that has not sense
enough to keep his mouth shut, or count five on his fingers ? Where
the devil in hell did Prieur pick him up, and what sort of a fellow
must Prieur be himself, to recommend him ? If he judges him
capable, he is a fool ; if not, he is worse. Damn him to hell ! I
wish he was dead. "*I would fain have him die, split me !*" Is not
this most terribly provoking ? for it seems to be a thing settled
that he shall go. What am I to do in this cursed dilemma, and
how came Madgett not to interfere in time ? I objected all along
to priests as the worst of all possible agents, and here is one who is
the worst of all possible priests. How the devil can I communicate
with such an ass ? It is impossible to conceive anything more
vulgar, ignorant, and stupid. If he goes to Ireland, the people
there will suppose that we are laughing at them, to send such a

fellow. What will Gog think? Yes, Gog will open his heart very readily to Mr. Fitzsimons. God rot him! I am in such a rage I know not how to leave off abusing him. Well, I am to dine to-day with Madgett, and please the Lord I will tell him a piece of my mind. Perhaps I may be able to put a spoke in Mr. Fitzsimons' wheel, if it be not, as I fear it is, too late. To give a specimen of his talents (because he amuses me): There happened to be some Portuguese despatches taken aboard a vessel going to Brazil. Sullivan, Madgett's nephew, was carrying them to the office to be translated, and Mr. Fitzsimons made the following remark: "You will have fine fun, making out what these Portuguese fellows say; are all those papers, pray, WROTE *in English?*" The despatches of the Portuguese Ministry to the Governor of Rio Janeiro *written in English!* Oh Lord! oh Lord! I thought I should have choked, endeavouring to smother the irresistible propensity I felt to laugh in his face. Yes, he is a pretty devil of an agent. I suppose he will talk Portuguese to the Irish, by way of keeping the secret. Damn him sempiternally! What the devil brought him across me?—Dinner with Madgett; after dinner began my remarks on Fitzsimons, and, after relating the anecdote of the Portuguese despatches written in English, told him plump I would not hazard the safety of my friends in Ireland, nor of the measure, by communicating with such an eternal blockhead. Madgett at first seemed inclined to make some defence for him, but the cause was too bad, and I was too determined, so he gave him up, and assured me he should not go; and there the matter rests, but I think I will go to-morrow to the Minister, and tell him a piece of my mind touching this said Mr. Fitzsimons. I must leave nothing to chance. I cannot conceive how Prieur could be mistaken in him. The fellow was fawning on me too, but I was as cold as ice, and stiff as a Spaniard, and would not understand the broadest hints. Hang him! I have taken up too much of my paper about him and his Portuguese written in English. Is it not strange, however, that Prieur and De la Croix and Madgett should be satisfied to let him pass on a business of such magnitude? I think I must go to the Minister, and make it a point that he shall be stopped. At all events, I will not communicate with him, "that's flat." After dinner walked for two hours in the Tuileries with Sullivan, talking red-hot Irish politics. Sullivan is a good lad, and I like him very well. Bed early.

April 4th. Called on Madgett at nine o'clock, in order to give him, in cold blood, my determination as to Mr. Fitzsimons, who, indeed, does not understand Portuguese. Madgett gone out of town *recruiting.* That is another scheme, which, as they are managing it, I do not like. I will go to Clarke again to-morrow, and protest against it, for I will not be accessory to spilling the blood of my brave and unfortunate countrymen. Poor fellows! and it would be the bravest and best of them ; whose lives, if they must be sacrificed, should be reserved for a better occasion. I will, on my part, leave nothing undone to prevent the infinite mischief which I see, in every point of view, resulting from introducing the spirit of *Chouannerie* in Ireland. I think I will go now and put my reasons against it on paper, in order to give to Clarke to-morrow. . . . Write my reasons, which are to be found in my memorandum of the 2nd, in the shape of five or six short propositions, and set off to give them to Clarke. Called, in my way, at the Rue du Bac, and saw the Minister. I told him that it was not a pleasant thing to speak hardly of anybody, but that my duty compelled me to tell him that Fitzsimons, whom I had seen and conversed with, was absolutely unfit for the mission on which it was proposed to send him ; that, as to his principles and honesty, I had no reason to doubt them, but, as to his talents, he was a downright blockhead (imbecile). That, consequently, I could not commit myself, or my friends, or the cause, to a person whom I found to be absolutely incapable. The Minister replied, that he did not know him at all ; he asked me then had I no person myself to recommend ? I told him I knew not a soul in Paris. He then desired me to look for a proper person (which I shall not do, for, in the first place, I know nobody, and, in the next, I will not make myself responsible by a recommendation), for, that it was absolutely necessary, he said, that the Government should be in-formed of the actual state of things in Ireland. He then asked me, had I not seen General Clarke?   I told him I had, by the orders of Carnot.   Well, said he, I suppose he told you that the affair is in train, that preparations are making, "*et j'espère que ça ira.*"   I told him I was very happy to hear it from him, and took my leave.   This short conversation took place in the court of his hotel, where I met him coming out of his bureau.   From the Minister I went to Clarke, whom I saw for two minutes, he being engaged with a general officer and his aide-de-camp.   I gave him my reasons, and he told me the plan was given up, which I am very glad to hear.   He also said he had not been yet able to find a proper person to go to Ireland.   I then mentioned that I had been with the Minister about Fitzsimons ; that he was utterly incapable, and that I mentioned it to him, lest he might be taken by surprise as to his appointment ; he then desired me to call upon him every three or four days, and so we parted.   I am heartily glad the system of *Chouannerie* is knocked in the head, and I hope it is partly owing to my representations against it. I am now absolutely idle for three or four days, and I am truly weary of this life.   "*Fie upon't, I want work !*"   Well, if ever I get to Ireland I shall have work enough to make me amends for this. Strolled, as usual, to the Champs Elysées, and dined alone. Delicious weather, and all the world diverting themselves except me.   "*Poor moralist, and what art thou ?   A solitary fly.*"   I declare I am as much alone here as if I were in the deserts of Arabia, and that is hard in such a city as Paris.   In the evening, *Comédie Italienne;* no great things.   The opera is the only spectacle for me.   Bed at ten.   "*Well, God's blessings be about the man,*" quoth Sancho Panza, "*who first invented sleep, it covers a man all over like his cloak.*"

April 5*th,* 6*th,* 7*th.*   Blank !   Blank !   Blank !   This is sad !

April 8*th.*   Strolled to the Palais de Justice, the Westminster Hall of Paris, because I have a sneaking kindness for the profession of the law, of which I was so distinguished a member in my own country.   Saw a man tried for stealing a plank ; he told his story very well, and he had a counsel who made a very good defence for him, and spoke extremely well.   I understood every

word of his speech, which I think is evidence that it was a good
one. The jury made a respectable appearance. They retired to
consider of their verdict, but I did not stay for the event. I suppose, from what I heard, the man was acquitted. The judge
charged them with great moderation, and exactly in the language
of the English law; told them it was their verdict and not his:
that the point for them to consider was the intention of the culprit,
as the fact was admitted, that if they believed he had no criminal
intent, but acted merely through ignorance, they are bound to
acquit him. All which I liked very well. I did not think they
had so much notion of criminal law in France, but that was
because I grounded my opinion on that consummation of all
iniquities and horror, the Revolutionary tribunal. The judges,
five in number, were dressed in black, *à la* Vandyck, with hats
decorated with the national feathers, and a tricolour ribbon round
their necks, like the collar of the orders of knighthood in England,
to which were suspended the fasces and axes in silver, the emblem
of their functions. The public accuser, or attorney-general, was
habited pretty much after the same fashion; the lawyers had no
discrimination of dress, which shows their good sense. It is the
same in America; the judges alone are distinguished by their
habits, and they are not disguised by that most preposterous and
absurd of all human inventions, the long full-bottomed wig.
Altogether, the appearance of the French tribunal criminal, and
the manner in which the trial was conducted, pleased me extremely.
Certainly every justice was done to the prisoner. I was astonished
at the purity of his diction and politeness of his manner in a short
discussion he had with the public accuser, who, on his part, showed
great lenity and candour. I am afraid an Irish thief would hardly
conduct himself with the same talents, or, at least, the same manners; but let that pass. Poor Pat is not to be despised because he
is not as polished as a Frenchman, and besides, who knows what
we may make of him yet? He has very pretty capabilities. Went
in the evening to see the *Déserteur*, at the *Théâtre des Italiens*.
Disappointed. A very poor performance; I speak as to the
actors, for the piece itself is inimitable. Even Chenard, who, in

general, is admirable, was very indifferent in Montauciel. His manner was dry and hard. The fact is, the French do not know how to represent a man drunk, which is owing to a defect in their education, for, as they never drink hard, they have no archetypes so they form some vague notions of the manner in which a drunken man walks and speaks, but this is all from the imagination, and the perfection of acting is to copy nature. If Chenard had the great advantage to spend two or three afternoons with P. P. and another person, who shall be nameless, I think it might very much enlarge and improve his ideas as to the manner of acting Montauciel. By-the-by, the character of Montauciel, which is so inimitably characteristic of the French soldier in the original, is miserably disguised on the English theatre ; they have carefully preserved, and, I must say, improved his drunkenness, which is but a subordinate and accidental trait in France, and they have suffered his gaiety, his *fierté*, his carelessness of manner, and his high spirit totally to evaporate. There is no character on earth more appropriate or better discriminated than that of a French Dragoon, as I have myself had one or two opportunities to observe. In that view Montauciel is inimitably drawn. Skirmish, the Montauciel of England, is nothing but a drunkard ; take away his bottle, and you take his existence. Montauciel can maintain himself without it. But I believe there is enough of criticism for the present, and, besides, I am sleepy.

END OF VOL. I.